Runaway

An AIRHEAD Novel

BOOKS BY MEG CABOT

CABOT

way

Point

Library of Congress Cataloging-in-Publication Data

Cabot, Meg.
  Runaway / by Meg Cabot. — 1st ed.
    p. cm. — (Airhead ; bk. 3)
  Summary: When sixteen-year-old Emerson Watts learns the truth about Nikki, the teen
supermodel into whose body Emerson's brain was transplanted, she finds that there is only
one person to turn to for help — especially since her loved ones seem to be furious with her.
  [1. Models (Persons) — Fiction.   2. Transplantation of organs, tissues, etc. — Fiction.
3. Identity — Fiction.   4. New York (N.Y.) — Fiction.]   I. Title.
  PZ7.C11165Run 2010
  [Fic] — dc22

                                                                        2009046813

ISBN 978-0-545-04060-0

12 11 10 9 8 7 6 5 4 3 2 1   10 11 12 13 14 15/0
Printed in the U.S.A.   23
First edition, May 2010

The display type was set in Century Gothic.
The text type was set in Adobe Jenson Pro Regular.
Book design by Kristina Albertson

FOR BENJAMIN

EXTRA SPECIAL THANKS TO JENNIFER BROWN.
THANKS ALSO TO BETH ADER, MICHELE JAFFE, LAURA
LANGLIE, ABBY MCADEN, AND BENJAMIN EGNATZ.

ONE

SO ACCORDING TO THE TABLOIDS, I'M on a secret love getaway (not so secret anymore now, though, is it? Thank you, *Us Weekly*) with Brandon Stark, the only son and sole heir of billionaire Robert Stark, currently the fourth-richest person in the world, after Bill Gates, Warren Buffett, and Ingvar Kamprad (who founded IKEA, in case you didn't know).

There are paparazzi staking out the oceanside mansion where Brandon and I are holed up. They're hiding in the dunes all along the beach. They're stretched out in ditches up and down the road, their telephoto lenses pointed through tufts of sea grass in the hopes of capturing me topless on a chaise longue by the pool (like that's going to happen).

I even saw one perched in a tree, trying to get a shot of me and Brandon Stark together that time we came out of the house to go grab some takeout at the local crab shack.

It's big news, I guess, the Face of Stark and the heir to the Stark fortune hooking up with each other over the holidays. My roommate, Lulu, texted me that she heard a picture of us together can fetch upward of ten grand . . . as long as I'm facing the camera and smiling.

So far, Lulu says, there hasn't been a single shot of me facing the camera and smiling. Not in any magazine or on any website anywhere.

I know people are wondering how that's even possible. I'm the girl who has it all, right? The little white poodle, yawning delicately at my feet; the thick, luxurious blond hair; the perfect body; the gorgeous boyfriend with the limitless credit card, who seems to care so much about me that he'll buy out the local women's boutique in my size just because I said I can't come down to dinner because I have nothing to wear.

That same gorgeous boyfriend was currently pacing up and down the hallway outside my room, so eager was he for me to join him that he could hardly wait to escort me down to the sumptuously set modern steel-and-glass table.

"How are we doing in there?" he asked, tapping on the door for the umpteenth time this hour at least.

"Not so good," I croaked. I glanced at my reflection in the mirror hanging over the dressing table in front of me. "I think I have a fever."

"Really?" Brandon sounded sweetly concerned. The best boyfriend a girl could ask for. "Maybe I should call a doctor."

"Oh," I said through the door, "I don't think that's necessary. I think I just need fluids. And bed rest. It would probably be better if I stayed in my room tonight."

I knew anyone who might have been watching — for instance, through a high-powered telephoto lens — could only have been thinking, *What is wrong with this girl?* After all, I was faking sick to get out of dinner with the hot son of one of the richest guys in America, while staying in his palatial, Frank Lloyd Wright–inspired mansion. It came complete with a huge heated outdoor pool (with vanishing edges, so that the water appeared to be dropping off into the horizon). Along one wall there was an aquarium big enough to hold Brandon's pet stingray and shark (it so figures that Brandon Stark would have a pet shark, doesn't it?), a home theater built to seat twenty, and a four-car garage that housed Brandon's European sports car collection, with a brand-new buttercup yellow Lamborghini Murciélago, a Christmas gift from Dad, of which Brandon was immensely proud.

Any other girl would have swapped places with me in a second.

But no other girl had my same problems.

Well . . . maybe one other girl.

"Don't think this means I like you," Nikki informed me, bursting into my room from the connecting door to hers, wearing a brightly colored maxidress, a leather motorcycle jacket, fringed wedges, and an enormous jeweled "statement" necklace that looked like a drunk frat boy threw up on her chest.

"No worries," I said. Nikki had made it more than clear that she doesn't like me — that she doesn't want to spend one waking minute with me unless she absolutely has to.

"It's just that your mirror is bigger than mine," she said, clip-clopping across my room to check out her reflection in my mirror, "and I want to see how I look in this."

"You look nice," I said.

I was lying.

Nikki beamed at the compliment I'd given her, though. This was a relief. It was the first time she'd smiled at me — or at least in my direction — since the private plane we took to get to this subtropical resort town touched down a few days earlier.

And who could blame her, really? It wasn't just that it was boring for her, being cooped up in this house, palatial as it was. She couldn't go into town, or one of the paparazzi might get a snap of her.

And even though they wouldn't have any idea who she was

if her photo showed up in a magazine, someone who had known her from her body's previous life might recognize her and wonder what the heck a girl who was supposed to be dead was doing walking around alive and kicking in ugly statement necklaces.

Because, like me, Nikki is a member of the Walking Dead.

But unlike me, Nikki's body was supposed to be dead and *buried*.

"You think?" Nikki stared at herself in the full-length mirror on the far wall of my room, across from a bank of floor-to-ceiling windows that face the curling waves of the Atlantic — black and ominous-looking this time of night — just a few dozen yards away.

Then she distractedly tucked a strand of her medium-length auburn hair behind her ear and made a face.

"Ugh," she said. "What is the point? Why do I even try?"

"What are you talking about?" I asked. "You look amazing."

Okay, I was exaggerating. But only a little. Actually, if she'd just worn makeup that suited her new skin tone, and quit flat-ironing her hair until it didn't have a hint of body left in it, and put on some clothes that weren't my castoffs from the boutique Brandon had raided on my behalf — which she didn't seem to realize were way too tight and long on her — she'd have been totally cute.

But no way was I going to tell her anything that wasn't one hundred percent positive. I wanted Nikki on my side even more than Brandon did.

"But do you think Brandon will like me in this?" Nikki asked anxiously.

Now we were getting to the root of the problem: the whole reason why I was faking sick . . . so she could get some one-on-one time with Brandon, without me being there to hog the limelight from her.

"Of course he will," I lied.

He'd better. I knew how desperately she craved Brandon's attention.

Not that I could blame her. Really, who wouldn't be in love with Brandon Stark? He had everything most girls could want in a guy: stunning good looks, an enviable sports car collection, a Greenwich Village brownstone *and* a beach house in the tropics, not to mention access to a private jet to go from one to the other.

Brandon really would make some girl a great boyfriend.

Except for the part about him being a low-down, two-faced snake, of course.

I stared at the back of Nikki's skull as she turned toward the mirror again. I couldn't help lifting my hand to finger the spot on my own scalp where, more than three months earlier, surgeons at the Stark Institute for Neurology and Neurosurgery had cut open my head, slipped out Nikki's brain, and inserted my own.

It sounded like something out of a cheesy made-for-TV movie, one that would be awesome to curl up in front of and watch on a rainy Sunday afternoon with a big bowl of popcorn.

Except for the fact that it was actually happening in my real life.

And little had I known that at the exact same time my brain was being inserted in Nikki's body, one of those neurosurgeons was secretly taking Nikki's brain and slipping it into the head of this girl standing in front of me.

Nikki — her brain, anyway — was supposed to have died.

And the secret she carried was supposed to have died along with her.

Unfortunately for Mr. Stark — but fortunately for Nikki — Nikki was still very much alive. Both her brain and her body. Just in two separate locations.

The secret she knows, however? That's still a secret.

And Brandon hasn't done a very good job of sweet-talking her out of it . . . mainly because he's been too distracted lately, trying to sweet-talk me.

And God knew, Nikki hated me way too much because of that to utter a barely civilized word to me, no matter how often I've tried to get her to open up to me.

I wondered how much of that is because her scar still aches sometimes, the way mine does.

"I'm sure you're right," Nikki said, her nose in the air as she left my room. "Brandon loves the color blue."

He does? This was news to me.

But I was finding out that there was a lot about Nikki Howard's ex-boyfriend that was news to me. His favorite color was the least of it, really.

What about the fact that he has a secret beachside lair where he likes to stash girls he's either kidnapped against their will, the way he has me, or intends to seduce, then blackmail to get what he wants, the way he does Nikki . . .

. . . which, in this case, is information to use against his father so Brandon can take over his company himself? Super!

Yeah. If it turned out Brandon Stark also likes to dress up as Strawberry Shortcake while playing croquet with his miniature pony collection, I totally wouldn't be surprised anymore.

"Em?" Brandon thumped on my door again.

"What?" I said, more sharply than I meant to. I had a headache that I really wasn't faking.

"I think I found a cure for what you have," Brandon said through the door.

I looked up in surprise at this.

Because there is no cure for what I have, since what I have is one hundred percent fake.

"Really?" I said. "What is it?"

"It's called you better get out here," Brandon said, in a different tone of voice, "or you'll be sorry."

Oh. Right. I forgot.

Because the tabloids have got it wrong.

I'm not on a secret love getaway. I may not exactly be behind bars.

I'm not sporting shackles or handcuffs.

There aren't even men in black suits standing on either side of me, speaking into little mini-microphones in their sleeves.

But I'm Brandon Stark's prisoner, just the same.

TWO

I OPENED THE DOOR AND STOOD THERE
in the long black velvet evening gown Brandon had had sent over
for that evening's festivities — a gourmet dinner being prepared
by the Cordon Bleu–trained chef Brandon had stolen away from
a nearby five-star hotel to come work for him for the week.

One thing about Brandon Stark: He doesn't mess around
when he's trying to impress a lady.

The question was, why couldn't he figure out the right girl to
impress? It was Nikki he was supposed to be trying to win over,
not me.

Not that he'd even have to try that hard with her. If he'd
expended *half* as much energy on her as he kept expending on
me, he'd have had her eating out of his hand.

Why couldn't he understand that?

Probably for the same reason he thinks it's cool to hang out in Ed Hardy shirts with reality show stars on his dad's yacht: He's kind of stupid.

And yet at the same time, he's completely evil.

It turns out the two combined are deadly. Well, for me.

Brandon didn't say anything for a minute. He just stared at me, his eyes blank as the spinning beach balls of death Mac users always got when an application on their computer wasn't responding.

Which was good. It meant plan B — which I'd come up with in case plan A, faking sick, didn't pan out — was working. I may seem like a defenseless blonde on the outside, but I actually do have a few weapons in my arsenal.

One of them was the Armani I was wearing. I realized the moment I saw it on the rack of clothes that had been sent over from the expensive designer boutique Brandon decided he was going to raid on my behalf that this particular gown was totally going to be my ally.

I may not have known a thing about fashion a few months ago when I'd been the worst-dressed girl in the entire eleventh grade at Tribeca Alternative High School.

But I've always been a fast learner.

"Brandon," I said to him. The long hallway — which was glass on one side so you could see the ocean and dunes (when it wasn't so dark out) — was empty except for us two (and the paparazzi, of course. But I'm fairly certain the private security guards Brandon had hired, who were patrolling outside of the house, had flushed out any photographers). I closed the guest room door behind me so there was no chance Nikki would overhear what I was about to say to him.

I figured it was probably useless. I'd tried reasoning with him before.

But never in Armani.

"This is ridiculous," I went on. "You're supposed to be trying to seduce Nikki, not me. She's the one with the secret your dad tried to have her murdered for. The one you want to steal so you can kick your dad out and take over?"

Brandon just stared down at me. He's no smarter, in some ways, than Jason Klein, the king of the Walking Dead (aka the jocks) back at my high school.

Just richer, and with fewer morals.

"Which is great, but I have to get back to the city," I said to him. I was trying to speak slowly and clearly, so he would be sure to understand me. "I have the Stark Angel fashion show in a few days. You know I can't miss that. This romantic getaway over the holidays with Brandon Stark? The press is eating it up."

Though the truth was, I couldn't imagine my mother was too happy about it. Not that I'd spoken to her. I'd been letting her calls go to voice mail. I knew if I spoke to her, the hurt I'd hear in her voice — *Really, Em. Spending the week with a boy? What's the matter with you?* — would be like a stab wound to the chest.

But what was worse was that no one else besides her — and, of course, Lulu and my agent, Rebecca, who'd called me approximately a zillion times — had left me a voice mail.

No one else, meaning the single person whose feelings I was most anxious about having wounded by taking off with Brandon Stark.

Right: Christopher Maloney, the love of my life, hadn't called.

I don't know why I thought he would have, after what I'd done to him — which was lie and tell him I didn't love him anymore . . . that instead, I loved Brandon. It wasn't like I *deserved* a call. Or an e-mail, or a text message, or anything at all from him.

I guess I just thought he'd get in *some* kind of contact . . . even if it was only to send me a letter of bitter recrimination or something. Sure, I wouldn't have enjoyed being on the receiving end of a *Dear Em: Thanks for ruining my life* e-mail. I mean, Christopher didn't know Brandon had forced me to say what I had.

But even a Dear Em letter would have been better than this cold stone silence. . . .

But no. Nothing.

Better not to think about that now.

Or ever.

"But eventually," I forced myself to go on to Brandon, "the people I'm close to are going to start getting suspicious. They know, Brandon, that you and I aren't . . . well, what you're trying to make them think we are."

I was lying, of course. The people in my life had no idea that I wasn't in love with Brandon, and that this whole thing was a fake. They didn't know. Hadn't I been the one going around basically hooking up with every cute guy I'd come into contact with ever since I'd gotten my brain slipped into this hot new bod? How was anyone supposed to have known which of those guys I actually cared about and which of those guys I didn't? Right: I had made the mess I was in right now.

And I was the one who needed to get myself out of it.

Which I was actually trying to do at the moment. Although it may not have looked like it.

"I've got to get back to the city," I said to Brandon again, stalling for time. "Just let me —"

Brandon reached up to lay a finger over my lips. And left it there.

"Shhh," he said.

Uh-oh. His reboot was apparently completed. His pupils

stopped looking like twin spinning beach balls of death. He'd taken a step forward.

Now he was standing just inches away from me, looking down at me with an expression I couldn't quite read.

But, like a lot of things about him lately, it scared me a little.

"Everything's going to be all right," he said in what I suppose he thought was a soothing voice.

Except I was about as soothed as a Dalmatian puppy at Cruella de Vil's house.

"I know what I'm doing," he went on.

"Uh," I said from behind his finger. "Actually, I don't think you do. Because Nikki's not going to tell you anything if you don't start paying less attention to me and more attention to —"

Then he removed his finger and started to lean his head down to place his lips where, a second before, his finger had been.

Ugh, no. Seriously? Again?

I had goose bumps, and not because I was in a sleeveless dress.

Look, I couldn't blame Brandon. I'd been giving him mixed messages for months. And straight up using him, basically. That's the kind of girl I'd turned into since I'd become Nikki. It wasn't nice to admit, but it was the truth.

But things were different now. I finally had my head — pun intended — on straight.

Nevertheless, I knew what I had to do. What I'd been having to do all week.

It's what models have to do all the time: pretend like we're actually comfortable in what we're wearing, or enjoying what we're eating, or aren't completely freezing standing there in the ocean, waves crashing over us.

It's not the hardest thing in the world. I've actually gotten pretty good at it.

And in this particular case, that was a really good thing.

Because prisoners are treated better when they get along with their jailors.

And there's more of a chance their jailor might slip up and let down his guard if he thinks his prisoner might actually like him a little.

And that would allow the prisoner to escape.

The problem is, I can't escape until I get what I need. Which happens to be the same thing Brandon needs: the piece of information that got me into this mess in the first place.

Which means no matter how bitchy Nikki is to me, I have to put up with her until she spills her guts.

So no matter how much Brandon grosses me out, I have to put up with him.

Nobody said it was easy being a prisoner.

So I did what I had to do: I let Brandon kiss me.

Fortunately, just as I saw Brandon's lips looming closer and closer to mine, I heard a nearby door thrown open.

It wasn't plan C.

But it was enough.

I hastily pulled my head back, relieved I had an excuse to, since even Brandon would have to admit he couldn't afford to let Nikki see him making out with me.

Footsteps — sturdy ones, not the tippity-tap of fringed wedges — sounded on the polished marble floor, and I turned to see Nikki's older brother, Steven, coming toward us.

"Hey," he said, nodding to us both at once.

"Hello," Brandon said, his response almost comical in its lack of enthusiasm. His attitude toward Steven this past week had been cool at best. While he had to pretend to be at least somewhat enthusiastic about seeing Nikki every time she came stomping into the room, he didn't have to pretend to be enthusiastic about seeing her brother.

"So," Steven said as he walked slowly by us. "What's up?"

"Dinner's being served downstairs in the dining room," Brandon said coolly. His tone clearly suggested, *So why don't you get down there and leave us alone?*

"Yeah?" Steven didn't look like he was in any kind of hurry. And why not? Steven, like his sister, couldn't leave the house for fear he, too, might be photographed and tracked down by

Robert Stark, who wasn't supposed to know where Steven or his mother was . . . or he might have them eliminated as well, the way he'd tried to do to Nikki.

"And what culinary delight are you going to stun us with tonight, Brandon?" Steven asked.

The funny part was, Brandon was too dumb to tell that Steven was totally being sarcastic. I had to hide my smile. Steven didn't care what was for dinner. He hated Brandon as much as I did. He'd never said so . . .

. . . but I could totally tell.

"She-crab soup," Brandon said, "and some kind of crab salad — peekytoe, I think — along with a foie gras or something."

As Brandon was speaking, Steven started heading for the floating staircase to the first floor. Because he usually left the room while Brandon was talking. That's how much he hated Brandon.

In my mind, I was screaming, *Don't go, Steven! Don't leave me alone with him!*

But of course I couldn't say anything like that. I had to be polite. On the surface.

"And then," Brandon went on, in a bored tone, "filet mignon. There's a chocolate soufflé for dessert."

"Sounds great," Steven said over his shoulder. He was

wearing some of the clothes Brandon had bought for him, a pair of black jeans and a dark gray cashmere sweater, the sleeves pushed up to the elbows. All of us — with the exception of Nikki and her mom, who'd had time to throw a few things into some bags before they'd left Dr. Fong's house — had arrived at Brandon's with nothing but the clothes on our backs (and our dogs . . . those of us who owned dogs), trying to escape from Robert Stark.

Brandon had been more than generous about making sure Steven and his mom had the things they might need, since they couldn't use their credit cards for fear Stark Enterprises might be able to trace them.

But I could sense that Steven seemed annoyed at being beholden to the son of a man who'd caused his family so much heartache. He never actually *said* anything that was outright rude to Brandon.

But he did *do* things that someone who was a little more self-aware than Brandon might have found rude. Such as walk out of the room while Brandon was still speaking.

"Filet mignon again. Great," Steven tossed over his shoulder as he headed down the stairs. "Oh, hey, Brandon," he added casually. "You know your Lamborghini is on fire, right?"

Brandon's hand went to the wire-suspended steel banister and froze.

"What?"

"Your new Lamborghini," Steven said. "I noticed it just now when I looked out across the driveway. It's in flames."

Yes. *Finally.* Plan C in action.

Brandon glanced out the bank of windows that looked over the front of the house, seeming a little scornful, like, *Yeah, right. My car is on fire.*

A second later his demeanor changed entirely. He let out a curse word that singed my ears.

"My car," he cried. "It's on fire!"

"That's what I said." Steven shook his head, looking up at me from the bottom of the stairs, as if to say, *What a loser.* "Isn't that what I just said?"

Brandon let out another curse and, grabbing his hair with both hands, tore past me, nearly shoving me down the stairs in his haste to get by, and then barreling by Steven.

"Call 9-1-1!" he screamed.

THREE

NIKKI CHOSE THAT EXACT MOMENT TO come out of her room.

"What's wrong with Brandon?" she asked as she click-clacked down the hall toward me.

"His car is on fire," Steven said with a shrug.

"What?" Nikki's voice rose to a high-pitched shriek. "Not the new Lamborghini!"

I had to flatten myself against the wall in order not to get knocked down as she hurried off after Brandon, her heels making a huge racket on the shiny marble floor.

"Brandon," she cried, racing after him. "Wait! I'm coming!"

I wanted to remind her not to go outside or the paparazzi might get a shot of her, but it was too late. She was already gone.

Cosabella, who'd followed me from my room, rushed down the stairs after Nikki, her claws skittering on the slick floor. She gave a few excited barks and then, when Nikki slammed the front door in her face, gave herself a good shake and came trotting back into the living room, looking proud of herself for a job well done.

"So." Steven folded his arms and stared up at me as I made my way down the long staircase. It was a little treacherous to navigate in high heels and a skintight Armani evening gown, I found. "You set the guy's car on fire?"

This caused me to freeze in my tracks.

"Me?" I arranged my face into a suitably shocked expression. "What makes you think it was *me*, and not one of the paps, trying to lure him outside so they could get a photo op?"

"Because I found your fuse," he said, holding up what used to be a wooden mixed-bead necklace Brandon had given me . . .

. . . at least until I'd rolled it in a mixture that included hot water, sugar, and another substance and let it dry overnight.

"You're a liar," I said when I reached the bottom of the stairs. I plucked the singed necklace from his hand. "You said you saw the car burning from the windows."

"Actually," Steven said, "I did. And I went out to investigate. That was a little while ago. I found it so interesting, I thought I'd let it keep going, to see what would happen. Where did *you* of all people learn to make a slow-burning fuse?"

"YouTube," I said. I dropped the charred necklace into the neck of a Greek amphora that was sitting at the bottom of the stairs. "And I resent the implication that a girl wouldn't necessarily know her way around explosives. I go to an alternative high school, you know."

"Of course." Steven nodded. "Stupid of me. But let me ask you a question," he said as he followed me into the dining room, where I'd gone to sit down at the massive, already set table. "Why would you want to blow up Brandon Stark's new car?"

Because he's holding us prisoner here. And Christopher doesn't love me anymore.

"It's not going to blow up," I said. "I just made a decorative design on the hood with lighter fluid. And there are plenty of fire extinguishers out there. I checked. If Brandon has any sense, he'll get the fire out before it does any permanent damage to anything but the paint job."

And I hadn't timed the fire right. It was supposed to have gone up *before* he got a chance to kiss me.

"You didn't need to destroy his car," Steven said, joining me at the table. "The guy is a tool, but that's going a little far, don't you think?"

"No," I said shortly. Cosabella curled up at my feet beneath the table.

"Wow." Steven stared at me. "You really hate him."

I pictured Christopher's face growing smaller and smaller in the distance as the limo Brandon had forced me into snaked its way down the road.

You have, my voice mail's robotic voice said in my head, over and over, *no new messages*.

Yeah. I guess I did hate Brandon.

"I told you," I said. "I was only trying to mess up the paint job a little."

Steven shook his head. "I'm not falling for it, Em."

Of course he wasn't. Nikki's brother is a trained naval officer. He isn't stupid.

But I widened my eyes and went for the innocent act anyway. Because of what Brandon said would happen if I didn't.

"I don't know what you mean," I said.

"Convincing," Steven said. "But spill now while we have five minutes alone together for once. You're not in love with Brandon Stark. What's going on, Em? Why are you pretending to be in love with Brandon on the one hand, then setting his car on fire behind his back?"

Whatever she knows about Stark Quark, if it's worth killing Nikki Howard for — and then giving her a brain transplant to keep her image alive — it's worth knowing. Believe me. And I want in, Brandon had whispered to me that cold gray morning back in New York, just a week ago.

Why should I help you? I'd demanded.

Because, he'd said. *If you don't, I'll tell my dad where the real Nikki Howard is. And,* he'd added, about Christopher, *no more of that other guy, the one in the leather jacket, who seems so into you. Just me. You're mine now. Understand?*

I'd looked up at him then like he was crazy.

But now I know better. Brandon Stark isn't crazy. Dumb, maybe. Desperate to leave his mark on the planet, the way his father has, but with no real idea about how to go about doing that.

But not crazy.

And if you tell them that I'm making you do it, I'll tell my father about the girl.

Would he? Would Brandon tell?

He certainly didn't care about Nikki — or about Steven or Mrs. Howard. Sure, he was willing to house — and clothe — them, since they had nowhere else to go, thanks to his dad's company essentially stalking them.

But he was only doing this because of what he thought he was going to get out of it: me (only not the real me. The me he thought I was, this made-up girl whose name he didn't even really know, who looked like Nikki Howard).

Oh, and whatever it was Nikki knew that he thought was going to make him so much money.

"Em." Steven was staring at me, his face — so much like the one I saw reflected in the mirror every morning when I put on my makeup, only masculine — tight with anxiety. "Whatever he's threatened you with, I swear to you, I can make it better. You just have to tell me what's going on."

I wanted to believe him. I really did. I'd never had a big brother before, but I was starting to really love Nikki's. He was so comforting, with his wide shoulders and steady gaze. I almost believed that he could make it all better.

But of course he couldn't. No one could.

And if you tell them that I'm making you do it, I'll tell my father about the girl.

Except Brandon wasn't going to tell his father a thing about Nikki. He couldn't. He needed her too much. She held the key to everything.

But Christopher. He'd tell his father about Christopher.

"Oh, there you are," Nikki's mother called as she came down the floating staircase, holding carefully to the handrail as both her poodles, Cosabella's siblings, skittered down the steps in front of her. "Is everything all right? What was all that ruckus I heard before?"

Talk about saved by the bell . . . a real Southern belle, as a matter of fact: Nikki and Steven's mom had the drawl and the gently fading beauty of one. You could see where both Nikki and Steven got their good looks. Mrs. Howard was still what my dad would call a knockout.

But before anyone could say anything else, the chef's assistant came out of the kitchen, holding a silver tray.

"She-crab soup," he said, trying to ignore the obnoxiously dancing poodles at his feet, all hoping they might be able to trip him and that he might spill some of what he was carrying. He seemed more disconcerted by the fact that there were only three of us than by the dogs.

"Oh," he said. "Is Mr. Stark not ready for dinner yet?"

"There was a little emergency," I said. "He'll be back in a few minutes. I guess you could tell the chef to go ahead and serve."

The assistant nodded, holding the tray for Steven and his mother to help themselves to the first course, then retreated back into the kitchen, his rubber clogs soundless on the black marble floor. Cosabella and Mrs. Howard's dogs, Harry and Winston, followed after him, still eagerly hoping he might drop something.

"What kind of emergency?" Mrs. Howard asked.

"Em lit his car on fire," Steven said.

Mrs. Howard, about to lift her shot glass of soup to her mouth, gasped instead. "Em! Why would you do such a thing?"

I shrugged. I couldn't tell her I'd done it because Brandon was a great big lying fake who'd caused me and my boyfriend to break up forever. She, like everyone else, thought I was in love with Brandon, and that he was protecting her and her daughter from his evil father.

And, in a way, he was.

I didn't want to worry her more than she already was. She'd left everything behind — her business, her home, her friends, her life — for her daughter.

Who actually didn't seem all that grateful for it, if you asked me.

"Shouldn't we call the fire department?" Mrs. Howard asked, still looking shocked.

Just as she was saying this, one of the glass side doors opened, and Brandon came in, Nikki tripping at his heels.

"I'm telling you, it was those jerks from *OK!*" Brandon said. "And I'm not standing for it. Not a second longer. I'm calling my lawyers. I'm suing for the cost of replacing my car."

"You're so right, Brandon." Nikki wobbled along after him in her too-high — and several sizes too big for her — platform wedges. "It had to be them. Who else would do such a thing?"

"Is everything all right?" Mrs. Howard asked. "No one was hurt, were they? Is the fire out? Nikki, no one got a photo of you out there, did they?"

"Oh, it's out," Brandon said as Nikki shook her head. Brandon had his iPhone glued to his face. "And Nikki's fine. But the paint job on my car is ruined. Ruined! Hello, Ken?" He started shouting into his cell phone. "Ken, it's Brandon. They trashed my car. What? The Murciélago, that's which one. Why? How the hell should I know why? To get a reaction out of me that they can plaster all over their damn magazine covers, that's why. Why else?"

"I don't know how any of us are supposed to be able to eat," Nikki said with a sigh as she sat down, unfolding her white linen napkin with a snap, "after what just happened. The paparazzi have just gotten so out of control. How could they do such an awful thing to poor Brandon?"

"What makes you think it was the paparazzi?" Steven asked, not looking in my direction anymore as the chef's assistant came into the dining room, carrying another tray. He was trying very hard not to trip over the dogs again.

"I don't know who else it would be," Nikki said. "Brandon's never hurt anyone. He's completely sweet and adorable."

I choked a little on the sip of sparkling water I'd just swallowed. If Brandon was sweet and adorable, I was Satan's bride.

"Maybe," I said when I'd recovered, "it was his dad."

"What?" Nikki looked confused. "Why would his dad send him a nice car for Christmas, then light it on fire?"

"Because," I said, "maybe Mr. Stark knows you're here."

Nikki turned visibly pale.

"You think he knows?" she asked.

Yeah. I was evil. I was a car-burning, lie-telling supermodel. Whatever. I didn't care anymore. They'd already given me a brain transplant, made me dump my boyfriend, and were going to make me parade around in a million-dollar bra on national television in a couple of days. What more could they do to me? Kill me?

Well, guess what? I was already dead.

"He could suspect," I said. "And if he does, we don't have much time. We need to know what it is he tried to murder you for. That way we can get the proof we need to prosecute Brandon's dad and have him put away where he can't try to hurt you anymore."

Nikki's chin slid out stubbornly.

"Like I already told my *mother*," she said, putting an unpleasant emphasis on the word *mother*, "when she tried to bring this up the other day: Brandon's dad did not try to have me murdered. I don't know where you all keep coming up with this story —"

"Because we all sat in the same room with Dr. Fong," Mrs. Howard explained patiently. "And heard him reveal that you didn't have an embolism, Nikki —"

"But they forced him to do the surgery, anyway," Steven interrupted. "They were going to *throw your brain away*. He saved your life by transplanting it into the body you have now. Why don't you get that? Just tell us what you were going to blackmail Robert Stark about, and we can all go back to our old lives."

"Oh." Suddenly, Nikki's eyes were bright with unshed tears. "Can we? Can we all go back to our old lives, Steven? I'm sorry, but you seem to have forgotten that that isn't possible for some of us. Because *there's another girl living in my old body*."

She shot me a look that sent chills up my spine. No one — not even Whitney Robertson, back at Tribeca Alternative, who I'm pretty sure had disliked me more than any human being in the entire universe, and only because when I was on her volleyball team during PE, I'd sometimes miss the ball — had ever given me a look of such pure, unadulterated hatred.

"So I can't go back to my old life," Nikki said to her brother. "That girl right there is living in my apartment, using my money, taking my gigs; even *my dog* likes her better than me." She pointed through the glass tabletop at Cosabella, who was sitting at the side of my chair, panting up at me eagerly, hoping I might slip her a piece of whatever food was about to be served (which, I have to admit, I'd been known on occasion to do).

"So excuse me," Nikki went on, "if I'm not exactly in a rush to get out of here. I happen to like things exactly as they are, considering the alternatives. Because if you think I'm going back home to live in redneck Gasper, USA, with you and Mom, Steven, well, you can just think again. I'm never going back there. *Never.*"

"Nikki," I said. I felt terrible about what had happened to her. I really did. Even though none of it had been my fault — hey, I definitely hadn't chosen to be the new brain behind the Face of Stark — I felt like I owed her something.

But I had to get out of Brandon Stark's control before I went crazy.

Or lit something else of his on fire. Like his pants, for instance.

"Maybe we could work something out." I lowered my voice just in case Brandon, even tied up as he seemed to be in his phone call, happened to overhear me.

She narrowed her eyes at me.

"What do you mean, work something out?"

"Well," I half whispered. "Like, I could give you the money back. The money in your bank account. I'd also offer you a cut of anything I make in the future. You know, from future jobs."

Nikki leaned back in her chair. The chef's assistant had set decoratively arranged plates of peekytoe salad in front of each of us, including in front of Brandon's empty seat. Brandon was still pacing at the bottom of the stairs, on the phone with his lawyer. Every once in a while a burst of his conversation would reach us. It sounded like, "What do you mean, I need proof?" and "No, I don't see why I should have to do that!" He was clearly lost in his own little world.

"That sounds fair, Nikki," Mrs. Howard said, moving some of her peekytoe salad around on her plate. "You really ought to consider it."

"I don't have to consider anything," Nikki said. "She's not offering me anything I wouldn't have if none of this had happened in the first place. She's offering me less, actually, than I would have had."

"But you ruined your career," Steven pointed out, his voice raised a little in frustration, "by trying to blackmail your boss. Which he should have fired you for. But instead, he tried to have you killed. Either way, Emerson's the one who would be doing all the work."

Nikki stared at him like he was stupid.

"You think modeling is work?" she demanded. "Getting paid to stand around in five-thousand-dollar dresses while people airbrush makeup onto you and compliment you while taking your picture? That isn't work. That's freaking fun, dude."

I had no idea what she was talking about. Modeling was totally work. Sure, it wasn't standing over a fryer at McDonald's in a polyester uniform, getting grease all over you, for minimum wage while people yelled at you that they wanted a Diet Coke with their Big Mac, fries, McNuggets, and apple turnover. And Supersize it.

But I had never worked so hard in my life on most of the shoots I got sent out on. That whole thing where Tyra was going on about smiling with your eyes? Yeah, not so easy, it turns out, when you're in nothing but a bustier and a thong and standing in freezing cold water up to your butt and you're shivering and all you want to do is go home and cry.

"Look, Nikki," I said, feeling like we were getting off topic. "With that kind of money you wouldn't have to live in Gasper. You could live in a duplex with a doorman and in-house gym in SoHo."

"And do what?" Nikki demanded.

"Go to college," Mrs. Howard said promptly.

Nikki snorted again. "Oh, right, Mom," she said, rolling her eyes.

"What's wrong with that idea?" her mother asked. "There's all sorts of things you could get degrees in, things you already know all about and could bring a specialized knowledge to because of your background . . . photography, fashion design or merchandising, business, publicity, media, entertainment law —"

Nikki cut her mother short.

"There's only one thing I want," she hissed.

"And what's that?" I asked.

Not the dog, I prayed. I wasn't sure I could part with Cosabella. In the months that I'd gotten to know her, the two of us had really bonded. True, it was kind of annoying having a four-legged little shadow follow me everywhere I went.

But I had kind of gotten used to it.

But what else could Nikki want? I'd already offered her all the money I had, and a split of my future earnings. Should I offer her *all* of my future earnings? It was going to be tough to figure out how I was going to pay the mortgage on the loft. . . .

Wait. Did Nikki want the *loft*? Was I going to have to move? What about Lulu? Lulu paid me rent to live in the loft.

Well, I guess we were just going to have to find some other place to live.

"What I *want*," Nikki said, in the nastiest voice I think I've heard — and that includes when Whitney Robertson used to ask me if I'd ever even heard of conditioner — "is my old body back."

FOUR

STUNNED, I LOOKED DOWN AT THE BODY
Nikki was talking about. *Her* body. The body I'd woken up in
so many months earlier, in so much confusion. The body I had
had to get accustomed to seeing myself in, to walking around in,
to *living* in. The body that had caused me so much pain and
heartache and astonishment as I'd tried to get used to it.

The body I had hated, railed against, refused to believe was
now my own, and had cursed.

The body I'd been convinced was ruining my life.

And then later, the body in which I'd experienced so much
laughter, having whipped cream fights with Lulu in the kitchen.
And wonder, as I'd felt what it could do on a treadmill, actually
experiencing runner's high for the first time in my life (I'd

certainly never exerted myself in my old body, especially in PE . . . except to try to duck the volleyballs Whitney Robertson spiked at my head).

And finally joy, as I'd lain beneath Christopher and felt his mouth moving over my lips, his heart drumming against mine.

And I realized, with a shock like the cold seawater I'd felt once pouring over me when I'd flung myself backward off a cliff into it, I wasn't giving this body up.

No way.

I may have hated it at times — I may have longed for my old life back.

But this was my new life. It was the only life I had.

I wasn't about to give it up.

"Over my dead body," Mrs. Howard burst out, basically summing up my feelings exactly.

"Well," Nikki said, looking over at her mother. "Good thing it's not your body we're talking about, isn't it? So why don't you just butt out?"

"Nikki," Mrs. Howard said. She'd pushed back her chair and risen from the table angrily. "Dr. Fong and I spent weeks nursing you after you nearly *died* the last time they did the surgery. Your new heart couldn't take the strain of being under anesthesia for so long. It was a miracle you even survived. And without brain damage."

"I'm not so sure she *didn't* suffer brain damage," Steven remarked, with the sarcasm only a sibling could display.

"Shut up," Nikki snapped at him. Her chin was sticking out again, a sign, I had figured out, that she'd made up her mind. To her mother she said, "I'm willing to risk it. I want my old life back. *All* of it. That includes my old body. Give it to me, or no deal."

Wow.

I had seen Nikki in a lot of moods since we'd moved into adjacent bedrooms . . .

. . . but I'd never seen her this adamant about anything.

"You're being ridiculous. I don't see how this surgery is even going to be possible," Mrs. Howard went on, throwing a beseeching look at Brandon, "considering the fact that the only doctors who can perform it work for Brandon's father at the Stark Institute for Neurology and Neurosurgery. And how is he possibly going to get them to do it without his father finding out?"

"Dr. Fong can do it," Nikki said. "He did it once for me. He can do it again."

Well. That much was true.

I looked down at the elegant hands I'd grown so accustomed to seeing at the ends of my slender wrists. The hands that had shaken so badly the first time I'd tried to feed myself. The hands with which I'd been forced to learn to write a new name —

Nikki's, not my own — on all the slips of paper autograph seekers had thrust at me every time I'd set foot in public. The hands that had slipped under Christopher's leather jacket — had it really only been a few nights ago? — and felt his skin burning beneath mine.

But I guess they'd never really been my hands after all.

They were her hands. Nikki's hands.

And now she wanted them back.

I clenched Nikki's hands into fists.

They may have been her hands.

But it was *my* brain that had made them do all those things.

"Dr. Fong doesn't have his own facilities to perform a complicated procedure like this," Mrs. Howard was saying. "You know he doesn't. Why do you think your recovery took so much longer than Em's, besides the fact that you nearly died during it, because the body you have now isn't as strong as your old one? Because he didn't have access to —"

"Well," Nikki said. "We can just set up an operating room here. If Brandon wants this information badly enough, he'll pay whatever it costs to give me what I want. Right, Brandon?"

"Oh, Nikki," her mother said. "Don't be so —"

"Right, Brandon?" Nikki said, interrupting her mother.

Brandon, who'd shoved his iPhone into his pocket and strode over to sit in his chair at the head of the dining table, looked up from his plate and said the words that sent a chill through my heart . . . Nikki's heart:

"Uh . . . I guess."

Wait — he was actually *considering* this? Did he even realize what we were talking about?

"See?" Nikki turned shining eyes on us. "It's all set, then." Her eyes, I saw, weren't shining because they were tear-filled. They were bright with triumph. *Goody,* her eyes seemed to be saying. "Now that that's settled —"

"Nikki," Steven said, raising his head and swiveling it to send a steely-eyed look at his sister. "No."

The word was simple. And final. Just *no.*

I realized then how much I loved Steven. He may have been Nikki's brother.

But he was my hero.

"What do you mean, no?" Nikki demanded, whipping her head toward her brother. No one ever said no to Nikki. I should know. "If they took it out, they can put it back in. You asked what I wanted in exchange for telling what I know, and that's what I want. I want my body back."

"Well, you can't have it back," Steven said. Steven's tone was brusque. "It could kill her. And you. You can't ask her to risk her life. She's already done it once. You can't ask her to do it again."

"*Yes*," Nikki said, her eyes narrowed, "*I can.*"

And in that *Yes, I can* I finally saw the girl from the tiny town who was so determined to make it big that she was willing to break her mother's heart by having herself declared an emancipated minor before the age of sixteen.

And had signed her first million-dollar contract a week later.

"*No*," her brother said, with just as much determination. And I saw in him the self-made man, the soldier with whom my loftmate, Lulu, was so head over heels in love, and about whom she asked me so breathlessly every time she called. "You're asking too much."

Now the shininess I saw in Nikki's eyes really was tears. She glared at all of us.

"Nobody thinks about *me*," she said. The flintiness wasn't gone. It was just being directed somewhere else. At forcing herself to appear sympathetic by crying, I suspected. "How *I* feel. I mean, how do you think it feels for *me*, to know I'm going to have to go around for the rest of my life in *this* body, looking like this hideous hag?"

She flung herself into the nearest chair, lowering her head onto the table, and burst into dramatic sobs.

Brandon and Steven exchanged incredulous glances, while Mrs. Howard hurried over to comfort her weeping daughter.

"Nikki," Mrs. Howard was saying. "How can you say that? You're a normal, healthy-looking girl. No, you don't look like you used to. But you're not hideous. You're still beautiful to me, just different than you used to be —"

"*Normal?*" Nikki echoed, in a tone that suggested her mother had used a dirty word. "*Healthy-looking?* Are you kidding me, Mother? I don't want to be *normal.* I don't want to be *healthy-looking,* or *beautiful to you.* I want to be freaking gorgeous, like I used to be! I don't want to be stuck in this stubby-looking body, with this plain-Jane face and this useless, ugly hair! I want to be hot! I want to be sexy! *I want to be Nikki Howard!*"

I don't know if it was my imagination or not, but the phrase *I want to be Nikki Howard* seemed to bounce off the cold hard windows around us and echo around the room. *I want to be Nikki Howard! I want to be Nikki Howard! I want to be Nikki Howard!*

"Well, you can't," Mrs. Howard said exasperatedly. "And you're not going to get anywhere if you don't stop putting yourself down. Just look in that window there and see what I see: a bright young girl, with so much to offer. . . ."

But Nikki wouldn't look up. She was too busy crying into her statement necklace.

Because Nikki wouldn't look up, I did. What I saw was my own reflection . . . the reflection Nikki used to have.

Perfect. Not a feature, not even a hair, out of place. Exactly what you would expect to see on the cover of a magazine or modeling an expensive dress or piece of jewelry in an ad. Telling you what to buy or where to go or what was hot now.

And because she looked so perfect — or what we'd been told for so long was how a perfect person was supposed to look — you would believe her. You'd want to buy whatever she was selling you, or go where she said to go. You'd want to make sure you had whatever it was she assured you was hot now.

If you weren't one of those people, like I'd always been, who hated her on sight. What did I need Nikki Howard for, telling me what to wear, what to buy, where to go? I'd never been able to stand the sight of her perfect, vapid face and body, towering over me on the sides of buildings or winking out at me from the pages of magazines.

And now that face and body were mine. I couldn't get away from them. No matter where I went, or how far I tried to run. Her face was my face. What she touched, I touched. What she experienced, I experienced.

But the thing was, I couldn't imagine *not* being her. Not anymore. She and I were one . . .

. . . and, I had to admit, I *liked* being her. I did. It wasn't always easy being Nikki.

But it was me. I was Nikki now.

Beneath me, I felt Cosabella — realizing I wasn't going to drop any food tonight — give up on her vigilant stand at my side and lay down to rest her head on my foot with a sigh. It was where she lay at every meal. It felt warm and natural to have her head there, soft as velvet. . . .

My heart jerked.

If what Nikki wanted to happen actually happened, I'd never feel Cosabella's head on my foot again.

Oh, I supposed I could get a new dog . . . if I lived through the surgery. She wouldn't be exactly like Cosabella, but it would be all right.

Wouldn't it?

Even if I ran — even if I took off tonight, with Cosabella — they'd find me. Where could I go that Brandon couldn't find me? I had the most recognizable face in the world. Maybe there was some tribal village in the wilds of the Amazon where they'd never seen Nikki Howard before.

But how long was I going to last without cable? I'm not even talking about the premium channels, but Bravo and BBC America? I started freaking out after even a few hours without the Internet.

I had to face it: I was screwed.

"No," Steven said again. "Nikki. It's not going to happen. It's too dangerous. And it's not medically necessary. No surgeon in his right mind would do it. Not even Dr. Fong."

"Why," Nikki sobbed, lifting her head and revealing that mascara had begun to run down her face, "does everyone hate me?"

"Nikki," her mother said. "No one hates you. It isn't that. It's because you two aren't —"

"*It's not up to you,*" Nikki yelled, just as the chef's assistant came out with a tray to collect the empty plates from the second course. "*It's up to Brandon!*"

The assistant turned around and headed right back into the kitchen, Harry and Winston looking after him disappointedly. Apparently, he'd realized now wasn't the best time to interrupt the conversation.

"Uh," Brandon said, shifting in his seat as he realized all eyes were on him. "If Nikki wants her body back, then that's what Nikki's gonna get. She's what matters here."

A coldness — like the cold of the glass tabletop beneath my fingers — began to seep into my heart. It felt as if it were spreading from my heart to each of my limbs. Soon the only warmth in my body was the warmth radiating from Cosabella's head resting on my foot.

"And Dr. Fong will do it," Brandon went on. "Or I'll haul his ass in front of the AMA for violating ten thousand different medical ethics in doing this whole switcheroo thing in the first place. Right, Nik?"

Now? He decides to start being Nikki's best friend *now*, right when I need him the most?

Oh, God. I was sure I was going to throw up.

Nikki stopped crying at once. Instead, she squealed with

excitement. She jumped up from her seat and ran over to where Brandon sat, throwing herself into his lap so that she could fling both her arms around his neck.

"Oh, thank you, thank you," she cried. "I love you so much, Bran!"

"I don't believe this," Steven muttered. He stood up and walked out without another word, heading up the stairs and back to his room.

Don't go, Steven, I wanted to say. *Don't go.*

But I couldn't speak. Because my lips, like the rest of my body, were frozen.

Nikki, noticing he was leaving, asked confusedly, "Steven? Don't you want to stay for filet mignon? I mean . . . we have something to celebrate."

"No," Steven said over his shoulder. "We don't."

A few seconds later, we all heard a door slam.

Nikki, still in Brandon's lap, threw an accusing look at her mother. "What's his problem?"

"He's upset, Nikki," Mrs. Howard said, looking distressed. "I'm upset, too. I don't think you or Brandon have thought this thing all the way through. Or considered poor Em. It's completely absurd — not to mention unethical — to perform a risky and life-threatening operation on two perfectly healthy young women because of *vanity* —"

"It's not vanity, Mother," Nikki said coldly. "It's my *life.*

And I want it back. Steven can pout about it all he wants, but he's never been in this situation. He doesn't *know*. Does he, Brandon?"

"Uh . . . ," Brandon said. He'd been texting someone on his mobile phone behind Nikki's back as she'd been talking. "What was that, babe?"

She turned her head. "Brandon. Are you *texting*?"

"Sorry," he said, grinning his perfect, boyish grin. "It's my lawyer. About the car. He thinks I may be able to pursue it in civil court."

"Oh." Nikki gave him a very brittle smile. "Maybe you should be calling Dr. Fong and starting to arrange having medical supplies shipped here instead."

"Uh," Brandon said. "Sure. Can we eat first?"

Nikki laid a loving hand along his cheek. "Sure, babe," she said, and kissed him very tenderly on the mouth.

I sat there. All I could think about was the weight and warmth of Cosabella's head on my foot. I didn't dare let myself think about anything else. If I did, I knew I would just start sobbing, the way Nikki had a few minutes earlier.

If anything could break through my frozen tear ducts, that is.

I don't know what I'd been expecting, really. I was a prisoner, after all. I always had been, ever since the surgery. I guess I just hadn't realized it until now. I had no rights, no say in what happened to me. If Brandon wanted to set up some whacked-out operating room in his garage and have a surgeon come remove my brain and stick it in some other girl's body, I guess I had to let him.

Didn't I?

Well, didn't I?

If I hadn't felt so isolated, so rigid — as if ice had formed in my veins — I might have been able to think straight.

But as I sat there, staring at my reflection in the plate-glass windows looking out over that cold black sea, I could think of nothing except how completely frozen and alone I was. . . .

I was on my own, and there was no one at all who was going to be able to help me out of this one.

FIVE

I WAS IN MY BED AT BRANDON'S BEACH house, and I was dreaming.

In my dream, Christopher had come to rescue me. He wasn't, it turned out, mad about the whole thing where I'd told him I loved Brandon and not him.

Quite the opposite, in fact. Our reunion was joyful . . . and passionate. It was turning the ice that had been flowing in my veins back to blood . . . warm, rich blood that was making me hot . . . shove-the-covers-down, hair-sticking-to-the-back-of-my-neck hot.

In my dream, Christopher was kissing me . . . gently at first, playful kisses on the lips, light as the down feathers in the comforter that I'd already pushed past my bare thighs.

Then, as I kissed him back, proving that it was true — I had never loved Brandon. How could I? — the kisses became longer . . . deeper . . . more passionate. My lips parted beneath his as his hands found their way into my hair — spread like a fan across my pillow — his mouth cool against mine because of the chill outside, the zipper from his leather jacket almost unbearably cold as it pressed against my warm skin as he leaned over my bed, whispering my name. . . .

I was so relieved to learn he hadn't even believed me that bitterly cold morning outside of Dr. Fong's house when I'd said I didn't love him. He'd known Brandon had been making me say it.

He just hadn't known why.

The reason he hadn't believed it was because he'd loved me — the real me — all along. Not me, Nikki, the girl who'd torn his heart out of his chest and thrown it to the ground and then squashed it underneath her Louboutins.

Me, Em. The girl in the photo he'd kept over his desk all those months.

The girl he'd thought was dead for so many months.

Except if that was true . . . if Christopher hadn't believed me . . . why hadn't he called?

Because, a voice inside my dream reminded me, *Christopher doesn't love you anymore.*

Wait a minute. I wasn't actually liking this dream after all.

I opened my eyes with a gasp to find a hand pressed to my mouth. This was no dream. This was really happening.

I knew who it was, of course. Who else could it have been? Who else had been trying my doorknob (unsuccessfully, since I'd been careful about locking it every night) all week? The hand over my mouth was masculine. I could tell that just by its size and heaviness, even if, in the darkness of my room, I couldn't see who owned it.

So of course I did the only thing I was able to: I clamped down on it with my teeth as hard as I could.

What else was I going to do? Brandon had snuck into my room in the middle of the night to do what guys like Brandon do to girls when they're asleep. How dare he try to take advantage of me when I was dreaming about someone else? Someone I actually *liked* . . .

I bit down and didn't let go until I heard bones crunch.

"Ow. Jesus, Em!" the voice cried in a hoarse whisper. The hand ripped away from my face, and for a second, I heard the sound of leather rubbing on leather . . . a sleeve lifting away from the body of a jacket as someone waved his hand back and forth.

Wait. My sleep-muddled mind tried to make sense of this. Why would Brandon be wearing a leather jacket *inside?*

"What did you go and *bite* me for?" Christopher wanted to know.

My mind reeled. Christopher? In my room? Here, at Brandon's house? What was Christopher doing here? How had he gotten in? Had I not been dreaming after all? Had he really been kissing me?

I sat up so fast, I jostled Cosabella, who'd been curled against my neck.

"Christopher?" I whispered. "Is that really you? Oh, my God, did I hurt you? Are you bleeding?"

"Of course it's really me," he whispered. He sounded so annoyed, I wanted to grab his face and go back to kissing it, just like in my dream . . . if that *had* really been a dream, and not real. Only Christopher could sound that irritated with me. Wonderful, amazing, easily annoyed Christopher. "Who else would it be? And don't tell me Stark has been sneaking in here. Was that why the door was locked? I had to use my library card to jimmy the lock. Seriously, if he's been trying to get in here, I'll kill him —"

I forgot that I was supposed to be giving Christopher the cold shoulder, on pain of Brandon destroying everything and everyone I loved.

I forgot that I was supposed to be pretending that Brandon and I were an item now.

I was so overwhelmed at finding Christopher sitting on the side of my bed, just like in my dream, that I threw my arms around him, pulling him close and swearing to myself that I was never going to let him go. I didn't even care that the metal rivets and zipper of his leather jacket were icy cold against the parts of my bare skin that weren't covered by the matching pink tank top and sleep boxers I was wearing. Just like in my dream.

"Oh, my God, Christopher," I whispered, breathing the crisp outdoorsy scent that was still clinging to his short hair. "I'm so glad to see you."

"I'm glad to see you, too," he said, putting his arms around me to hug me back. Hard. "And don't worry about my hand. I'm sure it's just a flesh wound."

I laughed. I think I was semihysterical.

But I didn't care. It felt so good to be in his embrace.

Christopher. Christopher was *here*.

"But what are you *doing* here?" I whispered.

His hold on me loosened just enough so that he could look down into my face. Sometime while I'd been sleeping, a partial moon must have come out. . . . I could see its faint glow through a crack in the curtains on the far side of the room. It didn't let in enough light for me to see him by, because his back was to it and he was thrown into silhouette by its glow. But he, I knew, could see me.

"Did you really think I'd believe you, of all people, were in love with Brandon Stark?" he asked in a softly chiding voice. "It may have taken me a while to figure out who you really are now, Em. But give me some credit. And now that I do know it's you, I'm certainly not going to let you go that easily."

My heart gave a little somersault inside my chest. I kept holding on to him. I don't think I could have let go of him, either, even if he'd wanted me to. Which, thank God, he didn't.

He leaned down and kissed me, and I realized, as our lips touched, that I *hadn't* been dreaming . . . that really *had* been him kissing me. Kissing me awake. No wonder I'd been so hot. . . .

And that his kisses were doing to me again what they'd done to me before, making me feel warm and protected in a way I hadn't felt since . . . well, since the last time I'd been in his arms, all too briefly back in my room at the loft during Lulu's holiday party.

And just like then, before I was entirely aware of what was happening, Christopher's hands were gently cradling my face as his lips moved over mine . . .

. . . and then I was sinking . . . sinking slowly back against the soft pillows behind me, with Christopher on top of me. Somehow he'd shed that annoying leather jacket, and he was half on, half off the bed.

But definitely half on me, a sensation I couldn't say I didn't find enjoyable. I knew there were things we needed to say. Things I needed to know, things I needed to tell him.

But how could I when his lips were doing such interesting things to mine, and his hands — oh, his hands — had moved away from my face to tug at my . . .

"Christopher," I said breathlessly, pulling my lips from his. It was the hardest thing I think I'd ever had to do. In the darkened room, there was nothing I wanted to do more than just let him keep doing what he was doing.

But I couldn't. Someone had to stay sane. And I had a pretty good idea that it wasn't going to be him.

"We have to focus," I said.

"Focus," he repeated. I could see that his blue eyes, so close to mine, were half-lidded and looked dazed. "Definitely."

He lowered his head to kiss me again.

But as much as I longed to let him, I knew I couldn't.

"No." I ducked out from beneath him and moved to the far side of the bed, where Cosabella was sitting, licking herself. I pulled her onto my lap to use her as a kind of doggy boy-defense shield. "I'm serious. I'm happy to see you, too. But we have to talk. What are you *doing* here?"

Christopher seemed to pull himself together. He lost the dazed look — well, some of it — and said, sitting up straighter,

"I think it should be obvious what I'm doing here, Em. I'm here to rescue you."

My heart gave another one of its crazy somersaults. Seriously, everything this boy said — and did — was causing my internal organs to do acrobatics.

"Rescue me?" Never in my life had anyone said anything as sweet to me. He had come all the way from New York to *rescue* me? Just when I had given up all hope that anyone I knew was even thinking about me. Except Lulu and my mother. And my agent, Rebecca, of course. "Oh, *Christopher* . . ."

It was all I could do to keep from crawling back across the bed and into his arms.

But that, I knew, would be a huge mistake. Because I wouldn't have the strength to crawl out of his arms again . . . not until things had gone way further than either of us were ready to handle . . . at least right now.

Pushing some of my sleep-tossed hair out of my eyes, I resolved to follow my own advice and focus.

"How did you even get in here?" I asked. "Brandon keeps this place locked up tighter than Fort Knox."

He pulled a small, sleek box from the pocket of his coat.

"Universal code grabber," he said. "Just the latest of my cousin Felix's many do-it-yourself hacking devices he's been working on to keep himself entertained. This one can run something like a million potential code combinations a second before it finds the right one. Used it to open Brandon's garage door."

I stared at the little metal box in his hand. Okay. *This* was definitely something I wouldn't dream. I wasn't so sure Christopher's cousin Felix belonged under house arrest in his mother's basement. I think maybe he belonged on the payroll of some tech corporation in Silicon Valley.

"I suppose that's how you bypassed the security system, too," I said.

"Oh, no," Christopher said, casually slipping the box back into his pocket. "I just typed in Brandon's password for that once I got inside. I figured he'd be stupid enough to use his own name — and I was right."

I couldn't help smiling at that one.

"So we're just supposed to walk on out of here," I said, "the way you came in?"

"Pretty much," he said. "You ready?"

I had to laugh. The idea of me just walking out of Brandon's house with Christopher and away from my problems like — well, like it was that easy.

Where could we even go? It wasn't, like, with my face, we wouldn't be instantly recognized anywhere we went.

And what about Steven, and Nikki, and their mom? I know I'm not related to them — except by blood — but I owed them something for the way they'd fought for me, even if it hadn't worked. Steven had gotten so mad at Brandon for agreeing to Nikki's insane plan, he'd finally had to leave the dining room entirely, for fear — he'd told me later — that he'd smash Brandon's face in. Later, he'd come into my room, telling me that we had to get out of there before both Nikki and I ended up dead.

But go where? Steven could always rejoin his naval unit and slip back under the sea in the submarine he'd left to look for his missing mother. But what about Mrs. Howard, who couldn't even use her credit cards or pay a bill for fear of Stark Enterprises tracking her down?

Or Nikki, who chose to remain so blindly ignorant of the role she'd played in causing all of this heartache?

I wanted to tell Christopher all these things.

But first, I had to tell him the most important thing of all — besides the fact that I was madly in love with him, which I was pretty sure from the previous few minutes' makeout session he already knew.

"Christopher," I said, breathlessly, "Nikki told us. She told us what she tried to blackmail Brandon's dad with. What she overheard that got her killed . . . and me into this mess in the first place."

He reached out and smoothed some of my hair away from my face. I closed my eyes for a second or two, relishing the warmth from his fingers as they swept my skin. A wave of desire slammed into me with all the force of a dodgeball hurled by Whitney Robertson.

Bad. I had it bad for this guy.

"Go on," he said.

"It just . . . ," I said, opening my eyes again when his hand fell away from my face. "It doesn't make any sense, is the thing. Nikki says she overheard Mr. Stark and a bunch of his cronies chuckling in his office over the fact that new Stark Quarks are going to arrive with some kind of undetectable spyware — bundled with the new version of *Journeyquest* — that's going to upload all of the information the user taps into it — any information he ever enters into any websites — Priceline, Facebook, e-mails, that kind of thing. And all of it is going to be stored on the mainframe at Stark Corporate. All of it."

I looked at Christopher and shrugged.

"That's it?" he asked, his eyebrows raised.

"That's it," I said, nodding. "Nikki swears. She didn't hear them say anything else. She says they were all congratulating one another and toasting over it. I mean, I guess an undetectable tracking software is pretty advanced, but one in three PCs in America has spyware on it already and their owners don't even know. What's the use of having all that information — and we're talking about data from hundreds of thousands of homes, maybe millions, because the Stark Quark is going to be the lowest-priced laptop in history — if Stark's just going to store it on the mainframe? It's not like they said they were going to use it for anything. And you know the people who are going to be buying the Quarks — they're pretty low-end — aren't rich. It's not like Stark's going to be getting the credit card numbers of, like, millionaires or anything. That's why I don't understand how this could be worth killing Nikki Howard over. What's the big deal?"

The moon had shifted. Now a shaft of its light fell full on Christopher's face, and I could finally see him properly for the first time since I'd woken to find him in my room . . . and in my bed.

And for a second, I thought I spotted a glimpse of the dark supervillain that I had been convinced he'd turned into after reports of my "death" and his decision to try to avenge it . . . that supervillain I thought was gone for good when he realized I wasn't dead after all.

But no. The darkness — and hate — were still there. Maybe they would never go away.

And I was going to have to live with the knowledge that I was the one who was responsible for that.

"Why does anyone commit murder?" he asked in a low voice.

"I —" I blinked. "How should I know?"

"Three reasons," Christopher said. He held up one finger. "Love." Another finger. "Revenge." And finally, a third finger. "Profit. They tried to kill Nikki Howard when she threatened to expose the truth about them."

"So?" I shook my head. "I still don't —"

"Robert Stark definitely has a plan for how he's going to profit from the information he's stealing from the people who buy his new PCs," Christopher said. "What we need to do is figure out what that is. And how we're going to make him pay. We've got a lot of work ahead of us. We better get on it. Get dressed and let's go."

I started disentangling my legs from the sheets. "Steven and his mom are going to be fine," I said. "I can probably get them up and out, no problem. But I'm not sure how we're going to convince Nikki to come along with us willingly. She likes it here just fine. And she's expecting a brain swap with me in the morning."

"Wait," Christopher said, putting a large hand on my shoulder. "What are you talking about?"

"Nikki," I said, looking at him in the moonlight. Something about his expression told me that the evil supervillain was not only back but here to stay. "Brandon promised her he'd get Dr. Fong to swap her brain back into her old body. This one. She's not going to want to go. But she has to, of course. It's not safe for her here."

"Em," Christopher said. His voice was cold. "I don't care about Nikki Howard. I'm here to rescue you. Not her."

"But." I blinked at him. "We can't just leave her behind."

"Oh, yes," he said, "we can."

SIX

I WAS TRYING TO WRAP MY MIND AROUND a world where the guy I loved would refuse to help a damsel in distress.

Although it *was* kind of hard to think of Nikki as any kind of damsel.

"If she wants to stay with Brandon," Christopher said, his tone uncompromising, "let her. Now go put some jeans on so we can get out of here."

"She's a severely damaged person," I argued. "She doesn't know what she wants. She's been through a lot."

"So have you," Christopher said. "And you aren't going around trying to blackmail people. Though I can't say I've been too impressed by how you've handled the situation so far."

I glared at him, stung. "What's *that* supposed to mean?" I demanded.

"You really thought I was going to believe you'd run off with *Brandon Stark*, of all people, because he's just so damned irresistible?" His tone was slightly scornful. "I'm not a complete idiot, you know."

My heart gave a warning *ker-thump* inside my chest. Uh-oh.

He sounded mad. Not just annoyed. But really, really mad.

And also, maybe, beneath the anger, a little hurt.

"Christopher," I said when I was able to find my voice, "I can explain all that. Brandon told me if I didn't pretend like he and I were —" I swallowed. Uh-oh. Snot. And some tears, too. Not a good sign. "You know. That he'd tell his dad where he could find Nikki."

"And you believed him?" Christopher demanded. "What was the likelihood of that happening, when Nikki holds the key to Brandon getting back at his father for taking away his Super Soaker when he was a kid, or whatever the hell it was Robert Stark did that Brandon's so mad at him for?"

Wow. Christopher was right about that one. Why hadn't I ever thought of that? For a smart girl, I can be really dumb sometimes.

I may be able to figure out how to make a slow-burning fuse by watching YouTube.

But boys? That's where I seem to have a big fat blind spot.

"He was really convincing, Christopher," I said. The tears were starting to overflow. I hoped he couldn't see them in the dark. I tried to hold them back. I felt so stupid. He was angry, and I responded by crying? How big a baby was I, anyway? No wonder he liked McKayla Donofrio better than me. I bet she never cried. She was too busy watching CNBC's stock market report and double-checking her retirement portfolio. "Brandon's dad tried to have Nikki killed. I think you're right, and he maybe even tried to have me killed . . . or at least that TV dropping on my head at that exact moment wasn't quite the accident everyone made it out to be. So how was I supposed to know he wouldn't try to have someone else killed, maybe even someone I love, like Mom and Dad, or Frida, or even . . . you?"

I thought that might cause him to warm up. I mean, I'd just admitted I loved him. You would think the guy would throw me a bone.

But no. He still wasn't having any of it.

"And you couldn't call or text me to tell me any of this?" Christopher demanded. "Seriously, Em? This past week, not a single message? What, Brandon's been watching you every second of the day?"

"No," I said, wiping tears from my face with the back of a wrist. I was mad now, too. Mad at myself for crying, but mad at Christopher, too. What did he want me to do? "But what was I supposed to say, Christopher? How do I know they aren't tapping your phone? You don't know what it's been like. It's like they're everywhere, watching. And besides, I promised Brandon —"

"Oh, you promised him," Christopher said. And this time, he wasn't being a *little* harsh. "Jesus, Em, for a smart girl, you can really be dense sometimes. Almost," he added, with a self-deprecating smirk, "as dense as I was for taking so long to figure out who you really were."

"Well, *you* never called or texted me," I said, a throb in my voice. I couldn't help it.

"You kicked me to the curb!" Christopher cried, spreading his hands out wide. I noticed for the first time that he was wearing black leather fingerless gloves, the kind cool bad guys — who always turn out to not really be bad — wear in movies. I supposed that's what Christopher was now, though.

Except that he was actually kind of bad. Or he was acting that way, at least.

"What am I," he went on, "your fricking dog? You can treat me like crap and I'm just going to come crawling back to you every time? Oh, no, wait — you treat your dog better than you treat me." He pointed at Cosabella, curled up beside me. "You let her in on everything."

I blinked at him. This had gone from really, really great to really, really bad in a matter of minutes. In my dream, Christopher had totally forgiven me. And then he'd made out with me.

But it didn't look like that was going to happen in real life.

"Face it, Em, you don't really love me," he said harshly. "You say you do, but you don't. You know how I know that? Because you don't trust me. Through this whole thing, you've never trusted me enough to let me in completely." He got up from the side of the bed. "Well, you're never going to be able to have a real relationship until you stop thinking Emerson Watts is the smartest person in the whole world, and start trusting other people, and letting them try to help you. It's called being an adult, Em. You might want to give it a try."

"Wait," I said, my voice cracking. "You're just going to *leave?*"

"Well," he said, "are you going to come with me if we don't take Nikki?"

"No," I said, lifting a wrist to wipe furiously at my eyes.

"Then yeah," he said. "I guess I am. Because you said yourself she's not going to leave willingly."

I couldn't believe this was happening. It was my big Princess Leia moment — I was being rescued, only not, thankfully, by my own brother — and I was blowing it. My rescuer was just walking out and leaving me behind like dryer lint.

But what was I supposed to do? I couldn't leave Nikki behind.

However much she might not deserve or even want my loyalty.

"Fine," I said. "I guess this is good-bye, then."

"I guess it is," he said.

And he turned and walked out of the room, closing the door behind him.

I sat there in my bed, expecting the knob to turn and for him to come back any minute. He'd be all awkward and sweet — or maybe still angry and defensive — and say it was my fault. Only, of course, what he'd really be saying was, *I'm sorry, Em. I still love you. Come with me. Please come with me.* Whichever. It didn't matter.

But he'd come back. Of course he'd come back.

He couldn't have just walked out. He couldn't be gone. He just couldn't.

But he was. The minutes on my bedside clock ticked by, and he didn't come back. The house was noiseless. Nothing. No sign of Christopher coming or going.

It took a while for reality to sink in, but eventually, it finally did. He'd ditched me. He'd completely ditched me!

I couldn't believe it. This was the worst thing that had ever happened to me.

Well, okay, not really. Getting a brain transplant in the first place. That was the worst thing that had ever happened to me.

But this was totally the second worst thing.

Besides the fact that tomorrow Brandon Stark was going to make me get a second brain transplant.

Yeah. I was a total idiot not to have gone with Christopher.

On the other hand . . . he'd clearly morphed back into the dark supervillain I'd seen hints of ever since I'd had my accident. I guess you can't really shake that kind of thing entirely. Maybe I'd been smart not to go with him. Of course I had! I couldn't have gone off with him and left the Howards behind. Because Steven and his mom wouldn't have gone without Nikki, either. How selfish would that have been?

No, I'd made the right choice. Christopher was the one with the issues, not me. How could he even have suggested otherwise? If anyone had any growing up to do, it was him, not me.

When I woke up — and I don't even know how I'd managed to fall asleep, with all the fuming I'd been doing — it was because Brandon Stark was rattling my doorknob, demanding to know when I was going to get up and come down to breakfast.

And a few seconds later, Nikki came barging into my room from the connecting door to hers, telling me to be sure not to eat too much, because she didn't want to get "her body" back too bloated.

And my cell, over on my nightstand, was buzzing. When I fumbled for it and squinted at the caller ID, I saw it was a text message from my agent, Rebecca, demanding to know when I was going to be back in New York.

Robert Stark was throwing a New Year's party at his

massive four-story town house preceding the live Stark Angels lingerie show the day after tomorrow, and it was important that I be there to meet the shareholders. If I wasn't there, I was going to be in violation of my contract. Not only was I going to be replaced by Gisele Bündchen (who'd managed to lose all the pregnancy weight in record time and changed her mind about agreeing to be in the show), but I was going to lose a lot of money.

Needless to say, Rebecca was unhappy with me.

I lay there and wondered how unhappy Rebecca would be if she knew how much her highest-paid client was about to *really* lose. As in, her life, if Nikki had her way.

Honestly, I don't know what I had been thinking. I've never considered myself the girliest of girls, or anything. I was born and raised in New York City, so I'd always thought I'd seen it all, including a broken bottle fight once outside our local Mexican restaurant (Señor Swanky's) between two men arguing over possession of a parking space.

So was it completely unnatural of me to think, when I'd woken in the middle of the night to find my boyfriend saying he was there to rescue me, that all my problems were over, and that everything was going to be all right?

Apparently so. Apparently, that Aretha Franklin song my mom liked so much was right, and sisters really did need to keep doing it for themselves.

Probably it was my fault for believing that those corny happily ever afters at the ends of the romance novels my sister, Frida, was always reading, where the hero was always saving the heroine — usually from dangerous situations she'd put herself into — could actually happen in real life.

Because it turned out all those books were wrong. It turned out, in real life, the hero had problems with the heroine's "trust issues."

Excuse me, but *I* have trust issues? I'm not saying I'm perfect. I'm not saying there isn't a possibility — a slight possibility — that what Christopher had said was partly true.

Maybe I do have difficulty letting other people in, or allowing them to get to know me, or help me, or whatever.

But Christopher thought *I* was the only one with a problem? Oh, that was rich. That was just hilarious, coming from a guy who kept a *code scanner* in his pocket.

And okay, Christopher had gone to a lot of trouble to rescue me.

But was I rescued? Um, the answer to that question would be no.

But I told myself I didn't care anymore. Not now that Dark Spider-Man had taken the place of my formerly sweet boyfriend.

Even if he had only been my boyfriend for about two minutes, total.

Why hadn't I just told Christopher last night that Nikki had demanded her old body back in return for her spilling her secret to Brandon?

Not that this would necessarily have made the slightest difference to him. Probably it wouldn't have, considering how much he hated me. Which was maybe why I didn't tell him. A girl had to have some pride. I mean, I didn't want him taking me back out of *pity*, or something. Nothing would be more disgusting than *that*.

So now he was gone and I was still here and I'd never know for sure if it would have made a difference or not.

And right now Brandon was probably having a secret laboratory set up where my brain was going to be sucked out and put into yet another stranger's body.

And who even knew if this time I'd recover from the surgery? I might be lobotomized or, worse, never wake up at all. I might end up in a vegetative state for the rest of my life. Or have that icky hair that Nikki had totally fried with the flat iron.

I'll just be honest: I wasn't that jazzed about being the new Nikki. No offense, but she wasn't showing too much potential, at least the way the old Nikki was dragging her around in my castoffs.

Plus, I had gotten used to being *the* Nikki Howard. Maybe it was shallow, and sure, I'd complained about it a few times.

But I don't care what Megan Fox or Jessica Biel say: There were definite advantages to being the hottest girl on the planet. Number one was that I got paid for it. A lot.

And number two was that people were just nicer to you when you looked pretty, as opposed to looking like the hot mess that I used to be, and that the old Nikki was now. They just were. It was a fact. Whitney Robertson was example A. Why would I want to go back to having volleyballs spiked at my head (on purpose), and my own sister refusing to be seen with me?

You could go on and on about how people were supposed to like you for what you had on the inside.

But if that was really true, why in the name of all that is holy would anyone have ever liked Nikki in the first place? I was becoming more and more convinced she was a cross between Heidi Montag and Hitler.

And I had no faith that Christopher would ever come back. We hadn't exactly parted on the greatest of terms, so it seemed unlikely I was ever going to see him again, except maybe in Public Speaking, if I got back to Tribeca Alternative. I couldn't believe he'd accused me of treating him like a dog when I most definitely had made almost every decision out of concern for *his* safety.

And okay, maybe, like he'd said, that *was* infantalizing him, just a little. After all, he was a grown man who could make his own decisions and didn't need my protection.

But in my opinion my trying to protect him only proved how deeply I loved him.

Wow. Maybe Christopher was right. Maybe I really *was* turning into one of those stupid heroines from Frida's books.

The thing was, I'd just felt so *happy* when I'd woken up and found him in my room. Everything had seemed so great. I wasn't all alone anymore . . .

. . . except, it turned out, I was.

And thanks to my own stupidity.

TSTL. Too Stupid to Live. That's what Frida said they called the heroines of her books who made choices that put their own lives at risk.

And those heroines aren't just in books, either. They're in horror movies, too. Like when the heroine of the movie hears a noise in the basement and thinks to herself that she had just better go check it out. Even though all the electricity in the house has blown out. And her flashlight is broken. And there is an escaped convict loose in the neighborhood.

Really, she deserves what's coming to her.

But did I? I mean, did I deserve to have my brain pulled out of my body *again* and have to learn to adjust to being a whole new person all over?

I texted Christopher an *I'm sorry. Can we talk? Where r u?* message, which I fully didn't expect him to reply to (he didn't), then took a shower and got dressed in a pair of designer jeans and a ruffly top the boutique had sent over, pulling on the boots I'd brought with me from New York.

As I blow-dried my hair, I tried to think about something other than myself. Like how Brandon's father could possibly be hoping to profit from storing all those people's data on Stark Enterprise's mainframe. Obviously, he wasn't going to use their credit card numbers himself. He was a billionaire. What did he need with a JCPenney card?

And most of the people buying Stark Quarks were college and high school kids. I mean, the Quarks only cost two or three hundred bucks, tops, and they came in colors like lavender and lime green.

So why was he collecting all that data?

I was still trying to figure it out when Brandon rattled my doorknob again.

"Hey," he called. "Are you coming to breakfast, or what?"

I strode over to the door and threw it open. Brandon was standing there, his hair sticking to his head because he'd just showered. He was wearing, of all things, another Ed Hardy shirt, jeans, and a thick gold chain around his neck. A waft of Axe assailed my nostrils.

Really, Brandon? I swallowed hard against the barf that rose up in my throat.

"I'm coming," I said, not smiling. "Is the doctor here?"

Brandon stared down at me blankly. "What doctor?"

I'd always suspected Brandon had been allowed to eat way too much sugar as a child.

But this was a bit much, even for him.

"Dr. *Fong*," I said, enunciating clearly so he couldn't misunderstand. "To perform the *brain transplant*."

"Oh," he said. "Uh . . . not yet." He glanced down the hallway to make sure Nikki wasn't around, then put one arm up against the wall behind me, leaning in close enough that I could smell the toothpaste on his breath. "Listen . . . you don't think . . . I mean, you didn't think I was actually going to go through with that crazy plan of hers to let you swap brains, or whatever. Did you? I mean —" He reached out and lifted the pendant I was wearing, some kind of crescent moon or something. "She's crazy. And you . . . you're the one I want."

I just stared at him. I would no sooner believe anything that came out of Brandon's mouth than I would believe something I saw on the cover of *Star* magazine about Jennifer Aniston's current state of pregnancy.

"Uh," I said. "You seemed pretty into the idea last night when you were talking about it with Nikki."

"How else was I going to find out what she was blackmailing my dad about?" he asked with a laugh. "I had to lead her on, you know."

I plucked the necklace out of his hand. Seriously, his cologne was so strong, it was making my eyes water.

"How do I know you're not leading *me* on?" I asked. "You two did used to go out. So you didn't always think she was so crazy."

Brandon stared at me with his mouth hanging open a little, giving me ample opportunity to observe his veneers.

"That was just," he said, his Adam's apple bobbing, "for sex."

"Charming," I said, wanting to throw up more than ever. "So what happens now? To Nikki, and Steven, and their mom? Are you going to go on keeping them forever, like your pet shark?"

"Well," he said, looking uncomfortable. "No."

"Then where are they supposed to go? They can't go back to their normal lives. Your father will find them. Do you want their deaths on your conscience?" I stabbed an index finger into the middle of his chest. "Do you? Well? Do you?"

"No," he said. He'd been backed up against the wall behind him. "Of course not. But that's not going to happen. Because your computer geek friend is gonna help me figure out how to use the information Nikki got about my dad and turn this all around to get back at him —"

"My computer geek friend?" I knew exactly who he was talking about. "And just why do you think he's going to be willing to help me, after what you made me do to him the other day?"

I didn't mention the part about Christopher's problem with my "trust issues."

"That's not my deal," Brandon said with a shrug. "You're the one who's supposed to figure out how to make that work. Or Nikki might end up exactly where you're so worried she will. . . ."

I don't know why I was so surprised. Everything in Brandon's life was disposable. Last night after he'd gotten off the phone with his lawyer he'd already begun making calls to purchase a new car to replace the one I'd burned up.

Why shouldn't he consider people disposable, too?

Just as he was making this casual threat, Nikki appeared in the hallway from her room, wearing a lantern dress that was exactly the wrong color green for her new complexion and patterned tights that made her legs look chunky. Her hair, as usual, was a disaster, and it looked like she hadn't even tried with her face. Maybe because there was no makeup artist around to do it for her.

"Good morning," she said. "Ready for breakfast?"

I gave her a tight smile. "Can't wait," I said, dropping my finger from Brandon's chest and brushing past him to head down the stairs. Behind me, I heard Nikki purr, "Hello, tiger." She was apparently speaking to Brandon. I hadn't any doubt from the slurping noises I heard next that she'd wrapped her arms around him for a big good morning kiss.

Was it everyone's intention to make me throw up before I'd even had my breakfast?

What I saw when I got to the dining room, however, made me completely forget what I'd just heard.

And that was my little sister, Frida, pouring orange juice into glasses at our place settings.

SEVEN

OH, SHE WAS WEARING A DISGUISE. OR
what I suppose she considered a disguise: red plastic-framed
glasses, black-and-white checkered pants, a white chef's coat, and
her hair was stuffed up into a tall white chef's toque, like the kind
they wear sometimes on the Food Network.

But other than that, she was very definitely Frida, a freshman
in high school, who was supposed to be at cheer camp over winter break.

There were any number of things I could have said or done
at that particular moment. Blurted out, *What are you doing here?*
Fainted. Stomped up to her and demand she get back home this
instant. Didn't she know how much danger she was in . . . how
much danger she was putting the rest of us in?

I didn't say or do any of those things. Instead, I just sank down into my seat — I'm pretty sure I couldn't have remained standing even if I'd wanted to — and sat there, staring up at her. I couldn't figure out what was going on for a minute or so. It isn't often you see someone from one part of your life in a completely separate part of your life and have to meld the two together, then try to make sense of what you're seeing.

Then slowly — more slowly than I would have liked to admit — I put two and two together.

It was all starting to make sense, though. The fact that Christopher had shown up last night, then left without me?

The fact that Frida was standing there in ill-fitting catering clothes, ladling out food to us — she was serving us scrambled eggs from a platter — trying not to make eye contact with me through the lenses of the red plastic-framed glasses?

I could see that she'd caught on to the fact that I'd recognized her. There were bright spots of color blossoming on either of her full cheeks, even though she was resolutely not looking my way.

My heart had begun to thump hard inside my chest. Not only was I afraid for Frida — afraid that Brandon (thick, dopey, dangerous Brandon) was going to show up any minute and recognize her — but I'd realized if Frida was out here, Christopher was in the kitchen. He had to be.

What was he thinking, letting my baby sister come here, of all places?

Worse, just the idea that he might be nearby was making my pulse speed up. How could I be so weak?

But I quickly put this thought out of my head. More important than that — more immediate than that — was the danger that Frida was in. My palms had gone slick with sweat. Didn't she have any idea how risky what she was doing was? If Brandon caught her . . .

. . . well, I didn't know what he'd do.

But I knew it wasn't exactly going to go over very well.

And what about Mom and Dad? Did they know where Frida was at this very moment? I very much doubted it. Because if they did, they wouldn't have allowed it.

She would be so, so dead when I got through with her.

"Is there anything other than eggs?" Mrs. Howard, already seated, asked politely, looking down at the yellow lumps congealing on her plate, her forehead slightly wrinkled, as if she were worried about actually tasting them.

Mrs. Howard, of course, had never met Frida. She had no idea my baby sister was the one serving her her breakfast.

"Pancakes," Frida said, in the fakest Southern accent I'd ever heard. She sounded like a bad Paula Deen. Did she really think just because she'd tucked her hair into a chef's toque and had on glasses that anyone was going to believe she was over four-teen? "I'll be right out with them, ma'am."

"Oh," Mrs. Howard said, moving bits of egg around with her fork. "That will be lovely." She didn't sound convinced.

Seated across the vast glass table from Mrs. Howard was Steven, who'd risen early to work out in Brandon's private gym, as he did every morning. I stretched out my legs as far as I could and tapped his foot, lightly, I thought . . .

. . . forgetting I was wearing pointy-tipped stilettos.

"*Ow*," Steven said, reaching for his injured leg. He gave me an aggrieved look, like, *What did you do that for? Aren't things bad enough? We're imprisoned in this guy's beach house mansion. Do you have to stab me in the leg with your shoes, too?*

I jerked my head in Frida's direction. Steven glanced at her, then gave me an annoyed *so what?* look, still rubbing his leg.

When I jerked my head back at Frida, Steven looked at her again. Recognition dawned.

When Steven glanced back at me one more time, his expression was one of alarmed disbelief.

I know, the look I gave him said. *What are we going to do?*

"What the hell is this?" Brandon wanted to know.

Brandon had disentangled himself from Nikki, and the two of them came over to sit down at the table.

"Is this juice fresh-squeezed?" Nikki wanted to know, before she gulped some without waiting for an answer.

"This doesn't look like waffles," Brandon said, glaring down at his plate.

"That's because it's eggs, sir," Frida said, giving him a slight bow.

My heart was now thumping so hard, I could barely breathe. Would Brandon recognize her? He had just seen her less than a week ago at the party Lulu and I had given at our loft — he'd danced with her, for Pete's sake! How could he not recognize her?

And if he recognized her, would he call the cops? Surely not, after what he'd said the night before about the Murciélago.

On the other hand, this was someone actually trespassing inside his house.

Would he have them rough her up? Over my dead body would any of them lay a hand on my sister. . . .

Of course, given the fact that I already was dead, this was sort of an empty threat.

"Eggs?" Brandon looked perturbed. "Since when were eggs ever on the menu? I hate eggs."

My shoulders sagged in relief. He hadn't recognized her. Of course not. Brandon paid no more attention to the help than he did to . . . well, Nikki, if he could help it.

"There's been a slight change, sir," Frida said. "Chef trusts you'll still find the food to your satisfaction."

Geez! Where had Frida learned to say all this stuff? She actually sounded like a real caterer. I couldn't believe it. My baby sister was all grown up!

Brandon looked down at the yellow goo on his plate. "No Belgian waffles?" he asked, now sounding slightly forlorn.

"This is disgraceful," Nikki said. "You really can't find good help anymore." She threw her napkin down beside her plate and started to get up. "I'm going to go give that chef a piece of my mind."

"No." I hastily threw my own napkin down, feigning indignation. "I'll do it. There's no reason why the rest of you can't stay here and enjoy yourselves."

I got up and made my way across the slick black marble floor toward Frida, with Cosabella, who had followed me downstairs, trotting behind me, her claws making familiar clicking noises on the marble. The whole time my heart was clattering along with my heels and Cosabella's claws. I was a little ashamed about what my heart seemed to be saying: *Chris-to-pher*, my heart beat in rhythm to my footsteps. *Chris-to-pher*.

It was ridiculous, I knew. Now was no time to be thinking about boys. Especially boys who'd abandoned me because of my alleged "issues." My sister was the one I had to concentrate on.

My sister who had stupidly, foolishly, amazingly put herself at risk because of me.

In a way, I was incredibly proud of her (not that I had any intention of letting it show while I was beating the crap out of her). How had she gotten here, all the way from New York City? She was only a freshman . . . a kid, after all. It seemed like only the other day she'd been begging me to go with her to see Gabriel Luna in concert at a Stark Megastore.

Or begging me not to go with her, actually, since she hadn't wanted me to be seen with her and embarrass her in public because I looked and dressed so badly. That had been before I'd become Nikki Howard, of course. God, how time flies.

"Come with me, young lady," I said, grabbing Frida's arm. "Let's just have a word with this chef of yours."

"Um," Frida said. She could barely keep up with me on her much shorter legs as I hustled her toward the kitchen. "Whatever you say, ma'am."

He wouldn't be there. I knew he wouldn't be there. I'd seen the look on his face last night when he'd told me he was done with me.

Not to mention the look he'd been wearing that morning by the limo outside Dr. Fong's house when I'd told him that things might have been different if he'd just liked me the way I was before the surgery.

But he hadn't, and so now it was too late.

No wonder he was so unwilling to forgive me . . .

. . . and was so convinced I had issues.

And okay, what I'd said to him by the limo had been a lie, though I'd told myself at the time that I believed it. I'd had to, in order to make myself say it.

The expression I'd seen on his face when I'd said it hadn't been the expression of anyone who seemed like he might later give me another chance.

Except . . . well, Frida was here. I never in a million years thought I'd see her. Miracles, it seemed, *did* happen.

So maybe . . . just maybe . . .

When I hit the swinging door to the kitchen with all the force I could, trying to give the impression, for Brandon's sake, of a billionaire's angry girlfriend, Lulu, in a white coat and toque that matched Frida's, let out a shriek.

My heart gave a deflated *zzzzzzzt* like a balloon some birthday clown had stepped on with his stupid giant clown shoes.

Christopher wasn't anywhere to be seen.

Instead, Lulu, letting out a sigh of relief, smiled like I was Ryan Seacrest telling her she was the new American Idol.

"Oh, thank God," she said, flattening a hand to her chest. "It's just you two. Oh, and Cosy! You *scared* me. Did you have to sneak up on me like that?"

My mind staggered as I tried to make sense of what I was seeing in front of me: my roommate, Lulu Collins — not to mention my sister — was in the kitchen of Brandon Stark's tropical beach house.

Of course. Of course they were. Where else would they be?

"What," I demanded, when I'd finally caught my breath from the lunacy of it all, "are you doing here? How did you get in? And where's the chef who was supposed to be here?"

"I don't know," Lulu said, answering my last question first with a shrug. She'd gone to turn off the stove, where she'd been frying something in a pan. It actually smelled delicious, like pancake batter. When had Lulu learned to cook anything but her signature dish, coq au vin? "I slipped him a check to take the day off. And we just borrowed his stuff and walked in. Well, drove in, actually. No one checked our IDs or anything. Em, are you okay? We've been so worried about you. You've been acting so weird! Cute top. Don't hug me back, I don't want to get pancake bits on you."

Lulu went to hug me. I stood there with her skinny little arms circling my neck, glaring over the side of her toque at Frida, who stood there smiling at me sheepishly.

"Do Mom and Dad know where you are?" I demanded, even though I knew the answer.

"Mom and Dad think I'm at cheerleading camp," Frida said. "And before you can get even more mad, Em, let me remind you that they put off their trip to Grandma's to stay in the city to be with you. But then you just took off to be with your new boy-friend, Brandon Stark. They're not exactly happy with you."

I blinked at her. "But —" I started to protest.

"Yeah," Frida said, nodding. "I know. But I couldn't tell them you weren't here of your own choice, could I? Or they'd start flipping out. So I had to be all *Oh, no, she's in love with Brandon now*. And go along with what all the tabloids were saying, just like everybody else. Even though I knew you didn't give a rat's butt about Brandon Stark. I could see it in your face, even if Mom and Dad couldn't. But just so you know, you're basically killing them, a day at a time. Happy?"

I blinked at her. So my boyfriend thinks I have trust issues, and I'm killing my parents? This wasn't exactly something I wanted to hear. Especially before breakfast.

"So when Lulu called me at camp — because Mom flipped out and said I was going to cheerleading camp, because, I think, she doesn't want me to turn into a boy-crazy freak like you, Em — to say she wanted to stage an intervention on you," Frida said, "I jumped at the chance. Because which do you think is more important: saving a beloved sister or learning to do a ball out to high splits?"

Since I had no idea how to answer this question — a ball out to high splits had to be some kind of cheerleading move — I blew some of my hair from my lip gloss and glared at them as

Lulu let go of me and stepped aside to move the heavy iron frying pan she'd been using off the heat of the stove. There was, I saw, a pancake in it.

Lulu really had been planning on serving pancakes.

Then, pulling herself up to her full height — which was more than eight inches less than mine — Lulu said, "Really, Em, you shouldn't be mad. We're here to rescue you."

I just stood there staring at them. I couldn't believe they'd done what they'd done — come all this way, just to bring me home.

"Come on, Em," Lulu said, making a little beckoning motion. "Get Steven and his mom and Nikki and let's go. Are you ready? That's a fantastic top, by the way. Did I say that already?"

"You guys," I said. I felt tears pricking the corners of my eyes. I couldn't help it. I couldn't believe how sweet they were being, especially after I'd been so sure no one cared. Well, except my mom. And Rebecca, my agent.

But my mom only cared because she had to . . . she was my mom. And Rebecca . . . well, she needed me for the money I made her.

At the same time, there was a hurt in my heart that I couldn't deny, and it had to do with the fact that, while they might have been there, a certain other person was so conspicuously absent.

Frida and Lulu, noticing the sudden tears in my eyes, exchanged glances.

"Uh," Lulu said. "Okay. Christopher was right."

My heartbeat sped up a little.

"You talked to Christopher?" I asked. "What did he say? Did he . . . tell you?" If he had told them about my alleged trust issues, I was going to kill him.

"Yes," Frida said. "He did. And don't worry. I've got this. We covered it in my Psych class. Em." She turned toward me, put her hands on my bare shoulders, and started speaking in an exaggeratedly slow voice. "What you're experiencing right now is called *Stockholm syndrome*. It's when you begin sympathizing with your captor because he's shown you kindness. I know Brandon might be hot, and he gave you that nice shirt. But he's still a bad guy. Just because he hasn't killed you doesn't mean he's your friend."

Shocked, I flung her hands off me. "Would you shut up? I'm not in love with Brandon. Ew, is that what Christopher said?" Talk about Too Stupid to Live. . . .

"Oh, phew," Lulu said, her fragile shoulders slumping with relief. "Good. Look, we don't have a lot of time. I chartered a jet to take us all back to New York, and it's waiting on the tarmac. They charge by the hour, so, you know, chop-chop. Go tell the Howards to come back here. By the way" — she dropped her voice — "has Steven asked about me? Did he like the eggs? I made them special just for him. He loves scrambled eggs. By the way, he knows I like him, doesn't he? I'm being too obvious." She poked Frida in the arm. "I told you scrambled eggs were too obvious. I should have gone for sunny-side up."

"Ouch," Frida said, rubbing her arm. "*Lulu.*"

"I peeked out a minute ago and saw him," Lulu went on. "He looks really hot in that sweater. It's cashmere and we're at the beach, for heaven's sake. Maybe he should take that shirt off. It would be all right with you if he went around shirtless, wouldn't it, Frida? See, Frida wouldn't mind. And what's with Nikki's hair? Is she not even trying? And that green is all wrong for her."

I took a deep breath.

"You guys," I said. "Seriously. We can't leave just yet. Did Christopher not tell you? We have to —"

"Are you all right?" Frida asked. She had taken off the red plastic-framed glasses and now she blinked at me, her eyes looking very dewy. I realized this was because there were tears in them. "Because you look horrible. I mean, underneath the makeup and everything. Do you realize you haven't smiled once since we got here?"

"You haven't smiled once since you left *New York*," Lulu said, accusingly. "I know, I've got you on Google Alert. I've seen every shot that's been taken of you, and you look totally miserable.

That's how we knew." She shot me a meaningful look. "That you needed to be rescued."

"Look." I took Frida and Lulu both by the arm and started steering them toward the back door, through which food deliveries were made. "Thanks a lot for trying to rescue me. I appreciate it. I really do. But we have to —"

Before anyone could say another word, the swinging door to the kitchen slammed open. Lulu let out a shriek . . .

. . . for which I couldn't blame her, since Brandon Stark was suddenly standing there in front of us.

EIGHT

"WHAT THE HELL," BRANDON DEMANDED, glaring from Frida to Lulu to me and then back again, "is this?"

"Oh," Lulu said. Her dark eyes had gone the size of the pancakes she was making. "Hi, Brandon. Did you like the eggs? I made them myself."

Brandon ignored the question. For which I couldn't exactly say I blamed him.

"What are you doing here?" He ripped his gaze from them and instead raked it over me.

I knew I had to act, and fast. It wasn't like I had a lot of time to think over how I was going to handle this, or what I was going to say or do. No one had told me there was going to be a second rescue attempt that morning. This wasn't like the car bomb thing, which I'd lain awake nights mulling over and planning. I mean, I really hated Brandon Stark, so I'd decided to do the meanest thing to him that I could think of, and that was light his favorite thing on fire.

But in this case, I didn't have a chance to come up with something as genius as a chemical-soaked beaded necklace slow-burning fuse. I just did the first thing that came to me.

I threw myself at him, draping an arm across his chest and snuggling my boobs up against his shoulder.

This was another advantage of being Nikki Howard. She was very distracting to men.

"My friends came for a visit, Brandon," I purred. "And they made breakfast. Isn't that a nice surprise?"

Brandon didn't look like he thought it was a nice surprise at all. In fact, he continued to look homicidal, completely ignoring my purry voice. And my boobs. Which was quite unusual for him.

"No," he said, fuming. "Where's the chef? I paid a lot of money for that chef."

"He'll be back tomorrow," Lulu chirped. "I promise. Look, Brandon. I was going to make you guys pancakes!"

Brandon seemed understandably unimpressed.

"Lulu," he said. "Were you the one who lit my car on fire?"

Lulu looked confused — which made sense, since she'd had nothing to do with the destruction of Brandon's Murciélago and had no idea what he was talking about.

"What?" she asked, setting the frying pan back down on the stove with a clang. "No . . . ?"

"I knew it," he said, reaching into his pocket for his iPhone. "I knew it wasn't the paparazzi who destroyed my car. That's it. I'm calling the police and having you all arrested."

I let go of him and took a step backward.

"Brandon," I said. "What are you doing?"

Except it was pretty clear what he was doing as the tones of 911 filled the air.

"Don't worry, babe," he said to me. "I have it under control." He pointed at Lulu and Frida as he said, "This is trespassing, you know, and that, my friends, was destruction of property. That Murciélago was worth over a quarter of a million dollars. Lulu, your dad can afford to pay that back, even if his last movie was a bit of a dud. Yes, hello," he said when someone on the other end of the cell phone picked up. "I'd like to report a —"

But before the last words were out of his mouth, a muscular, charcoal gray–clad arm appeared around his neck — seemingly from nowhere.

And Brandon's voice was cut off. He dropped the phone, reaching to claw at the arm.

But it was too late. A second later, Brandon closed his eyes. By then the arm had released him, and Brandon had sunk quietly to the floor, unconscious. Cosabella hurried over to him to sniff his ear, then give it an encouraging lick.

We all stood there, blinking down at him, completely unsure what had transpired — it had all happened so fast — until someone cleared his throat.

That's when we noticed Steven. He had apparently been standing behind Brandon the whole time he'd been talking to us. It had been his arm that had choked Brandon into unconsciousness.

"Steven," Lulu said, her face transforming into an expression I can only describe as unmitigated adoration. "Oh, hi!"

"Uh," Steven said, looking a little uncomfortable, "hi, Lulu."

"Oh, my God," Frida cried, snatching up a spoon and bending down to hold it in front of Brandon's nose, apparently to check and see if he was still breathing. "He's dead!"

"No," Steven said a little diffidently. "He's not dead. He'll wake up soon, no worse for wear. He won't even know what happened."

"Did you learn that choke hold in *military* training?" Lulu asked as she stepped over Brandon's prone body to come up to Steven and rub her body against his like a cat. I'm not even lying when I say her eyelashes fluttered.

"Uh," Steven said, eyeing her even more uncertainly than before. "Yes?"

"That was incredible," Frida said. She seemed just as admiring as Lulu. Maybe even more so. I flashed her an annoyed look. She was supposed to have a crush on Gabriel Luna, not Nikki Howard's older brother.

"So," Steven said, ignoring his new fan club. "Would someone care to tell me what's going on here?"

As he asked this, there was the sound of an explosion . . . so powerful, it actually rocked the kitchen a little, causing all the pots and pans hanging from a rack over the center island to clatter together and make a tinkling sound. I grabbed hold of the counter to steady myself on my heels.

"What was *that*?" I asked, alarmed.

"Oh." Lulu tugged on her chef's toque so it sat at a more rakish angle, and said, "That was just Christopher. He was supposed to blow something up to distract Brandon's security guards — and Brandon — so we could all slip safely out the back." She looked over at Steven adoringly. "But Steven already distracted Brandon, as you can see."

"Wait," I said, my heart stopping. "Christopher's *here*? With you?"

"Of course he's here," Frida said. "He said you two talked last night," just as Lulu was explaining at the same time, batting her big Bambi eyes at Steven, "We're here to rescue you. And your mom and Em." Then she added, with just a hint of distaste, "And your sister, too."

"Steven!" The kitchen door flew open. It was Mrs. Howard, looking pale, followed by Harry and Winston. "What's going on? What was that —" She looked down at the unconscious Brandon. He seemed to be sleeping gently as a baby. "Oh, dear . . ."

"He's all right, Mom," Steven quickly assured his panic-stricken mother. He went to put an arm around her. "Why don't you and Nikki go and get some things together? I think we're going to have to be leaving here in a minute or two."

Mrs. Howard shook her head, unable to tear her gaze from Brandon.

"We always seem to be fleeing places at the most unexpected times," she murmured.

But her reaction was mild in comparison to her daughter's, who came in a few seconds after her mother had left and whined, "What's going on? What was that —"

That's when her gaze fell to the floor, and she let out a blood-curdling scream.

"Brandon!" Nikki fell to her knees at her ex-boyfriend's side. "Oh, my God, Brandon! Are you hurt?"

Brandon actually appeared to be regaining consciousness as she asked this, partly because Nikki had yanked him into a sitting position. He rolled his head back and forth, murmuring something about how he didn't want any more peekytoe salad. When his eyelids fluttered open, he looked at Nikki and asked in a dazed voice, just like in the movies, "What happened?"

"Steven did a secret military move on you," Lulu volunteered to Brandon. "Don't worry, though. You're going to be fine."

"*What?*" Nikki cried, whipping her head toward her brother. "*You* did it? Why would you do that to Brandon, of all people? He's been so nice to us!"

Uh, maybe he'd been nice to her. To me? Not so much.

"Because he was going to call the police and have your friends arrested, Nikki," Steven explained. "And they're only trying to help."

"Help?" Nikki's flat-ironed hair flew around as she looked from Steven to Lulu and me and then back again. "Help how?"

"Help us get out of here, Nikki," I said. I didn't want to be the one to give Nikki the bad news. But someone had to do it. "Now that you told Brandon what you heard about the Stark Quarks, he has no use for you anymore. He's going to cut you and your family lose."

Brandon didn't dispute this. To be fair, he didn't look as if he was in the greatest shape to.

"No." She shook her head back and forth so rapidly that a lot of that shiny hair got a bit staticky and started sticking straight up into the air. She didn't seem to notice, though. "No, he's not. He's getting me my operation. Aren't you, Brandon? Tell them." Brandon was still a little groggy from whatever Steven had done to him, so Nikki, I guess to be helpful, gave his face a few smacks. "Did you hear me, Brandon? Tell them!"

"Uh, Nik?" Steven said. "Slapping him isn't really going to help."

It was at this moment that the back door to the kitchen tore open and Christopher came bursting in, a smudge of something that looked like oil on his cheek, his jeans dirty, and his leather jacket flapping open. He stopped on the threshold, apparently surprised to see us all gathered there, and particularly Brandon on the floor . . .

. . . and me, standing above him.

It only took him a second or two, however, to gather himself together.

And it only took a heartbeat for my breath to be knocked completely from me by the sight of him.

Which was infuriating. Because I was really, really mad at him. And I definitely wasn't in love with him anymore.

Why would I be in love with such an infuriating, stubborn person?

Or at least, that's what I told myself.

"Oh, good," he said. "You're all here. Let's go, then; we don't have much time. I'm pretty sure one of the security guards called 9-1-1. They're all over on the beach now, putting out the fire. Still, we need to go now."

Oh, the fire. Right. Of course.

"What do we do about him?" Steven asked, nodding at Brandon.

Christopher looked down at the heir to Robert Stark's vast fortune. "What happened to him?" he asked curiously.

"Steven used a secret military choke hold on him," Lulu volunteered again, just as chipperly as before.

"Excellent," Christopher said with a congratulatory nod at Steven. "Tie him up."

Tie him up? I stared down at Brandon, who looked about as freaked out as I felt. I couldn't believe Christopher — *my* Christopher — had just casually suggested someone tie up Brandon Stark. Who had Christopher turned into? A week ago he'd been a relatively geeky — if hot — straight-A junior at Tribeca Alternative High School in Manhattan.

Now all of a sudden he's John Connor from *Terminator Salvation?*

"Tie him up?" Nikki looked up with tears brimming in eyes that were already mascara smudged. "You can't be serious. You are *not* going to tie him up."

"Here's some cooking twine," Lulu said, after opening a few kitchen drawers.

"Perfect," Christopher said, and reached for the spool of twine Lulu handed to him. "Steven, want to help me out here?"

"It would be my pleasure." Steven bent over to begin wrapping Brandon's legs in lengths of cooking twine, while Christopher went to work on his wrists.

"Are you crazy?" Brandon demanded. He seemed to be coming around, but not enough to fight what was happening to him. Except vocally. "Do you know who I am? When my father hears about this —"

"When he hears about what?" Christopher wanted to know. "How you had a girl he tried to murder here in your house for nearly a week and never told him about it, because you were trying to get her to tell you what it was he tried to have her killed for in the first place?"

Christopher did have a point. On the other hand . . .

Frida edged over to me and whispered, "What's going to happen when Brandon gets out of that string, or whatever? I mean, isn't he going to be mad?"

"I would think so," I said.

"Then won't he just come after all of us?" she asked worriedly.

"Probably," I said.

This had been exactly what I'd been thinking. I was a little surprised Frida had figured it out. Frida had lately begun showing startling growth and maturity for someone who, just a few short months earlier, had been willing to stand for hours on line just to get the autograph of some guy I had never even heard of.

Suddenly, I became aware that Nikki's sobs had reached a pitch where they sounded like keening. I'd never heard actual keening before, but I'd read about it in books. It sounded like wailing, only higher pitched. Nikki was hugging herself and rocking back and forth on her knees like a little kid who'd had her favorite toy taken away.

"No, no, no, *no*," she was saying, the noes growing progressively louder. "I am *not* leaving here! Not without Brandon!"

Lulu, I noticed, was viewing Nikki's theatrics a little less sympathetically than anyone else in the room. Since I'd never seen Lulu behave anything but kindly toward anyone, I couldn't help feeling a little surprised when she said with more than a hint of prickliness to Nikki, "You seem awfully devoted to Brandon now, Nikki. But you weren't so devoted to him back when you were sneaking around behind his back — and mine — with my boyfriend, Justin, were you?"

This cut Nikki's keening off like a siren that someone had suddenly silenced — just as, in the distance, we heard the wail of a real-life siren.

The police were on their way.

Brandon looked over at Nikki in surprise — almost as if he were really seeing her for the first time.

"You?" His dark eyebrows furrowed. "And *Justin?*"

Nikki's mouth fell open, and she looked from Brandon to Lulu and then back again, seeming to be gulping a little for air, as if she were one of the fish from Brandon's aquarium . . . one that had accidentally leapt out of the safety of its soothing blue waters.

"You — you found out about that?" she asked, sounding a little stunned.

"He tried to perform mouth-to-mouth on Em," Lulu said, pointing at me. "Only she wasn't experiencing any trouble breathing, if you know what I mean."

I winced. I'd always wondered if Lulu had been looking out the window that day Justin had snuck up on me outside the loft.

Now I knew. Poor Lulu.

And poor Nikki. She blinked as if someone had slapped her. Her mouth was still moving noiselessly, as if she were trying to say something.

Only no words were coming out of her mouth.

"As much as I'd love to stand around and continue this very special episode of *America's Next Top Teen Supermodel*," Christopher said, "we need to get moving before —"

The doorbell rang.

"I think that's our cue," Steven said.

Mrs. Howard reappeared in the kitchen doorway, holding

the same bag I'd seen her leave Dr. Fong's house with nearly a week earlier.

"I'm assuming," she said, "I shouldn't get that."

"No," Christopher said. "You should not."

Nikki leapt to her feet and threw herself at her mother.

"Mom," she cried. "They're making us go with them! And leave Brandon behind!"

I looked at Christopher. I knew he hated me now, and everything. And maybe he had reason to.

But he still had to listen to me. Because this was my escape, too.

"We have to take him with us," I said.

Christopher looked back at me like he'd never seen me before in his life. In fact, it was a lot like those early days back in Mr. Greer's Public Speaking class, when Christopher hadn't known it was me, Em, looking out at him behind Nikki Howard's famous sapphire blue eyes.

"Absolutely not," he said, emphatically. "That is not part of the plan."

I walked up to him and stood so that my face was just inches from his.

"We have to change the plan," I said. "Because if we don't, the minute the plane lands, we're going to be surrounded by a bunch of feds. Brandon's going to call them. I guarantee it."

"He's not going to tell anyone," Christopher said. "He can't. What's he going to say? That he kidnapped you, and you escaped?"

"He'll make something up about all of us," I said. "He'll say horrible things about what we did to him, and next thing we know, Steven will be on *America's Most Wanted*."

"I don't think that show is even on anymore," Christopher said, looking down at me with his eyebrows furrowed. His lips, I couldn't help noticing, were very close to mine.

I hated myself for noticing this.

"Oh, that show is still on," I said. "And you know who's going to be starring on it soon? You, if you keep on the way you've been acting. What did you blow up, anyway, when you were out there 'distracting Brandon's security guards'? How do you know none of them got hurt?"

He bristled.

"Because none of them did," he said. "I was there. It was only a pipe bomb, and I threw it toward the beach, away from everyone."

"Including the paparazzi?" I demanded. "They've been hiding in the dunes."

"I checked it out beforehand," Christopher snapped. "No one was there. God, Em, what do you want from me?"

Obviously, I couldn't tell him what I wanted from him.

Because it wouldn't have been exactly appropriate to say in the mixed company in which we were standing, part of it having to do with his tongue in my mouth.

"I want you to be responsible for your actions," I said instead. I didn't know what was wrong with me. Why was I yelling at him when he was only trying to help me, which was quite generous of him, considering the fact that he didn't even like me anymore? "Not run around acting like your *Journeyquest* avatar, who by the way always attacked before thinking, too, which is exactly how you always got pwned —"

"You never pwned me," Christopher snapped. "I pwned you —"

"Um," Mrs. Howard said. The doorbell rang again. Now someone was pounding on the door, too. "I hate to interrupt. But I really think we ought to be leaving now —

"And I think taking Brandon along with us is probably the wisest course," Mrs. Howard continued. "Otherwise I think he might do something . . . impulsive."

"If you lay one hand on me," Brandon roared, thrashing on the floor, "I'll call my lawyers! I'm going to sue all of you! You, too, Lulu! Just because your mother and my mother both once lived in the same ashram, don't think I won't do it!"

Lulu looked down at Brandon with narrowed eyes. It was clear he'd made a big mistake bringing up her mother, about whom Lulu'd never been able to speak without emotion.

"He's coming along," she said, producing a dish towel from her apron pocket. "Gag him, Steven."

It only took a few seconds for Steven to thrust the dish towel into Brandon's wide-open, protesting mouth. The next thing I knew, he and Christopher were half dragging, half shuffling Brandon out the back door and around the side of the house toward a parked minivan. The sound of the waves hitting the beach a few dozen yards away was loud . . .

. . . but not as loud as the sound of even more approaching sirens.

The air outside was crisp and smelled of mingled wood smoke and salty ocean spray. Cosabella, excited to be on what she assumed was her morning walk, hurried along in front of me on the path, sniffing everything she came across and doing her business, along with Mrs. Howard's dogs.

Nikki kept stumbling as she walked in her platform heels and looked back at the house.

"My operation," she said faintly. "If we leave, I'm not going to get to have my operation."

"Yeah," her brother said, in a voice that was as unsympathetic as Lulu's had been over Justin. "Well, that's for the best. Mom said it would kill you, remember?"

"But," Nikki said mournfully, "I just want to be pretty."

I won't lie: When I heard that, *I* stumbled.

I could barely look at her. *I just want to be pretty.* Oh, my God.

Nikki didn't stumble again as we all got into the car (well, Brandon had to be scrunched down behind the backseats of the minivan, an indignity he did not seem to enjoy one bit, if the grunting that could be heard from back there was any indication) and started at top speed toward the airport, passing fire engines on our way.

Lulu, who still had on her chef's hat, waved cheerfully at the handsome firemen, some of whom actually waved back at her, blithely unaware we'd been the ones who'd set the fire they were racing toward.

But Nikki's face, when I glanced at it, was just about the saddest thing I had ever seen.

I just want to be pretty.

I may not have been a prisoner anymore . . .

. . . but Nikki suddenly looked as if she felt she were.

NINE

WE TOLD THE PILOTS AND FLIGHT ATTEN-
dants that the reason Brandon was tied up was because we were
taking him to rehab against his will.

They knew enough about Brandon Stark from having read
about him in the tabloids — and from even having flown with
him once or twice — to believe it. They walked around during
the flight shaking their heads to themselves as if thinking, *Oh!
Those poor, spoiled billionaires' kids! I'm so glad my own kid doesn't
have any of those kinds of problems.*

But that still left the problem of what Brandon was going to
do to us when the plane landed.

"Have each and every one of you arrested," he snarled at us
once, when he worked the gag out of his mouth.

Lulu, rolling her eyes, popped the dish towel right back in.

Mrs. Howard thought we should hold a press conference, like the impromptu one I'd held when I'd been trying to find her.

"Nice idea," Steven said, leaning his elbows on the slick table-top in front of him. "But what, exactly, are we going to say at this press conference?"

"Well, the truth," Mrs. Howard said. "That Robert Stark attempted to murder my daughter."

"And where's the proof?" Christopher wanted to know.

"You're looking at her," Mrs. Howard said, pointing at me.

Christopher had most definitely not been looking at me. He had been studiously looking everywhere *but* at me. Now that we were broken up — because of my alleged trust issues — he had taken the farthest seat from me on the large plane, at the dining table for six.

Not that I'd cared. Or pretended to, or even noticed. I'd taken a seat in front of the flat-screen TV and started flicking through the DVDs to check if they had anything new I hadn't seen yet.

"But she's clearly alive and well," Steven pointed out, nodding at me. "I think it's going to be a bit difficult for the average American viewer to understand that Em isn't Nikki Howard. I think by proof Christopher means something a little more sub-stantive than just Em's word that she's not Nikki on the inside. Because she actually is, on the outside."

"She's got a scar," Frida said. "Em could show them her scar from the surgery. Where they did the surgery."

"I suppose we need more," Steven said thoughtfully. "We need an actual *witness*. Maybe someone who was there when they performed the surgeries."

"Well, you can forget Dr. Fong," I said, moving back from the front of the cabin. I'd just hung up the jet's phone.

"They killed him?" Lulu cried in horror.

Steven gave her a wary look. I really couldn't tell whether he liked her or not. Sometimes I thought he did, and sometimes I wasn't sure. While I considered her an utter delight, Lulu seemed to scare Nikki's brother sometimes with her intensity.

I guess I could sort of see why. Since getting back onto the plane, she'd changed from her chef's uniform into a leopard print bodysuit and a purple tutu and sequined jacket, along with a cherry red beret that sat on her bleached blond pageboy at a rakish angle and brought out the café au lait tone of her skin.

Still, I thought she looked cute.

Steven, on the other hand, seemed to regard her as a sort of species he'd never observed before, in the wild or captivity or anywhere, really.

I suppose there hadn't been many girls in Gasper like Lulu.

"Uh, no," I said. "I think he's on the run, like we are. The operator says his house phone is no longer in service, and when

I called the Stark Institute for Neurology and Neurosurgery and asked for him, they said he had given notice."

From the very back of the plane, I heard a mournful sob. Looking around, I saw that it had come from Nikki, curled up in a seat by a window.

I guess I shouldn't have been surprised. Dr. Fong had been her last hope for getting her old body back.

I just want to be pretty, she'd said, in the most pitiful voice I'd ever heard.

Who didn't?

Well, okay . . . I didn't. Pretty was the last thing I used to care about. Back in the days before that plasma screen had hit me on the head, I never used to make any effort whatsoever to look good.

That's why Frida had never wanted to be seen with me. I'd just throw on whatever of my clothes was lying closest on the floor. A haircut was whatever was cheapest at Supercuts. Makeup was . . . nothing. I guess maybe I'd tried once or twice to make an effort, but only halfheartedly, and it had always ended in disaster. It was, like, I'd just decided, *Well, I can't look like Nikki Howard, so I guess I'll just give up completely.*

Which could be partly why the guy I'd liked had never noticed I was actually female. . . .

The trouble was, from what I now had been in a pretty decent position to observe, Nikki Howard herself had never been too pretty, either . . . on the *inside*, anyway. Maybe if she could just work on being that now, it might start showing on the outside, too. . . .

On the other hand . . . if I had to look at somebody else walking around in my body, I guess I wouldn't be feeling too pretty on the inside, either.

"What about the thing with the computers," Frida asked. She held up her Stark Quark, which she'd received as a gift from Robert Stark. "Can't we tell the press or the police about that? The thing Nikki overheard?"

"But we don't have any proof regarding that, either," Steven said, reaching for the laptop. "At least, not yet." He looked questioningly over at Christopher.

But all Christopher did was hold up both hands, still in their fingerless gloves, in a helpless gesture.

"Don't look at me," he said. "I'm out."

I narrowed my eyes at him.

"What do you mean," I asked, "you're out?"

Lulu looked at me and, pressing her cherry red lips together — she was using a pretty heavy hand with the gloss these days, due, I knew, to a certain someone whose initials were S.H. — said, "Christopher said he'd come with us to help get you away from Brandon, because he felt that was the right thing to do and he owed you that much. But after that he didn't want anything more to do with any of this."

"So," I said, still regarding him through narrowed eyes. I couldn't believe he was serious. "We're just supposed to figure out this whole thing with the Stark Quarks on our own?"

"Hey," he said. "You're the one who's so concerned about putting the rest of us in danger. It's probably for the best, then, that I just walk away. For my own safety. Right?"

I glared at him. "Whatever happened to *Take it down?*" I asked. "Wasn't that your plan? To take Stark down? You're just going to forget about all that?"

"Em Watts isn't dead anymore," Christopher said, giving me a brittle smile. "Is she?"

"So it's all good?" I couldn't believe what I was hearing. "What about that speech you gave in class? The three hundred billion dollars in profit Stark made last year that just went to line Robert Stark's pocket. The cheap, Chinese-made knockoffs they sell that our American-made products can't compete with. The locally owned businesses the Stark Megastores drive out of town. How, if we're going to keep from going the way of ancient Rome, with a collapsing economy and a society dependent on imported goods, we have to become producers again and stop consuming so much. . . ."

Christopher shrugged.

"Not my problem," he said. "You don't need my help. You don't even trust me enough to *ask* for my help. Remember?"

I looked at him, not sure if he really meant it or not. A part of me was pretty sure he did. His gaze on mine was steady and unblinking, and there was an upward curl at the corners of his mouth . . . he was smiling like he was actually *enjoying* this.

But I couldn't help feeling as if, behind those blue eyes, there was a different Christopher — the old Christopher — begging me to call him on his asinine behavior. To say, *I'm asking for your help now. Will you help us? Will you help* me?

Only I didn't.

Because I was too angry with him. Why was he acting like such a four-year-old? I'd already explained to him why I'd made the decisions I had. They'd been perfectly decent, rational decisions.

So why was he acting this way?

"We don't even know that they're necessarily doing anything wrong with the information, other than storing it," Steven said hesitantly. "Do we? If we just knew what they were collecting it for . . ."

I watched as Christopher turned his head to look stubbornly out one of the jet's many windows.

"*I don't care anymore*," he said to the window.

But I knew he wasn't saying it to the window.

He was saying it to me.

And it wouldn't be exaggerating to say it was like he had thrust his hand past my ribs, ripped my heart from the walls of my chest, pulled it out, and tossed it thirty thousand feet to the ground (I think we were somewhere over Pennsylvania at the time), just like I had that morning outside Dr. Fong's.

Really? All this because I hadn't wanted to leave without Nikki last night, and he'd had to switch to plan B, calling in Lulu and Frida for support?

Or was it really because of my *issues*?

Well, if you asked me, Christopher was the one with issues.

I glanced at Lulu to see what she was making of all this and wasn't too surprised to see her roll her eyes. *Boys,* she mouthed. Then she made a gesture like I should go over and sit down next to him.

I'm sorry, but had Lulu been nipping at the emergency oxygen? Because no, this was not going to happen.

Instead, I turned my attention back to the conversation at the table, ignoring Christopher, who was ignoring everyone else . . .

. . . even though I'd known what was coming. I'd known it before it had even come out of Frida's mouth.

"Maybe," she'd said, "maybe if Christopher doesn't want to help, his cousin could figure it out."

Of course. Christopher's computer genius cousin, Felix, who was already under house arrest for having bilked a televangelist out of tens of thousands of dollars by programming a local pay phone to autodial his show's 1-800 number several hundred thousand times in a row (who knew the owners of 1-800 numbers actually had to pay every time you called them?).

Why not drag Felix into all this, even though he was Frida's age? Felix had nothing more to lose, after all.

"No," Christopher said, turning his head back to face us, sharply. I knew he'd been paying attention. "If I'm out, he's out, too."

I couldn't help wondering how Felix was going to feel about this decision. Felix seemed like the kind of kid who, once involved in a project, wasn't going to let go of it quite that easily.

And Felix had already found a way into Stark's computer mainframe because of me.

I couldn't even deal with Christopher anymore. Instead, I decided just to ignore him. There were too many more important things to think about.

One of them was Brandon, and how we were going to get him to leave us alone. I decided I'd handle this one.

I sat down across from him in one of the Gulfstream's soft, cream-colored leather seats.

"Brandon," I said, leaning forward to lay a hand on one of his . . . which were getting a little puffy from having been tied up for so long. "If your dad's company goes down, there's going to be a great big opening for a new CEO. It would be a shame if you couldn't step into his shoes because you'd been arrested, too, for all the stuff you did to me. You know, like blackmailing me and threatening me and taking me across state lines against my will even though I'm a minor, and all. That's going to look *really* bad on Fox News. I mean, I don't *want* to press charges against you for doing all that stuff. Because the way I see it, you're still a Stark, which isn't exactly a good thing . . . but at least you don't seem to be into killing people. But I totally will go to the feds about you if you mess with my friends after we all get back to New York."

Brandon, looking at me with wide eyes above the huge green-and-white-striped dish towel sticking out of his mouth, said a lot of stuff.

But I couldn't tell what any of it was, on account of the gag.

"The thing you need to know, Brandon," I said, leaning back in the seat and crossing my legs, "is that I'm the one who set your Murciélago on fire."

Brandon's eyes got a lot wider, and he said a lot more things, in a louder voice. I still couldn't tell what any of them were, though. Well, any of them that weren't swearwords.

"Yeah," I said. "I know. You totally deserved it. You can't treat women — or anyone — the way you treated me. Do you understand? And no, I'm not going to pay for a new car for you. Instead, I'm going to do a lot worse to you if you mess with me again. I'm going to call Oprah's people and schedule an in-depth interview on her network about how you used me, and what a total and complete loser you are. You will become the most detested man in America. And then you will have zero chance of the Stark Enterprises shareholders letting you take over when your dad goes down."

Brandon quieted when I said all this. He stared at me with wounded eyes, looking almost like Cosabella when I scolded her for chewing on a pair of Jimmy Choos, which for some reason she seems to find irresistible.

"So, what's it going to be?" I asked him. "Are you going to play ball? Or are you going to continue going through life acting like a total butthead? Because at some point, Brandon, you are going to have to decide." I lifted both hands like they were the scales Lady Justice held. "Butthead? Grown-up? It's up to you."

He studied my hands. Then, nodding toward the hand signifying grown-up, he said something. Only of course I couldn't tell what, because of the gag.

"Did you say grown-up, Brandon?" I asked.

He nodded vigorously. I leaned over to remove the gag.

"Oh, thank God," he said. "And I forgive you for the Murciélago. Really, I do. I admit, what I did to you was really, really crappy. Like you said, I *can* be a loser sometimes. I really can. Now, could you please, please untie me and get the stewardess to get me a drink and a turkey sandwich? I'm dying here."

"Flight attendant," I said.

"What?" He looked at me like I was crazy.

"She's a flight attendant, Brandon," I said. "Not a stewardess. On your journey toward not being a butthead anymore, you might as well start using the correct language. Stewardess is sexist. And I will untie you and get you a ginger ale. We told them you're on your way to rehab so it would be better for you not to have anything alcoholic."

"Whatever," Brandon said. "Thanks. And I'm sorry."

Getting up from my seat, I stopped and looked at him in surprise. Those were the last two words I'd ever expected to hear from Brandon Stark . . . *I'm* and *sorry*.

Was it actually possible for guys like him to grow and change?

I glanced over at Christopher, who was bent over his cell phone, pounding away at the keys with his thumbs.

Hey, if guys could change for the worse, why couldn't they change for the better?

But maybe that was just wishful thinking.

TEN

IT FELT GOOD TO BE HOME.

Oh, there was a ton of mail I was going to have to go through — not just bills that needed to be paid but gift bags and packages from appreciative clients and sponsors and even, I supposed, some of Nikki's old friends, wanting to wish her happy holidays. Someone had sent her an entire case of Grey Goose vodka, someone else a $3,000 Chanel bag, someone else four different iPods, still in their boxes.

Happy holidays, indeed, for someone — at the Memorial Sloan-Kettering Thrift Shop, where I was going to donate all this stuff so they could sell it to raise money to give to people who needed cancer treatment (although I wasn't sure they'd take the vodka).

And of course I wasn't going to be able to avoid my voice mail — or Mom and Dad — forever.

But it was amazing to be in my own place, surrounded by my own things, in my own beloved New York City.

Except of course it wasn't *really* my own place.

And they weren't *really* my things.

And who knew for how much longer I was going to be able to enjoy any of them? I was still going to have to worry about giving them back to their rightful owner. Or maybe not, since I also had the whole my-boss-might-be-trying-to-kill-me thing to worry about, as well.

Because things hadn't ended particularly well with Christopher. Or Nikki.

I'd tried my best with both of them. I really had.

Now, stretched out on my bed, I remembered how, Brandon taken care of, I'd gone to try to make amends with Nikki. I don't know why I'd felt like I owed her something. She'd been nothing but nasty to me.

But I couldn't stand to see her sitting there crying in the back of the limo we'd taken into the city from the airport (well, all of us except for Frida, who'd taken the charter jet back to Florida, to finish out the rest of her week at cheerleading camp).

I just want to be pretty.

Hadn't all those times I'd sat in our living room, wishing

that Christopher would notice me as something more than just someone to play *Journeyquest* with, I'd sort of longed to be pretty, too? Frida had always been the one who'd said the actual words, though.

"I wish I could be pretty," she'd say, and sigh, looking at a photo spread of Nikki Howard in some kind of ridiculous, $20,000 gold metallic dress in *Elle* magazine.

Mom, feminist professor of women's studies at NYU, would always huff the same thing in reply.

"Don't be ridiculous, honey," she'd say. "Looks don't matter. What matters is the kind of person you are, how much character you have."

And Frida would snort: "Yeah. All the boys in school really care about my *character*, Mom."

"Looks fade," Mom would go on. "But intelligence lasts forever."

"But you do think I'm pretty," Frida would say. "Don't you, Mom?"

"Honey," Mom would say, cupping Frida's face in her hand, "I think you and your sister are both growing into strong, independent young women. And that's how I hope you'll always stay."

I'd always wondered if Frida had noticed how Mom never really answered the question.

I'd laid a hand over Nikki's and squeezed it, and said softly, "Nikki. You're going to be staying at Gabriel Luna's place for a little while until we can get this thing worked out."

This wasn't something Gabriel had been particularly delighted to hear. He'd been shocked when I'd called him from the plane and announced that the Howard family was coming to stay with him in his place.

On the other hand, he *had* offered to help back at Lulu's holiday party, when all of this was going down.

Well, we needed his help now. We couldn't exactly stash Nikki and Steven and their mom in a hotel — Stark was sure to be tracking all of our credit cards.

But hiding them directly under Robert Stark's nose, in the new high-rise, supersecure apartment (into which he'd had to move to escape his hordes of screaming fans) of Gabriel Luna, a recording artist on Stark's very own label? Genius, even if Gabriel had his doubts . . . not just about Stark not finding out, but about playing host to Nikki, who practically spat at him in response to his cheerful "So nice to meet you," before locking herself into his spare bedroom.

"Well," Gabriel had said. "This is going to go well, I see."

"I'm going to do everything I can to try to get you back all the things you've lost," I'd assured Nikki, back in the limo. Or attempted to, anyway.

"Really?" She'd whirled to look up at me with tears streaming from her eyes. "Like my face? You're going to give me back my face?"

"Well," I'd said, startled. My hand had risen unconsciously to my cheek. Or Nikki's cheek, I guess it was. "I'm not sure I can give you that, Nikki. But your money and your apartment — those things are yours."

She turned right back to the limo's window.

"Then we have nothing to talk about," she said coldly. "Because all I want is to be pretty again."

And kind of like my mom, I hadn't known the right thing to say. Because pretty was the one thing I couldn't give her. Because maybe pretty was something she had to give to herself.

Lying on my bed in Nikki's loft, staring up at Nikki's ceiling, with her dog snuggled against my neck, all I could think of was what she'd said to me in the car.

Then we have nothing to talk about. Because all I want is to be pretty again.

I had never seen anyone look as sad as she had.

I could understand her loss. I'd lost the same thing. Well, not quite the same thing . . . but sort of the same, if you counted the fact that I'd lost things I probably loved as much as Nikki loved her looks: my family, my home, my friendship with Christopher. . . .

I don't know how long I'd been lying there before Lulu popped her head into the doorway and said, "I'm starving. I'm thinking of ordering in. Do you want a banana split?"

I rolled over to look at her.

"Lulu," I said. "Banana splits are not a meal."

"Yes, they are," Lulu said, coming over to hop up onto my bed beside me. "They have fruit and nuts and dairy. So they represent most of the major food groups. If you include chocolate sauce. And I'm always full after I eat one."

"Go ahead and order me one, too, then," I said, giving up and rolling over onto my back with a sigh.

Lulu clambered over me to reach for the landline sitting in its cradle on the nightstand by my bed. She hit the auto dial for the deli on the corner and ordered us two banana splits for delivery. Then she hung up and looked at me.

"Are you thinking about Christopher?" she asked accusingly.

"No, I'm thinking about Nikki," I corrected her. Although of course I *had* been thinking about Christopher, even if only peripherally.

Lulu made a face. She evidently didn't consider her former roommate worth thinking about, much less discussing.

"He still loves you, you know," she said, about Christopher.

"Oh, really?" I asked, with a bitter laugh. "That's not what he says."

"He's just upset," Lulu said, "that you lied to him. Not just once, but a bunch of times. It's wrong to lie to the person you love. Unless it's to tell him that his hair looks good, even when it looks awful."

"What if it's to protect his life?" I asked, rising up on my elbows to look at her.

"Especially then," Lulu said, shaking her head gravely. "Guys *hate* that. They're supersensitive, especially now, with feminism and stuff. It's completely confused them. They don't know where they stand. Are they supposed to do stuff for you like open doors and pay for dinner when you go out, or let you do it all? They don't know. Then he tried to rescue you, and you wouldn't even go with him. So you're going to have to let him do things for you once in a while. Even if you know he's just going to screw it up. Especially when you, you know, have so much going for you, and he . . . doesn't."

I glared at her, feeling a little hurt. How dare she say my boyfriend (well, ex-boyfriend, I suppose, technically) didn't have anything going for him?

"Christopher has a lot going for him," I said. "He's a total computer wizard and he's really funny and sweet — when he isn't being all supervillainy about avenging my death and stuff. Or mad at me about running off with the son of his mortal enemy."

"I'm sure he is," Lulu said diplomatically. "But right now, he's hurt. And so you're just going to have to work on breaking through the protective wall he's built up around himself for fear of getting hurt again."

"Well," I said, collapsing back against the pillows. "It wasn't just to protect him. It was to protect my family. And Nikki, too. I explained that to him. And he still hates me."

"I told you." Lulu had found some black nail polish in Nikki's nightstand drawer, and now she was applying it to her toenails, having kicked off her purple platform mules. "He doesn't hate you. But you're going to have to find a way to make him understand how much you really do need him, so he can see how important he is to you."

"He *is* important to me," I cried. "I love him!"

"But he can't really *do* anything for you," Lulu said, concentrating on her toes. "You're the one with all the money and power. He's just a high school boy. He can barely afford to buy you dinner at Balthazar. At least, not dinner *and* an appetizer *and* the crème brûlée there. He probably couldn't even afford to buy a bottle of this nail polish." Lulu closed the cap on the bottle and shook it. "It's Chanel. More than twenty bucks. Like I said back at Brandon's —"

"But he had the opportunity to do something for me today," I cried. "To help with the Stark Quark thing. And he wouldn't!"

"He's still mad now," Lulu said. "Let him cool down. Boys need cooling-off periods, just like my nails are going to need to dry off before I can put my shoes back on and go over to Gabriel's to give Nikki a makeover. She needs one just like you and Christopher need some relationship counseling from Dr. Drew."

I gave her a dirty look. "Christopher and I don't need relationship counseling. He just hates me, is all."

"He does not. Going to rescue you was all his idea," Lulu pointed out. "He was the one who called me and was completely gung ho about sweeping in and getting you out of there. It was way Luke Spacewalker."

This made me want to cry, it was so sweet.

"Skywalker," I corrected her. "It's Luke Skywalker."

"So what are we going to do?" Lulu asked, looking at me with her huge brown eyes. For once, she'd foregone one of her many pairs of tinted contacts, which often gave her eyes an eerily catlike glow against her dark skin. "I mean, about this mess? We can't hide the Howards at Gabriel Luna's forever. Brandon's totally scared of you now since you told him you're the one who lit his car on fire, so he won't tell. But his dad —"

"— is the fourth-richest man in the world," I said. "And also the most powerful. I know."

I stared back at Lulu. Why was she asking *me* what we were going to do? I had no idea. I had never wanted any of this to happen.

And I had no idea how to fix any of it, either.

We were sitting there looking at each other blankly when something rang, loudly enough to make us both jump practically out of our skins.

"Ahhh!" Lulu screamed. "What *is* that?"

We jumped off the bed and began running around the loft, trying to find the source of the ringing, while Cosabella dashed up and down, barking.

"Is it the banana splits?" I asked. "Are they here already?"

"That's not the buzzer," Lulu said, meaning the intercom the doorman used to let us know when someone was waiting for us in the lobby.

"Then what is it?" I wailed as the ringing continued, loud as ever, at regular intervals.

"Oh, my God!" Lulu cried, stopping by a side table. "It's the house phone!"

"The house phone?" I didn't even know that we *had* a house phone, we were both so dependent on our cells. We only ever used it to call out for food. "Are you kidding me?"

Lulu reached down and picked up the phone. "Hello?" she said, a curious expression on her face. Someone said something, and Lulu looked over at me.

"Oh," she said. "Yes. Oh, hi! Of course she's here. Hold on one moment."

Then Lulu covered the receiver with her hand and said to me, in an excited way, "It's for you. It's your mother."

I immediately threw both my hands into the air.

"*My mother?*" I whispered back to her. "*I don't want to talk to my mother! Tell her I'm not here!*"

Lulu looked confused. "But I just told her that you *were* here. Why don't you want to talk to your mother?"

"Because she's mad at me!" I whisper-yelled. "I just spent the holidays at a boy's house without his parents being there! You might have read about it in every tabloid in America? I'm in big trouble with her."

"Ooooh," Lulu said, nodding, as understanding dawned. "I get it. Do you want me to explain that you were being blackmailed and that if you didn't do it, Brandon was going to tell his dad where he could find Nikki, and then Mr. Stark would kill her? I'm sure Karen will understand that." Lulu took her hand away from the receiver and said, "Hello, Karen? It's me, Lulu. Listen, if it's about Em going to South Carolina with Brandon Stark, I can —"

I don't think I've ever moved as fast before in my life. I literally dove for the phone in Lulu's hand, landing with it on the couch and then pressing it to my ear. Lulu looked down at me in shock as I said to my mother, "Hi, Mom!" in the fakiest voice you could imagine.

"Emerson," my mom said.

Uh-oh. This was bad. My mom only called me by my full name when she was really, really mad.

Plus, she wasn't even supposed to be using my real name on the phone, let alone on Nikki Howard's house phone.

Something in her tone, however, suggested that this might not be the best time to remind her of this.

"So," I said, lying full length on the couch, as Cosabella, excited by all the activity, leapt on the cushions around me. "How's it going? How's Dad?"

"Your father is fine," Mom said, in the tightest voice you could imagine. She sounded like she'd just gotten Botox in her lips or something, she was speaking in such a cold, controlled, tiny little voice. It was clear that she'd been bottling up her anger with me all week, just saving it for the moment when she could see me, so she could explode all over me like one of Christopher's pipe bombs. "Thank you for asking. I've been leaving messages for you on your cellular telephone. Have you not received any of them?"

Cellular telephone. She had actually said the words *cellular telephone*. I was so, so dead.

"Uh, no," I said. "You know what happened, actually? It was the funniest thing, I dropped my cell phone in the ocean, and I haven't gotten around to replacing it. . . ."

Beside me, Lulu stamped the floor and gave me a dirty look. *"No more lying,"* she mouthed. *"To anyone!"*

I rolled my eyes at her.

"Well," Mom said. Her voice was still insanely small and cold. "It's lucky I happened to catch you at home."

"Yes," I said, trying to get Lulu to go away by making shooing motions with my hand. Unfortunately it wasn't working, because she was still jumping around, going, *"Stop lying! Don't lie!"* which wasn't at all annoying (yes. It was). "So how's Grandma?"

"Your grandmother is fine," Mom said, still sounding as frosty as a lemon ice. "Emerson, your father and I would like to meet with you. Would fifteen minutes be enough time for you to get to the Starbucks on Astor Place?"

"What?" Feeling panicky, I flung a glance at the windows of the loft. It was, as usual for late December in Manhattan, sleeting outside. "Um . . ."

"Your father and I are already sitting here waiting for you," Mom went on, "since I understand from TMZ dot com — the only way I seem to be able to keep track of my own daughter's activities anymore — that you're back in Manhattan. The adult thing to do would be, of course, to show up to meet us. However, if you just want to leave us here waiting for you like complete idiots, that's fine. But —"

"Oh, my God, Mom," I said, sitting up. "I'll be there. I'll be right over. Is everything okay?"

"No, Emerson," she said. "Everything is not okay."

And then the line went dead.

I held the phone away from my face, staring at it.

"What's the matter?" Lulu asked, hopping around on her bare feet, probably getting black nail polish all over the white fake fur carpeting.

"My mom just hung up on me," I said in disbelief.

"She did?" Lulu shrugged. "My mom does that all the time. When she remembers to call me. Which is once a year, on my birthday."

Aw. I felt so bad for Lulu, I reached out to give her a hug.

"Well, my mom's never done that before," I said. "I think something might really be wrong. I mean, aside from the fact that she is supremely pissed with me for spending the week at a boy's house without his parents being there."

Lulu looked concerned. "Like you think Robert Stark might actually be there holding a gun to her head, making her call you, so it's actually a trap or something?"

"Oh, great," I said, giving her a sarcastic look. "I hadn't even thought of that. She says she's at a Starbucks. Why would Robert Stark be holding a gun to her head at a Starbucks?"

"Oh," Lulu said. She seemed a little disappointed. "Yeah. You're right. That's not very likely, is it?"

I gave her another hug. I just couldn't help it, she was so cute. "I gotta go. I'll see you later."

"But what about our banana splits?" Lulu called after me as I ran to grab my coat and hat, as well as a leash and coat for Cosy.

"Save mine," I yelled. "I'll be back for it."

"I hope so," I heard Lulu shout as I jumped onto the elevator.

She had no idea how much I hoped so, too.

ELEVEN

I FOUND MY PARENTS SITTING AT A TABLE in the back of the café, huddled over tall cups of coffee, looking extremely serious. Since they were both professors, they looked serious most of the time, anyway.

But this was out-of-the-usual serious. Dad had dark circles under his eyes, and it appeared to have been a while since his face had seen the business end of a razor.

Mom's hair could definitely have used some conditioning, and I don't think she was wearing a lick of makeup. Not that she'd ever been a close personal friend of Maybelline's.

But I'd come to find out that a little goes a long way when it comes to mascara and lip gloss, something about which someone might want to remind Nikki.

God, did I, Emerson Watts, just think that? What was happening to me?

Robert Stark, despite what Lulu had worried about, wasn't anywhere nearby. So they weren't being held hostage.

But they didn't say hi or even wave while I got my biscotti and herbal tea (caffeine is a big trigger for Nikki's acid reflux) and then joined them at their table. They acted like we were complete strangers.

Which is totally unfair because while I may not be related to them by blood anymore, I'm still their daughter. Even if I've shamed the family name by allegedly hooking up with Brandon Stark. Or so every major tabloid in the U.S. and most of the United Kingdom claims.

"So, hi!" I said, trying to act all cheerful, while I peeled off my leather jacket. Cosabella got to work prancing around and sniffing them excitedly, which Cosabella considers her personal life's work . . . sniffing everyone and everything, and basically making people smile, because she wants only one thing, which is food, and to be petted and admired.

Well, I guess that's two things. Or three.

"Hi," Mom said finally, while Dad was a little bit friendlier, saying, "Hi, honey."

"So," I said, when my coat was off and so was Cosabella's and we were all settled in and I'd had my first sip of tea and burned my tongue and everything. Why do they do that? Make their hot water so hot.

"What's up?" I asked. I thought that sounded nice and nonconfrontational.

Mom and Dad looked at each other, and I could see that they were giving each other the old *Go ahead, you start, No, you start* eye signal.

Then Dad was, like, "Em, your mother and I wanted to talk to you about something. We chose to do so here in this café because it's neutral ground, not our place or yours, and we thought it might be a little less emotionally charged than either of our apartments."

Whoa. My heart began to thump a little harder than usual. This sounded serious! Neutral ground? Less emotionally charged?

Wait . . . were they getting divorced?

I knew it. Dad worked most of the week in New Haven, teaching at Yale. I'd wondered when he'd taken the job if their marriage — always volatile, since they were different religions, and both academics, not to mention attractive — I don't know how they'd managed to have a daughter as plain as me — could survive the stress of so much separation.

And now the truth was coming out. It couldn't!

Or wait. Maybe it was me. Maybe it was me their marriage couldn't survive the stress of! Because of my accident and subsequent coma and then reawakening in the body of a major teen supermodel!

"The thing is," Dad went on, "we've been a little distressed about your behavior lately —"

Wait, I thought. My *behavior*? Oh, God! It *was* me! They were getting divorced because of me!

"Not just your behavior," Mom jumped in. "Your grades this semester were abysmal."

"My *grades*?"

When Mom had called to schedule this meeting (and then hung up on me), I had thought a lot of things must be going on:

Robert Stark was breathing down their necks, maybe making threats.

They'd found out their apartment was bugged, the way I'd found out mine was (why else the meeting in a Starbucks, instead of at home?).

They'd found out about Frida skipping out on cheerleading camp and flying to South Carolina to rescue me, and were naturally upset about their underage daughter jetting all over the place without their permission. This wouldn't be the biggest surprise. Frida had told the camp officials she was going to her grandmother's. I'd thought the whole thing sounded sketchy, but Frida claimed no one was going to find out. She'd be home in time for the Stark Angel show tomorrow night on New Year's Eve with no one the wiser.

Now, of course, I knew better.

Then I'd thought maybe they were getting a divorce.

Or even, God forbid, one of them had cancer.

Or was having an affair (Lulu's mom had left her dad for another man. And I wouldn't put it past Mom to announce she was turning lesbian. Hey, she wouldn't even tell her own daughters they were pretty. Why would she care about the sexual orientation of a lover?).

But I'd never expected it to be about my *grades*.

All this neutral-ground chatter for a talk about *my grades?*

I'm sorry, but a corporation was trying to kill my friends. The true owner of my body wanted it back. The love of my life had just unceremoniously dumped me.

And my parents wanted to talk about frickin' finals?

"How did you even find out about my grades?" I demanded. "You're not Nikki Howard's guardians. You're not even supposed to have access to —"

Mom pulled something out of her purse. It was a crumpled-up printout from the website TMZ.com. Someone (probably a reporter from their offices, though of course it didn't say that) had broken into Tribeca Alternative High School's main computer and accessed my (or more accurately, Nikki's) grades, then plastered them all over the Net.

And let's just say I wasn't doing so hot.

America's Top Model Not Quite Top of Her Class, screamed the headline.

I snatched the sheet from my mother's hands and scanned it.

"A C minus?" I was stunned. "Mr. Greer gave me a C minus in Public Speaking? That mall cop!"

Dad made a disapproving noise over his coffee. "Now, Em," he said.

"But seriously," I said. "It's *Public Speaking*."

"Exactly what I'm thinking," Mom said, pulling the sheet from my hands. "There's no reason why you shouldn't have gotten an A in it. You just have to stand up in front of the room and talk. You've never had difficulty standing in front of people and talking before. In fact, no one ever used to be able to get you to shut up."

"Now, Karen," Dad said, exactly the way he'd said *Now, Em* when I'd called Mr. Greer a mall cop. "I'm sure there's more to it than that."

"Yeah," I said, coming to my own defense. "You have to make up reasoned arguments, and —"

"What about all those subjects you formerly always did well in?" Mom demanded. "How do you explain the C minus in

Advanced Algebra? And the D in English? For God's sake, Emerson, English is your native language!"

I scowled. "I didn't have time to do the readings," I said. "It's not my fault —"

Mom gasped triumphantly and pointed straight at me.

"There!" she said, looking over at Dad. "She said it! Not me! She said it!"

I looked from Mom to Dad, not knowing what had happened.

"What?" I asked. "What'd I say?"

"I . . . didn't . . . have . . . time," Mom said, hitting the table with her palm to emphasize each syllable. "Face it, Emerson. You're letting your schoolwork go because you're spending too much time socializing."

"Socializing?" I made a face. "Excuse me, but I never get to socialize. I'm working so much, I never even get to see my friends!"

"Oh, I think you get to spend quite a lot of time with your *friends*," Mom said, reaching into her purse and pulling out a different sheet of paper. "Quite a lot of *quality* time."

She unfolded the page to reveal an *Us Weekly* cover that showed me in a bikini hanging out poolside at Brandon's beach house, and him standing right next to me, holding what looked like a cocktail.

Except that put in context, I knew that that cocktail was

actually a breakfast shake and that bikini was actually my workout gear after going for a perfectly innocent run on the beach.

But it would still look pretty bad to a parent, considering I had, after all, spent nearly the whole week at Brandon's without her permission.

And the fact that the headline splashed above the picture of us together screamed:

Back On!
Nikki and Brandon Rekindle a Love So Hot,
They Had to Take It South of the Border
(Islands)

I felt myself turning beet red. First of all, Brandon's house was on a barrier island. I didn't even know what a border island was. Could the press just write whatever it wanted and get away with it? Apparently.

And second of all . . .

"Look," I said, remembering what Lulu had said about telling the truth. "I can explain."

"There's nothing to explain," Mom said, folding the picture back up and putting it away again. "It's all perfectly clear to us. Isn't it, Daniel?"

Dad looked uncomfortable.

"Um," he said.

"Look," I said again. "It's not what you guys think. Brandon made me go with him to South Carolina. I didn't want to. And nothing happened. He and I aren't, you know, boyfriend and girlfriend. I mean, he and Nikki were. But he just wishes he and I were —"

"I don't want to hear it," Mom said, shaking her head back and forth and not making eye contact with me. Which, to be honest, is basically something she really hadn't done all that often since I'd woken up from my surgery. "I really don't. All I want — all I've ever wanted — is for all of this just to be over, and for things to get back to normal and for me to have my daughter back."

This kind of stung. Because the thing is, I *am* her daughter. On the inside. I've never stopped being her daughter. Even with the not-so-hot grades, I'm still her daughter.

So . . . what did that mean? She only loved me when I got above-average grades and was average-looking? Was this another thing about *character*?

I didn't get it. I really didn't. I felt like Frida and the pretty thing.

"Well," I said. "How do you think I feel? But that's not —"

"And so," Mom went on, completely ignoring me, "your father and I have decided to just pay it off."

I blinked at both of them. It was busy in the Starbucks they'd chosen. There were bloggers and NYU students everywhere, crowding every table with their laptops and expensive film equipment (the Astor Place Starbucks is right down the street from the Tisch School of the Arts, where the NYU film school is), looking all angsty in their hand-knitted woolen hats with the earflaps, and their facial piercings and their tattoos, which they'd all gotten to show off how individual they were.

Except how individual were they, really, *if every single one of them had facial piercings and tattoos?*

I was the only person in there under twenty who *didn't* have a pierced lip or eyebrow or any visible tattoos.

And I was also the one with the modeling contract with a corporation I bet all of them hated.

Not without good reason, of course.

But I'm just asking: Who was the biggest conformist there?

"What do you mean," I asked my mom, trying not to let all the bloggers and Eli Roth wannabes distract me, "you guys are going to pay them off?"

"Stark," she said. "We don't have much in our savings and our 401(k)s. But we're going to pull together what we do have and pay them off, so that you don't have to do this anymore. It won't be enough, we know, but it will be a start. You'll be able to go back to being yourself. Em —" Suddenly, I was back to being

Em. Mom even reached out and grabbed my hands, resting on the tabletop. "We're going to get you out of the contract."

I stared at both of them. I really wasn't sure I understood exactly what she was saying. I thought I did.

But it was so insane, I just assumed I was mistaken.

"Wait," I said, inching my hands out from under hers. "Are you saying . . . you want to violate the confidentiality agreement you signed about my not really being Nikki Howard and *pay Stark off?*"

"That's exactly what we're saying," Mom said, withdrawing her hands into her lap. "We want to get you out of this, Em. We never should have agreed to it in the first place. We only did it because we were scared, and . . . well, we wanted to save your life. But now we see that maybe . . . well, maybe it was the wrong choice."

The wrong choice? They should have let me *die* rather than be a model?

My shock must have shown on my face, since Dad leaned forward and said, quickly, "That's not what your mother means. She means maybe we made the wrong choice not negotiating more —"

"But." I tried to think back to what had been said in Dr. Holcombe's office that day my parents had told me about all the papers they'd signed when they'd agreed to the surgery that had saved my life. "You can't. You'll lose everything."

"Well, not everything," Dad said, in his usual cheerful manner, like we were talking about egg sandwiches or something. "We'll keep our jobs. And they can't take your mother's apartment, which is through the university. So we'll always have a place to live."

"But you'll go bankrupt," I protested. "That lawyer guy in Dr. Holcombe's office said you could even go to jail!" I didn't mention the part about how Robert Stark would have them both killed before he'd ever allow this to happen. If it were that simple — just paying back the money — I'd have tried to do it myself, out of the money in Nikki Howard's bank accounts.

"Well," Mom said, after she'd taken a fortifying sip of coffee. "I'd rather go to jail than see my daughter failing to live up to her potential, gallivanting around half naked with playboys on the cover of gossip magazines."

I have to admit, my jaw dropped when she said this. My mom's always been a feminist.

But I never thought she was a prude.

"Because you think I had sex with *Brandon Stark?*" I couldn't believe this was happening. "Mother, I did not have sex with him! That wasn't even a bikini. Those were my jogging clothes. I would never have sex with that ass clown!"

There's a possibility I might have said this a little too loudly, since a lot of the NYU kids turned around in their seats to look at us over their foamy nonfat cappuccinos. Some of them had their pierced eyebrows raised. I could see the bloggers beginning to blog furiously about what they'd just seen and heard. Even though they might have been hipsters, they loved a good scoop as much as the next blogger.

Twitter, I imagined, was probably on fire.

My mom, noticing this, hissed at me, "Emerson! Would you please lower your voice?"

"No, I won't, *Mother*," I said. If she was going to give me the full Emerson, I was going to give her the full Mother. Although I did lower my voice, a little. I mean, it *was* kind of embarrassing.

"For your information," I whispered, "the only reason I went anywhere with Brandon Stark was because he said if I didn't he would tell his dad where he could find the real Nikki Howard."

Both my parents stared at me blankly. Just as I'd known they would. Lulu's advice, to start telling the truth, was all well and good for her.

But her parents hardly even spoke to her. Her dad, a famous film director, just paid all her bills from whatever exotic movie locale he was working on, and her mom had basically disappeared off the face of the planet with a snowboard instructor who was nearly Lulu's age.

In some ways, Lulu was incredibly lucky. I knew she envied me what she considered my "normal" family.

But she didn't know how big a pain a "normal" family could be, how judgy and annoying they were half the time. I'd have given anything right then if my mother had just said that I'd looked pretty in that picture on the cover of *Us Weekly* and dropped the whole thing.

"Yeah," I said, to their uncomprehending stares. "That's right. The real Nikki Howard is still alive. I mean her brain is. It's in some other girl's body, obviously."

I saw my mom and dad exchange glances. It was one of those secret message glances people who are married or have been living together for a long time have with each other.

I could totally read what it said, too.

It said, *This girl is completely bonkers, and we're worried about her.*

Yeah. They didn't believe me.

Well, why should they have, anyway? Like Lulu had said, I should have just been honest with everyone from the beginning, instead of trying to protect them all like I was some kind of mother goddess.

"Em —" my mom started to say, carefully. "You've been under a lot of stress lately. It's obvious with your slipping grades, and the people you've been hanging around with — well, you're not exactly being the best example for your little sister now, are you?"

I have to admit, that hurt. Tears stung my eyes. *I wasn't being* a good example for Frida? Frida, who'd only ever aspired to go to cheerleading camp her whole life? At least I had a job!

"We think it might be better if, before Frida gets back from camp, you leave for a rest," Mom said. "A long rest somewhere you can be away from all the bad influences that have come into your life since you started working in the fashion business. Dad and I were thinking maybe a nice recovery center some-where in —"

Recovery center? Did she mean *rehab?*

"You know what?" I interrupted her.

Why was I even trying? What did I hope to accomplish? No matter what I said, my mom wasn't going to believe me.

And if I let them in on the whole *Nikki's-brain-was-totally-healthy-Robert-Stark-just-tried-to-have-her-killed-because-she-knew-that-the-new-Stark-Quark-PCs-come-bundled-with-spyware-that-Stark-Enterprises-is-using-to-upload-all-the-users'-information-to-their-mainframe-and-she-was-trying-to-blackmail-him-about-it-so-he-had-her-brain-removed* thing, they would just be two more people I loved put in danger.

That was it. I was done.

By not letting them in on the truth, I wasn't lying to them exactly.

I just wasn't necessarily being as open with them as I could have been.

But had they been as fair with me as they could have been? Believing what gossip sites said about me? Getting all raggy with me about my grades, when they knew the kind of pressure I had been under? It wasn't as if I'd had a *brain transplant* or anything this semester. A C minus grade point average was pretty good, if you took that under consideration.

"I just remembered something," I said, reaching around behind me for my jacket. "I have to go."

"Em," Mom said, no longer sounding like a crazy Icelandic elf, but more like her normal self, when she wasn't completely mad at me. She reached out and grabbed one of my hands again.

The thing is, it was too late. It wasn't her fault, necessarily.

But it was way, way too late.

"I'll see you guys later," I said. And I got up and started to sail out of there, Cosabella skittering along beside me.

But as I walked along, weaving my way through all the tables, I heard people whispering, "Omigod . . . it's Nikki Howard."

And, "Psst . . . that's *her!*"

And, "No way! Nikki Howard!"

And I realized I was doing it again. Running away from a problem.

When, really, that wasn't going to solve anything.

So I turned around halfway through the café and walked back to my mom and dad's table and stood in front of it.

"I'm not saying I don't appreciate what you're trying to do for me," I said. "Because I *am* in a jam — just not the kind you think. It's not drugs. I know you aren't going to believe me, but I'm going to ask you to trust me and believe me when I say I haven't done anything wrong. Please don't do anything like go to Stark and try to pay off my contract . . . not yet. It would be — well, it would be a really, really big mistake."

Looking up at me, Dad's expression was more concerned than ever.

"Emerson," he said. He was the one who hardly ever used my full name. When he did, it was a big deal. A really big deal. "What's going on?"

"I can't tell you," I said. "I'm just asking you to give me a few more days. And to trust me. Do you think you can do that?"

Mom opened her mouth — to argue, I'm pretty sure.

But before she could say anything, Dad reached out to take my gloved hand.

"Sure," he said. He gave my fingers a squeeze and smiled up at me. "We can do that."

Mom gave him a bewildered look. But then she, too, glanced up at me and smiled. It was a tight, nervous smile.

But it was a smile just the same.

"Sure, Em," she said.

I picked up the *Us Weekly* cover that had been lying on the table between us.

"Mom," I said, holding it up. "I know this is stupid, but . . . do you think I look pretty in this picture?"

She stared at it blankly. "Pretty?"

"Yeah," I said. "Pretty."

"You . . ." She seemed flustered. "You look like Nikki Howard," she said.

"I know," I said, gritting my teeth. "But do you think I look *pretty?*"

"Pretty," Mom said, looking confused, "is a patriarchal construct designed to make women feel less worthy unless they live up to certain standards established by the male-dominated fashion and beauty industry. You know that, Em. I tell you and Frida that all the time."

"Yeah," I said, putting the picture down again. "I know. That might be part of the problem."

And I turned and walked out of the restaurant.

TWELVE

SERIOUSLY, COULD I BE HAVING A MORE
messed-up day?

When I got onto the pavement outside the Starbucks,
swallowing down big gulps of cold air, that was all I could think
about. My sad, sorry, pathetic day. First I'd been dumped by my
boyfriend (although technically that had happened in the middle of the night).

Then I'd kidnapped a billionaire's son.

Now my parents thought I was a drug addict or
something.

Perfect. Great.

Had that been an intervention, or something, in there? In a
Starbucks?

God, my parents were such dorks. They couldn't even do an intervention right. Where was Candy Finnigan?

And why couldn't my mom just say Frida and I were pretty? Was it so hard? What was all this patriarchal construct crap? She always said butterflies were pretty. She said the material she'd picked out to reupholster our living room couch was pretty.

Why couldn't she say we were pretty, too? Why couldn't we be strong, independent, and pretty, too?

I was struggling to open my umbrella against the sleet — even my umbrella was broken. Fantastic — when I saw him. A guy in a black trench, standing across the street from me.

He wasn't directly across the street from me. He was sort of off to one side, and unlike me, beneath an awning, out of the freezing rain.

But I noticed him right away. Because he wasn't moving.

Of course we were in the middle of New York City (or the middle of Greenwich Village, to be more exact). The streets were packed with people. That's what caught my attention about him. The fact that he, like me, was standing perfectly still while everyone else around us was moving in one direction or the other.

And he was staring at me, as if waiting for me to decide which way I was going to walk.

And when I looked his way, he quickly looked back down at the cell phone he'd been tapping into.

At first I didn't think anything of it. I kept on struggling with my umbrella, no big deal.

Then something made me look again.

At his pants.

And I knew.

I just knew. He wasn't just some guy waiting for someone outside a store. He was waiting for me.

He was following *me*.

And he wasn't a stalker, either. I had had those before (or rather, Nikki Howard had). I'd had to call Stark security to get them off my back.

But stalkers were different. They didn't dress as well, for one thing. This guy's trench was impeccably pressed, as were his trousers. They were creased down the middle, the way only pants that had been dry-cleaned were. They even had a break in them where they fell over his shoes.

Every stalker I'd ever had wore his pants so short, the hem rose above his sneakers by at least an inch.

And none of them had bothered to get their pants dry-cleaned.

The guy standing across the street from me looked way more like Stark security than he did a stalker.

Suddenly, I went cold all over, and not because of the weather.

The pants were what had given him away. They were black, and perfectly tailored. They were, in other words, fancy.

I had a tail. A real, official, Stark Enterprises security tail.

And he didn't know I knew.

The two of us stood there on the crowded sidewalk across the street from each other. No way I was going to be able to go over to Gabriel's to see Steven and his mother and sister now, which was what I'd been considering doing.

It was amazing, but my first impulse was to call Christopher. Christopher, of all people! Who wasn't even speaking to me! Why would I call *him*?

And what good would calling Christopher even do? I mean, he'd probably only hang up on me. Just because he'd come to my rescue once didn't mean he was going to come flying to my rescue again.

Besides, I didn't even need rescuing. I was a strong, independent woman (according to my mother, anyway. And not pretty. Got that? *Not pretty. Pretty is a patriarchal archetype*). I could handle this all on my own.

Except . . . how?

Lulu, I thought suddenly. I needed to call Lulu and tell her not to go over to Gabriel's. Just in case they were following her, too.

I successfully finished putting up my umbrella, then centered it so Fancy Pants couldn't see me. Then I whipped out my non-Stark brand cell phone and swiftly dialed Lulu's number.

She answered on the second ring.

"Hey," she said. Her mouth was full. Of banana split, I didn't doubt.

"It's me," I said, through suddenly frozen lips. "Don't go over there."

"Go where?" she asked.

"To the place where you said you were going to go."

I was speaking cryptically not because I thought if they were already following me, my phone might be tapped, but because I'd suddenly realized the loft might be. We'd been gone for nearly a week. Who knew who'd had access to it while we'd been away? I had never even thought of that. They might have dismantled the acoustic noise generator Steven had installed. I'd never even checked. Had Lulu or I said anything about where Nikki and her family were hiding? I tried to think.

I was pretty sure we had.

"I'm being followed," I said.

Even the words sounded frightening. I clutched convulsively at Cosabella's leash. She, oblivious, was prancing along beside me, sniffing the wet ground for abandoned bits of street food, pretzels or hot dogs people might have dropped.

"You are?" Lulu sounded delighted. "Oh, my God! It's like something out of a Bourne movie! And you're like Julia Stiles! She's so pretty. Where are you?"

"Astor Place," I said. I was moving as rapidly as I could in the opposite direction to the loft and the Starbucks, trying to lead Fancy Pants away from the people I loved. Which was ridiculous, since of course Stark knew where my parents and I lived. "We need to make sure our friends are safe where we left them."

"Sure," Lulu said. "I can do that."

"*Subtly*," I said.

"I can be subtle," Lulu said, sounding hurt.

"I . . ." I didn't dare look back over my shoulder to see if Fancy Pants was behind me. But I was pretty sure he was. I didn't see him across the street anymore. "I don't know what to do. About the guy, I mean."

"Ooooh, I do," Lulu said, sounding even more delighted. This whole thing was a game to her, I swear. "Call Christopher."

"*What?*" I said. "Are you crazy?" I had no idea why I was asking Lulu this, since of course calling Christopher had been my first inclination. "Why would I do that?"

Lulu sighed deeply into the phone.

"We just talked about this," she said. "Remember? You have to give him an opportunity to feel needed, and to help you."

"I can't do that," I said. I was walking along so quickly, Cosabella was having trouble keeping up. "What . . . what if he gets hurt? Then it'll be my fault and I'll blame myself forever and *I'll* be the one who turns into an evil supervillain."

I didn't want to tell her the real reason I didn't want to call Christopher was that I was afraid he'd hang up on me, and I couldn't face another rejection from him.

"But what if *you* get hurt again?" Lulu wanted to know. Uh, that was exactly what I was worried about . . . only not by the people Lulu meant. "And he blames himself even more, only this time for your ultimate demise? And then he invents a reverse supernova death ray that sucks up all the sun's energy, and we all slowly freeze to death, and then the earth turns into a hollow husk and humanity ceases to exist and it's all your fault because you didn't call him?"

"Oh, my God," I said. "You've had way too much whipped cream."

"It could happen," Lulu said, defensively. "I saw it on TV once. *Call him.*"

"Fine," I said. There was no way I was calling him. "And, Lulu. Be careful what you say in the apartment. I think it might be bugged again."

"I'm always careful," Lulu said, sounding both hurt and

annoyed now. "I'm totally good at this spy stuff. I rented a whole plane and came and helped Christopher rescue you without anybody finding out, didn't I?"

Uh, I wasn't so sure about that. But I just told her thanks and hung up.

I walked blindly, not even looking to see where I was going, trying to figure out how this could possibly be happening to me.

Keeping my phone out, I did call someone . . . but not Christopher.

"So do you not hate me anymore?" Brandon asked, when he picked up.

"What?" I was confused.

"You're calling me," Brandon said. "So I figure you must not hate me anymore. Does this mean you wanna go out? I'm free tonight. I mean, I have plans, but I can break them. For you."

Oh, my God. Brandon was the biggest horndog in the world. It was totally disgusting.

"Brandon," I said. "You kidnapped me. And then you made the only person I'll ever love in my life hate me. I completely despise you."

"So . . . ," Brandon said. "I take that as a no, you do not want to go out with me tonight."

I held the phone away from my face to make sure it was working properly and I hadn't heard him wrong.

"No," I said, bringing it back to my face when I was sure cellular service to my area was fully functional. "I do not want to go out with you tonight. I called to ask why someone from Stark security is tailing me."

"How should I know?" Brandon asked. "Maybe because you're worth a lot to the company, and they want to make sure you don't get harassed by fans or hurt by the paps. Because everyone thinks you're dating me now. Even though you're not. You might want to reconsider. Private security's just one of the many perks of being Brandon Stark's woman. Hey, ow, not there."

I held the phone away from my face again. "What are you *doing* right now?" I asked.

"Getting a massage," Brandon said. "It kinda hurts to be knocked unconscious and then tied up half the day, you know. You and your friends play rough. Since you don't want to be with me, is there anything else? I really am kinda busy."

"If his assignment was to keep me from being harassed by paps or fans," I said, "he wouldn't be trying to keep me from noticing him, which is what he's doing."

"Oh," Brandon said, in a different tone. "That's different. Hey, you don't think my dad —"

"I don't know what to think," I said. "But do I think your dad is onto us? You tell me."

"Don't panic," he said. "My dad hasn't said anything to me about any of this. I'm sure he has no idea what's going on. What *is* going on, anyway? I mean, have you and your friends figured out what —"

I just laughed bitterly as I dragged my dog down the street. "Right," I said. "Like I'm going to tell you. When I'm ready to let you in on what's going on, Brandon, you'll know. That's a lot more courtesy than you ever offered me."

I hung up on him.

My fingers were trembling inside the gloves I had on as I dialed Christopher's cell. What other choice did I have? I didn't know where to go, and frankly, I was scared. Christopher, I told myself, would know what to do.

I had no idea at all whether he'd pick up. After the way we'd left things — he'd barely glanced at me as we'd gone our separate ways from Teterboro, where the plane had dropped us off — I half expected he'd let my call go to voice mail.

But, miraculously, I heard him saying "Hello?" in my ear.

"Christopher?" I said. I hoped I didn't sound as scared and shaky to him as I did to myself.

"What is it, Em?" he asked. He didn't seem surprised to be hearing from me. More like . . . resigned.

Great. My boyfriend — ex-boyfriend — was *resigned* to be hearing from me. Because I was such a drama queen? Like those girls I always overheard in the hallways at school blowing stuff out of proportion so they could get their boyfriends to pay more attention to them? *Oh, Jason, I couldn't get my locker open. . . . I know, I tried twisting it right, then left, but it wouldn't budge. I guess I'm just not* strong *enough. Could you help me? Please? Oh, great. Oh, Jason, you're so strong. . . .*

Seriously? That was me now?

On the other hand, a guy *was* following me. I'd stooped down to scoop up some of Cosabella's poo with a plastic baggie from my pocket and kind of looked over my shoulder in a surreptitious way while I was obeying New York City littering ordinances by tossing it into a nearby trash receptacle and there he was again, standing by the fence to a churchyard, totally pretending to be texting.

"I'm being followed," I whispered to Christopher.

"I can't hear you," he said.

"I'm being followed," I repeated, more loudly this time.

"Where are you?" he asked right away.

Not, *So what do you expect me to do about it?* Or, *I told you I don't want to be involved in this anymore.*

Surprised — and more relieved than I wanted to admit — I replied, "I'm on Broadway and Ninth."

"I'm not far from there," Christopher said. "Walk north on Broadway toward Union Square. I'll meet you." His voice sounded very soothing on the phone, even though I could tell he, like me, was on the street somewhere. I could hear traffic noises in the background. "How long's he been tailing you?"

"I don't know," I said. "About four blocks? I met my parents for coffee, and I noticed him as soon as I got out. He could have followed me there, for all I know."

"What does the guy look like?"

"Tall," I said, doing what he'd said, and walking swiftly north. "He stops every time I stop and pretends to be texting someone."

"What's he got on?"

"A trench coat and black pressed pants. That's what gave him away, actually. That he's someone from Stark."

"How's that?"

"Because of his pants. They're very fancy."

"His pants are fancy," Christopher repeated, and I realized I must sound like a mental patient. This was my day, apparently, for people thinking I was nuts.

"Seriously, Christopher," I said. "This guy is Stark security, not some Nikki Howard fan. Why would Stark security be following me?"

"That's something you might want to ask your boyfriend, Brandon," Christopher said.

"Oh, ha-ha," I said, trying to sound like I hadn't just done exactly that . . . and like what he'd said hadn't felt like a knife through my heart. "I told you, Brandon forced me to —"

"Save it, Watts, I heard it all the first time. Okay, I see you," Christopher said.

"What?" This startled me so much, I nearly dropped my umbrella. "You see me? How can you —"

But then Christopher turned the corner right in front of me and put an arm around me.

"Hi, honey," he said, and kissed my cheek. "Right on time."

I was completely shocked. His lips were warm against my icy skin. And the arm he'd slipped around me?

It felt like heaven.

Especially since I'd been certain I'd never feel his arm around me again.

"I already got the tickets," he said. He was talking in an inappropriately loud voice.

That's when I realized it was for the benefit of Fancy Pants, not me. Because tickets? What tickets?

"Great," I said, going along with him. I noticed he was carrying a plastic bag from Forbidden Planet, the comic book store, which was nearby. I remembered, belatedly, that Christopher had a mailbox there, where they held all the comic books he ordered every month. He must have just been making his weekly pickup when I called.

"So, are you ready?" he wanted to know.

He still had his arm around me. It felt so wonderful, I hoped he'd never let go.

But none of this, I knew, was because Christopher actually cared about me anymore. It was just because of old times.

Lulu had been wrong: Making a boy think you need him didn't do anything.

Except make you want him more.

"Sure," I said. I didn't see how any of this was going to work. Now Fancy Pants, who was standing over to one side of the sidewalk a few yards away, texting, was just going to follow us both.

Or so I thought.

Because a second later, Christopher dropped his arm from around me, and staring at the guy, shouted, "You. Hey, *you!*"

THIRTEEN

THE GUY WHO'D BEEN FOLLOWING ME
looked up from his cell phone, startled. Then he looked behind
him to see if Christopher was talking to someone else.

"I'm talking to you," Christopher cried, going right up to
Fancy Pants and shoving him on the shoulder. "Were you just
following my girlfriend?"

That's right. Christopher shoved the Stark security guy in
the shoulder.

He also called me his girlfriend.

My heart began slamming behind my ribs, and not from the
possible confrontation I knew was about to ensue.

Fancy Pants did *not* like Christopher calling so much attention to him. Either that, or he didn't like being shoved, even

though, to be truthful, it was only a little shove. He put his cell phone away and said, in a controlled voice, "I don't know you, son. Please take your hand off me."

"What do you mean, you don't know me?" Christopher asked, still using a voice loud enough to make everyone on the sidewalk look around at us. "You're sure acting like you know me. Or at least like you know my girlfriend, Nikki Howard. Because you've been following her for the past four blocks."

There! He'd said it again! *Girlfriend!* I definitely hadn't mistaken it.

When Christopher said the words *Nikki Howard,* a lot more people started paying attention. They actually slowed down on the sidewalk, or stopped walking altogether and stood there and started staring. One big burly guy who'd been unloading cans of soda from a truck on the corner actually came over and got in Fancy Pants's face.

"Hey!" Burly Guy said. "That true? You following Nikki Howard?"

Fancy Pants looked quickly around, as if for an escape route. He actually began reaching inside his coat — and not for a cell phone, which I'd already seen him drop into the trench's wide side pocket.

I was standing at just the right angle to catch a glimpse of exactly what it was inside his coat he was reaching for . . .

. . . a gun. In a shoulder holster, the handle nestled underneath his arm.

I gasped, and reached out to grab Christopher's arm, my fingers sinking into the leather of his jacket. I think I stopped breathing for a minute. I couldn't believe it.

A gun! He actually had a gun! He was going to try to shoot us!

But between Christopher, Burly Guy, the gathering crowd, and me, there were apparently too many witnesses. Because a second later, Fancy Pants's hand dropped away from the gun, and instead, he seemed to be looking for a different way out of his tight situation.

I continued to hold on to Christopher's arm, so freaked out I wasn't sure I could have remained upright if I didn't cling to him. A gun! He had a gun! And he'd been going to use it!

"That's not nice!" Burly Guy said, poking Fancy Pants in the chest — quite sharply, I thought. Especially considering the fact that he had a gun. "We leave celebrities alone around here!"

"True," Christopher said, shaking his head sadly at Fancy Pants. "We really do."

Fancy Pants looked perturbed.

But there was no way he could shoot his way out of this situation. Not unless he was some kind of psychopath. There were way too many people gathered around now, watching.

And I highly doubted Robert Stark would hire any psychopaths as part of his security team.

"I wasn't following her," he said, both to the burly man and to Christopher. "We just happened to be walking in the same direction, is all."

"So keep walking, why don'tcha?" Burly Guy asked him.

"Maybe I will, then," Fancy Pants said, looking injured. "Maybe I will."

But of course, he kept standing there.

"So go," Christopher said. "If you're in such a hurry."

"Yeah," Burly Guy said. "Go, why don'tcha?"

Fancy Pants, throwing us all a very dirty look, began walking slowly away. My heart continued to pound inside my chest as I watched him go, hoping he wouldn't turn back and start shooting.

"Faster," Burly Guy commanded.

Fancy Pants picked up the pace, walking off toward Union Square. He didn't look back.

"Thank you so much," I breathed, my grip loosening a little on Christopher's arm. My fingers felt sore from how tightly I'd been clenching him. I couldn't imagine how his arm must have felt.

But he wasn't complaining, I noticed.

"No problem," Burly Guy said. "We can't have people harassing our local celebrities. That's what makes New York different from L.A., you know? Here, people can walk down the streets and no one bothers them, ya know? Hey, I gotta say, my niece is about as pretty and talented as you are, and is going to be a superstar herself someday. Can I bug you for an autograph? You know, to inspire her."

"Of course," I said. "I'd be happy to. What's her name?" And when he told me Helen Thomaides, I scrawled, *For Helen, Reach for the stars. Love, Nikki Howard* on a page of his order form.

This, of course, opened the floodgates, and then everyone who'd been standing on the sidewalk watching our little confrontation with Fancy Pants wanted an autograph. Pens appeared from nowhere, and soon I was signing everything from people's drugstore receipts to the backs of their wrists.

As I signed, I tried to keep track of what was happening beyond the circle of autograph seekers around me. Where was the guy who'd been following me? Had he really just given up? Where was Christopher? Had he, too, given up on me? Or was he still there?

Finally, I felt a hand wrap around my arm. I looked up, startled. Fortunately, it was Christopher, not Fancy Pants. He'd scooped up Cosabella — thank goodness. Otherwise, she'd have been trampled in the rush toward me for my signature — and now he was saying, in a serious voice, "Nikki? I think it's time to go."

I looked over at the street and saw that he'd hailed a cab and that it sat with one of the rear doors open.

Christopher was helping me to escape? After telling me he wanted nothing to do with any of this?

I felt a rush of warmth toward him that was even greater than when he'd put his arm around me.

"Oh," I said to all the autograph seekers. "I'm sorry, I have to go."

"To a fitting?" one of the girls who'd asked me to sign her wrist wanted to know.

"To a photo shoot?" another one asked.

"Yes," I called to them all. What was the point in telling the truth? It would only disappoint them. "Sorry! Thanks so much! I love you all!" I blew them kisses just like I'd seen movie stars do on TV and ran to the taxi, ducking inside it, then scooting all the way across the seat to make room for Christopher, who was leaning inside to hand Cosabella to me.

"Come with me," I all but begged him. I could tell he was getting ready to bail, even though he'd done all those nice things for me already.

"Em," he said. His face had closed down, his blue eyes shuttered as if no one was home.

"Christopher," I said. "He had a gun. . . ."

"I know," Christopher insisted, glancing over his shoulder. "That's why you've got to get out of here *now*."

He knew? All that time, he'd acted so calm! He'd shoved the guy, knowing he had a gun? I couldn't believe it. He'd done it for me. Even though he claimed not to feel anything for me anymore. Anything but contempt. Maybe what he claimed and what he actually felt were two different things. I hardly dared to let myself hope. . . .

"I'm worried about *you*," I said. People who hadn't gotten my autograph, but had seen the crowd, were starting to drift over to the taxi, curious about who was inside it.

"Would you just go already?" Christopher said. "He's probably found a cab and is on his way back —"

"Please get in." Now I was begging. "I *need* you."

I don't care, Christopher could have said. *You're the one with a problem. Not me.*

But he didn't.

Lulu was right: Maybe guys just do want to feel needed sometimes. Not all the time. Because then you come off as a Whitney Robertson, all whiny and completely helpless.

But every once in a while, maybe you needed to stop running and tell other people you need them, and let them help you.

Including the guy you like.

Christopher got into the taxi beside me and shut the door.

He didn't act like he was too unhappy about it, either.

"Where are we going?" he asked.

"I *was* going to Gabriel's," I said. "I think . . . well, I don't know. But I'm worried Nikki might have said something to someone."

Just saying it out loud caused my mouth to go dry and my pulse to speed up. I couldn't look Christopher in the eye. Not so much because I was genuinely worried about Nikki and her family, which I was.

But because I was aware that we were alone in a nice, cozy cab together.

It was the first time we'd been alone together since he'd woken me up in my bed . . .

. . . and dumped me. Basically.

But now he'd just saved my life.

"You could be right about that" was all he said, though. "Considering the new friend you picked up back there. But I don't know how good an idea it is to head over there with Stark security on your tail."

"Where we headed?" the cabdriver wanted to know. He had to yell to be heard through the bulletproof glass between the front seat and the backseat. He'd released the brake, and we were cruising down Broadway, going the opposite direction Fancy Pants had walked off.

If he hadn't jumped into a taxi of his own, and was following us that way.

"Just keep driving," Christopher yelled up to the driver. He was evidently thinking the same thing I was. "We'll tell you when to turn."

"Do you think he's following us?" I asked Christopher, turning around in the seat to look.

All I could see, however, was the usual vast ocean of taxis behind us. There was no way to tell which, if any, of them held Fancy Pants.

"Probably," Christopher said.

"What do we do?" I asked anxiously.

"I say we go for a nice drive downtown," Christopher said, "and try to lose him just in case, then get out and jump onto the subway back uptown when it seems safe."

I couldn't believe Christopher was being so calm. This was obviously the new, supervillain Christopher, who was used to being in high-speed car chases.

Although we weren't really going high speed, considering we were stuck at a red light.

I looked down at Cosabella, who'd jumped onto my lap to peer out the window. Cosy loved being in any moving vehicle. Looking down at her was easier than looking into Christopher's face, which always just reminded me of how much I wanted him.

And how much he, in return, did not want me.

At least, up until a few minutes ago. I still wasn't sure if I should allow recent developments to give me hope that things were changing.

"What makes you think Nikki would rat us out?" Christopher wanted to know.

"She's mad," I said. "About this whole thing. The fact that she can't have her old body back. It's what she asked Brandon for, you know." I turned my head to look at him, feeling suddenly shy. "In exchange for telling him why his dad tried to have her killed."

Christopher stared back at me blankly. "She asked him for what?"

"Her old body back," I said.

His eyes widened. "Wait . . . she wanted you to —"

"Yeah," I said glumly. "She really hates the body she ended up with."

Christopher bristled.

"Did it ever occur to her that that's what happens," he said, "when you try to blackmail your boss? What did she expect?"

I goggled at him. "Well, not to have him try to murder her."

"Blackmail's against the law, you know," Christopher said. "It tends to make people angry."

"Well, whatever Robert Stark is doing is against the law, too,"

I pointed out. "I know two wrongs don't make a right, but it's not like Nikki knew any better."

"Uh, she's a member of the human race, isn't she?" he asked. "Plus, I thought she was an emancipated minor. So you can't say she didn't know better. She claims to be an adult."

"I'm just saying," I said, starting to feel a little less warmly toward him than I had when he had just saved me from Fancy Pants, because I was having such a hard time making him see how important losing her body would be to a girl like Nikki. "I know how she feels. It's horrible to have to give up your whole life because you made one stupid mistake."

"What was your mistake?" Christopher asked. "Pushing your little sister out of the way when that TV came loose so it fell on you and not her? Being in the wrong place at the wrong time? You didn't make any mistakes. And neither did Nikki."

The vehemence with which Christopher spoke surprised me. I hadn't known he felt that strongly . . . about anything other than avenging my death, which now was a moot point, since he knew I wasn't dead.

"I — I guess I never thought of it that way," I said, absently stroking Cosabella's woolly little head.

"So she lost her body," Christopher said. "She's still got her mind. Just because her former career was entirely based on her looks, that doesn't mean she can't have a new career, this time using her brains instead. Has she even considered that?

It's not like she doesn't have good business sense. As you might have noticed, considering the fact that she scared the owner of a multinational corporation into trying to have her murdered."

I blinked at him. It was true. Nikki had a lot more going for her than just her face.

But how was anyone going to convince her of that?

"If we could only figure out what Robert Stark was so scared of her revealing to everyone," I said slowly. The embryo of an idea was forming in my mind. "The thing with the Quarks, I mean. The fact that she was instrumental in discovering it . . . if we could uncover it and make it public, that might be enough to boost her self-esteem into not wanting someone to hack into my head and scoop my brain out of it again."

Christopher yelled at the cabdriver, "Turn right here!"

The cabdriver yelled back, "You are crazy! I'm in the wrong lane!"

"Just do it," Christopher yelled back. "There's an extra twenty in it for you."

Cursing, the cabdriver made a right turn so suddenly, Cosabella and I lurched over into Christopher. He threw an arm across my shoulders as, all around us, cars and trucks honked. Cosabella scrambled to find footing on the seat, which mainly involved stabbing her paws into my thighs.

"Sorry," I said, mortified that parts of my own body had gone flying into Christopher's. "I'm sorry."

"It's okay," he said. He was craning his neck to look behind us. "If he was back there, we lost him for sure."

"We did?" I tried to straighten up, conscious that Christopher hadn't moved his arm. It was horrible to be so hyperaware of these things, when I was sure he didn't care at all. "Well, that's good."

"And I get what you're saying," he said. "About Nikki. She has good instincts. They just needed to be guided in the proper direction. She was right to do something about what she overheard regarding the Quarks. She just didn't do the right thing. Blackmailing her boss instead of trying to stop him does nothing for the greater good . . . which is what you want to do."

"Robert Stark isn't collecting all that data for no reason, Christopher," I said, looking into his eyes. He still had his arm around me, so it was kind of hard not to. Also not to notice his lips, which were looking highly kissable. But I tried to turn my mind to higher things, such as saving Nikki and her family. "I was paying attention to your speech about him in Public Speaking. You don't get to be the fourth-richest man in the world by doing things for no reason. Tomorrow night I have to go to a party at his house. If there's going to be any chance of my finding out what it is he's doing, it's going to be then —"

"Whoa," Christopher said, his arm tightening. "You're going to confront him yourself?"

"Well," I said, "I think it's going to be our only chance of ending this. Otherwise . . . well, my parents are threatening to bankrupt themselves because they think they can just waltz into Stark Corporate, pay off my contracts, and be done with this. Which is so never going to happen. Steven and his mom are going to have to live in hiding forever, for fear of what Robert Stark and his cronies are going to do to them. And Nikki's going to get herself killed — or kill herself — trying to be who she used to be. So . . . yeah. I'm going to confront him myself. With your help, if you're willing. What do you think? Are you willing?"

Christopher didn't say anything right away. The cab rumbled along Houston Street, taking us God only knew where. I held my breath, waiting for his answer. I knew I couldn't do any of this without his help. I needed him — and his cousin Felix — to break back into Stark's mainframe and see what they could find out. I didn't think I'd be able to just walk up to Robert Stark and go, "Tell me everything." I needed to arm myself with some information first.

Information only they could get. If they looked in the right place. And it wasn't encrypted. Which it probably would be.

Still. The least they could do was try. . . .

"You're crazy," Christopher said. He seemed angry. At me. At himself. At the whole situation. For which I couldn't exactly blame him. "This whole thing has been completely crazy."

"I know," I said, with a shrug. Secretly, though, I was encouraged. A *You're crazy* wasn't a no.

"That guy back there had a *gun*," Christopher went on. "Brandon Stark didn't even have a gun, and he managed to kidnap you just by threatening to do mean things to your friends. How do you think you're going to cope with his dad, who's a *real* gangster?"

"Well," I said. Suddenly, I didn't feel quite so encouraged. There were actual tears in my eyes. "That's why this time I'm asking you for help. I know I can't do it alone anymore. I need you, Christopher."

"You're damn right you do," he said. "It's about time you realized it."

Then he pulled me roughly toward him and kissed me on the mouth.

FOURTEEN

"WHERE HAVE *YOU* BEEN?"

That's what Felix wanted to know when we showed up in his basement an hour later.

It was obvious from his tone that he didn't mean where had we *just* been — escaping from Stark security goons and making out (well, a little) in the back of a cab.

He meant where had we been since he'd last seen us.

In fact, I wasn't sure he'd moved from in front of his multi-screened computer command center since the first time I'd met him. He still seemed to have on the same clothes — baggy jeans, green velour shirt, and a lot of gold chains.

The only difference, really, was that there were a lot more

empty plates piled up around him. His mom had evidently been bringing his meals down to him.

Well, it was hard being a computer hacker under house arrest . . . though I guess there were some perks. Like sandwiches and brownies from Mom, upstairs.

"We just outran a guy from Stark security," Christopher informed him. "He was following Em. He had a gun."

"Em?" Felix spun around in his overpadded computer chair to look at me with narrowed eyes. Then he nodded. "Oh, that's right. I read the medical file. You're just borrowing Nikki Howard's body. Your real name's Emerson . . . Watts, right?"

"Uh, I get to have the body for keeps, I'm hoping," I said. "Getting your brain swapped into someone else's body is no picnic, you know."

"Especially if it's Nikki Howard's body," Felix said, and he made a growling noise. "Mamacita, I'd like to get me some of that!"

Christopher walked over to his cousin and slapped him on the back of the head.

"Hey," he said severely. "Show some manners. Just because you live in a basement doesn't mean you don't have to act like a gentleman around ladies."

"Ow," Felix said, reaching up to clutch his head. "Stop. I was only playing."

"It's okay," I said to Christopher. I actually felt a little sorry for his cousin. It had to be hard to be so smart and yet not have any outlets — positive ones, anyway — for all that intelligence.

"No," Christopher said, shaking his head at me. Felix might have been playing, but Christopher definitely wasn't. "It's not."

I blushed. Christopher was being chivalrous toward me now . . .

. . . but back in the cab, after he'd pulled me so roughly toward him and kissed me, he'd pushed me just as roughly away and muttered, "Sorry. I didn't mean to do that."

I'd stared at him in astonishment, my lips still tingling from where his mouth had bruised mine, and said, "Christopher. It's all right." Believe me. It was *more* than all right.

"No," he'd said. "It's not."

So. I still wasn't forgiven. Not yet. It was just that he couldn't help kissing me from time to time.

Boys are so weird.

Now he pointed at one of the computer monitors in front of Felix, which was streaming information.

"We're still on Stark's mainframe?" he asked.

"Yeah," Felix said. He sounded sulky. He leaned back in his computer chair so that he could rest his gigantic feet on one of the milk crates that made up his jerry-rigged command center, near some of the empty plates. "Not that they're doing anything interesting. I'm more bored with this hack than with all the *Stargates* combined."

"They're actually doing a lot that's interesting," Christopher said. "They're storing all the data people who bought the new Quarks are uploading."

This information startled Felix so much that he jumped, bringing his feet down from the milk crate and accidentally taking all the plates down, too, causing them to fall to the floor with a crash.

He didn't seem to care or even notice, however. His fingers began flying over the keyboard in front of the Stark monitor.

"Holy crap," he said, looking — for the first time — actually wide-awake and excited. "Why didn't you say so in the first place? What would they care about a bunch of data from some pissant plastic student laptops? It doesn't make any sense. Where are they storing it? I'm not seeing it." He took a slurp from one of the Cokes his mom had brought down to us (Aunt Jackie was super happy to see me. She'd gotten the complete Nikki Howard fragrance collection for Christmas from her husband and wanted me to sign the box with Nikki's face smiling alluringly up from it). "Where are they putting it?"

"What do you mean, you're not seeing it?" Christopher demanded. "Can you find the data or not?"

"Oh, it's on here," Felix said, slurping the Coke. "Their encryption is a joke. I've never seen a corporation so full of itself. It's like they think no one can touch them. And maybe that's because no one's ever cared enough before to try. But, I mean, I can't tell what they want all this crap for. They've got kids' Facebook and Flickr pages, even their damned *dental* records. What would they want *that* for? And here's a bunch of online budget travel reservations. Priceline and cruise ships and spring break school trips . . ."

"Maybe they want to get into the travel business?" I ventured with a shrug. "Stark doesn't have a commercial airline."

"Phoenix," Felix said.

"They want to base their travel hub out of Phoenix?" Christopher asked, confused.

"No," Felix said. His straw hit the bottom of his soda can. "That's what they're calling the database where they're keeping all these files. Project Phoenix."

Christopher looked at me blankly. "What's in Phoenix?"

I shrugged again. "Desert?"

"Senior citizens," Felix said, when Christopher looked at him. "Old people who drive golf carts. In pastels."

"Look it up," Christopher said to Felix.

Felix sighed, and typed the word *phoenix* into a search engine.

"*Phoenix*," he read, when the definition came up. "A mythical sacred fire bird with a thousand-year life cycle, near the end of which it builds a nest of myrrh twigs, then self-ignites, then is born anew from the ashes."

We all looked at one another blankly.

"Maybe it's a new video game," I suggested. "And the people whose data they've collected all have high scores on *Journeyquest* or something. And they want to send the game to them as testers."

"Then they should have sent it to me," Christopher said, looking (justifiably) offended.

"Yeah," Felix said, clicking on the Facebook page of one of the new Quark owners. "And no way does this loser play *Journeyquest.* Look at him. *Hi, I'm Curt. I like the Dave Matthews Band. I only drink organically grown coffee. I'm going hiking with my dog in Seattle at the end of the month. I suck.*"

I looked at Curt's profile. He definitely wasn't a gamer. He listed running and biking as his hobbies. He was attractive, without an ounce of body fat on him. He liked dogs and his nephews and wanted to save the whales.

All of which were admirable qualities and it was mean of Felix to be making fun of him.

"Show me another one," I said.

"*Hi,*" Felix said, clicking on another profile. "*I'm Kerry.* Oooooh, Kerry's hot. She likes writing and sunsets. I like writing and sunsets, too, Kerry. Look at that, Kerry's going to Guatemala to help teach children to read next month. That's nice of her. What else does Stark know about Kerry? Let's check her medical records. She had to e-mail them to the program she's going to Guatemala with. Oh, look at that. Perfect health. Not even a cavity. Surprise. Those Quark buyers are way too healthy. Eat a cheeseburger, Kerry, swimming in grease!" Felix was yelling at his monitors.

Felix got excited way too easily. Maybe it was all the caffeine and sugar in the Cokes he drank.

"It's weird," I said, "that they're all so crunchy granola."

"Or," Christopher said, looking at me, "someone at Stark is purposefully weeding through this data."

"And only saving the files on the healthy, attractive ones?" I squinted at Kerry's Facebook picture. She was standing in the sun on a hiking trail, wearing a T-shirt and shorts. She looked slim and fresh-faced and happy.

"But why?" Felix asked, reaching for the Coke I hadn't touched (Nikki's body couldn't handle caffeine or high fructose corn syrup). "I hate healthy people."

"I don't know," Christopher said. "But what else do they all have in common?"

"They take good care of their bodies," I ventured.

"They're all hot," Felix said.

"And they're all going places," Christopher said, "with their lives."

"Robert Stark is forming an army," I said with wonder.

"Yeah," Felix said sarcastically. "Of really boring people."

FIFTEEN

"OH, THANK GOD YOU'RE HERE," GABRIEL
said, opening the door to his apartment.

I couldn't figure out why he was so happy to see us. Not at
first.

I'd offered to come over to his apartment with some takeout,
having realized I was going to be no help whatsoever in solving
the mystery of Project Phoenix . . .

. . . at least, not by sitting around, reading over file after file
of incredibly attractive Stark Quark owners. That was something Christopher and Felix could do on their own.

So you could imagine my surprise when Christopher said he
would come with me to Gabriel's. Don't ask me why. He hadn't
grabbed and kissed me again, or supplied an explanation for why

he'd done so in the cab that afternoon. As far as I could tell, he still hated my guts and planned on continuing to do so indefinitely.

I couldn't help wishing I could be more like Nikki. I'm sure she'd had plenty of guys play weird mind games with her. She wouldn't put up with Christopher's guff for more than five minutes. I'd love to have asked her how she dealt with guys like him. I would have done so, in fact . . .

. . . if I thought I could get away with it without her punching me in the mouth and demanding again that I give her back her body.

Inside the Thai restaurant where we'd gone to pick up the takeout, it had been warm and dry and had smelled insanely good. I'd ordered one of almost everything to go, then sat waiting for the food on a red vinyl padded chair with Cosy on my lap while Christopher sat beside us, texting Felix on his cell.

After a little while of trying to ignore Christopher's presence — his highly kissable lips and big, raw-looking hands — it occurred to me: Wait a minute. I didn't have to ask Nikki for her advice. I could just come right out and demand an explanation from Christopher himself about where we stood as a couple. I deserved that, at the very least. I mean, we'd been friends for years before we'd ever been boyfriend-girlfriend (if we were even that).

What was I so scared of, anyway? He was just a high school boy. I was freaking *Nikki Howard*, supermodel.

Even if I wasn't, really.

Why was I so scared of what he was going to say, anyway? We'd already hurt each other as much as we possibly could. What more could we possibly do to each other?

And Lulu had said we needed to communicate more. Right?

"Christopher," I'd begun, after taking a deep breath and telling myself to be brave. After all, *he'd* kissed *me*, right? That had to mean he still liked me, at least a little. "What exactly —"

"Don't," he said. He didn't even look up from his cell phone.

"Don't what?" I asked, offended. I mean, really! The least he could have done was look at me!

"Don't start talking about our relationship," he said.

How had he known? How do they always know? What do they have, some kind of radar?

"Uh," I said.

Now I wasn't just offended. I was mad. I wasn't one of those whiny *I want to know where our relationship is going* kind of girls. I'd never brought it up once, not in the whole time we were going out.

Which, okay, had only been for, like, two weeks. And for a

large part of that time I'd been shacked up with Brandon Stark . . . against my will.

But still.

"I think I have a right to know where our relationship currently stands," I said indignantly. "Because I'll be honest: If you're going to keep playing these head games, I'm just going to start seeing other people."

Yeah! That sounded good. Like something Lauren Conrad or someone would say. Not that Lauren Conrad is this huge role model or anything.

But who else do we single girls have to guide us during these complex modern times? Seriously, everyone else is divorced.

Christopher lowered his cell phone and stared at me with an expression of utter disbelief.

"*What?*" he said. His voice cracked.

"I mean it," I said.

I didn't want to get into a huge fight in a Thai takeout place in Brooklyn.

But come on. A girl has to have standards.

"You can't just come rescue me — twice — kiss me a bunch of times, and then act like you don't even care about me." I tossed some of my hair. "I don't have time for this kind of game playing. I need to know. Either you're into me or you're not. If you are, great. If you're not, quit kissing me. It's only fair."

This was good. I had no idea where this stuff was coming from, or anything. But I liked it.

"Well," Christopher said. "To tell you the truth, right now, I'm really not that into you. Because you're acting like someone I don't even know. And it's not that cute."

Stung, I tried to pass off the tears in my eyes as a reaction to all the hot grease in the air from the frying. Maybe Lauren Conrad wasn't that great a role model after all.

"I'm not acting like anyone," I said. "Except myself. You said I needed to grow up, and that's exactly what I'm doing. I'm just requesting some honesty from you. I really love you, and I want to know if you —"

"Jesus," Christopher said. He lifted his cell phone into the air again. I couldn't help noticing he was blushing. "Would you stop saying that?"

"Stop saying what? That I love you?"

I had to admit, torturing him was kind of fun.

"Yes," he said, looking extremely uncomfortable. "You keep saying it, but then you don't act like it."

"How do I not act like it?" I demanded. Now *I* was blushing. I really hoped the cashier seated a few feet away who was staring into space didn't speak good enough English to tell what we were saying.

"By flying off to Brandon Stark's beach house, for one thing," he pointed out. "And letting the whole world think you're in love with him and not me, for another. Then, when I come to rescue you, you wouldn't even come with me —"

"Oh, would you let that go?" I demanded. "I already explained that!"

"You can't just say you're sorry for something and have it all be better," Christopher said. "You may love me, but you don't act like it. You don't trust me."

"I called you today when I was being followed!" I reminded him.

"Was I the *first* person you called?" he asked.

I felt myself blushing harder. How had he known I'd called Lulu first?

"You were the first person I *thought* of calling," I said. "But you were so mean to me on the plane. You have this whole evil supervillain thing going. It's not very attractive, you know."

It was sort of the opposite of unattractive, actually, but I didn't want him to know that. It would only encourage his bad behavior.

Like now. He rolled his eyes and turned back to his cell phone.

It was at that point that *my* cell phone rang. It was Gabriel, calling to ask how soon I thought we'd get there.

"Uh," I said. "Pretty soon."

"It's just," he said, "the sooner you get here the better, actually."

"Oh, why?" I asked.

"You'll see when you arrive" was all Gabriel would say, in a slightly agitated voice.

This had seemed very mysterious, but he wouldn't say anything more. We were going to take the subway to Gabriel's place to further throw off anyone from Stark who might be following us. But we ended up with so many bags of food, another cab seemed like the best idea, so Christopher finally flagged one down — our argument on hold indefinitely — and we made it to Gabriel's place without anyone seeming to tag along behind us. Nor, when we looked up and down Avenue A and Sixth, where Gabriel lived, did we see anyone who looked out of place — in pressed trousers and black shoes — lurking around.

When he opened the door to his apartment, I figured out everything about Gabriel's mysterious comment, however. He wasn't concerned about Stark security showing up unexpectedly. His anxiety was because his bachelor pad had been turned into an impromptu beauty salon.

Lulu was there, working her magic. Or trying to, anyway.

"Look," she was saying to Nikki. "You're just not cut out to be a blonde anymore, Nikki. Face facts."

Nikki, sitting on a stool in the middle of Gabriel's living room — his taste seemed to lean toward midcentury modern. He had a very fifties vibe going on, with low couches and a coffee table cut out like a kidney-shaped pool, and deeply piled shag throw rugs, modern art, the works. It was super old-school — was sulking.

"No," Nikki was seething. "I've always been a blonde. I'll always be a blonde. I want to stay a blonde!"

Nikki had foil packets sticking up all over her head, indicating something of a chemical nature was already going on with her hair. It just didn't appear to be what she wanted.

"Trust me," Lulu was saying. "You're going to look adorable. For once your insides are going to match your outsides."

This sounded ominous.

"Just give it a chance," Lulu said. "Like that purple eye shadow I was trying out on you. It's going to bring out the green in your eyes."

"I told you," Nikki seethed some more. "I want to be *blond*." She stabbed a finger in my direction as Christopher and I came in with the bags from the Thai restaurant. "Like *her*! Like I used to be!"

Steven, sitting at Gabriel's kitchen counter, thumbing through a magazine on architecture — Gabriel had dozens of them lying around — had leapt up as soon as he saw us.

"That smells incredible," he said, relieving us of all the bags we carried. "You two are lifesavers."

It felt good to be called a lifesaver, even if all we'd done was brought dinner.

Mrs. Howard had locked herself into one of the bedrooms with a migraine and wouldn't come out. I could totally see why. It looked like a tornado had struck Gabriel's apartment. There were shopping bags from stores like Intermix and Scoop scattered everywhere. How Lulu had managed to buy so much for Nikki in so little time, I'd never know.

"I don't even know why we're doing this," Nikki complained as Lulu sponged foundation onto her face, "since I'm just going to get my old body back soon. It's all a mute point."

"Moot," Gabriel corrected her, as he pulled plates down from a kitchen cabinet. "Moot point."

"That's what I said." Nikki glared at him. It was weird, but even with the foil packets popping up out of her head like alien antennae, she was already looking better. Lulu had put her in some kind of black halter top that accentuated her creamy shoulders and a pair of jeans that weren't hand-me-downs from me and actually fit the curve of her hips. She was starting to look . . . well, cute. Alien cute. But cute. "And nobody asked you, Prince William."

"Oh, that's very nice," Gabriel said. He was practically snarling at her. I'd never seen him looking so frazzled. "I give you shelter in my home, risking my life in doing so, and you make fun of my accent. You're extremely pleasant to have around, did you know that, Nikki?"

"Bite me, Harry Potter," she said, with a sneer.

He looked at me helplessly. "Do you see?" he asked. "Do you see what I have to put up with?"

I felt bad for having dragged Gabriel, who really had been an innocent bystander, in on all this.

"Have some pad see ew," I said, handing him a container. It was the only thing I could think of as a way to make it all up to him.

"Oh, thanks ever so much," he said. I was pretty sure he was being sarcastic.

An alarm went off. Lulu looked at her cell phone and squealed. "It's time to rinse," she said, and grabbed Nikki to pull her off the stool and into the bathroom. Nikki went with her, but not without grumbling. When the door shut, Steven turned to us and said, "If we don't find a way out of this mess soon, I think we're all going to go insane."

"I'll put a bullet through my own brain." Gabriel sounded grim. "Let alone wait for Stark to do it. Your sister will drive me to it, Howard. No offense."

"I know what you mean," Steven said as he took a seat at the kitchen counter and dug into a container of panang curry without waiting to put any of it on one of the plates Gabriel had provided. "She's always been like that, if she doesn't get what she wants."

"'That's how she got where she is today," I said. When everyone looked at me, I added, "Well, I mean, one of the highest-paid fashion models in the world."

"And also somebody one of the richest men in the world wants dead," Steven pointed out.

"Well, she's not getting her old body back," Christopher said, shoveling some pad thai into his mouth. "However much she might think otherwise."

I blinked at him. He claimed to hate me, then kissed me and came to my defense at every possible moment, while insisting we couldn't get back together because of my trust issues. What was going on with him?

"I know," Steven said. "But we can't go on living in hiding for much longer. And Gabriel can't be asked to put up with us forever."

The sound of shrieking came out of the bathroom. There was a bang, and then the sound of water spraying.

Then Nikki's voice screamed, "Lulu! *What did you do?*" Her voice was drowned out by the sound of a blow-dryer.

Gabriel looked toward the ceiling, as if praying for patience.

"Have either of you heard of something called Project Phoenix?" Christopher wanted to know.

"I went to Phoenix once," Steven said, chewing. "Nice weather."

"Is it a band?" Gabriel asked. "I think I caught them once in Wales."

"I'm fairly certain it's not a band," Christopher said. "It's something Robert Stark is working on."

"No idea, then," Gabriel said.

"What is it?" Steven asked.

Christopher filled them in on what little we knew so far about Project Phoenix. The explanation took us through most of the carton of pad thai and the remains of the pad see ew.

"It makes no sense," Steven said, when Christopher finished.

"It does," Christopher said. "We just can't see it."

"I saw on the news today," Gabriel said, "that they're building an elevator to space."

We all turned to look at him.

"Well, they are," he said, swallowing. "An American company. Rather than launching a shuttle every time we have to send something up to the space station, we'll just send it up in an elevator they're building from a mobile seagoing platform that will reach all the way up to space. It makes sense, don't you think? Anyway, maybe that's what Project Phoenix is. Robert Stark's own space elevator."

Christopher shrugged. "It makes more sense than anything else."

It was right then that the door to the bathroom opened and Lulu and Nikki came out.

Or at least, it had to have been Nikki. Because that's who Lulu had gone into the bathroom with.

But the girl with whom she emerged looked completely different. She had wavy dark hair, instead of Nikki's flat auburn hair, and a glowing complexion instead of Nikki's dead-looking, over-foundationed skin.

And there was a bounce to her step I'd never noticed in Nikki's before. She had on a flowy black empire-waist top and a pair of leggings that suited her figure perfectly.

Her step wasn't the only place where there was bounce, either.

"Geez," the girl said rudely, when she saw us staring at her. And by us, I mean mostly Christopher and Gabriel, though Steven and I were a bit slack-jawed as well. "Take a picture, why don'tcha. It'll last longer."

Okay. So it *was* Nikki, after all.

"Nikki," I said, feeling slightly dumbfounded. "You look . . . great."

"Chokers are so 2005," Nikki said, fingering the silver skull and crossbones on a black velvet ribbon at her throat. Did she really think we were only looking at the choker? "Which is what I told Lulu. But for some reason, this one works."

"The whole thing works," Gabriel said. I noticed he was holding a forkful of pad see ew frozen halfway to his mouth. He sounded slightly out of breath.

"I figure no one from her past life will recognize her," Lulu said, giving one of Nikki's new curls a pat, "in her new body like this."

"You can say that again," Christopher said.

I elbowed him, hard. "Oof," he said, and quickly closed his mouth after giving me a slightly devilish grin.

Gabriel, however, continued to stare.

"It's very retro," he ventured.

"Yes," Lulu said, glancing meaningfully around at Gabriel's decor. "Isn't it?"

SIXTEEN

WHEN I WOKE UP THE NEXT MORNING,
I wasn't in bed alone.

I don't mean just Cosabella, either.

Or, unfortunately, Christopher.

There was a five-foot-nine agent in a silk eggplant-colored
jacket and skirt sitting on the edge of my mattress, texting
madly, her hosed legs crossed and one Jimmy Choo bouncing
up and down on the end of her toes.

When she noticed my eyes were open, Rebecca paused, her
thumbs hovering over her BlackBerry, and said, "Finally. I
thought you were never going to wake up. Did you take a full
ten mils of Ambien or something? You should really cut back
to the fives. Well, are you going to get out of bed, or what? We

have loads to do, Nikki, and we don't really have all day. Get a move on."

Then she went back to texting.

This really wasn't how I'd dreamed of starting the morning. In my fantasies, I'd planned on waking with a hunky — albeit slightly villainous — eleventh grader between my sheets.

But I'd been unable to lure Christopher up to my apartment after we'd stopped by Gabriel's, since he'd decided to go back to his cousin Felix's to continue working on the Project Phoenix conundrum.

There was also the small matter of his continued disgust over my "trust issues."

You know if a teenage boy turns down an invitation to a single girl's apartment, it's bad. Really bad. The guy really must hate my guts. What was I going to do to convince him that I trusted him, already?

My relationship problems weren't exactly putting me in the mood for an early morning visitation from my agent.

"What are you doing here?" I asked Rebecca as I dragged a pillow over my head, disturbing Cosabella, who'd been sleeping soundly until I did this. Some watchdog she was. Robert Stark could have sent twenty of his henchman in to kill me in my sleep, and she wouldn't have done anything more than snort and roll over to make herself more comfortable.

"You have a big day today," Rebecca said, still punching her tiny keyboard. "The party at Robert Stark's. And then the Stark Angel lingerie show tonight. *Live,* in case you don't remember. It's New Year's Eve. The diamond bra? Your big television debut? A billion potential viewers? And let's just say you haven't been among my most *reliable* clients lately. All this running away to pop off onto private jets and to people's beachside compounds. I wanted to make sure you got up on time to get your hair and makeup and fittings done." She flicked a glance down at me. "Your roots are showing. And how long has it been since you had your cuticles trimmed? Your nails are a mess. And when was the last time you waxed *down there?* Need I remind you that you're practically wearing a thong on national television tonight? Really, what was that thing with Brandon Stark down in South Carolina? Not that I don't applaud your initiative. He's a wealthy boy. But can't you get him to buy a house somewhere close by? The Hamptons? All your *people* are up here, darling."

I knew what she meant by *people.* My hair people. My nail people. My waxer. My facialist. My stylist. My nutritionist. My trainer. My publicist. My agent. It takes a village to make someone look as good as Nikki Howard. It would be wrong to think she looked as good as she did *naturally.* I mean, there were some genetics involved, but teamwork (and Photoshop) had a lot to do with it, too.

But the one part of being at Brandon's that had been kind of nice was that for once, I hadn't been surrounded by all those people. I'd just been . . . well, me again.

For a change.

I lay there, not moving. Who had let Rebecca in? Karl, the doorman? Because he knew her so well? Well, Karl and I were going to have words. Because this was unacceptable.

Lulu? I highly doubted it. Why wouldn't she have woken me up to tell me Rebecca was lurking around? This was so not like Lulu . . . and so not how I'd wanted to begin my day. I'd wanted to lie around, hugging the memory of Christopher kissing me so roughly in the cab (why couldn't I rewind time and go back to that moment and do it all again, only right, so we didn't fight afterward?).

Except I couldn't. Because Rebecca was leaning over and smacking my butt.

"Get up! And be sure to eat a big breakfast. And lunch. I don't care if you show a little tum on TV tonight, I can't have you passing out on me again, like you did at the Megastore opening. No hypoglycemia today. Work! Work, work, work!"

Rebecca got up and teetered out of my room in her insanely high heels.

"The car's coming to pick you up for the Stark party at seven," she bellowed. "Be here, or I'll chop you into little bits and feed you to the other models I represent. Believe me, they're hungry enough to eat up every little bite."

She clip-clopped out of the room. A few seconds later, I heard the elevator doors opening, and her stepping into it, talking loudly on her cell phone.

"What?" she was saying. "No, not the python. I said the lizard skin. Can't anyone follow simple instructions anymore? What is wrong with the world?"

Sighing, I got out of bed, Cosabella darting quickly after me because morning is when she gets her first bowl of food of the day (I have no idea how Cosabella eats so much and stays so thin. Possibly it's because she never stops moving, except when she drops off into an exhausted sleep on my neck at night).

As I opened Cosabella's can in the kitchen, I wondered if Christopher and Felix had made any progress trying to figure out what Project Phoenix was. Obviously, I was going to do as much snooping as I could when I got to Robert Stark's Upper East Side town house. But it would have been nice to have some clue what I was supposed to be snooping for.

I was scooping some of Cosy's nasty-smelling food into her bowl when I heard a sound and straightened up, only to see a very large, almost naked male figure sneaking out of Lulu's room.

I screamed as loudly as I could, causing Cosy to jump about a foot in the air, and the male to shriek almost as loudly as I had.

"Em, it's me!" the male cried, and when my eyes had had time to focus after they were done spinning around in circles of shock, I saw that it was, indeed, someone I knew.

Someone who was, in fact, Steven Howard, Nikki Howard's brother.

In an undershirt, boxer shorts, and a pair of socks.

Coming out of Lulu's bedroom! With his blond hair sticking up all wild, like he'd just woken up!

And now Lulu was coming out of her room right after him, wearing one of her fancy negligees and rubbing her eyes all sleepily, going, "Stevie? Is something wrong? I thought I heard screaming."

Oh, no. No, I could not handle this. Not first thing in the morning (even though a glance at the clock on the microwave told me it was closer to noon than morning).

Steven and Lulu? I mean, I'd known she'd *wanted* it to happen — wanted it to happen more than anything — but . . .

"Oh, hi, Em," Lulu said, giving me a drowsy smile. "I didn't know you were home."

But Steven was . . . well, he was . . . he was my *brother*!

Wasn't he? Maybe not technically, but —

Actually, yes, he was. Technically. This was so . . . so wrong. So gross. So . . .

. . . so typically Lulu.

"Steven spent the night," Lulu said, like it was the most natural thing in the world, going over to the refrigerator and pulling it open. "We're a couple now. What do you guys want for breakfast? Scrambled eggs? Steven likes his eggs scrambled, don't you, Steven?"

Steven was standing there in his socks and underwear, turning bright, bright red.

But not as red as *I* could feel myself turning.

"Uh, hi, Em," Steven was saying. He'd gone to sit behind the kitchen counter on one of the stools, so the fact that he was in his underwear wasn't *quite* so apparent. "I'm really sorry about this. We didn't know you were home. I, uh, checked the acoustic noise generator. It's still working. There are no bugs in the loft. So we're safe here."

"Well, that's good, I guess," I said. I was glad I had on my flannel rainbow pajamas. They covered me from neck to foot.

"Steven and I are so in love," Lulu said, smiling ecstatically as she piled eggs, butter, cheese, and cream next to the stove. "He told me he loved me after I gave Nikki her makeover yesterday. She looks so good now. She was so happy. She was really happy, wasn't she, Stevie?"

"She was," Steven said. He was still blushing. It was weird to see his cheeks turning the same color pink as my pajamas. "It was weird to see Nikki happy, for once."

"She says she's going to go to college," Lulu said. "Business school. That was Gabriel's idea. She and Gabriel get along weirdly well. When she isn't calling him names. I wish she weren't quite so abusive toward him, it's not very nice. But I guess we can't expect miracles. Oh, Em, are you all right?"

I think I was staring at them so hard, I'd forgotten to breathe. I closed my mouth shut with an audible snapping sound.

"Uh-huh," I said, and nodded.

"Is it Steven and me?" Lulu asked, glancing over at Nikki's brother, like she couldn't understand why I was so surprised. "He said he was sorry for blurting out that he loved me, that it had just slipped," Lulu went on, cracking some of the eggs into a bowl. "But I wouldn't let him take it back. Would I?"

Steven shook his head. "She wouldn't," he said.

"I knew he really meant it, and that we were meant to be together forever. Because I'm the future Mrs. Captain Steven Howard." Lulu looked thoughtful as she switched on the coffeemaker. "Wow. Is it just me, or does that sound really hot? Mrs. Captain Steven Howard." She glanced over at me and Steven. "I'm going to keep my maiden name for my albums, though, of course."

I widened my eyes at Steven. Did he even know what he'd gotten himself into, I wondered?

He gave me a sheepish smile.

"What can I say?" He shrugged his broad, bare shoulders. "I love her."

I shook my head in wonder. Stick a fork in him. Steven was *done*. Lulu had caught him, reeled him in, stuffed him, and served him up with a nice lemon-and-garlic sauce.

And he looked really happy about it, aside from the blushing thing.

"Wow, you guys, that's so sweet," I said, meaning it.

I wandered out of the kitchen and back into the living room, because I had a lot to do. Rebecca had left a list. Apparently, there was a stylist coming over with a selection of gowns for me to choose from to wear to Robert Stark's party, not to mention my waxer — Katerina, who normally performed this service for Lulu and me, had apparently been pink-slipped . . . at least in the waxing department. Which was just as well. It was a bit odd to have the person who cleaned your toilet also waxing you — hairstylist, and nail people. . . .

"You know what?" Lulu went on, making Steven a cup of coffee. "I never noticed before, but you two have the same color eyes. Robin's-egg blue. That's my favorite color. Both of you." She turned from me to Steven with the dopiest smile I'd ever seen. "It's like the sky is in your faces!"

Oh, wow. And I'd thought Steven had it bad? Lulu was done, too.

Was this what people who were in love were like? Maybe it was just as well Christopher and I couldn't work things out. I didn't want to become a zombiefied dope like those two.

The buzzer on the intercom went off. Still feeling a little dazed from my discovery, I wandered over to it and picked up the receiver. It was Karl, letting me know my first appointment had arrived . . . Salvatore, with the clothes.

I thanked him and said to send him up.

"Uh, guys," I said, to Lulu and Steven. "My clothes guy is here."

"Oooh," Lulu said, going over to Steven and putting her arms around him. "Fashion show. Fun."

I guess Steven really *was* my brother, because the sight of him snuggling with a girl — even a girl I really liked, such as Lulu — skeeved me as much as it would have skeeved me to see Frida making out with someone.

"Yeah," I said. "Okay. If you two could just hold off doing that until after I've had breakfast, that would be great."

"Sorry," Steven said, looking like he meant it.

"Oh, I'm sorry, Em," Lulu said, pulling her arms away from Steven like he'd electrocuted her. "I forgot you still haven't found love like we have. I shouldn't rub it in."

"No," I said. "I've found love, and everything. Christopher and I just still need to work out a few things."

"Oh." Lulu looked sad. "I feel so bad for you."

"Yeah," Steven said. "Do you want me to, I don't know. Put him in a choke hold, or anything?"

I couldn't help smiling at that.

"I don't think that's going to help," I said. "But thanks. Maybe if you two went and put some more clothes on for when the guy comes? Because he's going to be here any minute."

They scooted out of the room — well, Steven stomped more than scooted, on account of his size — just as the elevator doors opened to reveal Salvatore carting a wheeled rack of dresses and gowns for Robert Stark's party.

"Ciao, bella," he said, kissing me on both cheeks. His assistant, a stick-thin woman with dark hair, began unzipping the garment bags to show me what was inside them.

"Very chic, this," Salvatore said, fingering the sleeve of my pajamas. "I have seen in this month's *Vogue*, yes?"

"Very funny," I said. "Thanks for coming over. Would you like some coffee?"

Salvatore and his assistant did want coffee. And so, later, did the waxer, hairstylist, and their assistants when they showed up. And the nail tech and her assistant. I seemed to spend my entire day making cups of coffee — and sandwiches — for people, in between getting primped and styled for the evening's command performance, and trying to avoid seeing Lulu and Steven with their tongues down each other's throats.

This, however, proved harder to do than I thought, since they were kind of all over each other, and Steven wouldn't go back to Gabriel's place. Lulu made him stay to help pick out what I was wearing to Robert Stark's party — a short, black, spangled dress by Dolce & Gabbana. Then she made him stay because she decided she wanted him to come to Robert Stark's party as her escort.

"I think that would be a really bad idea," I said. And not just because I didn't want to be distracted from my snooping by her and Steven making out all night. "What if someone recognizes him?"

"Oh, baby," Lulu said, holding Steven's face between both her hands, then giving him a big kiss. "I didn't think about that."

Gag.

"It's better that I stay with my mom and Nikki, anyway," Steven said. "I haven't seen them since yesterday."

Yes, I thought. Go back to Gabriel's now.

The buzzer on our intercom went off. I went to the receiver to pick it up, just as my cell phone vibrated.

"Yes?" I said, lifting the receiver to the intercom. I checked my cell. It was Christopher.

"Brandon Stark is here, Miss Howard," Karl said. "To take you to his father's party."

Perfect, I thought, rolling my eyes. Brandon had been completely ignoring me since my phone call to him yesterday. It was so like him to think his reward would be that it would be all right to show up at my apartment to escort me to his dad's party without even asking.

"Tell him I'll be right down," I said, and hung up the intercom to answer my cell.

"Christopher?" I said.

"Em," he said. "You can't go to that party tonight."

"Uh," I said. "I have no choice. The million-dollar bra has been taken out of the vault. I've been waxed and buffed and shined. I'm in my borrowed dress. The car is here."

I didn't mention the part about Brandon being in it. Christopher and I were fighting enough as it was.

"Em," he said. "You don't understand. *You're* Project Phoenix."

SEVENTEEN

"WAIT," I SAID, GRIPPING THE PHONE more tightly to my ear. A chill had passed over my body.

But that was surely only because I was standing there in a too-short sleeveless dress on a chilly December 31st evening.

"What are you talking about?" I asked. "How can I be Project Phoenix?"

"I don't know," Christopher said. "I don't — we don't — still even know exactly what Project Phoenix is. But we've found a link from it to the Stark Institute for Neurology and Neurosurgery. And your name."

"*My* name?" I echoed. "Emerson Watts? Or —"

"No. Nikki Howard. Em, think about it. Think about what all these people have in common. They're young. They're healthy. They're attractive."

"So?"

"Just like Nikki Howard."

"What are you guys talking about?" Lulu asked me curiously, adjusting one of her fishnets, which had gotten twisted around her leg.

"Nothing," I said to her. "Go on down to the car and let Brandon know I'll be right there, will you?"

Lulu shrugged. "Okay."

"No!" Christopher cried, overhearing me. "Em, you can't go to that party!"

"Christopher, I have to," I said. "If I don't go, Robert Stark will know something is up." And a billion fans would be tragically disappointed. Not to mention the show's sponsor, De Beers jewelry. "And, anyway, I don't see what the connection is between the Stark Institute and all those other people and me."

"You don't?" Christopher sounded slightly hysterical. "Em, don't you get it? Curt? He's just going on a hiking trip in the Cascades. By himself. He goes missing, who's going to know what really happened to him? Kerry, going to Guatemala to teach the children to read? She disappears along the way? She's one of thousands who go missing every year. Same with all these other people. It's freaking genius, Em. Young, healthy kids . . . and Stark has its pick. They may have been doing this for years. All these pretty missing girls we hear about on CNN every day . . . for all we know, Stark may have been behind it all along."

"Christopher . . ." I shook my head. I loved my boyfriend. I really did.

But his hatred for Stark — because of what he'd seen them do to me — may have caused him to go around the bend.

I guess I could understand it. He'd seen me get crushed to death right in front of him. The post-traumatic stress this had inevitably caused him had to have been severe. I loved him, but he was one messed-up dude.

And then he'd found out the accident had been no accident at all but had been caused by Stark. And that I wasn't dead at all but living in some other girl's body.

No wonder he'd lost his mind and morphed into Iron Man.

Only without the supersuit and in teenage form.

"Em," Christopher said. He was still speaking fast and still panting a little. "Listen to me. Robert Stark is a marketing genius. He's dedicated his life to finding a demand, then supplying the product for that demand at a price that drives all other competitors out of business. The question isn't *whether* he's doing this. *It's why hasn't anyone caught him before now?*"

The buzzer to my intercom went off again. It was Brandon's driver, I knew, wanting to know where I was. Lulu had already gone down.

"Look," I said. "You're probably right."

What else was I going to say? I had to just play along with him. Was this what it was like, I wondered? To be Lois Lane or Lana Lang or Mary Jane Watson or any of those other women who were the girlfriends of superheroes? I mean, those guys were crazy, right? The men who thought they were superheroes. How were you supposed to deal with them? You didn't want to upset them or get them riled up, or they'd just go and put on their capes and jump out the window to go get shot at.

So you just went along with their craziness, trying to soothe them as best you could in the hopes that they'd stay home, where it was safe.

Then you went out and did whatever you wanted behind their back.

"We'll talk about it when I get home," I said, in the most soothing voice I could summon. "We'll figure out the best thing to do then."

"What?" Christopher cried. "Em, *no* —"

"You can't do anything about it now, anyway," I said. "I mean, what are you going to do? Call the cops? You don't have any proof. Are any of those people missing yet?"

"Well," he said. "No. And technically there's no proof

except what happened to you. Which wasn't an accident, either. But —"

The buzzer went off again, for a much longer time.

"Right," I said. "Look, I've got to run. Everything's going to be all right. I'll call you from Robert Stark's to prove it."

"Don't go to that house, Em." Christopher sounded mad. He sounded more than mad. He sounded furious. And also scared. "I'm warning you, Em. Don't you even think about —"

"Love you," I said, grabbing my bag and faux fur and running for the elevator. "Bye."

"Don't you hang up," Christopher said. "I mean it. Don't you dare —"

"Oh, I'm in the elevator," I said as I pressed the button. "You're breaking up. I'm losing you. . . . "

"You are not losing me," Christopher said. "Em, don't be stupid. I —"

I hung up.

Really, I wasn't trying to be mean. It was just that I didn't have time for Christopher's supervillain stuff right then. Rebecca's warnings from that morning were still sounding in my ears. I had to get to Robert Stark's party, and then to the studio where the lingerie show was being broadcast, or my butt was toast. I completely valued my relationship with Christopher, and I totally thought something was up with Robert Stark.

But I had my professional obligations to fulfill.

And besides. What was Robert Stark going to do to me? That he hadn't done already, I mean.

"Where *were* you?" Lulu wanted to know, when I finally fell into the back of the limo.

"Sorry," I muttered, climbing over Brandon's outstretched legs. "Important call. Would you *move?*" This last was directed at Brandon.

"My bad." Brandon was clearly already drunk. Since this was how he was anytime he had to see his father, it was no surprise.

"But really," Lulu said. "What did Christopher want?"

"I have no idea," I said truthfully.

"He wanted to come," Lulu said sympathetically. "Didn't he? As your date?"

Brandon looked up from his highball glass at this. "You're back together with that guy? Leather jacket guy?" He looked disappointed.

"None of your business," I said, wagging a finger at him. "Go back to your drink."

Brandon glared dopily down at his whisky.

"Guys who wear leather jackets always get the girl," he muttered.

If only he knew the truth.

Robert Stark's huge, ten-bedroom, four-story gray town house, with its subdued black trim, private garage, and indoor pool, ballroom, and vast private back garden, was about as far uptown as you could get from my place. Just off Fifth Avenue, it was steps from Central Park and the Metropolitan Museum of Art.

His annual New Year's Eve party was so popular, and attended by so many celebrities and wealthy politicians and Stark shareholders, there was already a traffic jam just to get to his place. Lulu and Brandon and I had to get out and walk the last block, and then fight the crowd of paps that had gathered outside.

The whole time — well, during the walk to his dad's house, anyway — I quizzed Brandon, trying to see if he knew anything about Project Phoenix.

"What is that?" he'd asked, still slurping scotch from the glass he'd brought along for the stroll from the limo. "A new stadium someone is building in Arizona?"

Seriously. A band? A space elevator? And now a stadium?

"No," I'd said. "It's something your dad is doing using data from people who bought his new Quarks."

"How's that going to work?" Brandon wanted to know.

"That's what I'm asking you," I said, frustrated.

"Well, if I knew that, would I be here with you?" Brandon asked. "No, I'd be in my dad's office, telling him I knew and to get the hell out. Right? So try again."

I hunched along beside him, defeated. Christopher and Felix

had to be onto something . . . but that *I* was Project Phoenix? It was all just too crazy.

Still, at least Christopher was trying.

Which was more than could be said for me. I was at a *party*. Worse, a boring party for celebrities. I saw Madonna getting out of a limo right in front of the red carpet leading up the steps to the wide-open front door (which was a bit weird, because she lived right around the corner. She could almost have walked. Although not in those heels, I realized when I looked at her gladiator platforms). The governor of New York was going inside just ahead of her.

"There's Nikki Howard!" the paps gathered on either side of the gold security ropes cried when they saw me with Brandon. "Nikki! Is it true you and Brandon Stark are engaged?"

"Absolutely," Brandon said drunkenly into the first microphone thrust in his direction. "Hey, watch the drink."

"No," I said. "We're just friends."

"I'm engaged," Lulu said to a reporter who had asked her whether her album was ever going to drop. "Well, okay, engaged to be engaged someday. I'm a bit busy at the moment to be thinking about getting married, recording my new album."

"Lulu," I hissed at her. "Can it on the engagement stuff. No one's supposed to know about You Know Who."

"Oh, the identity of my husband-to-be is a secret," Lulu squealed as I dragged her past the uniformed security guards posted on either side of the door and into the town house. "He's very shy. *You* know. Not used to life in the spotlight yet."

Inside the Stark mansion, there were models in Stark Angel bra-and-panty sets, complete with wings — not any of the models from the show I was going to do later, though, and their wings were smaller, for better maneuverability — to offer glasses of champagne to everyone and take people's coats as soon as they entered. Farther into the house, which was sumptuously decorated and made up entirely of marble and black wood paneling, were magicians, jugglers, a fire-eater, and acrobats from Cirque du Soleil.

Lulu took one look at the fire-eater, who had quite a circle of admirers, and said, stomping her foot, "I *knew* I should have a fire-eater at my party."

Brandon, who'd traded his empty glass from the limo for a flute of champagne from a passing Stark Angel's silver tray, made a face.

"Fire-eaters suck," he said. "Your trapeze girl was great."

"Really?" Lulu looked skeptical. "I don't think anyone even noticed her. She was hanging way above everybody's heads."

I stood there holding my champagne, which of course I wasn't drinking, wondering what I was even doing there. We'd meandered into Robert Stark's cavernous ballroom — the ceiling was twenty feet high, at least, and painted with cherubs that looked like chubby versions of the Stark Angels who were wandering around (minus the bras) and dotted all over with humongous crystal chandeliers that glittered like the drop earrings I was wearing. All around us were celebrities who were drinking and chatting and crowding the impressive buffet, where paper-thin curls of roast beef and fat ruby-red strawberries and caviar in gold bowls with mother-of-pearl spoons and huge pink shrimp sat curled in chilled bowls and were being served on fine china plates by caterers in white suits. I saw Madonna again, this time talking to Gwyneth Paltrow, and Jay-Z hanging out with Bono. Everyone was there, at least for a little while. It didn't seem like the kind of party you stayed at for a long time . . . just one of those parties where you stopped by, said hello, and left. . . .

Part of that might have been because the French doors leading from the ballroom out to the back garden were wide open, and a chilly breeze was coming in. Then again, the room was roastingly hot because of all the bodies in it. People were milling in and out of it, not even bothering to get their coats to go outside.

"Oh, look," Lulu said, pointing at someone over by the buffet. "There's Taylor Swift. I'm going to go tell her about Steven. She's going to be so happy for me."

I grabbed Lulu's arm before she got more than two inches away.

"Would you stop?" I whispered. "No one's supposed to know about Steven."

"I won't tell her his last name, silly," Lulu said. "But I'm just so happy. I'm busting to tell everyone I know!"

She wrenched her arm out of my hand and hurried off. There really wasn't anything I could do to stop her, beyond tackling her and sitting on her, which I was pretty sure wouldn't go unnoticed.

Brandon, who'd disappeared for a minute or two, reappeared holding a plate of shrimp, which he chewed noisily in my ear.

"Have you tried this shrimp?" he asked. "It's freaking amazing."

"Would you get away from me?" I said irritably. "I hate you."

"You're so moody," Brandon remarked, chewing loudly. "Just because I kidnapped you and tried to force you to be my girlfriend. I thought you'd be over that by now. Here, just try a bite." He waved a shrimp in my face. "The cocktail sauce is really good."

"Stop," I said, and stepped away from him . . .

. . . right into the path of Rebecca, wearing a long black evening gown, which fit her body like a second skin and had a slit up to her pelvic bone, practically.

"Oh, good, there you are." She grabbed my arm. "I've been looking everywhere for you. What are you doing, hiding in this corner with Brandon? Why aren't you mingling? You're here to mingle. You're the Million-Dollar-Bra Girl."

Brandon let out a giant horselaugh at that.

"Million-Dollar-Brawr Girl!" he said, doing a pretty good imitation of Rebecca. "Better get cher brawron!"

Rebecca sent him a withering look.

"Brandon," she said severely. "Are you drunk?"

"Of course," he replied, licking a shrimp.

"Get out of my sight, then," Rebecca said. She began steering me away from Brandon, toward the center of the room. "Mr. Stark Senior has been asking for you all night. He wants to introduce you to some of his shareholders."

I hurried along beside her, practically having to jog. I had no idea how she walked so fast in such high heels. We were approaching a group of tuxedoed men and women in evening gowns.

"Found her," Rebecca called in her Brooklynese.

The people turned and the group broke apart a little. I saw that at the center of it was Robert Stark, looking as absurdly handsome — only older, of course — as his son. He smiled at me, his teeth startlingly white against his tanned, weather-beaten face. He'd been using his own Stark brand teeth-whitening strips, I saw.

"Ah, there she is," he said, and put his hand on my bare back. "Nikki Howard, everyone, the star of this evening's performance."

All the old people smiled at me. They looked kind and

attractive and rich. Very, very rich. The ladies had a lot of diamonds dripping from around their necks, and the men's faces were very puffy and red, like they'd had too much to drink already.

"So nice to finally meet you, dear," one lady in a long beige dress that was tastefully decorated in sparkles at the bottom said, reaching out to shake my hand. She said her name, but I instantly forgot it.

"Nice to meet you, too," I said.

She seemed to hold on to my hand for way too long. It was creepy. I wanted to get away from her, and from Robert Stark and the rest of his friends. Or shareholders, I guess they were.

Except that two things happened at once.

One was that I glanced down at our clenched hands and noticed that around her slender, blue-veined wrist was a black velvet cord, and that from the cord dangled something that looked to me like a gold bird that was on fire.

Or, you know. A phoenix.

And when I looked up, wondering if I was interpreting what I was seeing correctly, I noticed someone over her shoulder, just coming into the ballroom.

And that was Gabriel.

Who, like me, was undoubtedly being forced to come to this party by his agent.

Except that he was with someone. A pretty brunette of about average height, who was wearing a purple dress with a black corset laced up *tight* to flatter her cute figure, and matching purple eye shadow. It took me a second to recognize who she was, Lulu's makeover had been so complete:

None other than Nikki Howard.

EIGHTEEN

"EXCUSE ME," I SAID TO THE WOMAN who was still holding my hand. "I actually have to go make a phone call."

I didn't want to say I had to go say hi to someone I knew, because I didn't want to draw Robert Stark's attention to Gabriel's date. I had no idea whether or not he'd been alerted to the fact that Nikki was still alive, or if he knew whose body she'd been put into or what she looked like.

But I figured the less attention I drew to Nikki, the better.

But Robert Stark, it turned out, wasn't done with me.

"Oh, I'm sure your call can wait," he said, putting his arm around me and turning me so I couldn't even see Gabriel or Nikki anymore. "There are some more people I'd like you to meet. This is Bill and Ellen Anderson, also Stark shareholders, as I'm sure you know."

I found myself shaking the hands of more old people in evening wear . . . again dripping in diamonds and rosacea . . . and again with black cords around their wrists with what looked to me like a gold phoenix dangling from them.

Hey, I was no expert on mythological birds. But if it had fire shooting out of its wings, was it not a phoenix?

It seemed like everyone Robert Stark dragged me around the room to introduce me to that evening had a phoenix either on her wrist or hanging from her clutch. It was so bizarre!

I hadn't seen any gift bags being given out at the door. But maybe I'd just missed them. Maybe Christopher was completely wrong, and Project Phoenix was some kind of charity and all the Stark shareholders were donors.

It seemed kind of rude to ask, especially when they were being so gracious to me, taking so much time to ask how I was and saying how nice it was to meet me, and all of that. My mom had always told me to be kind to the elderly. I couldn't exactly run away, even though I really wanted to. I was dying to ask Gabriel what he was thinking, bringing Nikki here.

Was she going to cause a scene? Confront Robert Stark about what he'd done to her? Didn't she know he'd just have his security staff drag her out? No one would believe her, anyway.

Finally, Robert Stark seemed to be satisfied that I'd met enough of his shareholders, and he said, glancing at his platinum watch, "Well, I'm sure you'll be needing to leave for the studio to get ready for tonight's show."

He wasn't kidding. I saw that the hands of his watch said it was close to eight thirty.

"I do have to go," I said. "It was really nice meeting your friends."

"Shareholders," he corrected me. "Never mix business with friendship, Nikki. That's something you never could keep straight, isn't it?"

I stared at him. Was he kidding me? Did he really think I was Nikki? I mean, the real Nikki? Did he really not remember?

"Uh," I said. "I'm not Nikki. You know that, right? You know I'm really Emerson Watts?"

You killed me, I wanted to add. *You killed me and put my brain in Nikki Howard's body because she was blackmailing you. The real Nikki's here in this room, you know. She can back this whole story up. Do you want me to get her?*

But my heart was thumping so hard just from the few words I'd said, waiting for some response from him, some acknowledgment. I couldn't get further than *You know I'm really Emerson Watts?* before Robert Stark lowered his sleeve over his watch, looked over my shoulder, and smiled broadly.

"Ah, Gabriel," he said. "So good to see you. Thank you for coming. Can't wait to see your performance tonight. Who is this lovely creature you've brought with you?"

I spun around slowly, hardly daring to believe any of this was happening. Robert Stark. Robert Stark, the man who had ruined my life, was actually about to speak to Nikki Howard — the *real* Nikki Howard, the one he'd tried to have murdered.

And he didn't even know it.

Nikki looked even more amazing up close than she had from across the room. It wasn't that she appeared so different than she had before. She did, obviously, because she'd gone from looking like a washed-out rag to a punk rock princess.

Her hair, now dyed almost jet-black, had been scrunched dry rather than flat-ironed, so the natural waves framed her heart-shaped face in a more flattering way.

And her makeup, rather than being a carbon copy of how she used to do it when she was in her old body, had been done for her new face, so that the tones played up her new eye color and emphasized the curve of her lips and cheeks.

It was more like she was carrying herself differently. She seemed . . . proud. And playful. And, yes . . . hot.

Suddenly, I could see why all those guys — even other girls' boyfriends — had gravitated to Nikki. It was totally obvious to me now that it had never just been about her looks. It was about something more. Something I knew I didn't have, because I had something else. Something that was essentially, irrevocably . . . Nikki.

"Why, hello," Nikki said, extending her hand toward Robert Stark. Not in a handshake. So that he could kiss it. "You can call me Diana Prince."

Diana Prince? *Diana Prince?* How did I know that name?

Oh, my God.

Diana Prince? That was Wonder Woman's alter ego.

Nikki Howard had named herself after Wonder Woman.

"So nice to meet you, Miss Prince," Robert Stark said. And he actually raised her fingers to his lips and kissed them. "Have we met somewhere before? You seem familiar."

"Oh," Nikki said, with a kittenish smile. "I think you would remember having met me."

"I certainly would," Robert Stark said, smiling back. "Well, Gabriel, like I said . . . good luck tonight. Miss Prince . . . Miss Howard . . . good evening to you both."

And he walked away, toward a set of his guests who were waiting for him by the ballroom doors.

It was only after he was out of earshot that I realized I'd been holding my breath the whole time, and released it.

"Oh, my God," I cried. "You guys. I nearly had a heart attack just then. Nikki — I mean, Diana. What are you *doing* here?"

"Oh," Nikki said, looking after Robert Stark, her purple-lined eyes narrowed. "I just wanted to see his face one last time. Before it's behind bars."

"I tried to keep her from coming," Gabriel said. It was only then that I realized how highly frustrated he looked. "But she insisted. Loudly. I think my eardrums are broken."

But now I was beginning to suspect his frustration had nothing to do with disliking Nikki. The opposite, in fact.

Nikki rolled her eyes dismissively in Gabriel's direction. Turning to me, she said, "Please tell me your friend with the leather jacket came up with something we can use to put that scumbag in jail. Other than our word that what happened is true."

"He has," I said. "Some kind of theory, anyway." I didn't want to tell her that Christopher's theory was totally insane, and that it revolved around . . . well, the two of us. "But he has no proof. . . ." I let my voice trail off as I stared toward the ballroom doors, having just noticed something.

"Or maybe he has," I added thoughtfully.

Nikki and Gabriel turned to look in the direction I was staring.

"Oh," Nikki said, still bored. "That's nothing. The old people are all leaving. They always do that. Because it's after eight. Way past their bedtime."

"It's not just the old people," I said. "It's only the old people I just met. The Stark shareholders. Where are they going? They aren't getting their coats."

I started walking swiftly toward the doors myself.

"Uh, Nikki," Gabriel said, conscious that, despite the mass exodus of the shareholders, the ballroom was still crowded with people who might think it strange if they overheard him calling me Em. "Where are you going?"

"I'll be right back," I said to him. I was jogging now. Which wasn't easy in heels.

But when I got to the hallway the shareholders had disappeared into, it was empty. Well, except for a staircase cordoned off by a velvet rope and manned by a Stark security guard.

"Excuse me," I said, going up to him. "Did you see Robert Stark go by here?"

"Yes, ma'am," he said. "He's upstairs."

"Oh, great," I said, finger combing some of my hair out of my eyes in a manner I hoped he'd find irresistibly fetching. "Can you let me up to see him for a minute? I'm Nikki Howard. I just have to tell him something about the show tonight. It'll only take a second."

"I know who you are, Miss Howard," the security guard said, with a polite smile. "Unfortunately, I can't let you up. Authorized personnel only."

As he said this, Mrs. Whatever Her Name Was, with the blue veins and the sparkles around the bottom of her skirt, came hurrying up.

"Oh, hello again," she said to me, with a vague smile.

"Hi," I said, smiling back.

Then, to the security guard, she said, "I'm so sorry I'm late. I had to go to the little girls' room."

She actually said that. The little girls' room.

Then she did something extraordinary. She held up her bracelet. The one with the phoenix — or what I thought was a phoenix, anyway — dangling down from it.

And the security guard said, "Of course, madam."

And he undid the velvet rope and let her up the stairs.

Now of course I was bursting with curiosity to get up those stairs and find out what was going on up there.

Because it seemed like, without a doubt, those bracelets or whatever they were had some kind of significance.

I turned around and, ignoring the guard who'd snubbed me, hurried back over to Gabriel and Nikki, who'd been waiting for me back at the doors to the ballroom.

"What was that all about?" Gabriel asked.

"There's something going on upstairs," I said. "We need to get up there."

"Em," Gabriel said, pulling out his cell phone. "We're needed onstage for the Stark Angel show, which is going on live in approximately . . . two hours."

"Where's Brandon?" I asked. I looked around the ballroom and finally saw him, slow dancing with someone who looked a lot like Rebecca. I was halfway across the room before I realized it *was* Rebecca.

When she lifted her head from his shoulder after I poked it, her shrug was eloquent.

"What can I say?" she asked. "I've still got it. He thinks I'm hot. And anyway, what do you care? You don't want him."

"I didn't say anything," I said. "I just need to borrow him for a minute."

"Well, make it snappy," Rebecca said. "And you better not be having second thoughts about his three hundred million. You let them slip through your fingers, missy. You can't blame me for scooping up your leftovers."

I knew she was referring to Brandon's money, which she'd always encouraged me to try to snatch up by getting myself engaged to him. I guess she figured if I wasn't going to go for it, she would.

"You're entirely welcome to him," I assured her. I'd take penniless supervillain Christopher, whom I wasn't even sure wanted me, over multimillionaire Brandon any day.

I only wished Christopher would realize it.

"Fine," Rebecca said. "Brandon, Nikki's here. She wants to ask you something."

Brandon looked scared. "Oh, no, not Nikki. She's a bitch." Then, when he saw me, he smiled. "Oh, *that* Nikki. Okay. Hi! Have you got your brawron?"

"Oh, for God's sake." I grabbed Brandon by the arm and steered him a few feet away from Rebecca so we couldn't be overheard. "Brandon, I need you to get me upstairs. Your dad's having some kind of meeting up there, and I want to see what it's about without him knowing I'm there. Is there some way I can get up there other than the main staircase? He's got a guard there, and the guard won't let me by."

"Sure," Brandon said. "Servants' staircase, in the back. This way."

He slipped an arm around my shoulders and led me from the ballroom and toward the French doors out to the back garden. I'm sure everyone who saw us must have thought we were leaving the party to go hook up. Even the people who were in the garden with the fountains and the architecturally sculpted bushes would have seen Brandon lead me from the ballroom, down the paved path, and up to a door the caterers were using to bring the food in and out . . . it led straight into the massive, industrial-size kitchen. Everyone in there working stared at us as we walked by the chilled trays of shrimp and tiny goat cheese– filled canapés in our evening wear.

"Hey," Brandon said, spying these. "I didn't see those." He plucked up a few and popped them into his mouth while I rolled my eyes.

Then Brandon opened a door and we were in a dingy hallway, with a narrow stairway that curved upward.

"See?" he said. "Servants' staircase. I used to spend hours playing in here when I was a kid. I pretended I was an orphan and some loving parents were going to come and adopt me and take me away from this terrible place. *Ha!*"

His bitter *ha!* echoed up and down the staircase.

"Thanks, Brandon," I said. "Would you let Gabriel and Nikki know I'll be back as soon as I can? And that if I'm not . . . they should call the police?"

"Sure," Brandon said affably. "That's Nikki back there, with the black hair?"

"Yeah," I said, not sure I wanted to hear what he had to say about that.

"She looks kinda hot now," Brandon said. "But you know who's really hot. Your agent. What's up with that?"

"Yeah," I said, *really* sure I didn't want to hear about that. "I don't know, Brandon. I have to go now."

"Okay," he said. "You'll let me know if you find out anything I can, you know, use to send old Robert to the big house. Because I really hate that guy."

"Consider it done," I assured him.

Then I started climbing the twisted staircase. . . .

I wasn't quite sure what I expected to find when I got to the top. Certainly not what I found.

Which was a maid in a black uniform and a white apron opening the door just as I was about to. She was so startled to see me, she nearly dropped the entire tray of empty champagne glasses she was holding.

"Oh, my goodness!" she cried. "Can I help you?"

I had no idea if she'd recognized me, let alone what I should do. I didn't want her to turn me in to the security guard.

But I wasn't sure that she didn't know I had no right to be on that floor.

"I — I think I made a wrong turn," I stammered. When all else fails, and you're a blond supermodel, acting like an airhead never fails to work wonders. People pretty much expect it of you, anyway, and invariably find it charming. It's stupid and sexist, but it works.

Even on other women, especially if they're older than you. It brings out their maternal instinct or something.

Well, it probably wouldn't work on my mother. But it works on almost everyone else.

"I — I was looking for — for the little girls' room," I stammered.

Thank you, Lady Whose Name I Forget.

"Oh," the maid said, with a laugh. "It's two more doors down, honey."

"Oh, sorry," I said, giggling. "I'm such a ditz. I was wondering where all these stairs were going. Thanks so much."

"You're so welcome," she said warmly.

It had worked. Thank you, God.

I slipped past her and out into the hallway. Unlike the scene downstairs, it was hushed and quiet. There was deeply piled carpeting on the floor — gray, of course — and stark seascapes hanging on the walls, each lit with its own individual painting light . . . the only lighting to see by. I waited until I couldn't hear the maid anymore on the stairs, then listened to hear if I could detect any other sounds.

And soon enough, I heard it: the drone of a human voice coming from a room a few doors down from where I stood. I padded toward it, my stilettos silent on the plush carpeting.

Pressing my ear to the thick door, I listened as closely as I could. It was a woman's voice. It sounded nice.

But I couldn't tell what she was saying. I could hear no other sounds.

What should I do? Open the door and go in? Who knew what lay on the other side? What if I walked into some kind of

Stark shareholder business meeting or something, and everyone turned and looked at me?

And Robert Stark — who had to be in there — had one of his security goons shoot me?

Or worse, drag me out in front of everyone? I'd be so embarrassed. Getting shot would be preferable. Then I'd just be dead, not mortified.

What if it wasn't just a business meeting, though? What if Project Phoenix was really what Christopher said it was . . . whatever that had been? I had a moral duty to go in there and find out. He was trusting me to find out. My whole relationship depended on it.

Turning that doorknob and seeing what was going on in there was what I'd gone to all this trouble for in the first place, right? I had to do it.

My heart was beating so hard in my chest. I was acting, I realized, like one of those heroines in Frida's books — the Too Stupid to Live kind. Going into that room would be a stupid thing to do. Any girl who'd do it was an idiot. If I was watching this unfold on a movie screen, I'd yell, "Go home!" at the TV.

"Excuse me?"

I jumped nearly a mile and whirled around, then relaxed a little as I saw that the maid with the tray was behind me. Only she'd restocked her tray with glasses that were now full to the brim with sparkling champagne.

"I just have to get by you," the maid said, sounding embarrassed.

"Oh, of course," I said, and then, like it was the most natural thing in the world, I opened the door for her, since she had her hands full.

And after she went in, I followed her.

NINETEEN

IT WAS DARK INSIDE THE ROOM.

That's because it was some kind of media room, like the one Brandon had at his beach house, for showing movies. There was a huge screen at one end of the room, where images were flashing. All the Stark shareholders — even in the dark, I recognized the ladies I'd met downstairs from the diamonds around their necks — were seated in wide, comfortable, red velvet-covered chairs in front of the screen. They were watching the images flashing on the screen with rapt attention.

I shouldn't have worried about anyone noticing me come in. No one cared. They were too busy watching the presentation.

I found an empty chair and sat down to watch the show. The maid, noticing this, offered me a glass of champagne, which I accepted with a smile, just to be gracious. There was a little table next to my high-backed theater chair on which I could set the glass, so I did, knocking something over in the dark. This was embarrassing. Also dangerous. I didn't want to draw attention to myself, even though I was in the back, and there were only a few other people seated in my row.

I scrambled around on the carpeted floor for whatever I'd knocked over. I found it almost at once. It was some kind of gaming joystick, I realized as soon as my fingers closed over it. It had a cord attached to it that disappeared into the floor, but only a single button on the joystick. I was careful not to press the button, but I kept the joystick in my lap, since I noticed everyone else in my row was doing the same thing.

After that, I turned my attention to the presentation that was going on. The nice female voice I'd heard out in the hallway was much louder now. It belonged to an immaculately dressed, very beautiful Frenchwoman who was standing to one side of the screen. She was in charge of the presentation, I saw. She was holding a joystick, too, but it was more of a clicker, like the kind you use during a PowerPoint presentation. In fact, that's what the presentation we were seeing was. PowerPoint.

I had to stifle an automatic yawn. Seriously? PowerPoint? I almost wished someone *would* shoot me.

Then I saw what the PowerPoint was about and sat up a little straighter in my seat.

The slide the stunningly beautiful Frenchwoman was showing us was a photo of a muscular, slim-hipped young man who wore cargo pants and no shirt, grinning into the camera with his arms around a collie. The collie had a bandanna around its neck.

"This is Matthew," the Frenchwoman said in her cool, emotionless voice. "Matthew is a twenty-year-old college student studying philosophy and is on his dormitory's Frisbee team. Matthew is six foot two and one hundred and seventy pounds and has a small tattoo of a fish on his left ankle. Matthew is a vegetarian and believes in abstaining from drugs and alcohol to keep his mind and body pure."

With fingers that felt numb, I opened my purse and took out my cell phone. It wasn't easy to do without drawing attention to myself.

But I found the film application. And I pressed record.

I wasn't sure what was happening. But based on what Christopher had said on the phone, I was beginning to have a very creepy feeling.

And I just wanted to be on the safe side.

"Matthew has no history of heart disease or cancer in his family," the Frenchwoman went on. "And will become available when he leaves for a trip to Honduras to volunteer for Habitat for Humanity over spring break this April. Matthew's starting bid is at five hundred thousand dollars. Please begin your bidding now."

Around me, I heard the sound of clicking joysticks. I looked up from my cell phone, wondering if what I thought was happening could really be happening.

Because it just didn't seem possible to me that Christopher could have been right.

"Five hundred fifty," the Frenchwoman said tonelessly. She was staring at a little computer monitor on her desk. "Six hundred. Six fifty. Do I have seven hundred? Seven fifty. Eight hundred. Eight fifty. Matthew has a naturally fast metabolism and grew up in an area with fluoridated water, so no cavities or dental issues at all. He really is a prime specimen. You could not ask for a healthier young man. Nine hundred thousand. One million. I have a bid for one million dollars. Matthew, going once. Going twice. The bidding for Matthew is now closed at one million dollars. Thank you."

The image of Matthew vanished from the screen, and the clicking of the joysticks around me stopped. Almost immediately — way before I'd even had time to process what I'd just witnessed — a new image appeared on the screen. It was of a young woman with long, straight black hair. She was lying on a bed, laughing up at the camera, holding a gray-and-black tiger-striped cat. She was wearing a pair of cute shorts and a tank top. On her wall was a poster that said *Save Tibet.*

"This is Kim Su," the Frenchwoman said, in the same slightly bored but completely businesslike voice. "She is nineteen years old and is five foot two and weighs one hundred pounds. She has no tattoos and is a lifelong vegetarian. She has no health problems, including no history of dental issues. She's a freshman at a prestigious university and works out regularly. Her family is extremely long-lived, including one set of great-grandparents who are still living and are now in their hundreds. Having yourself transplanted into Kim Su would make an outstanding investment, as she has not only incredible beauty but longevity on her side. Because Kim Su is such an amazing find, the starting bid for her is eight hundred thousand. Kim Su will become available this summer when she leaves to be an au pair in the Hamptons."

The clicking was even more enthusiastic for Kim Su than it had been for Matthew. Bidding immediately went into the millions. I wasn't that surprised when the lady with the sparkles on the bottom of her dress got her for a cool three point five.

"Yes!" she cried, almost jumping out of her seat.

Several of the other ladies leaned over to congratulate her on her excellent buy.

I just sat there, feeling kind of sick. I think maybe I was in shock. I couldn't believe it was true. It was all true, everything Christopher had said on the phone. Project Phoenix was exactly that: people buying more attractive people's bodies to have their brains put into them.

Those kids we'd seen online — well, most of them had been kids. Teenagers, really — all the ones who'd bought Stark Quarks. The reason Stark had saved their information . . . the reason they'd combed through it so carefully, saving some and not others? It was because Stark considered them donors.

Like me.

I was Project Phoenix. The prototype.

Of course. The doctors at the Stark Institute for Neurology and Neurosurgery had said there was a waiting list of wealthy candidates wanting the surgery — candidates with perfectly healthy brain function but whose bodies maybe weren't all that they used to be — a little flab here, a little wrinkle there. Maybe some male pattern baldness. And that the only thing stopping the institute from doing more surgeries was a shortage of donor bodies. And that the donor bodies they had weren't always the most desirable . . . the body Nikki got was of a drunk driver killed in a DUI.

And Nikki nearly died during her surgery because the body she got was so unhealthy. So why wouldn't Stark do this? What was stopping them?

Nothing. Nothing at all.

I felt cold all over. And it wasn't because of my way-too-short dress.

I don't know how long I sat there, watching image after image flicker across the screen and get bid on, before my view was obscured by a large male figure.

Not one of the males on the screen that I'd just seen sold off, either.

This was a male dressed in Stark security garb.

"Miss Howard?" he said softly. "Will you come with me, please?"

I was busted. I shouldn't have sat there so long.

But how could I move? What Robert Stark was doing . . .

. . . it was the most disgusting thing I'd ever seen in my life.

All the Stark shareholders turned to look as I was escorted from the room, even though the Frenchwoman said in her calm voice, "Please pay no attention to the slight disturbance in the back. It is only a minor interruption. Shall we turn to the next candidate?"

I heard the murmurs and whispers. And then I heard Robert Stark himself assure his shareholders, in his booming voice, "Don't worry, everyone. It's only Nikki Howard. You've all met her! She's one of you . . . or what all of you will be shortly. She just wanted to stop by to make sure you're choosing wisely!"

This caused a ripple of laughter through the room.

I didn't hear any more. That's because by then the guard had pulled me out. I stood there in the hallway, staring at the floor, not really caring what was going to happen to me next. So what if Robert Stark had me killed, like he'd tried to do to Nikki?

I wasn't sure I wanted to live in a world where people did this kind of thing, anyway.

"Well, that wasn't smart, now, was it?"

I glanced up from my feet to see Robert Stark himself standing in front of me, adjusting his tuxedo's bow tie, looking like a cat someone had stroked the wrong way.

"What did you hope to accomplish in there, anyway?" he asked. He leaned over and snatched my purse away. Then he opened it and dumped the contents on the floor. My iPhone fell out with everything else. He leaned down and picked it up.

"I suppose you were recording all that," he said. "And thought you'd be slick and send it to someone. CNN? Well, nothing's going to come of that."

With surprising force, he turned and hurled the phone as hard as he could toward the far end of the hallway. It smashed into a thousand pieces when it hit the wall.

I flinched. The phone exploding reminded me of the way my body must have looked to Christopher, exploding under the weight of that plasma TV.

No wonder he was so messed up now.

Except . . .

Except that everything he'd been insisting was true about Stark Enterprises?

It had actually been true all along. *He* wasn't the crazy one.

The rest of us were, for not believing him.

"And not just because you don't have the recording anymore," Robert Stark said, turning back to me. He was speaking absolutely without rancor. That was the scary part. He wasn't even mad at me. He didn't care. He was completely cool and collected.

Except for the part about destroying my phone.

"Those kids you saw in there?" he went on. "The ones my friends just purchased? They're going to meet with accidents during their travels soon. The same kind of accident your sister is going to have this evening on her way back from her trip to cheerleading camp if a word about any of this gets out. Do you understand? Because believe it or not, I have people who would happily bid on her, as well."

I stared at him, my heart suddenly feeling frozen. How had he known about Frida and her cheerleading camp?

But of course.

Frida had a Stark Quark. Robert Stark himself had given her one.

I nodded slowly. I understood. I understood perfectly well.

"One word," he said. "One word tonight when the Stark

Angel show goes live — even though you might want to get cute and try something? — and your sister never makes it back tonight to that little apartment she and your parents share down at NYU. Understand?"

"I understand," I unglued my tongue from the roof of my mouth to say. "You don't want me to tell anyone that Robert Stark is providing his shareholders with healthy donor bodies so that they can have their brains transplanted into them and be young again. If I do that, my sister dies."

Robert Stark just looked down at me. His expression wasn't as cool and collected as it had been before. Now one of his dark, slightly graying eyebrows was raised a little.

"You just don't get it, do you?" he asked. "We gave you an incredible gift — the gift of beauty — something most women would kill for. Do you know how many women would die to be in your shoes right now? You have the world on a string. And all you can seem to think about is bringing me down."

"What about Matthew?" I asked him. "And Kim Su? Do you think they're going to appreciate your *killing* them so that those rich old folks in there can live their lives for them?"

"Oh, they're not going to be living their lives for them," Robert Stark assured me. "They'll be living their own lives, just with new bodies. Sure, they're going to have to explain to their friends about how they had more than a 'little work done.' But that will only bring more clients in to me. And it will be worth it, not to have to wake up every morning with creaking joints, to have to take nine different kinds of heart medications — believe me, it will be worth every penny to them."

"But what about Matthew's family?" I asked. "What if they see him one day, walking around with some other guy's brain in his head, and he doesn't recognize them?"

"These people live in far different social strata," Robert Stark said with a sneer, "than the donors' families. They'll never see one another. You can be quite sure of that."

I shook my head at his snobbery.

"You're going to get caught," I said. "It's murder. You can't keep it a secret forever."

"Why not?" he asked. And now both eyebrows were lifted. "I've managed to so far. How long do you think we've been doing this, anyway?" That's when he laughed. "Nikki — and to me, darlin', you'll always be Nikki — we've been doing this for years. *Years*. With this latest technology, we've been able to offer our clients a more diversified and unique selection of products over a broader range, while still increasing our profit margin."

Then he looked at the security officer and said, "Clean that up" — he meant the mess emptying my bag had made on the carpet — "and escort her back downstairs and to the car that's waiting to take her and her friends to the studio. She's late enough for the Stark Angels show as it is."

To me, he said, "The least you could do is say thank you, you know."

Now it was my turn to raise my eyebrows. "For *what?*"

"I've given you the greatest gift anyone could ever give another human being," he said. "A second chance at life. Only this time," he added, "you get to do it beautiful."

I just stared at him. Honestly, what could you even say to that?

I thought about spitting in his face.

But it didn't seem like the right thing to do.

Especially since he'd just said he knew my little sister's travel plans.

Did I really want to see Frida up there on that screen, being bid on like some kind of Ming vase at Sotheby's . . .

. . . only to have her skull sawed open and her brain lifted out to have it replaced by that blue-veined lady's?

I took back the purse that the security guard handed to me — minus my iPhone. Meanwhile, Robert Stark was already walking away, back into his macabre auction room. He never once looked over his shoulder at me.

Not that I'd expected him to, I guess.

It was just as well that he didn't. He'd have seen the murderous look in my eye.

And he wouldn't have liked it. He wouldn't have liked it one bit.

The security guard took me by the arm and began guiding me down the stairs. Not the back stairs Brandon had shown me, but the wide main staircase I hadn't been able to get up before, because I'd lacked a phoenix bracelet.

The other security guard was still standing at the bottom of it. He looked confused to see me being escorted down by one of his colleagues, but lifted the velvet rope and let me pass.

"Here you go," the security guard who had my arm said, when we reached the coat check, where Gabriel and Nikki were standing waiting for me, with Lulu, who had my coat. They were all three flanked by other security guards.

"Oh, my God," Lulu whispered, holding my faux fur coat out for me. "Are you all right? You look pale as a ghost. Are you going to throw up?"

"Let's just get out of here," I whispered back. "Where's Brandon?"

"I don't know," Lulu said. "He disappeared a while ago with your agent."

"Great," I said sarcastically. The security guards were hustling us down the red-carpeted steps and out to the limo that was idling outside. Paparazzi snapped dozens of photos as we ducked inside the car, all calling out, "Nikki! Where's your boyfriend?" and "Nikki! Did you have a nice time at the party?"

Once we were inside the car and the doors had been closed, Nikki said, "It's so weird how they do that."

"Do what?" Gabriel asked.

"Yell *my* name. But they're talking to *her*." She pointed at me.

"It must be weird," Gabriel said, but his voice was softer than when he'd ever spoken to Nikki before, as if he were sympathizing with her for once. "You must miss it."

"That?" Nikki's eyes widened. "Being screamed at by the paps? *You* probably like it. But I'm sort of starting to appreciate this anonymity thing for a change." She looked over at me and demanded, "So? Did you find out anything?"

"Oh," I said, leaning back against the leather seat and taking a long, cleansing breath. "I learned a lot."

"Oh?" Gabriel asked. "Care to enlighten us?"

I reached into my bra and pulled out my Stark brand cell phone. "You have no idea," I said. "Can I borrow your phone? This one is bugged. I need to call Christopher."

Gabriel fumbled around in his pockets, while Nikki just rolled her eyes.

"No one will let me have a phone," she said. "I'm not to be trusted, evidently."

"Oh, for Pete's sake," Lulu said, opening her gold Prada clutch and tossing me her phone. "But you better tell us what you heard up there. . . . "

I was already dialing.

"Oh," I said. "You're going to find out, all right. Hello, Christopher?" He'd picked up on the first ring.

"Em?" he said, confused, because his caller ID had said Lulu's name.

"Yeah," I said. "It's me. Listen, you were right. About all of it. Project Phoenix is exactly what you said it was. And I've got proof. On film. The problem is, I got caught. By Robert Stark himself."

"Jesus Christ, Em." Christopher sounded like someone had punched him in the stomach. "Are you all right?"

"I'm fine," I said. "So far. They think they destroyed the only proof. That's why I can't e-mail it to you or anything . . . because if I do, it will totally send up a red flag. Because it's on a Stark brand phone they've got bugged, so that means it's also on their mainframe, I'm pretty sure. Which means Felix could probably pull it up . . . but then they might notice. So just in case, I'm going to hand deliver it to him right now with Lulu and Nikki." I looked at the two of them questioningly. They both glanced at each other, then nodded eagerly. "So can you be there in, like, twenty minutes, Christopher, and be ready for it?"

"I'm already at Felix's," Christopher said. "He's ready for whatever you've got. What are you going to be doing in the meantime?"

"The Stark Angel lingerie show," I said, unable to keep the sarcasm from my voice. "Live."

"We're already tuned in to Channel Seven," I heard Felix yell in the background. "All ten monitors! High def!"

I heard a crunching sound, then a cry of pain. I assumed Christopher had hit his cousin.

"Never mind him," Christopher said. "If you don't want us to be watching, Em, we won't watch. Besides, it sounds like we're going to be pretty busy."

"No," I said. I had to be mature about this, I realized. It was just a body. My body.

And with any luck, Christopher was going to be seeing it naked someday, anyway.

"You can watch if you want. Just do this other thing first. Only . . . whatever you're going to do with it," I said, trying to control the shaking in my voice, "can you wait until Frida's plane lands, and she gets home safe? Because Robert Stark said —" Suddenly, I was holding back a sob.

"What, Em?" Christopher asked. He sounded as worried as I felt. "What did Robert Stark say?"

The tender concern in his voice only made it harder to speak. I couldn't believe this was the same Christopher with whom only an hour or so ago I'd been arguing.

"He said if anything about Project Phoenix gets out," I answered, trying to keep from crying, "he'll . . . he'll . . . "

"Don't say another word," Christopher said. "I know what to do."

"But." How could he know? I hadn't told him what Robert Stark had said he'd do. Something so awful, I couldn't even think about it.

"Em," Christopher said. His voice was warm. Warm with love for me. For *me*. "I know. Don't worry. Consider it done. Frida will be fine. We've got it handled here, okay? We're professionals."

"But," I said again. Now I couldn't help smiling a little. The idea of Christopher and his cousin as professionals was ludicrous. "One of you is wearing an ankle bracelet."

And one of you is an archvillain, with fingerless gloves and a dark streak a mile wide.

"She's going to be all right," Christopher reassured me. "You did your part. Tell Nikki and Lulu to get here with that cell phone. And I'll do what I have to do. And, Em?"

"Yes?" I asked in a shaking voice.

"I'm really proud of you," he said. "Mad as hell at you for putting yourself in danger. But really, really proud."

"Yeah," I said. Now the tears were coming.

But they were tears of happiness.

"Me, too," I said.

TWENTY

IT WAS CHAOS AT THE STARK ANGEL
lingerie show. For one thing, Ryan Seacrest was there to emcee
it. He hadn't been there for the two dress rehearsals earlier in
the month because . . . well, he was Ryan Seacrest. He was a
busy man.

For another thing, Gabriel and I were more than two hours
late for our call time. That hadn't caused too much anxiety on
the part of Alessandro, the stage director. He basically wanted
to kill us.

"Dressing rooms for makeup and costumes," he yelled
when he saw me and Gabriel slinking in through the stage
door. "Now."

I figured if Alessandro had his way, we'd never be asked to participate in another Stark production ever again.

Then again, after tonight, if things went the way I hoped they would, there wouldn't be any more Stark productions. Not ever again.

Jerri, the makeup artist, came darting in as I was wiggling out of my party dress, and the costume ladies were fretting about what to do about the indentations the seams of my panty hose had left on my belly. Seriously. These are the things we under-wear models have to worry about.

"No worries," Jerri said. "I'll airbrush it. No one will see a thing."

Jerri had a little machine that sprayed out liquid foundation the way self-tanning machines airbrushed bronzer on people. It was basically the same principle, only Jerri planned on spraying the foundation over my entire body instead of just my face . . .

. . . which was what she did for most of her clients, a lot of whom were male sportscasters.

"They have to look good, too," she explained. "Now that everyone has high-def TVs. You can't have any blemishes, or anything. I do their hands, too, for when they're holding the microphones, interviewing people. If you don't spray, you don't play."

It was amazing. Here I'd been thinking Jessica Biel and all

those movie stars had perfect bodies, when it wasn't true. *Everything* on TV was fake.

Make that everything on TV, in magazines, and in the movies, too. No wonder those Stark shareholders felt like they needed to murder young people and steal their bodies.

"Oh, sure," Jerri said as I stood there in my bra and panties, feeling the cold spray go all over my body. "All the actresses do it, for their nude scenes? They're all sprayed. It covers your cellulite, too. Not that you have cellulite. Oh, wait. Yes, sorry. Even Nikki Howard! Ha, wait till I tell my sister. She thinks you're perfect. Not that you aren't —" Jerri popped her head around to look up at me. "You know, you almost are."

I smiled down at her queasily. "It's okay. Can I borrow your cell phone?" I asked. "I need to make a call. It's local."

"Oh, go ahead, darling," Jerri said. "Make as many as you want. I'm getting holiday pay for this, it being New Year's Eve and all."

She gave me her phone, and I quickly dialed my parents' number. My mom picked up after the second ring.

"Hello?" she asked curiously, not recognizing the number on the caller ID.

"Hi, Mom," I said. "It's me." I didn't say it's me, Em, because Jerri was there. "I was wondering . . . do you know if Frida made it to her plane all right?"

"Well, of course she did," Mom said. "She called me from the runway three hours ago. She should be landing at LaGuardia any minute. The girls are all sharing cabs back into the city. Why do you ask?"

"I just haven't heard from her in a while," I said, trying to sound casual. "That's all. Do you think you could have her call me the minute she walks in the door?"

"Of course," Mom said. "But aren't you a bit busy? I thought you were doing that, er, lingerie show tonight, on Channel Seven."

Damn. I was kind of hoping that Mom had forgotten about that.

"I am," I said stiffly. "But that doesn't mean I don't worry about my little sister."

"Well," Mom said, "I'll be sure to have her call you."

Belatedly, I remembered I didn't have a cell phone. One was smashed to bits on the carpet in Robert Stark's upstairs hallway. And the other was on its way to Felix's basement in a cab with Lulu and Nikki. Hopefully it was there by now.

"Actually," I said, thinking fast, "could you have her call Lulu? My cell is messed up." I gave her the number. "It'll be better, anyway, in case I'm onstage."

"All right," Mom said. In typical Mom style, however, she didn't sound like she thought it was all right. "Listen, honey, while I have you on the phone . . . about yesterday."

"Yeah," I said. I was conscious that Jerri was working her way up toward my head with the spray gun. "I'm really sorry —"

"No," Mom said. "*I'm* sorry. I realize now that when you asked me if you were pretty — well, that's such a loaded question, honey. I mean, for me. I don't want you girls to judge one another by your looks —"

"Mom," I said. I couldn't believe we were even having this conversation. My boss had just threatened to kill my little sister if I exposed the fact that he was basically a murdering sociopath.

And if things went the way I hoped they would, I was just about to do exactly that.

And my mom wanted to have bonding time over the phone.

"I really don't have time for this. I just wanted to check on Frida."

"But this is important," Mom went on. "I realize that maybe, at your school, that's what all girls do. Judge one another by their looks."

"Not just at school, Mom," I said. "Try all of contemporary Western society."

Hello, Mom? This is America. Welcome. This is called a McDonald's. Can you say that word? Mc-Don-ald's. They serve cheeseburgers here. And fries. Can you say the word *fries?*

"I know," Mom went on. She sounded like she was practically crying. "And it's just so wrong. I don't *want* you girls to judge

269

yourselves that way. There's so much more to you than that. You're both just so amazing, you and Frida, so smart and strong and creative. I wanted to emphasize *that* part of you. But every time you turn on the television, what do you see? Well, skinny girls with big boobs, in tight pants with shirts cut down to their belly buttons. And every time I'd take the two of you to the store, you'd both want exactly what those girls — Nikki Howard — was wearing. You eventually grew out of it, but Frida — it's like a mother can't win. And my mother said I was exactly the same way, and that's why she stopped telling me I was pretty — that I let it go straight to my head when I was growing up. . . . "

This was news to me. Grandma? Grandma always told Frida and me that we were pretty. So much so that it really didn't mean anything. Of course we were pretty. We were her granddaughters. It doesn't mean anything when your grandmother tells you that you're pretty.

But Mom? Mom never said we were pretty, or looked good. It was always, "Your mind is all that matters!"

And of course that's true.

But it would have been nice to have heard our hair looked good, once in a while.

And now that I knew Mom had liked girlie clothes? Mom, who always dressed so sensibly in gray suits and low-heeled shoes? Grandma had had to stop telling Mom she was pretty because she got so conceited about it?

This was fantastic stuff. I couldn't wait to tell Frida.

If I ever saw her again.

"And I guess," Mom went on — she was practically babbling — "I just thought if I followed her lead, you two would turn out like me . . . more interested in things academic than . . . well . . ."

What? What had Mom been like as a girl? I was dying to find out.

But by then Jerri had gotten to my head with the spray blower.

"Look, Mom," I said. "I have to go get ready for the show. I understand everything you're saying. I know it's all fake. No one knows that more than me. But it's still nice to hear your mom say you're pretty once in a while, you know? But don't worry about me, okay? Everything's going to be fine." This was a bold-faced lie. I had absolutely no way of knowing this. But what else was I going to say? Look, Mom, because of my jackassery, my boss may be about to kill your youngest daughter? "Just call Lulu as soon as you hear from Frida."

"I will," Mom said. She hesitated, then said, "I love you, Em. In case that wasn't clear. No matter what you look like. Or what you wear."

This brought tears to my eyes. Because I so didn't deserve it.

"Thanks, Mom," I said. "Me, too."

I hung up and handed the phone back to Jerri.

"Moms," I said to her, rolling my eyes in an effort not to burst into tears.

"Tell me about it," Jerri said, tucking her phone back into her pocket. "Mine smokes a pack of Camel Lights a day. Can I get her to stop? No way. Close your eyes now, hon, I'm gonna do your face."

Forty-five minutes later — which Jerri claimed was a speed record for her — I was out of hair and makeup and tucked into the diamond bra and panties, my wings attached and floating behind me. I looked, when I saw myself in the mirror, like a cross between an angel and . . . well, a girl wearing a diamond bikini.

Oh, well. Hopefully, Mom wouldn't be watching.

I strode in my platform heels toward the soundstage as Jerri trotted alongside me, blotting on the last dab of lip gloss.

"There you are." Rebecca appeared as if from nowhere, still in her black evening gown with the slit up to here. "I heard you were late. What did I warn you about? Did I tell you not to be late? Did you eat anything? I can see your hip bones. I know you didn't eat anything. If you faint on me, Nikki, I swear to God . . ."

"I'm not going to faint," I assured her. "Is Brandon here with you? Because I really need to talk to him."

"As a matter of fact, he is," Rebecca said, looking demure. Or as demure as it was possible for Rebecca to look, which wasn't very. "You might as well know, we're an item now. And I know there's a bit of an age difference, but honestly, I think he could use a mature woman in his life. No offense, Nikki, but you haven't exactly been the most steadying influence on him. And he needs stability."

"I really don't care about that," I said. "You can have him. That isn't what I want to talk to him about. It's about his dad, actually."

"His dad?" Rebecca shrugged. "Not exactly his favorite topic. But it's your funeral." She pulled her BlackBerry from her Chanel bag and began banging on the keyboard. "You sure you want to get into this now, right before the show? Can't it wait? You're onstage in five. And don't talk to Ryan, all right, darling? All the girls are talking to Ryan, and it's getting on his nerves."

I looked up and down the hall. There were models in Stark brand underwear and wings everywhere. I saw Kelley, my friend from the dress rehearsal, wave her cell phone at me and set off her ringtone. It played the *Journeyquest* Dragon Battle Cry. Kelley laughed and pointed at me, then gave me the thumbs-up. I smiled at her like *Ha! That's funny.*

But mainly I was thinking how much I wanted to throw up.

"I won't," I said.

Rebecca shrugged and kept banging on the keyboard.

What was Robert Stark doing right now? I wondered. Was he trying to kill my sister?

And what about Christopher? Had Lulu and Nikki gotten him my cell phone? I felt so vulnerable not knowing what was going on.

I wasn't the only one. Gabriel stepped out of his dressing room in full makeup and his tux. He was with his band — all of whom were good-looking enough to cause a ripple of excitement to pass through the other models, Ryan Seacrest suddenly forgotten.

But Gabriel ignored it. When he saw me, in fact, he said to the rest of his guys, "Hey. I'll be right there," and fell back to whisper to me, "So? Have you heard anything?"

I shook my head. "Nothing. You?"

He shook his head. "I'm sure it will be fine."

"Or," I said, "we'll walk out onto the stage and a boom will fall on us, killing us both instantly, courtesy of Robert Stark."

"It's always good," Gabriel said, tugging on his lapels, "to think positive."

"Brandon will meet you after the show," Rebecca announced, reading from the screen of her BlackBerry.

"But I really need to talk to him now," I said, unable to keep the dismay from my voice.

"Well." Rebecca shrugged. "What do you want me to do? The man says he's busy. He'll meet you upstairs in the Stark Sky Bar, he says. There'll be champagne for all of us to toast in the New Year. It's where we're all going to watch the Times Square ball drop. There's a perfect view from there —"

"Places!" Alessandro came scurrying down the hallway, clapping his hands. "All of you. Backstage, now! What are you dillydallying for? Are you trying to give me a heart attack? The show's started! We're live! No more talking once you get through the soundproof door. Go! GO!"

I reached instinctively for Gabriel's hand. My own was ice-cold. But his felt warm . . . just like his gaze when it met mine.

"It's going to be all right," he assured me, with a smile. "You did the right thing."

"Did I?" I asked. I wished I could believe him. In theory, I did.

But Frida! My own sister! How could I have been so stupid?

"Oh, God," Rebecca said, noticing our clenched hands. "What is going on here? Are you two an item? This is perfect. Can I announce it to the press? Do you have any idea what this is going to do for your sales numbers, Gabriel? You're already in the stratosphere, but this, honey, we're talking Mars —"

275

By this time, I was going through the studio doors, and all the cameramen and sound engineers were shushing Rebecca to be quiet.

Still, she stood behind the doors, even as they were closing, whisper-yelling, "You can't hide things from me, Nikki! You can't run away! I know all your secrets!"

If only she knew.

Inside the backstage space of the studio, where we were all gathered to wait our turn onstage, it was so quiet, I could almost hear my own heartbeat. It was the front of the studio, where the stage was, where it was another matter entirely. There, it was thunderously loud. The live audience was screaming with appreciation for Ryan and the models who were already strutting out onto the stage, doing their catwalk up and down the runway, showing off their different bra and panty sets.

Gabriel and his band had ducked back behind the revolving set, to reappear on stage right as soon as it was their cue to begin playing Gabriel's number one hit song, "Nikki."

This wasn't going to happen until the second-to-last commercial break. As I stood there waiting for my musical cue, I noticed Veronica, the model who'd hated me so much — because she thought I'd been e-mailing her boyfriend, Justin, when actually, that had been the real Nikki — standing in front of me. She was pointedly ignoring me.

Because I needed something to take my mind off the fact that my sister, at that very moment, might be dying, I tapped her on the shoulder.

"Hi," I said. "I was just wondering. Did the e-mails stop?"

Veronica looked around. Her eyes grew huge when she saw me.

"We — we're not supposed to be talking," she stammered.

"I know," I said. "But did they?"

"Yes," she said, and turned back toward the show, nibbling on a press-on nail.

Ha. Because Nikki had better things to do these days.

Like torture Gabriel Luna.

A few minutes later, Veronica got her cue to walk — and she sashayed out onto the stage. And then I heard it.

"Nikki, oh, Nikki . . . The thing of it is, girl . . . in spite of it all . . . I really do think . . . I love you."

My cue.

For a second, my heart hammering, I hesitated. I thought I was going to throw up. What was I doing? Who *was* I? Was I, Em Watts, the girl who wouldn't even shower in front of other girls during PE, really going to walk out onto that runway, in front of millions — maybe even a billion — of television viewers, not to mention however many people were in the live audience, wearing nothing but a pair of panties, a bra, a set of wings, and a lot of body spray?

"It's not the way that you walk, girl . . . the way that you smile or the way that you look . . ."

On the other hand . . .

. . . if things went the way they were supposed to, and Christopher did what he said he was going to, because of me, Robert Stark, the fourth-richest man in the world, was going down tonight. What had happened to me was never going to happen to another person again.

And there might never even be another Stark Angels lingerie show ever again.

That would certainly make my mom happy.

"It's just the way you move me . . . the way that you move me . . . that makes me say, Nikki, oh, Nikki . . . The thing of it is, girl . . . in spite of it all . . . I really do think . . . I love you."

"Nikki," Alessandro whispered from somewhere in the darkness behind me. "GO!"

I walked out into the blinding lights of the stage, moving my hips in time to the music, trying to follow the markings on the runway and step exactly where they'd told me to step and not run into Ryan Seacrest.

The reflections from the diamonds on my bra were making me crazy. I could hardly see where I was going. If something were to come loose from the ceiling overhead and tumble down, smacking me in the head, I would never know it. I was completely blind.

Who would wear one of these stupid things in real life? And *why?*

"Nikki, oh, Nikki . . . The thing of it is, girl . . . in spite of it all . . . I really do think . . . I love you."

At least I had Gabriel's voice to guide me. The weird thing was, he actually sounded sincere.

But isn't that what musicians do? Like models and actresses, they make you believe what they're telling you.

Unless . . . he really did love Nikki. Not me. But the real Nikki.

Wouldn't that be funny? That as much as the two of them fought, they actually loved each other? They certainly seemed to be at each other's throats enough.

But wasn't that true of me and Christopher? We were always fighting. Always!

But then, when it came down to it, we really loved each other. At least, I really loved Christopher.

I hoped he really loved me. I thought I'd heard his love for me on the phone when we'd spoken just now. I'd know for sure the next time I saw him . . . whether or not he really loved me. I'd be able to see it in his eyes. I was sure of it. We may not have had the easiest of romances, but it was one, I felt sure, that was going to last forever.

If Nikki and Gabriel fell in love, it would kill my sister, Frida.

Oh, God. *Frida. Why did I have to think about Frida?*

"It's not the way that you walk, girl . . . the way that you smile or the way that you look . . ."

"Ah, look at her, ladies and gentlemen," Ryan Seacrest was saying. "The number one supermodel in the world, Stark's own Nikki Howard. She's wearing over a million dollars' worth of diamonds, ladies and gentlemen. I don't know when I've ever seen anything quite so beautiful. Except possibly for the low, low interest I'm receiving on my Stark credit card. Apply now for exclusive cardmember-only sales and special financing offers throughout the year. . . ."

Getting to the end of the runway, I looked out into the screaming, cheering audience and saw him. Robert Stark. Just sitting there, looking up at me.

Grinning. Grinning the way only someone who knows he's won can smile.

Why was he grinning like that? What had he done?

Gotten away with murder, that's what.

Except he hadn't.

Not yet. Not if I could help it.

Frida, my heart was crying the entire time I was out there. *Please let Frida be okay.*

I made it off the runway without tripping or anything falling down onto my head. Only my heart hammering in my throat.

And no one, I was certain, had even been able to tell that much.

Because I was a professional now.

I was Nikki Howard.

It wasn't until I got to the Stark Sky Bar a half hour later — the diamond bra and panties handed back over to the security guards who'd been assigned to guard them, the angel wings put away, and my street clothes put back on — that all hell broke loose.

TWENTY-ONE

THE SKY BAR, WHICH WAS A HUGE, CIR-cular restaurant at the top of the Stark Building, the walls made of floor-to-ceiling windows all the way around, so you had an unimpeded view of the sparkling lights — or, in this case, the crowds at Times Square, and the New Year's ball drop — was crowded. Ryan Seacrest was there, along with his agent and his manager, enjoying some Dom Perignon. I spied Rebecca there as well, hanging on to Brandon like they were attached at the hip — gross — and Gabriel and his band.

Everywhere else I looked were celebrities from the party at Robert Stark's house, as well as the shareholders I'd met.

The same ones who'd been bidding on "donors" for their brain transplants. Of course they didn't know that I'd filmed their little auction and smuggled that film out and that two computer geniuses were (hopefully) at this very moment doing whatever it is those kind of people do with that kind of thing.

What *were* they going to do with it? I wondered.

"Hey," Gabriel said, coming up to me with a glass of sparkling water a few minutes after I'd walked in. He was a welcome sight. I'd been surrounded by Stark shareholders wanting to chat with me some more.

I knew what they really wanted, of course. To talk to the Project Phoenix prototype, a living, breathing, actual brain transplant recipient. They didn't say as much, but it was totally obvious. They were dying to know what it was like to die . . . and then be resurrected as someone totally hot.

If they'd come right out and just asked, I could have told them: It was hell. And heaven. At the same time.

Would I do it again?

Not a chance.

"Glad we're not down there," Gabriel said, indicating one of the many flat-screen TVs that hung from the ceiling, showing close-ups of Anderson Cooper reporting live on the impending ball drop from Times Square. It was so cold, you could see Anderson's breath.

"Me, too," I said.

"Have you heard anything?" Gabriel wanted to know. He wasn't talking about the ball drop.

"I don't have a phone," I reminded him.

"Right," he said, wincing. "Sorry, I forgot. I haven't heard anything, either." His gaze drifted toward Robert Stark, who was laughing at something Rush Limbaugh had said, and slapping him on the back.

"Nikki!" Robert Stark cried, having spotted me over Rush's shoulder.

I winced. Brandon's dad held an arm out, beckoning for me to come over, a big smile on his face. Surrounded by adorers, he was holding court. Everyone was smiling and holding champagne, clearly enjoying themselves.

And, of course, there was a bunch of photographers there, itching to take some publicity pictures for tomorrow's papers.

"Oh, no," I said, under my breath. Gabriel looked sympathetic.

"Here she is, the star of the night," Robert Stark called, waving to me again to come over. "Nikki Howard, ladies and gentlemen. Wasn't she lovely this evening? Didn't she look beautiful in all those diamonds?"

I had no choice but to go over to him. What else could I do? I tried to plaster the nicest smile I could onto my face. I knew what was going on.

And I knew the role I had to play . . . at least until I found out whether or not Frida was safe: Robert Stark was showing me off. I was his finest product.

I was the original Phoenix.

When I got to his side, Brandon's dad slipped his arm around me. It was like being embraced by a python.

"Such a great girl," Robert Stark said, hugging me to him. "So glad to have her in the Stark family."

I kept the smile plastered on my face. Flashes went off. The photographers said encouraging things like "Great! That's just great, Nikki, Mr. Stark. Over here, now. Sir, could you put your chin up? Chin down now. Nikki, look over here. Great. Fabulous. You two look great together. Thanks so much."

But the whole time, all I could think about was how much I wanted to throw up.

When the purple splotches from the flashes faded, out of the corner of my eye I thought I saw some people coming into the restaurant. I had to do a double take, not sure I believed my eyes, before I registered who they really were. . . .

Lulu, in her outlandish black cocktail dress with its bright red crinoline, sassily striding up to the bar and demanding a cocktail, pulling Steven Howard — *Steven Howard* — in her wake . . .

Steven's sister, Nikki, with her jet-black hair and matching black corset, sashaying up to the bar behind her brother like she owned the place . . .

And Christopher — *my* Christopher — escorting a very young-looking girl with curly hair who was peering all around

285

the place with her mouth slightly ajar in the manner of someone who seemed *way* too excited to be there . . .

Frida. *My sister, Frida.*

I'm pretty sure some throw-up *did* come up into my mouth when I saw that. Frida? They'd brought *Frida* here? Were they crazy? Hadn't they registered the part where I'd told them Robert Stark had threatened to *kill* Frida?

"Um," I said, ducking out from beneath Robert Stark's arm. "Will you excuse me?"

"Of course," he said, looking a bit confused as I darted away.

I raced toward Frida until I was able to grab her by both arms and spin her around — she'd been pressed up against one of the vast windows, looking down over Times Square at the crowd below.

"Frida," I cried frantically. "You're all right?"

"I'm great," she said, pushing away some of the hair I'd caused to fall into her eyes by the violence of my gesture. "What do you think? Those guys came and got me. Em, what's going on? No one will tell me. Is everything okay? And what happened to Nikki? She's all hot now. Also, have you seen the way Gabriel looks at her? It's not fair, I saw him first —"

I hugged her to me.

"Never mind about Gabriel," I said into her hair. "He's too old for you, anyway."

"What?" Frida said. She was hugging me back, but obviously had other concerns. "He's only, like, eight years older. That's nothing."

"Seriously." I pulled her away from me and looked down into her eyes. My own were filled with tears. "There will be lots of boys your own age who are going to be crazy for you. So just shut up."

Christopher had come over, holding two glasses of soda. "Problems, ladies?" he asked lightly.

"None at all," I said, turning my tear-filled gaze toward him. "Is everything —"

"Oh," he said, handing one of the glasses to Frida. "It's all good. Look up."

"Up?" I looked up, not knowing what he was talking about. But all I saw were the flat-screen TVs hanging overhead.

"That's right," Christopher said. "Keep watching. Hey, has anyone talked to Brandon?"

"Brandon?" I took the sparkling soda he offered me. I'd lost the one Gabriel had given me a long time ago. "Why?"

"Because he just might want to prepare himself for —"

That was when all the television screens in the room started showing that the Times Square ball was beginning to drop. And everyone began hurrying toward the windows to see it for themselves.

"Ten," everyone began to chant. "Nine . . ."

Everyone, that is, except for Nikki — the *real* Nikki. She walked right up to Robert Stark with a great big smile plastered across her bright red lipsticked mouth.

"Hello again," she said, grinning at Robert Stark.

He seemed a bit startled to be interrupted while counting down to New Year's. But not unpleasantly so, because Nikki was one hot little number.

"Well, hello there," he said, grinning back at her. "Miss, er . . . Prince, is it?"

"That's right," Nikki said. "Good memory. But that's not actually my real name."

And she lifted the remote she'd snagged from the bar and turned up the sound on all the TVs.

"Five," everyone was screaming. "Four . . ."

"It's not?" Robert Stark asked, seemingly only interested for politeness' sake. "What is it, then?"

"Nikki Howard," she said. "You should have just paid up, Robert." Then she cocked her head to look at him a little bit harder. "On second thought . . . I should have just turned you in in the first place."

"Happy New Year!" everyone screamed.

Over by the bar, I saw Lulu throw her arms around Steven and kiss him. Rebecca and Brandon had already wrapped themselves into such a tight clench, I had to look away, a little shocked. Even Nikki scampered off from a confused-looking Robert

Stark to go up to Gabriel Luna, who was hugging his bandmates, pull him away by his shirtfront, and plant a huge kiss right on his lips . . . much to the dismay of Frida, who let out a faint whimper at the sight.

Christopher, meanwhile, was grinning down at me. He looked more devilish than boyfriend-like. I was so alarmed by everything that had just happened in the past five minutes, I took a step away from him. I really wasn't sure how much more I could take.

"Oh," I said, holding up both hands to ward him off, my heart having begun to stutter. "No . . ."

But it was too late. He'd already caught me around the waist and hauled me back toward him, crushing my body to his and then dropping his mouth over mine.

I think I let out a whimper that was not unlike Frida's — only for different reasons, of course — before I found myself melting, as always, at the touch of his lips. Why couldn't I resist him? It was so infuriating! Was this how it was always going to be between us? We were always going to be making each other mad, then kiss and everything would be fine . . . *more* than fine, actually?

Christopher had his arms around me, seeming to be in no hurry to finish our New Year's kiss. Not that I minded.

Who knows how long we would have stood there kissing (and in front of poor Frida! I did feel bad about that) if right then every single television in the room hadn't flashed the same orange message: *Breaking News*, and a news anchor hadn't come on to say, urgently, "We're interrupting our New Year's Eve coverage to inform you of a breaking story out of New York City concerning Robert Stark, the entrepreneur who founded Stark Enterprises, known worldwide for its chain of large discount department stores."

A ripple of excited chatter went through the Stark Sky Bar when this announcement was made. Rebecca and Brandon actually disattached themselves long enough to pay attention to what was going on. The Stark shareholders all stood looking up at the television screens in confusion, some of them weaving on their feet a little, because they'd had so much to drink.

Robert Stark stood absolutely still, staring in shock at what he was seeing.

I reached for Christopher's fingers with one hand and Frida's with the other. Frida glanced at me and asked, in a whisper, "Em. What is this?"

"Just watch," I whispered back. I'd be lying if I said my heart wasn't hammering a little, though.

"This evening," the news anchor went on solemnly, "CNN has exclusively obtained video — video CNN can verify is authentic — that proves that Stark Enterprise shareholders, including Robert Stark himself, have been knowingly participating in a highly experimental surgery known as a full-body transplant —"

Somewhere in the room, a woman screamed and dropped a glass, which smashed to the floor.

"— in a secret laboratory in Manhattan called the Stark Institute for Neurology and Neurosurgery. Here's CNN chief medical correspondent, Dr. Sanjay Gupta, to explain this controversial — not to mention illegal — procedure."

"Thank you, Wolf," a new voice said. "In a full-body transplant, a patient's brain is completely removed from his or her body and placed into a new body, usually from a donor who has been declared brain-dead. In the case of something the corporation was calling Project Phoenix, however, living donors were being handpicked from —"

"What is this?" Robert Stark thundered, whirling around to glare at the rest of us. "What is this? Turn it off. Did you hear me? I said turn it off!"

No one moved to turn the televisions off, even though I was pretty sure the bartenders had the remote controls. In fact, I saw Nikki lift one of the remotes and deliberately turn the volume up.

"— in this exclusive video, representatives from the corporation can be seen auctioning off the profiles of young people who, it is alleged, will be placed into a vegetative state at a later date so their bodies can be harvested for the highest bidder, to have their brains transplanted into them when —"

The footage I'd shot at the auction began to play as the news announcer went on. I have to say, that Stark brand cell phone had done a pretty good job of capturing what I'd wanted it to. The images of Kim Su, the Frenchwoman presenting her, and the shareholders bidding on her were clear as day. You couldn't really see their faces, but you got the gist of what was going on really well.

And the sound, after I'd had to slide the cell phone into my bra to hide it?

Still crystal clear.

Hey, Stark:

Can you hear me now?

"*You*," Robert Stark raged, whirling around to face me as the recording of him — recognizably the deep voice of Robert Stark — was saying, *They'll be living their own lives, just with new bodies. . . . And it will be worth it, not to have to wake up every morning with creaking joints, to have to take nine different kinds of heart medications — believe me, it will be worth every penny to them. . . .*

I stumbled back a step. He looked angry enough to lift me up and throw me bodily out one of the plate-glass windows that were all around us, like in one of the *Die Hard* movies. I totally wouldn't have put it past him.

I wasn't the only one who noticed, either. Christopher moved in front of me, placing himself as a human shield between me and the billionaire who wanted to kill me.

If that wasn't love, I don't know what is.

"You," Robert Stark growled again, completely ignoring Christopher. "*You* did this! I destroyed that phone! How is this even possible?"

On the television screen, our voices went on — his and mine, with a written transcript provided for the viewer, in case anyone couldn't understand what we were saying on the tape.

"*You're going to get caught. It's murder. You can't keep it a secret forever.*"

Did I really sound like that?

No. Of course I didn't.

But Nikki did.

"*I've managed to so far. How long do you think we've been doing this, anyway? We've been doing this for years. Years. With this latest technology, we've been able to offer our clients a more diversified and unique selection of products over a broader range, while still increasing our profit margin.*"

Profit margin. That's all it had ever been about for Robert Stark.

And that's what was about to destroy him.

"You destroyed my iPhone," I said to Robert Stark, in the steadiest voice I could summon, speaking from around Christopher's broad shoulders. "But you didn't find my Stark brand phone."

"The one you've been bugging all this time," Christopher added. "All that film and audio was up on your own mainframe. We just transferred it over to CNN. Wolf Blitzer has it all now. And after this, the world."

Robert Stark stared at us like we'd just told him Mariah Carey was really a man.

"Stark!" one of the red-faced shareholders shouted. "You told us this would never get out! You swore!"

"— two teen hackers in the New York City area who discovered that the new Stark Quarks actually contain spyware that enables the corporate giant to upload all the users' data to their mainframe," Wolf Blitzer went on, "and sent us this recording of Robert Stark and supermodel Nikki Howard at a Project Phoenix auction this evening . . ."

The Stark shareholders, I noticed, were suddenly beginning to head for the doors of the Sky Bar, their expressions panic-stricken.

But it was going to be difficult for them to leave.

Because just then the doors were thrown open, and dozens

of New York's finest, in their dark blue uniforms, began to stream in, their gold badges gleaming under the disco lights.

"Everybody stay where you are," one of them said, using a megaphone to be heard over the sudden cacophony of shocked partygoers. "Nobody's going anywhere."

"I need my blood pressure medicine," the husband of the lady with the sparkles at the bottom of her skirt screamed.

"We'll make sure we get it for you," a cop assured him, "over at Rikers."

"Is this really happening?" Nikki came over to ask me.

"I think it is," I said, feeling as dazed as she felt.

Over by the bar, Brandon, finally realizing this was his big moment, hurried to face the photographers who'd been taking the publicity photos of me and his dad earlier.

"In light of the recent discoveries about my father," he said, suddenly sounding as if he hadn't had a single thing to drink all night, "with whom my relationship has always been troubled, I'd just like to say that I'll be taking over the day-to-day operations of Stark Enterprises for the foreseeable future, and that I'll be doing my best to make Stark a greener, more earth-friendly corporation. I'll definitely be thinking of the employees, who for so long have labored without a union or proper health care. I'll be working to correct that, as well as the impression Stark may have given that it doesn't care about the small business owner —"

But none of the reporters was listening. They were only interested in what was happening in the center of the room.

"Robert Stark?" asked a police captain, striding up to Brandon's dad and showing him his badge. "We'd like to ask you a few questions downtown, if you don't mind."

"Not without my lawyer," Robert Stark bristled.

"I wouldn't dream of it," the police captain said politely.

That's when he handcuffed Robert Stark and led him away.

TWENTY-TWO

IT WAS MONTHS BEFORE IT ALL SET-
tled down.

And even then, I couldn't go anywhere without someone wanting to shove a microphone into my face to ask me
about it.

I wasn't allowed to discuss it, though, because of the testi-
mony I was scheduled to give against Robert Stark — and
all the Stark shareholders who'd been at the auction the night
of the Project Phoenix auction, and Dr. Holcombe, and yes,
Dr. Higgins, too — at the grand jury.

I wasn't the only one testifying, of course. Because of
what we'd done, Dr. Fong was able to come out of hiding and
tell what he knew about the goings-on at the Stark Institute

for Neurology and Neurosurgery, too, in exchange for immunity from prosecution.

Some of the surgeries, he maintained, had been medically necessary to save the life of the patient, and completely aboveboard.

But a lot of them . . .

Well, let's just say, not so much.

The families of some of those "donor bodies" had come forward to testify as well. According to the legal experts I saw occasionally on the news, this wasn't something Robert Stark was going to be able to wiggle his way out of. This was multiple counts of murder, attempted murder, and in Nikki's case, assault with a deadly weapon (a scalpel).

Robert Stark, formerly one of the world's most powerful men, was going to go away for a long time.

A long, long time.

Dr. Fong wasn't the only one who was safe now. Nikki, Steven, and Mrs. Howard were safe, too, because of what we'd done, and able to go back to their normal lives.

Except, of course, that for some of them, this wasn't so simple.

Mrs. Howard was excited and eager to go back to Gasper and her dog-grooming business.

I was sorry to see her go. I'd really grown to think of her as a second mother.

But Gasper was the place she knew and loved, and where all her best friends were. And Harry and Winston didn't like being cooped up in tiny New York apartments. They missed having a yard to play in.

I went with her to the airport and hugged her good-bye. It was sad, but it was better for everyone all around, especially Mrs. Howard. Too much togetherness with her daughter had been giving her chronic migraines, and was perhaps too much for anyone to put up with, long-term . . .

. . . including Steven, since he went back to his naval unit. He sort of had to. I guess it had something to do with the fact that he'd signed up to be on this submarine and couldn't exactly just leave, especially now that he'd found his mother and sister, which was the only reason they'd let him off in the first place.

Lulu was devastated. I had to order her a banana split every day for almost a week before she started to look on the bright side.

"At least," she pointed out, "he can't cheat on me. There aren't any girls on his sub."

In the meantime, she says she's really and truly going to finish her album. She's already finished a song based on their (daily) e-mails to each other called "Hot Love Down Under (the Sea)."

I don't know. I think it's got real potential. I'm not the only one. She was the first artist to be signed on the Stark label under Brandon's new management as CEO.

He hasn't actually done a bad job of being in charge now that his dad's in jail (without bail). Of course, Brandon has a lot of talented people to help him (not the least of which is Rebecca, from whom he's seemed to become inseparable. In fact, she's quit the agenting business. But that's all right. Really, it is. I like waking up to find only people I've invited over in my bedroom).

One of the first things Brandon did upon taking over Stark Enterprises was hire Felix and Christopher to come up with a free software patch for all the people who purchased the Stark Quarks to download, so they could fix the pesky little spyware problem. This was a far better strategic move than recalling all the PCs (which was what a lot of people advised him to do), and went a long way toward improving consumer confidence in Stark after everything his father had done to ruin the company. Because of the free patch and all the publicity the case is getting, the Stark Quarks are actually the highest-selling PCs of all time.

Which just goes to show: There's no such thing as bad publicity.

Felix and Christopher did such a good job coming up with the patch solution so quickly (not to mention bringing down his dad as CEO) that Brandon hired them as heads of Stark's IT department, since whoever was running it before sucked so badly, a couple of teenagers could break into the mainframe and basically run rampant through their entire network.

Now Stark's firewalls are impenetrable, their encryption codes unbreakable, and their IT department takes a two-hour lunch every day so they can have *Journeyquest* marathons.

And Felix, who got his ankle bracelet removed a few weeks ago, has started bathing and wearing a suit to work. He actually looks almost presentable. . . .

And because of Stark's newly implemented sexual harassment training seminars (mandatory for all staff administrators — Christopher's suggestion), Felix can actually speak to women without making lewd and offensive innuendos.

Which still doesn't make it okay that he asked my sister, Frida, to his alternative high school's prom.

"It's not like a real prom," Frida said, when I made a big deal about this while we were shopping at Betsey Johnson the other day. She was actually planning on getting something there to wear to Felix's prom with high-tops (thus the "not like a real prom" part. If it had been a "real prom," she said, she'd have worn heels). "We're not *going out* or anything."

"But it's still a prom," I said. "He's still *Felix*. He's going to try to kiss you. Probably worse."

"And that is a bad thing . . . how?" Frida replied.

"You'd let Felix kiss you." I could not believe this was happening. "Christopher's *cousin?*"

"You let Christopher kiss you," Frida pointed out, flicking through a rack of off-the-shoulder numbers with big poofy skirts. Total prom wear. "All the time, I might add. I hardly ever see you two when you *aren't* kissing. Including in school. Which isn't *too* disgusting."

"That's different," I said huffily.

And it was. Christopher and I had known each other our whole lives, practically. We were made for each other. We finished each other's sentences.

Sure, we still fought sometimes.

But what two headstrong people deeply in love don't fight from time to time? Especially two people who'd been friends for so long before falling in love. We knew each other so well, we could tell what the other person was thinking half the time.

Like just the other day, in Public Speaking, when Whitney Robertson poked me in the back before class even started and leaned over to ask, "Hey. Is it true, the rumor I heard . . . that you had one of those brain transplants they're talking about on the news all the time, and you're really . . . um, *Em Watts?*"

She said my name like it was a dirty word.

Also, I could tell there was no way she believed it was true. How could I, Nikki Howard, lithe, swanlike creature, ever be associated with someone as odious as that hideous, hobbitlike Emerson Watts?

It had been Christopher who had leaned forward in his seat and said to Whitney, with obvious pleasure, "You know what,

Whitney? It *is* true. And because you were always so mean to her when she was Em, you can pretty much kiss away any chance you might ever have had at getting to meet Heidi Klum and Seal at any of the fall fashion shows. Right, Em?"

Whitney and her little crony, Lindsey, had both turned their horror- and guilt-stricken gazes toward me. You didn't have to be a mind reader to see what they were thinking: *Please let what he said not be true. Please!*

I thought about putting them out of their misery. But the other thing that had come out of all of this (besides an end to Robert Stark's newest commercial sales campaign, to sell hot young bodies to his old friends, for them to be hot and young again) was an end to all the lies.

"He's right," I'd said, with a shrug. "I'm really Em Watts. I just use Nikki Howard as my modeling name now. And I'm not really interested in being BFFs with you guys. Unless, of course, you stop spiking volleyballs at other girls' heads on purpose. And torturing them about the size of their butts in the hallway. You do remember when you used to do that to me, don't you, Whitney?"

Now Whitney's eyes were the size of quarters.

"B-but," she'd stammered, "I — I was only kidding around."

"Huh," I said. "Did you notice how I wasn't laughing back then? It doesn't hurt, you know, Whitney, to be kind to people, no matter what they look like. Especially because, these days? You never know who they're going to turn out to be later."

"I . . . " Whitney blinked. "I'm so *sorry.*"

"Yeah," I said. I believed she *was* sorry. Now. "I bet you are."

The best thing about everyone knowing who I was — who I *really* was — was that my old grades were combined into my new ones and brought my grade point average up quite a bit. Suddenly, I went from being a mediocre student to an above-average one. Not straight As, by any means, like I used to be.

But considering what I'd been through, and how many classes I'd missed, it was still a relief. With hard work, I'd managed to keep my head above water, gradewise . . . hard work, and Nikki's career management skills.

Because Nikki, another witness in Robert Stark's grand jury trial, had decided not to go back to Gasper but stick around in New York . . . as my new agent and manager.

Well, why not? She knows everything about the modeling business — especially as it concerns Nikki Howard — and obviously has a shrewd business sense (except when it comes to blackmailing people, which she swears on the Lady Clairol Midnight Sky she uses to keep her hair so dark that she's not going to do anymore).

She turned out to be serious about business school. She took her mom's advice and enrolled in classes and is already making her professors miserable.

Hey. No one can say Nikki Howard's not bossy and doesn't know how to get what she wants . . . especially for her clients (of which, so far, I'm the only one. But she's working on that).

It made sense that I give Nikki a cut of what I earned, anyway, since my career was the one she'd launched. We worked out that she got a percentage of all my future earnings, plus everything that had been in the accounts I'd found when I'd been declared "legally" Nikki Howard.

And since, immediately following the makeover Lulu gave her, Nikki regained her va-va-voom factor with men, she lost all interest in swapping brains (not that we'd have been allowed to do this, even if we'd wanted to: There's been a total ban on the surgeries, except in the case of life-threatening injury). I don't know how much of this had to do with the fact that Nikki seemed to get really into being Goth "Diana Prince," the name and persona she took for her new body, and how much of it had to do with Gabriel Luna being . . . well, into *her*.

But I do know she has no interest whatsoever in selling the loft. She's perfectly happy staying where she is, living in Gabriel's apartment, driving Gabriel nuts by taking up all his closet space and insulting his bandmates . . .

. . . and he, in turn, is the most creative he's ever been, having written three new *albums* of songs — all about the same wacky girl he lives with — in four months.

Instead, I'm paying Nikki rent, same as Lulu.

My living situation had been the source of heated discussion with my parents, who'd assumed I'd move back home once my true identity was revealed.

But to me, in a weird way, the loft *was* home now. How could I leave Lulu, who had no family other than me and Steven, who was still away at sea?

"Maybe when he comes back," I'd explained to Mom and Dad over pizza at their place one night — pizza I could now enjoy without worrying anyone was spying on me. "And he and Lulu do get married someday. . . ."

Frida snorted. "Right."

"What's that supposed to mean?" I demanded.

"You're not coming back, even if Lulu does get married. You like living in a bachelorette pad," Frida said accusingly. "Face it, Mom and Dad. She only wants to stay there so she can have Christo —"

"That's not true!" I interrupted, although it was, of course, partly true. "And it's not that I love you guys any less. It's just that I still have a very busy schedule, what with work and school and —"

"Oh, please," Frida snorted.

"She's gotten used to being in her own space," Mom said very diplomatically, "and wants to keep it that way. We understand."

Dad didn't look like he understood, exactly, but he didn't say anything. He clearly felt that he was outnumbered by females in this instance, as often happened in our household.

"I don't care," Frida said, shrugging. "So long as I get invited over for your parties once in a while . . ."

"Done," I said. Like I said, Frida had really gotten very mature lately.

". . . and I can bring Felix."

"Oh, my God, no! Are you serious?"

"Felix saved my life," Frida said truculently. "And yours. How can you be so mean about him?"

"He didn't save your life," I said. "*I* did. Felix and Christopher helped. A little."

"That's not true. They were equally as important as you. He told me all about it —"

"Girls," Mom said. "Please. Both of you are smart, vibrant, beautiful girls with wonderful, talented, handsome boyfriends. Please stop fighting and clear the dishes so your father and I can have some alone time."

Alone time is important if you want to build a strong romantic relationship. Christopher and I try to grab as much as we can. Especially at Balthazar, which is one of our favorite restaurants to go to together for dinner . . .

. . . with an appetizer, *and* dessert, despite Lulu's assertions that high school boys can't afford to take their girlfriends there (they can, if they also work part-time in the IT department of a major corporation. And their girlfriend insists she pay once in a while, because I work, too, and it's only fair for the girl to pay sometimes. I don't know where this archaic idea that the boy always has to pay comes from).

It was at Balthazar the other night that I was sitting across from Christopher, happily stabbing a piece of lettuce and goat cheese, when a little girl came up to our table, holding a pen and a piece of paper.

"Excuse me," she said to me shyly. "But are you Nikki Howard?"

I looked over at her, surprised. She couldn't have been more than seven or eight years old. I saw her parents sitting at a neighboring table, smiling at her encouragingly.

The truth was, I didn't know what to say. I was Nikki Howard . . . sort of.

Except I also wasn't, anymore.

But the little girl's expression was one of such hopefulness . . . she was in New York City for the night, all dressed up (she was probably going to a Broadway musical later).

And here she was in a fancy restaurant, and she'd spotted a celebrity. What was I going to do? Say, *No, little girl. Actually, I'm Em Watts.*

"Yes," I said. "I am."

Her face burst into a delighted smile. She was missing her two front teeth.

"Can I please have your autograph?" she asked, shoving the pen and paper at me.

"Of course," I said, darting a look at Christopher, who just grinned and kept on eating his salad. "What's your name?"

"Emily," the little girl said.

I refrained from saying, *Em is my name, too,* and wrote *Best wishes, Emily, love, Nikki Howard* on her piece of paper, and handed it and the pen back to her.

"Here you go," I said. "Have a nice night."

"Oh, thank you," she said, and scurried back to her table and her parents, looking overjoyed.

"That was nice of you," Christopher said as soon as she was gone.

"What was I going to do?" I asked. "Kick her in the face?"

"To tell her you were Nikki Howard, I mean," he said.

"I *am* Nikki Howard," I said. "As long as I'm stuck with this face, I'll always be Nikki Howard."

"Yeah," Christopher said. "But it's not such a drag, is it? I mean, being Nikki Howard has its perks."

"It does," I said, smiling. "But it has its drawbacks, too. As you might have gathered, since even the real Nikki Howard doesn't want to be Nikki Howard anymore."

"Well," Christopher said. "Maybe this will make you feel better about it."

And he reached into the pocket of his jacket and pulled out

a long rectangular velvet box, which he slid across the table toward me.

"What's this?" I asked, surprised, since we weren't exactly the kind of couple who showered each other with gifts. We sort of had everything we'd ever wanted . . . which was each other.

"Open it and see," he said, a mischievous twinkle in his blue eyes.

I widened my eyes at him in mock astonishment, then opened the box . . .

. . . and my astonishment turned to the real thing.

Because lying there inside, on a whisper-thin necklace chain, was a heart-shaped platinum tag, surrounded by tiny diamonds, on which the words *Em Watts* had been inscribed in elegant cursive.

"I thought if you wore that, no matter what face you saw every morning in the mirror," he said in his deep voice, "you'll never forget who you really are."

My eyes filling with tears, I held my hand out across the tabletop. He grasped my fingers, his grip strong and reassuring.

"As if I ever could," I said, my voice clogged with emotion, "with you around to remind me."

HARD COVER

HARD COVER

A Marc Portman Thriller

Adrian Magson

This first world edition published 2016
in Great Britain and the USA by
SEVERN HOUSE PUBLISHERS LTD of
19 Cedar Road, Sutton, Surrey, England, SM2 5DA.
Trade paperback edition first published
in Great Britain and the USA 2016 by
SEVERN HOUSE PUBLISHERS LTD

Copyright © 2016 by Adrian Magson.

British Library Cataloguing in Publication Data
A CIP catalogue record for this title is available from the British Library.

ISBN-13: 978-0-7278-8607-1 (cased)
ISBN-13: 978-1-84751-710-4 (trade paper)
ISBN-13: 978-1-78010-771-4 (e-book)

This is a work of fiction. Names, characters, places and incidents
are either the product of the author's imagination or are used fictitiously.
Except where actual historical events and characters are being described
for the storyline of this novel, all situations in this publication are
fictitious and any resemblance to actual persons, living or dead,
business establishments, events or locales is purely coincidental.

All Severn House titles are printed on acid-free paper.

Severn House Publishers support the Forest Stewardship Council™ [FSC™],
the leading international forest certification organisation.
All our titles that are printed on FSC certified paper carry the FSC logo.

MIX
Paper from
responsible sources
FSC   FSC® C013056
www.fsc.org

Typeset by Palimpsest Book Production Ltd.,
Falkirk, Stirlingshire, Scotland.
Printed and bound in Great Britain by
TJ International, Padstow, Cornwall.

To Ann, who in between everything else,
finds the time to make this stuff better

ACKNOWLEDGMENTS

With grateful thanks to Geoff Weighell, all-round pilot and CEO of the British Microlight Aircraft Association, for his helpful advice and information. Any perceived errors are mine alone and/or a case of creative licence on my part.

Thanks also to KM and EB; two people I never thanked enough for what they did.

ONE

Cuidad Madero – Gulf Coast of Mexico

C ompetence. It's a sure-fire way to get yourself noticed by a suspicious security professional.

Most people on the street look unassuming, engrossed in their own brand of the everyday. They don't have what's called 'presence' – at least not the threatening kind. Many professionals on the other hand, if they're not mindful, look anything but. Something in their training and motivation gives them an indefinable aura that sets them apart from those around them.

To a watchful eye, it's the heads-up, can-do attitude that spells potential trouble. Like a wolf in a woolly coat, it might look like a sheep and smell like a sheep; but if it walks like something hairy, it's time to take a closer look.

Which was why I was shuffling along with my head down, hiding beneath a grubby two-sizes-up faded and beat-up camo jacket and hood with make-do patches on the elbows. I was stopping every now and then to change hands with the box I was carrying, an old television carton which looked a lot heavier than it actually was. But that was part of the plan. Looking vulnerable, which I did by stopping every few yards and flexing my fingers, means you don't appear to be a threat.

The man standing outside the gates of the workshop yard didn't look the sympathetic type. The bulge under his coat told me and anybody who cared to look that he was armed, and he worked hard on living the image; he was big and shaven-headed, and sneered every time I stopped. When he spat on the ground and it landed too close to my foot to be an accident, I figured it was his way of passing the time and intimidating people he didn't like the look of.

Sophisticated.

I dropped my shoulders and wrapped a piece of my sleeve

around my hand, then grabbed the string again and went to shuffle past him. By then he'd lost interest and turned his head to check the street the other way.

Big mistake.

Just before I drew level with him I pushed my fist through a slit in the cardboard and pulled out a piece of four-by-two hardwood timber I'd found in a dumpster back down the street. It was eighteen inches long and had a nicely balanced feel to it, although I doubt the guard would have agreed. When I swung it at the back of his head he went down and out without a sound.

I dragged him off the street and through the pedestrian door set in one of the gates, and rolled him behind an old car body that was slowly rotting into the ground. I slapped a length of heavy tape across his mouth and did the same on his wrists and ankles, and just for luck used a further length to secure both ankles and wrists together so he couldn't kick out when he woke up.

Inside his coat I found a Czech-made Browning semi-automatic in a nylon holster. It was a nice piece but hadn't been cleaned in a while. In his side pocket was an unopened packet of condoms and a fat silencer the size of a small beer bottle. It looked professionally made but unbranded. It didn't smell used, so I figured he probably got it out when he wanted to impress the ladies, with the condoms on stand-by in case he got lucky.

I stripped out the magazine and tossed it out of sight behind the car, and threw the gun through the window into the rotting interior. I pocketed the silencer and went back outside for the box. I'd already scanned for cameras on an earlier pass when a couple of cars had driven through the gates, and it had given me a brief glimpse inside before the guard had slammed them shut. I hadn't spotted any obvious lenses, but that meant the place I was about to hit was either innocent of any wrongdoing or the owners didn't feel the need because they had a tight control on the entire area.

I figured the second option.

I dropped the box out of sight inside the gates and closed the pedestrian door behind me. I took a semi-automatic out of my coat pocket and tried the silencer for size. It had a rubber insert which fitted tightly around the barrel, and the silencer was probably good for one-time use only. But since I wasn't planning on starting a long shooting war, it would do fine.

The building had once been a metal workshop, evidenced by a rack of rusting metal sheets at the back of the yard and the remains of an overhead pulley system for hauling heavy loads through a set of sliding doors at the front. These were shut tight with a heavy coating of grime over the inspection glass set in one side. There were no windows overlooking the yard, although I figured there had to be an office of some kind on the first floor – a further indication that the people here didn't concern themselves with snap inspections by the local police or on anybody else busting in uninvited.

It told me everything I needed to know about them and this part of the city.

A set of metal stairs in one corner led up to the first floor and a walkway running out of sight on the side of the building. It would be the obvious way in but I gave it a miss. In old buildings the vibration set up on metal stairs the moment you step on them is a clear give-away.

Instead I walked down the side of the building, stepping past a pile of twisted metal and ancient car parts, following a concrete path that looked like it had been recently swept of rubbish.

I came to a window and ducked beneath it. A conversation was going on inside, but it was just a rumble of voices and I couldn't understand the words enough to follow the subject. I counted three different speakers, all male. One of them sounded pissed off and kept interrupting the others, who shut up the moment he began speaking. He was either the boss man or the biggest and meanest; it didn't make much difference to me.

I crept along to the rear of the building and found another door and a path leading to an outside toilet. It smelled awful and hadn't been cleaned in years. No surprise there.

I turned back and tried the door handle. It felt smooth and well-used, and moved without a sound.

The door opened outwards, and brought with it a smell of mould, damp and oil – and cigarette smoke. I slipped inside and found myself in a tiny lobby with a wooden door facing me. A flight of concrete stairs to one side led up to the first floor.

The voices were coming from the other side of the door.

I took the stairs on my toes, careful to avoid a layer of grit where the plaster had crumbled off the rotting walls, and reached a single door on a small landing. It was open a crack and I edged it back until I could see inside.

The room had once been an office. All it held now was an armchair, a wooden table and a camp-style bed. The air seeping out from inside smelled of stale bodies, ditto food and quiet desperation.

The armchair was currently filled with a reclining twin of the gate guard downstairs, dressed in creased pants and a filthy shirt. He had a three-day growth of beard and a big gut and was snoring softly, and sporting a pistol on his chest with one hand resting on the butt.

The bed held the slim form of a teenage girl, her hands tied with rope. Her name was Katarina, and she was the thirteen-year-old daughter of local federal judge Antonio da Costa. Just weeks before, the judge had declared war on the cartels in the region and vowed to bring them to justice for their murderous, racketeering activities.

Kidnapping Katarina had undoubtedly been intended to ensure that particular war got stopped in its tracks. The message was simple: Judge da Costa either pulled his head in or he never saw his daughter alive again. The tactic had worked before in other parts of Mexico, and the kidnappers were probably counting on a satisfactory repeat outcome.

The grim truth, however, was that the judge would probably never see his daughter again, whatever he did. The cartels didn't take prisoners for fun and rarely returned them even when they'd got what they wanted. To them, violence of a kind that would have made I S look almost restrained was the only thing that mattered, and they performed it with chainsaws, just so everybody got the message.

I'd been called in on this job by a local security contractor working for da Costa. He'd quickly found he and his colleagues were too well-known, so he needed an outsider. He told me that the kidnap gang had been identified as a small spin-off cell from the Los Zetas cartel centred on Mexico's Gulf Coast. Formed after the arrest of the cartel leader, Alejandro Morales, or 'Z-42' as he was known, this particular cell was taking a huge risk, not least from the Los Zetas, who were still a ruthless force throughout the country, but from the northern-based Sinaloa Federation who were looking for a way of taking over the Los Zetas business and would deal ruthlessly with any competition.

The security firm had discovered through a local mouthpiece that Katarina was being held on a little-used industrial area on the south-eastern edge of Cuidad Madero, where the sprawl of low-cost housing began to leech into the surrounding hills. The infrastructure here was poor and the area almost abandoned by the local politicians, and the only people remaining on the industrial site, which was gradually being cleared by heavy-handed developers, were a few die-hard businesses and homeless families with nowhere else to go. It made a police or army raid virtually impossible to carry out successfully as these hangers-on had no choice but to do the bidding of the cartel.

Thus it had to be a one-man mission and pray for good luck.

Katarina looked okay to me. It was hard to tell, but her clothes were still clean and she didn't look in pain, so I was guessing the men hadn't touched her. What her state of mind might be was a different thing altogether. Right now, though, she was looking straight at me, eyes bulging imploringly over the gag that had been stuffed into her mouth and secured by wire looped around her head and cutting into her cheeks.

I held a finger to my lips and signalled for her to turn her head away. If the guard woke up and saw her face, he'd know instantly what was about to happen. I also didn't want her to see what would go down if things went wrong.

I checked the wooden floor in front of me; it was bad news. The planks looked thin and unstable, warped by time, heat and decay. The moment I stepped through the door, unless the men downstairs figured it was Mr Sleepy up and about, I'd

be on a twenty-second countdown to get the girl off the bed
and out of here.

And our only way out was back down the stairs.

TWO

T
he rumble of voices was still going on, with the main
man still holding forth. I had no idea what they were
discussing but it had to be what they were planning to
do with the money. There had been a ransom demand of $3
million, along with the judge's promised silence against the
cartels, but that was pretty much standard; in the end, unless
the judge openly gave up his daughter's life for the sake of
his job, they'd get what they wanted.

Getting the girl back in one piece still wouldn't happen.

That was why I'd been called in; the judge knew perfectly
well the kind of people he was dealing with, and whatever
their demands he was well aware of the likely outcome. His
daughter would be found, like so many previous kidnap
victims, in a storm drain somewhere, and it wouldn't be pretty.

I took a deep breath. These men were highly dangerous and
would be ready to start shooting at the slightest provocation.
If the ones downstairs realized I was up here, they wouldn't
bother coming up to find me first; they'd start shooting through
the floor.

I stepped carefully across to the man in the armchair, testing
the boards for give. As I did so he stirred, alerted by a sixth
sense to danger. He came up out of the chair in a rush, lifting
the gun off his chest towards the girl on the bed, and I knew
his instructions had been simple: at the first signs of a rescue
attempt, waste the hostage.

Holding the silencer in place I shot him twice. The gunshots
were muffled, no more than a snapping sound. But his body
tipping over the arm of the chair wasn't. He hit the floor hard,
his gun skidding out of his hand and bouncing across the
boards like a drum roll.

Instantly I heard a volley of shouts from downstairs demanding to know what was going on and what Carlos was doing.

The girl turned when she heard the shouting and looked to see what had happened, her eyes growing wider as she saw the dead guard with his head covered in blood. I bent and hauled her off the bed and tucked her behind the door where she would be most protected. Then I cut the ropes around her wrists and signalled to her not to move and to put her fingers in her ears. A split second later a volley of wild shots were fired through the ceiling downstairs, ripping up through the planks and filling the air with splinters and making Carlos's body jump.

Showed how much these guys cared about their colleagues. He should have joined a friendlier gang.

I fired back, spacing out my shots across the floor with a concentration around the door. I heard a scream which told me I'd been lucky, but no more shots.

They were on their way up.

I reloaded and grabbed the table, hurling it through the doorway onto the landing. I was counting on the element of shock and surprise as it hit the wall of the stairwell and crashed down the stairs. Somebody got the message and began yelling and firing like it was the fourth of July, and I heard the vicious spit and whine of shells taking pieces out of the walls and ceiling, and the clatter of brick and plaster rubble falling into the well. I waited for the shooting to stop, then stepped out and fired back, using the walls to bounce shells around the small lobby like shrapnel. There was more shouting, and I recognized the boss man's voice telling somebody to call for backup.

I had to get down there before that could happen, and there was only one way to do it. I ran down the first set of six stairs, my feet skidding in the dirt, and rounded the corner to face the door where the men had been talking. As I did so a chunk of plaster and brick dust exploded near my head and I saw a man in grubby jeans and shirt lying in the corner of the lobby, firing up the stairs. He had blood on his shoulder and was screaming something I didn't understand.

I shot him once and scooped up his gun as I ran past, and hit the door running, rolling across the concrete floor into what had once been the workshop. One man was lying on the floor, eyes wide open, my lucky shot from upstairs. Another was frantically stabbing a cell phone with his thumb while juggling a pistol with his other hand and trying to bring it to bear on me.

I pointed my gun at him and shook my head. He didn't look like a pro, more a talker than a fighter. But even talkers can be dangerous.

He dropped the phone and bent to put the gun on the floor, shaking his head at me and imploring me not to shoot, his jowls quivering like jello. He was quite a surprise. He was dressed in a smart suit and white shirt, with flashy-looking brown loafers polished to a high shine. All in it would probably have cost him a couple of thousand dollars. He was short and fat and had more of the sleek look of a businessman or politician than a kidnapper.

Maybe the local grab-and-ransom business was moving upmarket.

As I got to my feet I heard a noise behind me.

I spun round, finger tightening on the trigger.

It was Katarina. She'd followed me downstairs and was holding onto the door frame and doing her best not to fall over. She looked ghostly pale and ready to throw up, but had clearly got the guts to drag herself down here, ready to face whatever was waiting. But the look on her face wasn't just the expression of a traumatized kidnap victim; she looked genuinely appalled and was staring past me at the fat man as if she couldn't believe her eyes.

'*Tio*?' She whispered. Uncle. Then she held out her hand and screamed, '*Non!*'

I turned in time to see the fat man going for his gun. In his haste he fumbled it, juggling with both hands to turn it the right way and pull the trigger. He looked terrified and I realized why: for whatever insane reason – undoubtedly money – he'd arranged via this group of misfits for the kidnap of his own niece. It wouldn't be the first time family had turned on family for profit. It also explained why the goons he'd used were low-level quality and not cartel guns. But one thing was certain: he might have stayed in the background so far, only now the game was truly up.

He lifted his gun towards the girl with a scream of rage as if I wasn't there, clearly intent on killing her to wipe out any evidence of his involvement.

The silencer on my gun had dropped out of alignment and was likely to deflect a bullet if I fired, so I snapped it off the end and squeezed the trigger three times. The reports were deafening in the room and made my ears hurt, and the smoke residue clouded the air between us.

But not enough to hide the fat man's expensive jacket and shirt jumping with the impact of each shot, or the way he flipped over backwards and dropped the gun.

I turned to the girl and grabbed her round the waist. We hadn't got a lot of time before somebody came to investigate the noise, and we had a long way to go.

'Come on,' I said, hustling her out of the door. 'Let's get you home.'

THREE

I'm a close protection specialist. I run security, evaluate risks in hostile situations and, where needed, provide hard cover. To do my job I have to look ahead of where a principal is going to be at any one time, checking details, terrain, routes in and out – most especially out – and providing the best possible solution for a happy outcome. If it works the principal won't even know I'm there and will go home happy. If it doesn't, I get involved.

And that's where the hard cover comes in; it means I have to take a more direct course of action and fight back.

Two days later, after returning Katarina safely to her family, I had my feet up in my New York apartment evaluating a couple of jobs I'd been offered on the security contractor network, when I received a call.

'Yup.'

'Well, at least I now know you're home.' The voice was unmistakably British and I recognized it immediately. It belonged to a man named Tom Vale, a senior officer with the UK's Secret Intelligence Service or MI6. I'd worked with him once before and we'd got on fine, mainly because he didn't try dictating my every move once I was in the field. I wasn't sure what his current role was, only that he was a former field officer of some note and now close to retirement, and had been retained after a more senior colleague had been forced to stand down.

'I'm on a break,' I replied, although I knew that was going to be short-lived. Tom Vale didn't call freelancers like me unless he had a job that needed doing. I could refuse if I didn't like the sound of it, but we both knew that was unlikely.

'Glad to hear it. You know where the local CIA office is.' It wasn't a question. 'Can you be there in one hour?'

He could only be talking about New York. I'd been to the NY office before, which was located in Manhattan, where I'd picked up a previous job, so I guessed he'd been briefed on that.

'Will you be there?'

'Of course. I hope you can make it. There's a bit of a rush job on.'

He disconnected and left me wondering why an MI6 officer would be calling me in to a CIA front office. He'd either been given the task of contacting me because I was known to be a little sceptical of CIA procedures after my last assignment with them, or his star had risen in the intelligence world and he was now a major player with a foot in both camps. Knowing the rivalries that existed in their world, I was betting on the former.

A bit of a rush job. It was very British and Vale-speak for a major assignment.

I got there within the hour and was escorted through the security screen and up to a small office on the fifteenth floor. It could have been any government office in the country, with the same lack of design features, minimal furniture and an atmosphere of apparent calm overlaid by the hum of air-conditioning. But I knew there would be a hustle going on behind the doors and partitioning, and the building would be alive with electronic activity from all the terminals and computer screens being fed a torrent of information and raw data.

The office had three people present, all drinking coffee. Two men and one woman. Vale stepped across to shake hands and handed me a takeaway mug from down the street. He may have been a visitor here and British, but he was the type to make it his business to know a man's preferences. He stepped back and introduced the other two.

'This is senior CIA Assistant Director, Jason Sewell.' He indicated a comfortable-looking man in his mid-fifties, with a genial smile and watchful eyes. Sewell lifted himself off the chair and shook hands, and I moved the likely importance of this assignment several notches up the scale. For a man of his rank to be here in person, instead of on the other end of a video-conference line, this had to be a real zinger.

'And this is Angela Thornbury. She's a senior political analyst from the State Department, currently on attachment as an advisor to the White House. Ms Thornbury – Watchman.'

He hadn't used my real name and I guessed that was because he didn't think Thornbury needed to know it. Sewell probably did, but he didn't seem about to give the game away.

Thornbury was short, neat and serious-looking, in a grey suit and white blouse. She hesitated before reaching out a tentative hand, but stayed where she was so I had to reach across the table. She had a loose grip which lingered about as briefly as her smile, as if she wasn't quite comfortable being here. I didn't blame her; the environs of the White House were probably a lot more genial than the front office of one of the nation's foremost spy agencies, and outsiders like me were probably treated over there as on a par with pit bulls.

Introductions over, we all sat down. This time it was Sewell who did the talking and he didn't waste words. He took a photograph out of a folder in front of him and slid it across the table towards me. I noticed Vale and Thornbury had similar folders and photos.

'This is Leonid Tzorekov. He's a former KGB officer who met Vladimir Putin in the nineties before moving into a senior intelligence planning role. He resigned eight years ago and took on a senior post with Russia Bank and moved to London, where he set up ActInvest, a finance and securities operation. He's done very well for himself and now spends much of his time between London and New York, where ActInvest has a small office.'

Tzorekov looked to be in his late sixties, maybe older. He was lean and fit, with the air of an ageing athlete, and had the steady look of a man who has achieved much in his life and is not about to retire and take up gardening.

'He's seventy-four and extremely active,' Sewell continued, reading my mind. 'For some years since leaving Russia Tzorekov hasn't figured on anybody's radar. He appears to have distanced himself from the activities of other bankers with open and obvious ties to Moscow, and there's been nothing to suggest he is even remotely connected still with the KGB or any intelligence-gathering activities.'

He hesitated just long enough to suggest that there was a 'but' lurking in there somewhere, so I gave him an opening. 'However?'

He ghosted an appreciative smile. 'He was already a senior instructor in the organization when Putin was recruited, and helped train Putin's intake. The two became friends. It's thought Tzorekov saw Putin as a younger version of himself and took him under his wing, mentoring him through the critical stages of his career and preparing him for the future. That meant providing political protection when it was needed and pointing him in the right direction to move up the KGB ladder, which he did.'

'Things changed for Tzorekov just recently,' said Vale, taking over, 'with rumours of two attempts on his life. Both were passed off as accidents – one in London and one here in New York. The first was a mugging near Grand Central Station. He was attacked by two men. He was lucky, as he had this man with him.' Sewell was already sliding another photo across the table. The photo showed a younger man with a receding hairline and the slight build and pallid cheekbones of a ballet dancer. 'His name is Arkady Gurov. He's also ex-KGB, forty-two years old and listed as a security and IT manager for ActInvest. We're ninety-nine per cent sure he's Tzorekov's bodyguard.'

'And the other incident?'

'That was near Canon Street underground in London. A cab mounted the pavement as Tzorekov was walking to the station. It killed a news vendor and seriously injured two other members of the public. Gurov hustled Tzorekov away and the cab driver disappeared in the melee. The cab was found to have been stolen just an hour before from a garage in Southwark. It looked like a straightforward theft and joyride until the police found no fingerprints.'

'None?'

He shook his head. 'In view of who Tzorekov is, and the severity of the incident, the Metropolitan Police went over the vehicle three times and even tracked its progress on cameras from the accident back to the time it was stolen. There were no clear shots of the driver, which in itself seemed too unlikely to be a random car-jacking, and the fact that keys were involved suggest the vehicle had been stolen to order from the garage where it was being serviced. They discovered fresh traces of a cleaning agent on the door handle and steering wheel – nothing to do with the garage, as it happens – and concluded that the driver cleaned it after stealing the vehicle as a precaution, then wore gloves to drive to the area and make the hit.'

'Sounds organized. What did you mean "who Tzorekov is"?'

He shrugged. 'He's one of a large number of Russians working and living in London. We're aware of his KGB history, which Jason has outlined, although that doesn't seem to have prevented him voicing the occasional disagreement with his country's activities. He has family connections in Ukraine, for example. Because of that and following the murder of Litvinenko, his name was automatically placed on a watch list of prominent Russians in the capital. He's very rich and although he doesn't always speak highly of his mother country or of their politics, it could be a clever cover. But that doesn't explain the attempts on his life. There could have been other attempts, of course, that we don't know about.'

I had an inkling of where this was going, so asked, 'Are you saying they're still in touch?'

'Interesting question,' said Vale. 'We believe they never actually broke off contact altogether, but Tzorekov's move to the UK would have made it difficult for Putin to maintain open relations with a man generally seen as no longer accepted – an outsider, a dissident, even.'

'But?'

'We know messages have been passed to and from Tzorekov over the years, with a connection in Moscow. It probably isn't Putin himself tapping away on a keyboard, and although it's infrequent, it's enough to suggest that he is still talking to somebody over there.'

'What makes you think it's Putin and not a family member?'

'Because the messages are delivered in person, not by phone or email – a measure of the precautions being taken by both sides not to be seen talking to each other. We believe they're carried by a man named Valentin Roykovski. Roykovski has been to the UK on several occasions, and was once recorded visiting ActInvest's office in London. That by itself wasn't unusual, because many Russians in London bank with them. But shortly afterwards, Roykovski was spotted in a restaurant in Mayfair. Tzorekov was sitting at the next table but they ignored each other.'

It was an old-school method but still worked well if done correctly. A brush contact allows two people to exchange information or objects such as documents or a USB stick without actually being seen to meet. It's best done on the move, such as in a busy subway station or airport, but sitting at adjacent tables somewhere quiet is just as good.

'So Roykovski's a conduit.'

'We think so. The interesting thing is, Roykovski never goes anywhere near the Russian Embassy. He flies in, does what he has to, and flies out again. Like a bag man.'

'Is that significant?'

'It is,' Sewell put in, 'when you consider that Valentin Roykovski used to be Putin's driver back in the KGB days, and almost certainly knew Tzorekov pretty well, too. He's long retired now but he's been seen close to Putin's home at odd times and the general consensus is that he's almost certainly on a retainer of some kind. We're keeping a watch on him to see what he does over the next few days. If he moves, ten to one it's because he's acting on instructions from Putin. He'll be our marker.'

'So what is it you want me to do?'

'Personally, I don't. No offence. But others do.' He looked at Angela Thornbury with raised eyebrows.

She cleared her throat and asked, 'Have you ever heard of a group called the *siloviki*, Mr . . . Watchman?'

I ignored the obvious tone of condescension and doubt in her voice. She also sounded pissed by the obvious use of a code name. 'Well, I'm guessing they're not a group of travelling musicians. Could you enlighten me?'

Actually, I had heard of them, but I saw no reason to make this a spitting contest with a member of the State Department. The *siloviki* were rumoured to be mostly intelligence or military officers close to Putin, and considered to be part of his inner circle. If he needed advice, the senior members were the ones he went to, and usually held posts that decided policy at the very top of the government tree. They were also regarded as hawks and not friendly to the US or the European Union.

Which was pretty much what Thornbury went on to tell me at much greater length and detail, until Sewell jumped in to halt the flow.

'We don't know for sure,' he said, 'whether Leonid Tzorekov was, or is, part of this inner circle – a *silovik*. All the evidence says he isn't, although he must know some of the current members pretty well. But even though he's now gone to the outside, he evidently feels he may still be in a position of some influence. He recently approached the authorities in London and offered his services in talking to Putin and trying to counter the hawks who seem intent on driving a hard wedge between Moscow and the West. As we all know, they're doing a great job of talking up threats against Russia after the problems in Ukraine and the annexation of Crimea, mostly as a smokescreen. We know the sanctions are hurting them economically and, for some of the hierarchy running the state apparatus and big business, personally. Tom, here, got involved and brought us in so we could work together to find a way to use this opportunity.'

'Could Tzorekov have a vested interest in being a go-between?'

'We don't think so. He might want to improve his reputation among those who regard him as a deserter, but that's unlikely to work. There are those around Putin whom we know would actively strive to ensure there were no contacts from anybody outside the Moscow circle; they especially don't trust those who moved abroad and regard them generally as having been infected by living in the west.'

'But that's not the only reason?'

'No. Most importantly they wouldn't want their own influence over Putin threatened in any way – they'd have far too much to lose.' He blinked. 'So much so, we believe they would probably take extreme action to prevent a meeting happening at all.'

Extreme action. Another term for assassination.

I was beginning to see where this was leading. A zinger indeed.

'And you want me to do . . . what, exactly?'

Sewell lobbed the ball to Vale this time, who leaned forward and said, 'The general consensus is, it would be useful if somebody could follow Tzorekov into Russia and make sure he gets to Putin in one piece.'

FOUR

'You say Tzorekov is coming home. Is it really true or a foolish rumour?' The speaker stood up and walked out from behind his ornate desk and poured himself a glass of water. Evgeniy Koroleg was a major player in the Russian gas and energy industry. Of medium build and sporting a heavy moustache and a day's growth of stubble, he deliberately affected plain, off-the-peg suits and heavy-soled shoes. His general demeanour and manner of dress generally marked him out to strangers as a lower-rank manager in a manufacturing plant, rather than the powerful man he really was. It had proven useful in the past and allowed him to pass among competitors unremarked and overlooked . . . until he needed to turn the tables to his advantage.

He turned and stared out of the window across Kutuzovskiy Avenue towards Poklonnaya Hill and the Great Patriotic Museum. Right now he wasn't sure if being one of the most powerful yet unremarked men in Russian industry was likely to be of much benefit if certain things came to pass. Things such as the outsider Tzorekov being allowed to worm his way back inside the Moscow ring. For Koroleg and a few others like him, that could prove extremely problematic, especially if it resulted in a downturn in the sale of energy supplies due to aggressive outside corporations and investors being allowed to enter the game. While he could stand some of the effects of the sanctions being aimed at Russian businesses and ventures overseas, including his personal portfolios, he had come to rely on the status quo in Russia and in the surrounding countries still allied to their old giant neighbour.

'All our information points towards it being so.' The man on the loudspeaker console on Koroleg's desk was trying to sound relaxed, even unconcerned, but failing. His name was Broz Scechin, an FSB surveillance operative in London tasked with, among other duties, watching certain wealthy Russian business nationals who had moved abroad, to gauge their sympathies and future plans. He reported by order to his FSB controllers, but on certain issues and the receipt of payments, his actual loyalties lay with Evgeniy Koroleg. And the well-connected energy mogul's reputation for hard-headed business dealings was equalled only by his rough treatment of employees and others who displeased him or failed to meet his high standards.

'Then it must be so.' Koroleg finished the water. 'Tzorekov has been quiet for too long, happy to be making money like the happy capitalist he really is.'

'Of course, you're right. I—'

'Who else knows of this?'

'I have a technical assistant who provides the recordings and transcripts, but that is all he does. He takes no interest in these matters.'

'Make sure it stays that way. What about others?'

'I suspect the British . . . and possibly the Americans. They discuss such matters but I have no way of proving they have discussed this particular subject.'

'Never mind. We will soon know if they have done so.'

'Apart from them, I do not think it will become common knowledge. Tzorekov has kept a low profile for many years, so in spite of his background, he is not newsworthy here or in the United States.'

'Let us hope so.' Koroleg watched two drivers on the side of Kutuzovskiy Avenue having a heated discussion over a bent fender, and wondered how long it would be before a traffic cop appeared and settled it by a traditional example of Russian negotiation involving money changing hands, mostly to the cop. 'How did you come by this information?'

'By chance, from a phone conversation he was having with an unidentified contact. He mentioned going home . . . which I judged by the way he was talking to mean Russia. He sounded determined and intense. He said he felt he had a duty.'

'To do what?'

'He didn't specify. He mentioned only that he had to try to avert a confrontation, and how too many voices were pulling the world towards the brink of disaster. I can send you a copy of the recording, if you wish. The conversation was rather fragmented.'

'Don't bother. I believe you. But keep it in case I need it for later.'

'Of course.'

'Was there any mention of when this return might happen?'

'Not for certain, but it seemed reasonably imminent. The following day he made an international call to an unidentified number and asked for a location and a date. He didn't say why and the person on the other end seemed to know what he was referring to and ended the call after saying he would be in touch with the details.'

'That sounds like there is to be a meeting.'

'I think so, too.'

Koroleg nodded to himself. 'How long have you been monitoring him?'

'For the last three months, and on a few occasions before

that. His name is on a random watchlist with others. We check his phone calls and emails, but not constantly; there's a risk he has people who will notice too much regular attention. Until now there has been nothing in the transcripts to gain our interest – mostly business and family matters. But this seemed different.'

'How so?'

'He sounded . . . emotional. And there have been no previous discussions of a similar nature. I believe he has come to a decision very recently and is acting on it. There is another month of monitoring to go . . . unless you feel we should continue beyond that. We could, of course, go back over the recorded data to see if there was anything we might have missed. However, he keeps changing his passwords,' the man added quickly, 'so there are some gaps in our information.' His voice dripped apology, but Koroleg ignored it; the technical resources and manpower available were not unlimited and he wouldn't have expected anything less than such caution from a man with Tzorekov's background.

'Of course he keeps changing them. And he does not have to rely solely on "people", as you call them, to tell him that – he's KGB-trained from way back. Is there any chatter from among the community?'

There was a slight hesitation. 'You mean here in London?'

'Of course in London – it's where he lives, is it not?'

'Yes . . . yes, of course. So far we have picked up nothing.'

'In that case it proves he is planning something out of the ordinary, otherwise he would not be so coy.'

'Have you any specific instructions?'

Koroleg returned to his desk. He had much to do and a shortlist of trusted people to talk with. 'Yes. Bump Tzorekov's name from occasional monitoring to primary. Check his office computers and look for airline tickets outside his usual travel schedules. I want to know his whereabouts and movements day-to-day until further notice, but do not share this with anybody else. My eyes only, you understand?' The instruction was blatantly clear, in case the man on the other end harboured any doubts; he might be FSB with a clear reporting line to his superiors in Moscow, but he now had specific orders which meant he kept all mention of Leonid Tzorekov strictly to Koroleg.

'I understand.'

Koroleg hit the disconnect button and sat down behind his desk with a sigh of frustration and an acute feeling of discomfort in the pit of his stomach. There was a list of people who would not be welcomed back to Russia under any circumstances now they had left. Some were considered traitors with only self-interest at heart and were despised, their unwelcome back home made abundantly clear. Others were looked on as a direct threat to everything Russia was becoming on its way back to its rightful position as a powerful and prosperous superpower. In the eyes of a few well-placed individuals inside Russia with their hands holding the strings of influence, this second group were considered deserving of a fate far worse than mere loathing, as some had already discovered.

And then there was Tzorekov. Friend of the powerful and a man of influence still, yet with a disturbingly benign view of the West, if the stories about him were true.

He began considering a plan of action based primarily on an approach to life being one of prevention rather than cure. If he had to draw up a list of people who should never be allowed to exert pressure or influence on anybody inside the Moscow establishment – especially at the very top – then in Koroleg's opinion, Leonid Tzorekov had just earned himself the number one spot.

FIVE

'I have some conditions,' I said, once the silence had gone on long enough; once I'd digested the magnitude of what they were asking me to do.

'Conditions?' Sewell blinked. I guess he wasn't accustomed to field personnel trying to negotiate their orders. Except that I wasn't part of the CIA, so if I didn't like the assignment I could always get up and walk away. And he knew it.

'Let's hear him out,' said Tom Vale. He was trying not to smile and I figured a former field man like himself understood what I was thinking. Setting a few rules is never a bad thing, and going into an assignment like this without knowing the parameters would be crazy.

'Before that, where exactly will I be going?'

Sewell looked pointedly at Angela Thornbury, who seemed surprised at being brought back into the discussion. She shifted in her seat before saying, 'Um . . . we're not sure at this point. Mr Tzorekov is trying to confirm that information right now. As soon as we know . . . so will you.' She glared at Sewell, meaning it would be his responsibility to pass on the information.

'Why?'

'Pardon me?'

'Why is Tzorekov telling you? If he's going in the hopes of meeting Putin and making a difference, he must know this could end in disaster. He might never come out again. Does he expect you to lift him out if it all goes belly-up?'

'No, not at all.' She glanced at the other two as if for help, but Vale and Sewell were studying the ceiling and the table with great interest. 'He doesn't want his efforts to go public, but he wanted us to know what he was attempting to do. He firmly believes in this.' She shrugged and looked a little defensive. 'We have no idea what his deepest motives are, but we do believe he's sincere and want to facilitate his safe journey.'

'Sincere. For a former KGB man.'

She flushed a little. 'Yes. I suppose so.'

I turned to Vale. 'Does he know I'll be watching him?'

'God, no. I think he'd be shocked if he thought he was dragging a posse with him – especially foreigners. As Ms Thornbury said, he's doing this because he's convinced he can make a difference; Ms Thornbury and her colleagues have requested that we provide a covert backup to help in that aim.' He gave a chill smile. 'Not that I think he'd object too much if you did have to step in and help him out of a sticky situation. He knows the risks better than anyone but I doubt he has a death wish.'

As plans went it sounded a little loosely-packed, but I'd worked with far less. And this one had a greater benefit potential if it could be pulled off. 'Do we know if he's already in touch with Putin?'

Thornbury again, now on the relatively safer ground of political intrigue and motivation. 'Not directly. It's a very sensitive situation; Tzorekov is regarded by those around Putin as an outsider – a man who has turned his back on his country. It would be almost impossible for him to make a direct approach, and neither can Putin be seen to be talking with such a person. Tzorekov will have to use an intermediary close to the president and he will advise us as soon as he has confirmation of a safe entry. If he can, of course,' she added. 'Putin might refuse to see him.'

'What's the likelihood?'

'Fifty-fifty. But we have faith in Tzorekov's shared history and friendship with Putin; he knows as well as we do that Putin is being influenced by some very powerful figures around him. They're military as well as government, but there are a few very tough business leaders in there as well who are using economic and commercial arguments in favour of standing up against what they see as threats by the West. Putin is his own man, but there seems to be evidence that even he is in danger of being persuaded to take a much tougher line generally than is healthy for us all. If Tzorekov can pull him back just a fraction from being too confrontational, it will give us time to work on a wider diplomatic solution.'

So, jaw-jaw instead of war-war. Where had I heard that before everything went belly up because politicians thought it was a game? 'And if the meeting goes ahead?'

'It will probably be away from Moscow, somewhere towards Saint Petersburg, close to the border with Finland. Putin has a *dacha* in the area and holds some of his more private meetings there. It would be the most likely area for a meeting like this.'

'You're talking about the Ozero Cooperative.'

I saw a grin spread across Vale's face at Thornbury's look of surprise. Clearly she hadn't expected me to know about that, but I do read the newspapers, and had picked up a mention some time ago about a cooperative of rich men around Putin buying up sites around a lake – *ozero* – in the

north-west of the country. These were reputed to be businessmen and ministers who had all prospered in the new Russia
and on whom Putin relied for economic and commercial
support in building Russia's economy. Putin himself had a
house there, thought by some to be his own way of keeping
an eye on the movers and shakers on which he relied, and
making sure they knew it.

'Yes. The members are thought to be different to those of
the *Siloviki*, although it's almost impossible to be certain.
Undoubtedly there are some who share the same aims and
business interests.' She checked herself, then added as if as
an afterthought, 'There's a strong belief that apart from the
Siloviki and the Ozero Cooperative, there's a third grouping;
this one much smaller but just as diverse, which may include
selected members of the other two. They're rumoured to call
themselves the Wise Men and have connections in industry,
government and the military.'

'You make them sound significant.'

'That's because they are. If anybody in the Russian hierarchy
has a profound desire *not* to permit a meeting between President
Putin and Leonid Tzorekov, it will be this group. They don't
want the situation to be "normalised" or rendered anything
other than what it is. On the other hand, neither do they wish
to supplant Putin. He's the leader they need and they merely
want to steer him in the best direction that suits them. For the
same reasons I'm sure you've had outlined to you already, they
have too much to lose by Putin turning friendly to the West:
military budgets, defence spending and the supply of armaments and energy to the surrounding countries fearful of a
confrontation of any kind – all that would fall by the wayside.'

'They undoubtedly have investments outside their own
borders,' Sewell put in, 'being good capitalists at heart, but
not enough to make good any losses they could suffer at home.'

I nodded. I was beginning to lose interest, not because the
venture didn't wound worthy – it certainly did – but this was
entering the area of 'too much information' for the job I
was going to do. I got the impression somebody might have
ramped up the argument to sell this mission, and it was feeding
all the way down the line.

In any case, my decision was already made. I was in.

'I'll need to work with people I know and trust. I'm going to need good intelligence and first-rate comms backup.'

He lifted his eyebrows. 'For instance?'

'Brian Callahan and Lindsay Citera.' Callahan was a CIA Clandestine Service Officer, and knew all there was to know about field operations. He was sharp, incisive and didn't take needless risks with personnel in the field. So, too, was Tom Vale, but I was pretty sure he wouldn't be involved except in an advisory role. Lindsay Citera was a communications operator working with Callahan and had proved a real boon the last time I'd worked with her as my unseen 'voice'. She was smart and cool under pressure, and although fairly new to the task, she had proved to have an instinct for working at long range with an operative in difficult circumstances. She also had a sense of humour, which was pretty useful when the going got tough.

Sewell shifted in his seat and like all good administrators, tried to dodge the point. 'I don't think we can nominate any specific persons at this stage,' he muttered, and looked at the other two for support before adding, 'in any case I'm not sure they're available. We do have many other very competent people who can do just as good a job.'

'I'm sure you have.' It wasn't an acceptance and he knew it from my tone of voice.

After several moments, Vale said pointedly, 'Is it a deal-breaker?'

'Yes.' I wasn't being difficult; this wasn't a friendly country I was being asked to enter, nor was it a place I could easily blend in and move about at will. Russia is one of the toughest environments for outsiders to move in and possesses several highly efficient government agencies with a wide network of resources to call on. If the Wise Men Thornbury had mentioned were as well placed as she said, they probably had the resources to drop a net on anyone of interest. If they wanted a city or area closed down, they could most likely do it very quickly. I would need to know exactly what was going on around me and have absolute faith in the people I was going to work with.

Sewell looked hesitant but he could see this wasn't going his way. 'Very well. Callahan and Citera. Anything else?'

'No. Anything I need I'll source myself.'

'Like what?' Thornbury looked alarmed. I could see by her face that she was trying not to think about things that go bang and the possible consequences of somebody going off on a Rambo-style mission in the Russian heartland. Typical State Department; we want you to do this for us but please don't make a noise doing it in case we get embarrassed.

'Stuff. A vehicle, clothing . . . resources.' When she didn't lose the frown I explained, 'I'll have to go in light, so it'll be easier to get what I need over there.'

'Are you saying you have contacts there who can do that?'

'I do.'

'Who are they? Can they be trusted?'

I smiled and said nothing. Silly question; my life depended on trusting people to do what I wanted and not turn me in, and most of the time they didn't let me down. Maybe they didn't have the same ethos in the State Department.

But she hadn't finished grandstanding yet. 'Very well. I have a couple of conditions of my own. Under no circumstances are you to engage in any form of conflict with local forces, nor are you to come to the attention of the authorities. I understand you're accustomed to operating below the radar, is that right?'

'That's correct.'

'Good. Make sure you keep it that way. This mission is of vital importance and I don't want anybody taking the potential outcome lightly – and that will surely be a bad one if you should allow yourself to be compromised.'

'I don't think that's likely.' Tom Vale looked annoyed, but she waved a dismissive hand as if he were of no importance.

'The White House,' she continued grandly, 'wants this to succeed without any unpleasant consequences or adverse publicity. That means nobody can know that the US is involved in any way whatsoever. I hope I make myself clear?'

'Sure,' I said. 'Which would you prefer me to do if I am careless enough to get caught – take a cyanide pill or shoot myself?'

At that point Jason Sewell levered himself out of his chair

and said, 'I think we're done here. Brian Callahan will give
you a briefing as soon as we're ready for you to go. Ms
Thornbury, may I have a word outside?'

The way he said it and the look on his face made it an
invitation she couldn't refuse. As he walked out leaving her
to trail along behind, I wished I could have been a fly on the
wall.

SIX

Out in the cool air of the corridor, Sewell waited until
they were only a few steps away before turning on
Thornbury and fixing her with a cold stare that left
her in no doubt about how angry he was.

'Now, listen to me, ma'am. I have great respect for your
position and the desires and hopes of the White House in this
matter. But let me level with you: you may have an inside
track around the Oval Office, but out here in the real world,
we treat people a little differently. The man you've just spoken
to with such disrespect is highly experienced in conducting
covert operations in hostile terrain. He knows what the score
is and yet he will still do his job. I trust him and so do a lot
of other people around here.'

'That's as may be, but I have a duty—'

'I haven't finished.' He waited until she reluctantly clamped
her lips shut before continuing. 'The man sitting alongside
him, Tom Vale, who you seem to have ignored as if he weren't
there, has operated undercover himself for over thirty years
and has been inside Russia on covert missions more times
than you can even begin to imagine. He came to us with this
information, so talking as if this is entirely *our* mission or *our*
doing, is unhelpful in the extreme. In fact it's downright arrogant. We do not hold the only stick in this corn-beating contest
and we need men like Vale to remain onside. Both these men
know the consequences and importance of this venture; they're
intelligent and experienced enough to understand without being

told like high school kids on a fifty-cent tour of the White House.' He leaned forward and added softly, 'If Watchman can pull this off, we will all have cause to be very grateful to him and to Vale. So pissing them off is what we around here call counter-productive. I hope I've made myself clear on that.'

With that, he turned and walked away, leaving Thornbury in stunned silence alone in the corridor.

SEVEN

When it was clear neither Sewell nor Thornbury was coming back, I stood up ready to leave. But Tom Vale waved at me to hold on.

'Are you sure about this?' he said. 'Don't get me wrong, Marc, I'm not trying to put you off and we'd be crazy to pass up this opportunity of getting some influence over there. But this isn't going to be a stroll in the park. You know that, don't you?'

I nodded. If anybody knew about the risks of operating undercover in Russia, it would be Vale. He'd been there and done that and got the snow on his boots to prove it. 'That's why I need Callahan and Citera. They'll give me the edge I need.'

'I've been thinking about that. I might know of people with some local knowledge. If I can get hold of any useful information I'll pass the details to Callahan.'

'Thank you. What exactly is your role in this?'

He smiled. 'As low-level as possible if I can help it. We call it reciprocal trading. Two heads are better than one and so forth. But it helped that Tzorekov approached us first to test the water, and we brought the State Department and Sewell into the game.' He shrugged. 'I'm happy to let him do the running on support; he has the manpower and technology. But the simple fact is, we all stand to benefit by helping Tzorekov succeed.'

I let that one go, although I knew Vale was being modest. He and MI6 had some very tricky technology of their own, and some extremely capable people using it. But it was good to know he was there in the background if I needed some extras.

He must have read my mind because he said, 'Is there anything I can help with? Don't worry – nobody's listening, and if they are, what I'm offering isn't against the rules.'

'Good to hear. I guess, papers. passport, driver's licence . . . you know the stuff.' It was backup material, in case I had to change cover while in the field. Having a fallback position is always good trade craft and a boost to the confidence to know you have it in your back pocket if needed.

'No problem.' He paused. 'I'm not going to ask why you haven't asked Sewell for it; I heard about your last outing with them. A little unfortunate.'

A little unfortunate. There he was with his understatement again. It had certainly come close to the wire. A leak of information had nearly been the end of me in an assignment in Ukraine, not helped by a crooked senator in Washington who had an agenda against the CIA and an eye for making some quick money out of a bad situation. 'It's not Sewell I don't trust,' I said. 'Once bitten twice shy, is all.'

'Fair enough. What level of papers do you need?'

'A working stiff – maybe a low-level or supervisory role. If it's outside the Saint Petersburg area I'll need something that allows me to move around in that region. There's a lot of forest up that way.'

'Sounds good. They'll be with you by tomorrow morning.'

I realized by his smile that he was ahead of me; the job had already been done.

'Thank you. Why are you doing this?'

'Because we owe you. And the people in the Basement would never forgive me if I didn't make the offer. I can't extend it to supplying any operatives to come with you, although they'd do it in a heartbeat if I asked them. But I'm sure you know that, anyway.'

The Basement was a small team of special forces operatives working for MI6 – their hard action branch on call twenty-four-seven and similar to the CIA's Special Activities Division. I'd helped one of their men and an MI6 officer on a previous job and they clearly hadn't forgotten it.

'I appreciate that.'

He seemed to hesitate, then said in a soft rush, 'Just be careful, Marc. There are some very powerful people on both sides of this argument who want Putin to continue banging the war drum.'

'Why? What do they stand to gain?'

'If it goes too far, not a thing and everything to lose, God help us all. But in the short term, more armaments, increased budgets and a huge increase in military spending generally on all sides.'

It was crazy, of course, but I knew he was right. All wars, no matter how hot, cold, small or large, meant somebody somewhere stood to make a quick buck.

'Don't forget,' Vale continued, with a hand on my sleeve, 'no general or politician *ever* considered every consequence of playing this game a shade too far. They all thought they could control it down to the wire – but they never have. And some poor innocent has to pay the price.'

I thought he was about to say more, but a rush of voices outside the door signalled the approach of visitors, so he merely nodded. 'Come on, let's get you an escort out of here.'

EIGHT

I thought Leonid Tzorekov looked drawn and tired as he left the arrivals hall at Saint Petersburg's Pulkovo International airport and headed towards the exits. It might have been the lights, which cast a sickly aura over everyone, or maybe now he'd stepped off the plane and had solid ground beneath his feet – Russian ground at that – he was beginning to regret his decision to come back. If he was nervous, though, he was hiding it well enough not to have attracted attention from the watchful eyes of the Border Service personnel. Maybe being an older man, he'd got passed over as a potential threat.

Seconds later I spotted Arkady Gurov. He was trailing in his boss's wake by several yards and didn't look the part of

anybody's bodyguard. But as a former member of Russia's
Federal Protective Service or FSO, he'd have been well-trained
in how to keep a low profile and melt into the background.
He was pushing a baggage trolley with two bags on it, and I
wondered how long he was planning on staying. He moved
easily, with a slight spring in his step, and in spite of the flush
of other passengers, he was managing to stick close enough
to his boss without seeming to be with him.

Tom Vale had passed me the heads-up about their travel
arrangements from Heathrow, which had been via Paris and
on separate flights. From there they had gone to Frankfurt,
then taken a late afternoon flight to Saint Petersburg. They
could have travelled direct but I figured it gave Gurov a greater
opportunity of spotting anyone taking too much of an interest
in his boss. They were travelling on Israeli passports, which
Vale seemed to think was OK with him, and I didn't bother
asking how they had arranged visas; Tzorekov undoubtedly
had his own methods of arranging them but it gave me a hint
about how long he must have been planning this venture.

Vale had also told me a little about Gurov's background. It
seemed that several years ago, Tzorekov had paid for an
emergency heart operation on Natalia, Gurov's wife, followed
by a lengthy convalescence in a Swiss clinic. She had since
died but Gurov had never forgotten it and now seemed welded
to Tzorekov for life.

It said a lot about the bond between them, and the extent
to which Gurov might go to protect his boss. It was worth
bearing in mind if we ever met up.

They made their way to a car rental agency and I hung
around long enough to see Gurov indulge in a neat piece of
theatre. While waiting his turn, he began chatting to an older
man – Tzorekov – in the queue behind him, and found they
were travelling in the same direction. He offered him a ride,
which the old man duly accepted with a lot of nods and smiles.
The rental agency lost out on a second deal, but Russians are
generally an agreeable and friendly people, especially towards
the older generation, and nobody seemed to mind.

Gurov had bypassed the various family-type sedans on
the list and selected a dark green VW Touareg. It was an

understandable choice; tough enough for the roads in the region yet not so unusual that it would stand out if they were heading into the back-country around the lakes.

I'd arrived the day before and had my ride close by, along with a few items I'd arranged through a contact in Moscow before leaving home. On paper Yuri was in the tool and plant hire business, but the bulk of his real turnover was done beneath the counter and had nothing to do with construction work.

'No problem,' he'd said easily, when I got through. 'What do you need and where?'

I'd prepared a list and we negotiated a price and collection point. He expressed neither surprise nor curiosity at my requirements and where I was headed, but I hadn't expected anything less. He operated in the kind of world where showing too much interest in his clients' needs was a dangerous way to live. And since most of them lived and worked well outside the law and had their own ways of dealing with loose tongues, he was hardly likely to go telling tales to the authorities.

Yuri had fixed me up with a collection point in the industrial zone near the docks on the west of the city, where I'd also found a UAZ Patriot pickup with a small logging company's decals on the door panels. It had a lot of miles beneath the hood and a suitable collection of bruises to the bodywork, but in this region and especially out of the city, it would blend in perfectly. It also had a spare set of magnetic decals in the back and I could change the profile of the car within a couple of minutes if I had to.

All that, however, would have been wasted if I hadn't had the right level of paperwork coming through the airport. With modern technology, passing through identity checks on false papers is a high-risk venture. But it's not impossible if the preparation is right.

No border force can track a line back from a presented passport if the available supporting documentation is solid enough. For one, hardly anybody carries that much history with them on trips abroad. Even checking with a source-country's authorities takes time, because most forces don't have the resources to do it quickly unless they have a specific reason for jumping through all the procedural hoops required.

Just ask travellers who have been asked to prove who they are by some picky immigration officer; it's suddenly impossible to remember dates and details you had at your fingertips the day before.

But Vale had made sure I wouldn't have that worry. He'd got me a full, verifiable legend or history, right down to the bits and pieces, like a personal letter from my mother, an unopened utility bill I clearly hadn't had time to open on my way to catch my flight and a couple of photos in my wallet that were duplicated on my cell phone. The visa was bona fide and had been arranged on a just-in-case basis. I was going to switch to another set of ID once I got moving inside the country, but they'd be good for the duration of my stay here.

I gave the two Russians a decent lead and followed them out of the airport. They turned onto the main ring road around the city and headed east, crossing the impressive cable suspension bridge over the Neva River. The direction fitted what the CIA analysts had suggested was one likely heading, picked up from a mention of 'the lakes' in an intercept on Tzorekov's phone. The problem was, lakes were numerous to the north of Saint Petersburg, some of them vast, their numbers extending hundreds of miles to the north coast beyond Archangel and the White Sea off the Kola Peninsula. Exactly where these two men were headed was still unknown, because Tzorekov himself didn't yet know; hopefully that would soon become clear.

Until then I had to stick to them without being seen and wait for developments.

As it happened, they didn't go far. After a couple of miles they signalled and took an exit ramp. I slowed, keeping a couple of trucks between us, then followed. As I left the ramp I spotted their car pulling into the parking lot of a motel called the Solokna. It looked new and what they like to call boutique.

I found a spot nearby where I watched them carry their bags inside, then left my car out of sight and walked across the lot until I could see through the main entrance. Tzorekov and his shadow were walking away from the reception desk. I waited until they were in the elevator before booking a front room at a smaller hotel opposite.

It could have been almost any hotel area anywhere in the world, with lots of parking, exit and approach roads, suitably neat flower beds and that air of anonymity that exists in places where nobody actually lives and the turnover of people is constant and mostly private.

After checking the room I went for a stroll around the area, fixing my bearings in case I needed to make a quick exit. I was also wary of having tripped an alarm bell somehow on my own passage through the airport, and wanted to make sure I hadn't picked up a tail. But nobody stood out and I didn't get that buzz behind the ear when I feel I'm under surveillance.

Back in the hotel I ordered a meal from room service via the reception desk and settled my bill ready for an early start, then ate with one eye on the parking lot and the Touareg. If Tzorekov and his muscle had a change of plan and made a move, I needed to know immediately, otherwise I'd lose them before we even left the city.

For now, though, I had a way of controlling that. Once it was good and dark I took a small item from my bag courtesy of Yuri, and made my way across to Tzorekov's hotel parking lot. The Touareg was parked by a spread of bushes, but they weren't big enough to shield me if he happened to look out of the window. Fortunately the lighting was spare and if I was lucky I'd be there and gone in a few seconds. Then I had a stroke of luck: a coach pulled into the lot and parked up against the Touareg, effectively blocking it – and me – from the hotel.

The coach passengers were too busy piling off and grabbing their bags to be looking my way, so I stepped up close to the Touareg and leaned down as if I'd dropped something. The underneath of the vehicle was nice and clean, courtesy of the rental company, and the powerful magnet on the tracking device fixed itself in place with a soft clunk. I'd pushed it right up behind the muffler, out of sight unless they put the vehicle on a hoist or got down in the dirt and crawled around to make a comprehensive search.

That done I returned to my room and checked my cell phone, pulling up the app for the tracker to make sure it was working. If they took off now, I'd be able to see where they went and follow. I'd been told the tracker's battery was good for a twenty-mile range and twelve days of life, but I didn't plan on letting them get that far or staying around that long.

Before going to sleep, I checked in with Langley on my encrypted phone.

'Go ahead, Watchman.' It was the familiar voice of Lindsay Citera. I hadn't seen where she worked, but I knew it would be a small space full of monitors, speakers and a whole array of computer equipment that I neither understood nor wanted to. It would be oppressive to most people, lacking natural light and air and therefore mostly sterile, but it allowed the operators to focus their entire attention on the job in hand.

'I'm in place and signing in,' I told her, and gave her the name of both hotels and the description and number plates of my car and Tzorekov's Touareg. From this point on, Lindsay would be locked in to my moves twenty-four-seven and ready to respond. Her task was to monitor the area and the roads ahead once we were on the move, and to check news feeds and local intel chatter between the police, army and FSB. There were a few other agencies to be wary of but these were the primary causes of concern in the area I was about to enter. Any one of them might pop up on the radar, but as long as I kept my eyes open and Lindsay kept an overhead watch for traffic and movements, I wasn't too worried. We'd worked together once before, and in this game you learned to recognize a good connection when you made it.

'Likewise, Watchman. Is it bad karma to wish you luck, break a leg or stuff like that?' I could hear the hint of a smile in her voice and figured there was nobody else close enough to hear. Maybe Brian Callahan would have approved dropping the recognized formality for a moment but I wasn't sure some of the other stiff-necks in Langley would have felt the same way. For me, though, it was a welcome sound; I knew she would be on top of her game once we got going.

'Every bit helps. Thank you. Speak soon.'

I cut the connection and put my head down, instincts tuned to be up and on the move at a moment's notice.

*   *   *

As it happened, my instincts were on top of their game, too. Something woke me less than three hours later and I slipped out of bed and looked through the curtains. Some of the parking lot lights were out in my hotel and across the way, throwing several vehicles into patches of shadow.

I was wondering if it was a cost-cutting exercise on the part of the hotels' managements, when I saw movement on the sidewalk, near a patch of shrubbery.

A group of four men were huddled together apparently in conversation. But I'd seen this kind of scenario before. The men were in pairs, each one looking past the man opposite. They were checking out the vehicles in the parking lots of both hotels.

As I watched, one of the pair facing my hotel peeled away and walked across the parking lot. He stopped by my pickup and tried the door.

NINE

'Can we really trust this "Watchman" of yours?'

Jason Sewell suppressed a sigh of irritation. Angela Thornbury calling yet again. He thought he'd made the situation very clear outside the meeting at the front office in New York several days ago, when Watchman had signalled his agreement to shadow Leonid Tzorekov into Russia. But she seemed to be having difficulty getting the message and had been bugging him on and off ever since. He thought they'd covered every question she had to ask, from demanding detailed information about Watchman's background, which he'd fielded through Brian Callahan, the Clandestine Service Officer who would be running him, to seeking assurances he couldn't give about what might happen if Watchman or Tzorekov were intercepted by Russian security forces.

'I think you may rest assured that we're OK on the trust thing,' he said mildly, aware that this call, like all the others, was probably being recorded by Thornbury for posterity. If this venture did go wrong, there would be no shortage of names being thrown around in her risk-averse world of the civil service, with himself at the top of the blame tree. There wouldn't be any responsibility attached to Thornbury herself, of that he was certain. Few people got to be assigned to the White House without learning ways of sidestepping trouble along the way and knowing how and when to duck out. 'And he's not my man.'

'Well, I can't say I'm comfortable with it.' She sounded just as bullish as the first time he'd met her, as if all the decisions had been made unilaterally by him with no negotiation. It made him wonder who else was in the room with her right now, listening in as a useful witness if the dirt hit the fan and she wanted to show her hands were clean.

He didn't know Thornbury well, but he didn't have to; he'd been around Washington long enough to recognize the signs of ambition on steroids when he saw it. She was merely preparing the ground around her like all good politicos, for a potential crash of career-ending proportions – as long it was somebody else's career on the line.

'Is it the man you don't trust or the job we've asked him to do? Sorry – the job *you* asked us to arrange,' he amended bluntly. Record that and swallow, he thought savagely. It was mid-afternoon in Langley, Virginia, but still too early in the day for this kind of political skirmishing, and he had too many other fights to referee to waste time on this one.

'The man, if you must know. And why wasn't I given the courtesy of being introduced to him by his real name – I assume "Watchman" is some sort of code name? I asked around and nobody's heard of him. Frankly, I find these boys' games a little insulting.'

'Ma'am, in my line of work we often have to rely on, and place trust in, people we've never heard of before. It's not called the secrecy business for nothing – something you might care to remember while you're talking about people like him. And we don't use his real name for the same reason. So feel insulted if you must, but that's the rules. What's your point?'

Sewell wondered who she had asked and how openly. There was no shortage of back-office pretend spooks in the Washington arena, and he hoped she hadn't bandied the code name around like yesterday's news. Freelance operatives like Portman did their best work by staying in the shadows and not beefing up their image as some kind of celebrity action figure. Staying out of the limelight was how the good ones survived, and Portman was one of the best. Even Sewell had expressed some doubts about the man when he'd first heard of him, but he'd proved himself more than capable and reliable.

'Of course. I promise, I never mentioned it outside—' She was suddenly gabbling, taken aback by his obvious reproof.

'Instead of the White House,' he interrupted her, 'you might like to have a word with your own people in the Truman Building.' He wanted to tell her to get a grip and stop playing with people's lives, but armed as she was with the undeniable authority of the White House, he was forced to bite his tongue.

'Pardon me?'

'Try Ed Travis. I didn't see any reason to mention him before, but one of Watchman's recent successes was hauling one of your colleagues out of Ukraine at great risk to himself – but I'm sure you must have heard about that.' He was pretty certain she hadn't; the State Department was a big place, especially once you got a foot on the glittery trail to the White House and left ordinary duties behind. The least she could have done was checked some facts before voicing her doubts.

He fielded a couple more queries, then politely disconnected and pushed the phone away. Time to go check the troops – and put himself out of reach for a few precious minutes. He left his office with instructions to his secretary to hold calls unless it was from the president, and made his way down to the Operations Centre. At the end of a corridor, silent apart from the rush of air-conditioning, he found a smallish room where Lindsay Citera, Portman's comms contact, was sitting surrounded by a state-of-the-art collection of computers, monitors, recording and editing equipment.

It had been a while since he'd sat at this kind of desk and he was ready to confess that he had at best only a working knowledge of what each box of tricks did, so quickly was this technology evolving.

'How is it going?' he asked genially, and waved a hand

when the young woman made to take off her headset and stand up. 'Relax, relax – I'm just visiting, which is a euphemism for getting away from my desk and the darned phone. Any contact with Watchman yet?'

'Just twenty minutes ago, sir,' she replied. 'He's in the Saint Petersburg area and sitting on Counselor's location.' Counselor was the code name they had assigned to Leonid Tzorekov. 'It's—' she glanced at a digital clock above her monitor – 'twenty-two hundred hours over there and they've checked into a motel just outside the city.'

'Good to hear.' He turned as footsteps sounded in the corridor and Brian Callahan appeared. The CSO was tall and lean, grey hair cropped short and neat. He had a relaxed air about him but Sewell knew the man had a tight hold on every detail of the various missions he was directing at any one time. It had been Callahan's early confidence in Portman and Lindsay Citera that had persuaded him to let them carry this assignment through to what he hoped and prayed was going to be a successful conclusion.

'They chasing you for updates?' Callahan asked with a knowing smile. As a long-time officer he was well acquainted with the pressures that could be brought to bear on the agency, seeking details and reassurance that often weren't there to give.

'Something like that. You got everything you need?'

Callahan nodded. 'We're good to go.'

'Glad to hear it. This is critical, you realize that? Call me if you have to – no matter what.' With a nod to Lindsay, he turned and walked away back to his office.

Callahan watched Sewell disappear down the corridor and turned to Lindsay, who was frowning. 'Don't worry,' he said. 'It's his style – and he's covering our backs. If it wasn't him it could be someone who might not be on our side.' He studied some notes Lindsay had brought up on a separate screen. It consisted of details on two vehicles, the names of hotels and their location. 'You got all that from a brief conversation?'

She smiled. 'The cars and hotel names, yes. The hotel addresses came from TripAdvisor.'

He grunted. 'Good thinking. You planning to follow both vehicles?'

'If we can, sir, yes. The Touareg is Counselor's car. Watchman has placed a tracker on board. It's got a twelve-day battery and should be easy to follow from the air once they get away from the city.'

'Are the Pathfinders in place?'

'Yes, sir. In place and ready with the drone – and a route out across the border in case of problems.'

She was talking about a new generation of 'cloaked' and near-silent mini-drone, originally designed to track devices used for monitoring animal movements in the wild. Watchman would be following the same signal from the ground, but once the target vehicle was well clear of the Saint Petersburg area and into the open country, its course would also be monitored by a pair of covert operators from the British Pathfinder Platoon, part of 16 Air Assault Brigade, who had 'wandered' across the border from Finland ostensibly on a wildlife photography trip. Trained in covert activity and escape-and-evasion techniques, their task was to deploy and operate the drone to lock on the signal from the Touareg. From there they would feed back data to Langley via GCHQ – the Government Communications HQ in Cheltenham, England – in case Watchman lost the signal and needed help picking up their trail again.

'You haven't told Watchman about the tracking team,' Lindsay said.

Callahan shook his head. 'Not yet – and I'd rather not. He's got enough on his plate and doesn't need to know. Once we feel they've done their job we'll tell them to pull out; they're not there to get involved. Any questions?'

'This could be pretty dangerous for him, Port– Watchman, right? Being in Russia, I mean.'

'Potentially, of course.' He gave her a searching look and sat down on a chair nearby. 'Did I do the wrong thing, asking you to meet up with Watchman last time?' His voice was low. Concerned.

'No, sir. Of course not. What do you mean?'

'It was a risk worth taking, putting you face-to-face with

an operative like that. I had knowledge I wanted him to have without bringing him into the building, and you were the best person to give that to him. The fact is, Lindsay, support staff like you very rarely get to meet field operatives, and that's for a good reason; it's easier for them to interact at a distance, especially when the dangers are considerable, if they don't have any . . . personal knowledge of each other.' He raised a quick hand as she went to speak. 'I don't mean that in any unprofessional way – please don't misunderstand me. I guess we never covered this issue before, but maybe now is the right time. If you feel . . . compromised or conflicted about supporting Watchman in any way, I can re-assign you without impacting on your performance or professional standing here.'

'Sir, no.' Lindsay leaned forward and said, 'I'm good. I'm fine with this, I promise. I was just . . . concerned, that's all. The same as I would be with anybody else.'

Callahan gave a hint of a smile, his features softening. 'Really? The same?'

She returned the smile. 'Well, maybe a little bit more. But that's only because you teamed us up last time and Watchman was my very first assignment.' She shrugged. 'I do feel kind of . . . responsible, I guess.'

'I did that, didn't I?' He stood up. 'Fine. The partnership works. In fact it works very well.' He walked towards the door, where he turned and said quietly, 'Let's keep it that way.'

He disappeared upstairs, leaving Lindsay alone with the electronic hum filling the air and the distant murmur of other communications specialists like her, talking to their contacts around the globe. The sound made her realize once again the almost intimate nature of her work, attached by a tiny thread of electronic signals to another person so many miles away who had only himself and her skills to rely on.

The thought instantly brought Watchman's face to mind. As Callahan had said, it had been on his orders, in Washington. It had been a risky thing, coming face-to-face with and making real the somewhat detached human being she had been talking through the most dangerous of situations over several days.

But it had been a necessary meeting to pass on some vital information. And she had found him to be very . . . human. She hadn't known what to expect, having only recently gone through training with the CIA before being dropped into a situation where she had some responsibility for a man's life. Her knowledge of covert operatives, whether special forces or spies, had been limited until then to films, books and the occasional 'outed' intelligence officers who hit the headlines, and the scuttlebutt from other trainees wondering what real CIA spies were like. If she had expected to meet some kind of super-agent, a robot in a nice suit and with the personality of a computer chip, she had been pleasantly surprised. Portman had been neither of those. He had been almost . . . ordinary, and yet possessed of some inner energy, like the quiet buzz of electricity.

Partly because of that she felt conflicted about Callahan not telling Watchman about the two British Pathfinders. True, if Watchman knew about the two other men, and he was caught, they could end up being taken as spies. But she couldn't help wondering if Watchman wasn't the best judge of that. He was professional and knew the risks, as did the two other men.

She pushed the thoughts aside and began checking the equipment around her. No distractions, that was the rule. She'd found Watchman, or Marc Portman, as she now knew him, to be a pleasant, mildly funny and not a bad-looking man. But she also acknowledged that thinking of him as anything other than a professional operative was a strict no-no. He had his world and she had hers. And although they were connected by work for short periods of intense activity, mixing them in her own mind was something she was determined to avoid at all costs.

She focussed on familiarizing herself with the screens. So far she had researched the area stretching from Saint Petersburg to the White Sea and the Kola Peninsula, and as far east as a line from Archangel in the north to Vologda in the south. She now had live screens showing the terrain, localized maps and all roads, with whatever military or police bases she had been able to pull off current records. The area around Saint Pete was the most complex, as she'd expected, but out to the north and east, which was heavily rural and wooded, with a spread of lakes and rivers, not so much.

She had also pinged all known training facilities in the area where the Russian forces carried out winter survival exercises using the forests and lakes. None of them should present a problem for Watchman, but any hazards involving the Russian military were best avoided.

That done, she dimmed the lights and went to the camp bed in the corner and lay down, one ear listening for the first indication of a contact.

She smiled in the gloom, a thread of excitement running through her. This was her world now; a million miles away from anything she'd ever known before, in a job few of her family or friends would imagine or even comprehend. She felt an almost fierce sense of pride in working with Callahan and Watchman once more, in knowing that along the corridor, others like her were following the same procedures, harbouring the same concerns and tensions, anxious above all to not screw it all up.

TEN

I threw on some clothes and hit the stairs. If somebody was about to jack my vehicle, I'd lose that and whatever equipment I'd left in there. And it was too late to go hunting for replacements. By the time I got re-kitted, Tzorekov and his buddy would be long gone and the tracker would be as good as useless.

I walked past the reception desk, where a night porter was watching a small television and blatantly ignoring what was happening right outside the building. A camera monitor on the wall showed a nice view of some bushes at the side of the hotel, well away from the current action. He looked surprised to see me, then alarmed, his mouth opening and closing rapidly when he saw I was going outside. That told me he was in on the deal. I left him flapping and slapped the button to open the door, and stepped into the night.

The three other men had now joined the one at my car. One man moved to stand by the trunk, while another hovered by an Audi two spaces away and the fourth wandered off towards the outer edges of the parking lot with a cell phone glued to his ear.

It was a neat set-up and well-rehearsed, each man with an assigned role to play. On the signal to go from the lookout with the cell phone, the man by the car door would open it, the guy by the trunk would jump in, start the car and drive it away. The break-in specialist would then move on past the Audi and open an older Volvo next to it, and his pal would drive that away. All the time, the lookout would be ready to run interference on anybody who happened along.

Somewhere nearby I was betting there would be a car transporter, ready to take anything these guys could lift. They weren't playing sophisticated or going for the expensive vehicles; that was obvious by the way they'd ignored the Audi and a couple of BMWs in the same lot and gone for the beat-up but still very useful and saleable UAZ. These guys were working on quantity; quick to steal and easy to sell, they undoubtedly had a dealer lined up ready to move the cars on within hours of being lifted. It was the crude end of the business, but at six to eight cars in one sortie, all taken within twenty minutes, it was easier than stealing one high-end vehicle with anti-theft systems and a possible tracking device and getting peanuts for their trouble.

'Hey.' The international language of 'Hey, what the fuck are you doing with my wheels?'

The four men froze. They hadn't expected anybody to be up and about this late; even less had they figured on anybody challenging them while they went about their business. Hell, what idiot hotel guest faces down a gang of car thieves in the middle of the night?

The man at the door to my car was the first to react, but he was quite calm about it. Or maybe he didn't recognize real opposition when he saw it. He signalled to his pal by the trunk to dump me in the bushes and turned back to opening the door.

I let Trunk get right up close, then double-stepped and body-checked him low down, hitting him hard with my shoulder and lifting him off his feet. He grunted once and hit the ground on his head. He didn't get up. I carried on moving, which put me close to Door, who looked amazed to see I'd got past his pal in one piece. He spun round to face me, bringing up his hand, and I caught a glimmer of light shining off steel. A knife man. Luckily for me he was at a disadvantage by being between two vehicles, and couldn't manoeuvre for more space, which knife fighters like to do, if only because it looks good.

I waited for him to commit with the blade, slapped his hand aside and punched him hard in the throat. He gagged and tried to breathe, which is not so easy when you've taken a hit like that. For good measure I bounced his head off the roof of the UAZ and heard the knife clatter away in the darkness.

Two down.

A rush of footsteps told me the man by the Audi was coming in fast, so I turned to greet him. He was trying to untangle something from his coat pocket while he ran. I took that as a sign of intent and ran to meet him. It's the last thing an aggressor expects, especially when accompanied by a trio of buddies. It's simply not supposed to go down like that. He made the mistake of still trying to get whatever he was carrying out of his pocket while simultaneously throwing a wild punch at my head. That was never going to work.

I took the hand he offered and let his own forward momentum do the rest. He glanced off my hip and landed on his back with enough force to crack the concrete. To be fair, he tried to get up, but his body wasn't in it. Just to make sure I followed him down and slammed a palm-heel into the side of his head. He grunted and stopped moving.

Number four was nowhere to be seen, but I heard the sound of footsteps running away along the street.

I walked back to the hotel and found the night porter staring at me with his mouth open.

'You saw that?' I said. 'Any of it?' I pointed at the monitor, which still showed the bushes.

'No, sir.' He shook his head. 'Nothing. I see nothing, I . . .'

He stopped speaking, no doubt wondering if I was going to call the cops.

'That's good,' I told him, and stepped up real close, which made him shrink away. 'You keep it that way, you hear? Otherwise I'll come back and see you.'

He nodded, and I hoped he was more scared of me than he was of his pals.

ELEVEN

Evgeniy Koroleg was in an early-morning meeting listening to plans for the replacement of a new gas pipeline damaged by the fighting in southern Ukraine, when he felt his cell phone buzz in his breast pocket. He signalled for the others to continue and took the call. It was Broz Scechin in London.

'Yes. Speak.' At least this promised to be a little more interesting than engineering problems and broken gas pipes.

'Tzorekov has already left London.'

'What?' Koroleg spoke more sharply than he'd intended, and noted the sudden lull in conversation around the table. 'Wait one minute,' he told Scechin, and made a rolling motion with his hand to continue without him and stood up and left the room. Whatever else he did today, this would take priority.

Once he was back in his office he kicked the door shut and demanded, 'How did you not know of this before?'

'He laid a false trail,' said Scechin. 'He even fooled his office staff. He claimed he had a bad back and said he was working from home. But I now know he travelled from London Heathrow to Paris, then to Frankfurt and on to Saint Petersburg, arriving yesterday evening.'

'How?'

'I discovered the ruse when a security cop at Pulkovo thought he recognized Arkady Gurov leaving the arrivals hall. He knew of Gurov from a few years ago – they served together for a while. He had no reason to suspect Gurov of anything but reported it on his daily log as a sighting of interest, as he was required to do.' He added slyly, 'I took the precaution of having Pulkovo security office send me their daily summaries along with passenger lists and reports for the past three days.'

Koroleg ignored the hint for praise. The man was doing what he was paid for. 'And?'

'Gurov wasn't listed.'

'Of course he wasn't. The man's not an idiot – he'll be using false papers. Give me a minute.' He took a tour of his office to think, this time ignoring the view across Kutuzovskiy Avenue. This news had suddenly shrunk his world to a bubble within his office, pushing out all other thoughts. Where Tzorekov went, so did Gurov, he knew that. And what might have been a vague plan, an idle boast in the mind of an old man with mawkish dreams of his homeland and maybe an egotistical sense of his own position in the world, had now morphed into a reality he didn't want to contemplate. Yet he had to face up to it. There was too much to lose if he ignored it.

Arkady Gurov. He'd never met the man, but knew enough about his background from the extensive file he'd had built on Tzorekov and his entourage. Attached like a limpet to his boss's every move, he was almost the antithesis of the public perception of hulking KGB/FSB officers. Slim and boyish, almost effete, he looked unobtrusive and could no doubt slip by unnoticed in a crowd. Yet more by luck than skill, he'd been spotted by somebody who knew him. He swore, forgetting he was still holding the phone.

'Sir?'

'If Gurov is here, then Tzorekov is, also. They will have been on the same flight. If not, he won't be far behind. Find out what names they were using. Check the passenger lists from Heathrow through Paris to Frankfurt and Pulkovo and pull up any names appearing on all four.' He knew it might be a wasted exercise, since both men had probably switched to fresh papers by the time they left the airport. But any action was better than none.

'Yes, sir. Anything else?'

'No. Nothing. Thank you, Scechin. Good work.'

He disconnected and this time went to the window, finding

the breath sticking in his chest. Solving problems involving hundreds of miles of pipelines, of contracts and schedules and workforces in hazardous areas – all that was relatively simple compared to what he knew lay before him. Scechin had done as much as he was able in providing this information; but now Koroleg needed some bodies closer to home to do a different kind of job. This matter was in danger of getting beyond his means to deal with. He dialled a number and waited. It was picked up and a man's gravelly voice answered.

'You're not calling me to discuss the weather, I trust?'

'No. I'm not.' Koroleg breathed more easily now. The man on the other end of the line was a fixer by nature and an industrialist by chance. Built like a bear and twice as tricky, Victor Simoyan was one of the new breed, like Koroleg, who had found fortune inside the country rather than seeking more by taking their wealth outside. Simoyan ran one of the fastest-growing armaments development companies in Russia, and had the ears of those who mattered. If there was a person who shared Koroleg's own fears about the danger Tzorekov represented, Simoyan was one of them. A sudden reversal in the race to build more arms would see his fortunes crushed in more ways than one. He had invested heavily in new manufacturing facilities and there were rumours that he had been forced to borrow heavily from some highly questionable sources, of the kind who would not wait long for loan repayments to be made, no matter how well-connected the borrower might be.

Dead was dead, even in a fancy suit and a big office.

The positive side to Simoyan was that he had, over the past years, harvested connections running deep inside the military and intelligence world, and made no secret of his belief in taking action and not leaving matters to chance. Koroleg's reach by comparison was far more commercial by nature, while Simoyan could get things done that required an entirely different kind of contact.

'Well, don't keep me in suspense, Evgeniy. I'm not getting any younger.'

'The problem I told you about? It's arrived.'

'What?' Simoyan swore beneath his breath and Koroleg heard

a chair creak as the big man sat forward. 'That's not good. Where is he?'

'That I don't know. He was at Pulkovo yesterday evening with a man named Arkady Gurov – his security man. They could be anywhere by now.' Like heading for the lakes, he thought, and maybe one lake in particular. He wondered where Putin was and made a mental note to check the president's itinerary over the next few days. Surely the man couldn't possibly think of meeting with Tzor—

'It's true, they could be,' Simoyan agreed pragmatically, interrupting his thoughts. 'But all is not lost. They must have hired a vehicle from the airport. I'll have someone pull up the security videos from the rental agencies. That will tell us when and the plate number. He could have purchased a map – you know how sketchy satellite signals can be. It might give us a clue where he went.'

It was something Koroleg should have thought of; he could have used Scechin. But he was happy to let Simoyan deal with it; the man was clever and knew all the tricks. Thinking of ways of gaining access to information was as normal as breathing for him, and he would know who to go to without wasting time. If Tzorekov or his minder had hired a car, pictures of one or both will have been on a hard drive somewhere, waiting to be accessed.

Damn. Could it really be this simple? Was it a problem solved?

'I'll get a team together,' Simoyan continued. 'I take it we want him found, right?'

'Found, yes.' Koroleg felt almost breathless at the speed with which things were moving. From hearing the information provided by Scechin just minutes ago, to now hearing that a team would be assembled. A team . . . to do what? He really didn't want to think about that side of things, although he knew they would all have to, eventually. 'We should tell the others. Get their opinions first.'

'Share the responsibility, you mean?' Simoyan chuckled, and Koroleg had an instant image of the man, larger than life in his vast office, already building a picture of what had to be done and who he could trust to go with him. Simoyan could read minds like no other and understood the psychology of covert groups and the way they thought.

'It makes sense. You and I are not the only ones who would be affected by this.'

'What – that a certain person might be persuaded to have a reversal of attitude? Damn right we're not.' Simoyan cleared his throat as if dislodging Putin's name where it had got stuck. 'Very well. I will call them together for a video conference tonight – no, this afternoon. Make sure you come. I'll get Solov to attend in person as well; we need him to influence any doubters.' Simoyan's office was in an old printing works in the Mozhaysky District a few miles away in the suburbs. It was neither smart nor especially prestigious, but it was his own fiefdom where he liked to hold court and pretend he was a man of the people. It was also far enough out of the city to remain off the radar of news media and security people alike, especially useful for gatherings of the kind Simoyan was now planning.

'What is this team you talk of?'

'Four men should do it. I'll get them on standby. I know a few good men who are looking for work.' He grunted. 'Don't worry – they're highly trained and know what to expect. They're also trustworthy as far as it goes and . . . untraceable.'

'What does that mean?' Koroleg sometimes found Simoyan's convoluted way of expressing himself like listening to experimental music: painful and impossible to fully comprehend, and in the end, being not much wiser.

'It means what it says; they will do the job and disappear.'

'But we haven't decided anything yet.'

'Not yet. But we will, once I've spoken to the others. All we need to do then is give them the green light and let them loose.'

TWELVE

It was just after six in the morning when I saw a slim figure emerge from the hotel across the way. The sky was a dense mass of brooding cloud cover dumping a curtain of rain across the parking lot, making it hard to get a clear view. But

I recognized Arkady Gurov's walk as the bodyguard took a tour around the lot, checking the place out before walking across to the Touareg, shoulders hunched against the downpour.

I threw on a dark green waterproof coat and grabbed my bag, keeping an eye on Gurov as he checked the car over. He was good; he made it look natural, bending to check the tyres, at one point pretending to put his ear to one of the side walls as if listening to a slow puncture; but I knew he was peering under the vehicle for any additions made since last night.

He evidently failed to see the tracker and I gave a sigh of relief. He stood up, then opened the door and climbed in. A puff of fumes from the exhaust, followed by a single flick of the wipers as a signal, and Tzorekov walked out of the hotel to join him. Unlike last night the banker looked surprisingly spry and no longer shuffling along like an old man.

I had to give him ten out of ten for a convincing act getting through the airport.

Both men, I noted, were dressed in similar clothing; waterproof jackets and pants like those used by hunters and weekenders, walking boots with thick soles, and waxed caps. They were carrying small bags only, and I figured they must have kept a reservation and left their travel clothes at the hotel for their return trip.

By the time I got downstairs and out to my car, they were turning onto the access road to the elevated section of the highway. I watched to make sure they were heading up the ramp and not into the city, then followed at a discreet distance, merging into the mountain of spray being thrown up by the traffic thundering by.

I plugged in the phone and switched on the tracking app, and watched a little red dot heading east. For a while this might be the only connection I had with the two Russians, and I was anxious not to lose it.

There were lots of trucks about, taking advantage of an early start to circumnavigate the city before the smaller commuter traffic began to clog up the roads. That and the heavy rain made following the Touareg easy enough without being seen, but the downside was not knowing whether anybody was on my tail, hiding behind the spray blanking out the road behind me.

I focussed on the road ahead and decided that I couldn't obsess about what I couldn't see; that way was madness. If a tail did materialize I would deal with it.

Without knowing where the two Russians were going, I knew their choice of routes was fairly limited. Saint Petersburg was located close to the southwestern corner of the vast Lake Ladoga, more an inland sea than a lake. A number of smaller lakes were situated in the area, one of them Lake Komsomolskoye, where Putin and his friends had built dachas – the so-called Ozero (lake) Cooperative.

If they took the northern circular highway close to the city, it meant they were probably heading for the area west of Lake Ladoga which also housed Lake Komsomolskoye. But their actual destination could be anywhere to the north right up to the border with Finland, although I thought that was unlikely. As controlling as he was, Putin was in a difficult situation; if he did contemplate meeting with his old instructor and mentor, such was the paranoia of political states such as Russia, he couldn't simply disappear from sight for long without a lot of speculation from local and foreign media alike.

Tzorekov's alternative direction was to turn east along the E105 and head towards the smaller Lake Onega, swinging north from there. Either way led to a vast area of countryside and a limited network of roads.

Ironically, I realized that by a twist of fate, Vladimir Putin might now be in control of my future movements. Go figure.

A flash of signals up ahead showed through the gloom. It was the Touareg heading off to the east. At least they were moving away from the city, which was an indication that they now knew where they were going. All I had to do was stay with them and remain invisible.

As I followed them round the loop I dialled up Langley. It was time to give Lindsay a fix on our movements.

'Go ahead, Watchman. What's your situation?' Lindsay sounded alert and ready. It would be late at night back in her electronic bubble, and she'd probably been catnapping since I'd called in last night. But that was no substitute for real sleep.

'Currently heading east on the E105,' I told her. 'About eight miles to go before a possible turn-off to the north.'

'Copy that. Any developments?'

'Nothing yet, but I get the feeling they might have a destination in mind.' I was more convinced when I saw the Touareg pull into the outside lane and pick up speed, blowing a billowing wall of spray in its wake. I was pretty sure they'd done it for no other reason than to avoid the trucks, which weren't always being driven in a straight line. But I stayed where I was in case they were running a check for tails. I made sure to check my mirror as well, waiting to see if another vehicle would slip past or had slotted in behind me.

So far nothing doing, which was good.

'We have a note from London, courtesy of Tom Vale,' Lindsay continued. 'A known asset was seen checking out Counselor's London apartment and his house in Surrey.'

A known asset. That meant somebody working out of Moscow's London embassy. If they were checking on Tzorekov's movements, it had to be on orders from somebody at home, and was unlikely to be a coincidence.

'They know he's on the move. That's a pity.'

'Correct. We're checking with London to verify the source, but you should be aware that they will probably manage to track Counselor all the way.' She hesitated as if embarrassed. 'Sorry, I . . . you'll know that better than me.'

'No need to apologize. If you think something needs saying, say it.' The checking would be made by someone in the US embassy in London's Grosvenor Square or whatever other resources they had in place around the capital. They would send people round to all of Tzorekov's known haunts, his office and related workplaces, the aim being to pick up on anybody asking questions about his movements. Put a face to that person and they might get a line back to whoever was issuing the orders. It was an inexact science against a security apparatus well-versed to operating in secrecy, but the effort was always worthwhile because it offered the opportunity and hope of putting another face on the map for future reference. And you never knew when that might be useful.

It was part of the long game of counter-espionage and information-gathering.

I signed off from Lindsay and checked the road both ways. Traffic was beginning to thin out, but I still had plenty of cover. Hopefully Tzorekov and his minder, if they could see me at all, wouldn't concern themselves too much with a logging contractor's battered vehicle on the same stretch of road and heading into a region thick with forest.

A few miles later I had at least one answer about Tzorekov's journey: he ignored the turn-off to the north and continued east without losing speed. It meant he wasn't going anywhere near Lake Komsomolskoye and the area where Putin had his dacha, but heading instead round the other side of the vast Lake Ladoga and probably to the north. It was a huge land mass to be aiming at with few decent roads, and those that were there were often poorly maintained with few facilities, which was why I'd stocked up on bottled water, food supplies and fuel.

It made the task of following somebody very risky but I didn't have much choice. Wherever Tzorekov went, I was going with him.

THIRTEEN

We were approximately ninety mostly grindingly slow miles and four hours out from Saint Petersburg when I noticed Tzorekov's car beginning to waver, causing a bunching of the other vehicles between us. I figured he'd either detected something was not quite right or he was about to take a turn off the road.

I dropped back, pulling briefly onto the side of the road to allow a couple of heavy Kamaz trucks to go by. If Tzorekov had detected a presence, the trucks would do as extra cover until I figured out what he was up to. So far I had nobody obvious on my tail, unless the opposition were being cute and using trucks now as surveillance vehicles.

The road had dropped many miles ago from a four-lane highway separated by metal barriers, to a standard two-way road with heavy markings to show the edge of the blacktop. That and the continued rain had slowed our progress dramatically, although it hadn't prevented some crazy manoeuvres by truckers in a hurry, overtaking where death seemed a high probability. However, there was nothing much I could do about them but hope nothing would alert Tzorekov and his pit bull to my presence.

We were now moving through a long corridor of trees crowding the road, with a narrow gravelled shoulder on each side. A few wooden houses could be glimpsed dotted about in clearings whenever the rain slackened, but for the most part we were in a dark world of noise and tail lights, exhaust smoke, of giant radiator grills too close for comfort and the ever-present squeal of wipers and the hum of the heater trying to do a job against the odds.

Then I glimpsed a flash of colour through the gloom. It was a battered sign with a gas pump image. We were approaching a service stop.

The Touareg signalled to turn off. Beyond it I spotted an access road to a Statoil gas station with a restaurant at the rear. There were rows of big trucks and several cars, but nowhere was there sufficient cover if I followed them off the road. I was going to have to go on by and hope there wasn't a back road out.

I kept going, sticking close to a rust-covered truck with a low skirt that was throwing up a wall of spray. From the corner of my eye I saw the Touareg had slowed to a crawl just inside the access road, with a figure in the front turning to study the traffic going by.

I gave it ten miles before I pulled into a side road leading to a collection of small wooden houses, each with a patch of garden. I found a concealed gateway where I could keep one eye on the main road, then jumped out and did some stretches to loosen the kinks, before taking the spare decals from the back of the pickup and changing my profile from a logging company to a construction firm. The decals were fitted with magnetic strips, and fitted easily over the existing signage, including a third on the tailgate for good measure.

Next I went to the rear of the pickup and unscrewed the nearside tail light unit. In the body space behind it was a canvas bag holding a Yarygin 'Grach' 9mm semi-automatic and two spare clips. I took the gun out and replaced the light unit, then moved across to the other side.

The space behind the right-hand unit held a Saiga semi-automatic rifle with a wooden stock and butt. It came with a night vision scope and three spare magazines. It felt light and comfortable and I was hoping I wouldn't have to use it. I'd left it to Yuri to specify the type of rifle depending on avail-ability, as long as it was accurate and didn't look as if I was about to start WW3. Hunters in Russia are a common enough sight, especially those hunting grouse and blackcock. If I did get stopped with a rifle, even if I was slightly out of season, I figured offering an on-the-spot fine and having a nice polished sporting-style rifle would get me off more lightly than toting an all-composite plastic assault rifle with night sights, an extended magazine and a grenade launcher.

I put the Saiga back in its space but kept the pistol and scope tucked inside the door panel. I was now ready for what-ever lay ahead. I took a drink then hit the road again, but at a slower speed. The rain had slackened off, but the road surface here was bad, with the edges merging into the verge in a string of puddles, beneath which lay the potential for burst tyres and damaged suspension. More experienced drivers in the region had developed a habit of hogging the centre line, which was alarming to the uninitiated, especially when the vehicle coming at you was a ten-ton truck with battered front fenders. The additional worry was the constant clatter of loose gravel and crushed stone on the underneath of the bodywork, with larger pieces skidding out from other vehicles like shrapnel.

I was beginning to worry about where the Touareg had got to. The red light indicator showed me that it was some way behind me, but not moving closer. I slowed some more, in case they had decided to turn off or double back, and allowed a few vehicles to go by in the hopes of seeing them coming.

Then the picture changed dramatically. The tracking light began to move up fast on the small screen. Fifteen minutes later the Touareg came blasting by, lights full on and kicking up a storm of spray. I caught a brief glimpse of Tzorekov slumped against the door, head thrown back in sleep, and Gurov at the wheel. He didn't even spare me a glance.

'Watchman, stand by for an update.' It was Lindsay. I slowed and turned up the volume over the rush of road noise, and flicked my indicator for a following truck to get off my tail and go by.

'Go ahead,' I said, as he cruised by just inches away, the slipstream rattling the pickup like a dog shaking a rabbit. The passenger looked down at me from his perch and laughed. Maybe he had something against construction companies.

'I'm patching Tom Vale through. Please hold.'

A click and a buzz and Vale was on the other end. 'Sorry to burden your morning – I gather it's wet out there.' He sounded a little tense, in spite of the humour.

'What's up?'

'You heard about the asset checking out Tzorekov's place? We now have confirmation of a phone call from London to a Moscow number that they're on his trail. Pulkovo was mentioned, so you should expect company anytime soon.'

It was to be expected. Having a figure like Tzorekov go on the move without warning or detail would have sounded alarm bells for anybody watching him. After what amounted to years of private banking and commercial activity, all open to scrutiny like any other businessman, and little apparent interest in his homeland, having him and Gurov suddenly duck out of the limelight would have been instantly noticed. All it remained for me to find out was who was going to be involved and how good they were in chasing him.

'Any mention of where they were heading?'

'Nothing yet. I'll keep you informed.' He disconnected and I had Lindsay back on, this time with information on weather patterns over the next forty-eight hours.

'Rain,' she told me briefly. 'Lots of it. It's unlikely to lift for several days, according to long-range forecasts.'

It wasn't ideal, but there was good as well as bad. I didn't mind poor weather conditions so much; in the current situation, bright sunshine and clear visibility for miles could be a disadvantage. Keeping Tzorekov's vehicle in sight wasn't essential at the moment until the opposition showed up. Then a lot would depend on whether they were expecting him to have company and what their intentions were. I didn't think for a moment, after the briefing in New York, that there would be a welcoming committee. But they would be under orders from whoever was controlling them, and I doubted the decision to eliminate a figure like Tzorekov would be taken lightly. The fact that he was now on Russian soil would raise a degree of caution in some minds, no matter how opposed they might be to allowing him anywhere near Putin. But not all minds were so restrained. There would be some who would go for the nuclear option, which meant despatching Tzorekov and ending the problem once and for all.

'You might like to keep an eye out for air traffic in the area,' I suggested. 'They won't want to lose any time.' I was counting on the opposition not being local. Tzorekov's move had probably taken the Russians by surprise as much as it had everyone else, so having someone deal with the situation would mean bringing in people from outside.

'Copy that, Watchman. I'm tracking all light aircraft. There's a pattern of regular private flights and more regular military traffic in the region, but the bad weather has currently closed down a lot of non-essential movement.'

Well, that was useful. It might keep the bad guys off Tzorekov's back for a while, although if somebody really wanted him out of the picture badly enough, I couldn't see them adhering to any regulations. Getting up here by road would take too long in these conditions, so an overland hop, as risky as that might be in poor weather, was the most likely option, dropping them by air as close as they could to their target area.

'What about Impaler?' I said, using the code name we'd agreed for Putin. It wasn't the best I'd ever heard, but it would do.

A tapping of keys and she came straight back. 'He's in

Moscow at the moment. He's expected to attend a veterans' rally in the city tomorrow, with other ministers and military top brass. Immediately after that he's scheduled to take a flight to Kursk in the south to address army units based there.'

Kursk. That wasn't far from the border with Ukraine. But it was a long way from where we were now heading. It was probably a 'well-done, guys' visit to the troops in the south, for reasons I could easily guess, and Lindsay confirmed it.

'It's believed they were among some of the units used across the border in Ukraine. If true, they lost a few men. Impaler's been under pressure from some quarters to recognize their efforts without confirming to the world that they had used regular forces. This could be the first move. He's also visiting some oil and gas infrastructures in the area, and bolstering support among the locals. This is expected to take him over the next three days, according to an agenda released this morning.'

Interesting. If the plans were true, then it would appear to put any idea of Putin meeting with his old mentor out of the question. He could hardly be in two places at once. But given a fast flight and the might of the office of president, using a supposed and publicised visit to troops in some southern outpost followed by a detour to check out some energy pipelines in the region, would allow him time to disappear off the radar for a while without arousing too much suspicion.

It made me wonder whether he had, as some observers had suspected in the past, resorted to using a double to give himself maximum coverage in what was a vast land mass and a lot of fires to fight in a very mixed population. Saddam Hussein had elevated the practice to an industrial level, but Putin wasn't Saddam.

I signed off and got back to watching my nose and tail. Right now the machinations of the various parties to this picnic were unknown and therefore not worth worrying about. Being unseen and remaining that way was my priority.

Up ahead, a line of tail lights flared bright red in the gloom.

FOURTEEN

Leonid Tzorekov came awake with a start as Gurov
was forced to brake sharply. A line of red brake lights was
glowing through the spray some way ahead, lending the
trees either side a ghostly glow.

'What is it?' The older man sat up and rubbed his eyes.
'Why are you slowing down?' He sounded irritable, an
impatient old man scornful of their slow progress and his loss
of sleep.

'I don't know.' Arkady Gurov appeared relaxed, but he was
as watchful as always. He slid his hand towards the door
pocket where he had placed a GSh-18 semi-automatic. It was
loaded and ready to go, although the two men had had some
disagreement over having a weapon of any sort with them on
this trip.

'We are here to stop a war,' Tzorekov had protested, when
Gurov had first shown him the gun. 'Not start one.'

'I know. Don't worry, I don't intend to use it unless I'm
forced to.' Gurov's voice carried a tone of respect as always,
but there was also a measure of steel. His boss's safety was
his one and only concern, and always had been. He didn't have
to say how dangerous this venture was, because the old man
knew that perfectly well. But sometimes Tzorekov forgot what
the old country was like, and ignored what it had become.

A phone call before leaving Saint Petersburg had tracked
down a dealer and a time and location, and had taken Gurov
to the service area washroom shortly after entering the restaurant. He had returned after a few minutes, the gun heavy in
his coat pocket.

'I hope that does not happen. It's more likely to get us killed.'

'It's an insurance policy, that's all. You know the risks we
are taking.'

'Insurance? For what? Against what?' He sounded petulant,
as if unable to comprehend their situation.

Gurov had touched the old man's hand in reassurance, acutely reminded of his boss's age and underlying fragility. It was hard to see in a man he'd known for a large part of his life, when all he'd known was his toughness and resilience and sense of purpose. 'I can already feel them out there. They know we're coming.'

Tzorekov puffed out his lips, but said nothing. Then he nodded and gripped Gurov's hand in return, as if confirming his utter faith in the younger man, who was like a son to him. If Gurov thought he needed a weapon, the gesture said, then so be it.

Gurov dropped the window and leaned out. He couldn't see much through the haze, just a vague line of vehicles crawling along, tail lights flickering, and the same plunging rain that had dogged them ever since their arrival. Then he saw a flashlight being waved and figures in uniform walking down the road, peering through vehicle windows. They were armed, he could see that, but their insignia was impossible to distinguish at this distance.

'It's either police or military,' he said calmly, and pushed the gun out of sight.

'Out here? What can they want?'

Gurov shrugged. There could only be one kind of authority out here: military or intelligence. They were the same thing, really. 'It's probably a security exercise. Relax – they're not interested in us.'

The line of traffic slowed to a stop and the Touareg was quickly enveloped in a new haze, this of exhaust smoke from the stationary line of vehicles. Gurov switched on the air-conditioning to keep the cabin free of the diesel fumes being belched out by a large haulage truck immediately in front as the driver kept stabbing at the gas pedal to keep the engine turning over.

The first figure arrived alongside and peered into the car. He was dressed in dark camouflage gear and carrying a subma-chine gun across his chest. Gurov recognized the model as a Vityaz-SN with an extended magazine. The man wore the badge of a military police unit.

Gurov dropped the window. 'Problem?' he asked.

'There's a deserter on the run in the area,' the soldier replied, peering past Gurov's shoulder to check the rear seats and footwell. 'We're trying to make sure he's contained and doesn't get away. There's no need for alarm.'

'What did he do, this man?'

'He ran away – it's what deserters do. Only this one raped a fifteen-year-old girl first. Where did you begin your journey?' The soldier stared past Gurov at Tzorekov, who ignored him. 'And what's your business in this area?'

Gurov almost told him Finchley Park in north London, but stopped himself in time. 'Saint Petersburg,' he said instead. 'We're on a last camping trip.' He gave a brief nod towards Tzorekov who had turned his head away, and touched the side of his own head.

The soldier pulled a sympathetic face. 'Shame you didn't choose better weather for it, then. Have fun. By the way, the guy's desperate so don't pick up any hitchhikers. Before you go, I need to check the back of your vehicle. Is it open?'

'Help yourself,' Gurov replied. 'It's only our gear. Forgive me if I don't get out, though.'

He watched in the side mirror while the soldier walked to the rear of the car and opened the door, and moved their bags aside to make sure nobody was hiding there. Moments later he slammed the door and waved them on, then turned and strode along to the next vehicle in line.

'Do you believe that rubbish?' Tzorekov muttered sourly, turning to look back as the traffic moved forward and picked up speed. They passed several soldiers standing on the verges either side, most of them looking bored and wet. 'This many men for one deserter?'

'What else do you think they were doing?' said Gurov. 'If it was us they were after, why would they let us go? Anyway, there are training camps in this area; there's always one bad apple in a hundred men.' He nudged the old man's knee, aware that the tension of this trip was making his boss see dangers at every turn, even while objecting to Gurov taking basic precautions on their behalf. 'You're a suspicious cynic, you know that?'

Tzorekov sniffed and wiped away a film of moisture on the

car window. 'Maybe I am. Are you saying you don't think they will try to stop us – that there are those who won't feel threatened if Putin is persuaded to soften his stance?'

Gurov said nothing. He knew the tone of voice too well. A response wasn't expected.

All the same, he had a pinched feeling in his gut that the ball had been set in motion. As sure as the sun set in the evening, somebody, somewhere, if they weren't already on the move, would shortly be on their way to intercept them.

Behind them, the soldier checking the traffic told the next driver in line to stay in his cab, before walking to the tailgate. Once he was out of sight he took out a cell phone and dialled a number. It was answered after three rings.

'Report.'

'They're on their way through,' the soldier said, and recited the licence plate number. 'A green Touareg. The tracker's in place.'

FIFTEEN

Four hundred miles away in the Golyanovo District of Moscow's north-eastern suburbs, four men were gathered around a table in a rundown, first-floor apartment. In the street outside, the squeals of children could be heard, and the relentless, high-pitched whine of a starter-motor failing to catch echoed up right beneath their window.

'Why doesn't that dickhead give it a rest?' muttered Andrei Kruglov. 'It's never going to start, even I know that.' He was sitting with shoulders slumped, staring into an empty glass that had been full of vodka, and rubbing the side of his head against a blinding hangover from the night before. Lean and hungry-looking, he had a shaved head and the small stylized tattoo of a parachute on the side of his neck.

'You could always lean out the window and toss an egg under the hood,' said his close friend and 'twin', Jacob Ignatyev.

'I'm sure I've got an RDG-5 around here somewhere. That would get it moving.' He was referring to the Russian hand grenade, which all four had used many times in their military careers.

'Listen up, children.' The man at the head of the table, a tall and imposing figure with broad shoulders and a beak of a nose, snapped his fingers twice. His name was Alex Chesnokoy, a former master sergeant, and it was his customary signal for a briefing. The other men stopped talking immediately. 'Good news: we have a job to do.'

'Great,' said the fourth man, a squat, bullish individual with a widow's peak and dark, intelligent eyes. His name was Georgi Gorin, a former junior sergeant but now, like the others, unemployed. 'I could do with some work.'

Each of the four men had been together for a long time. They had been released from their original units to serve in the 3rd Spetsnaz Brigade based near Stavropol in the south west. After serving in several conflict zones, including Africa and Chechnya, they had now left the military looking for more lucrative contract work outside. So far, that had led to precious little that didn't involve working for one of the many mafiya gangs in the country.

'Damn right.' Kruglov tapped the table and sat upright, eyes gleaming in spite of his hangover. 'Who are we taking down?'

'Who said we were taking anyone down?' Chesnokoy queried. 'Did I say that?'

'Well, why hire us otherwise?' Gorin murmured with a knowing grin. 'If it was for anything less they could use a bunch of women.'

Chesnokoy smiled indulgently. 'You're a cynic and a sexist, Georgi. But you're not wrong.'

'I knew it,' said Ignatyev. 'Tell me it's some jihadi bastard. I could do with taking one of them out. Every one counts, right?'

Chesnokoy waited for silence, then said, 'It's not a jihadi. And it's not one target, but two.'

'Same difference. Twice the fun. Who are they?'

'How about former KGB?'

A stunned silence. Then Ignatyev shrugged. 'That's cool.

I've never dropped a KGB thug before. Is it anyone we know?'

'No. Not unless you're a lot older than you look.' He handed each man a sheet of cheap photo paper showing a series of monochrome shots of two men, one old, one young. They were full-facial and side shots, and looked like file photos from military service records. The last ones were different; they were in colour and had clearly been taken in the street by a covert camera, and both men looked slightly older. 'Their names are Tzorekov and Gurov. Tzorekov is the main target and used to be an instructor in the old KGB. The younger one, Gurov, looks like a ballet dancer but don't be fooled; they say he's very good at what he does.'

'And what is that, exactly?' said Gorin. He was staring at the photos as if to commit them to memory.

'He's Tzorekov's bodyguard.'

'You're right, boss,' said Kruglov, tapping the photos. 'Gurov's a shuffler. Put him in tights and a frilly shirt and he'd be a lead in the Bolshoi.' He shrugged at the looks from the other three. 'I read books, OK? You clowns should try it some-time – you might learn something before you die. Oh, I forgot, you can't read.'

'Enough.' Chesnokoy said softly. 'These are serious people. Make no mistake, you sad bastards are going to have to be on top of your game for this job. You hear me?'

They all nodded. Chesnokoy had never been known to exaggerate or underplay an opponent's skills or capabilities. If he said they were good, you had better believe it.

'So, just because one target is old and the other looks soft, doesn't mean we take them for granted. Remember they will have had tough training and they won't have forgotten it. Once KGB, always KGB. If you screw up, they'll send your balls back home in a plastic bag.'

'They'll need a big bag for mine, then,' muttered Ignatyev, clutching his groin with both hands and grinning lewdly. Kruglov sniggered in response.

'There's one other thing. This job pays top rates – better than top rates, in fact. But it carries one specific condition: we all have to disappear afterwards. For a long time.'

The silence lasted a lengthy few seconds as each man considered the implications of that statement. None of them was married – or, at least – not with any great conviction, and their homes were wherever they happened to put their heads, like this squalid apartment which had been sub-let while the official tenant was in hospital. But disappearing for a long time? That was an unusual demand to make of anyone.

'Like where?' said Gorin. 'And how long is long?'

'Where you go will be up to you, and however far the money will take you. As for how long, you should think about retiring . . . while you still can. On the other hand, if you have a low boredom threshold and a hunger for more action, you could try taking a job with one of the American security contractors. They're always looking for gun-fodder.'

Gorin glanced at the others. He hadn't said much but he was looking serious, the thinker of the group. He put a finger on the photo and said, 'If the payment you're talking about is big enough to take us away for a long time,' he said quietly, 'and presumably overseas, if I read you right . . . that's a ton of money.'

Kruglov leaned forward. 'So what? That's good, right? At least we can get out of this dump and a dozen others like it.'

Gorin shrugged, conceding the point. They'd all had a tough time since leaving the military. In uniform they had been accorded the respect they had earned in tough campaigns, and regarded by other units with something approaching awe. Here they were nobodies. He looked at Chesnokoy. 'So who are these two really, Alex? I mean, if the money's so good, what's their status? Are they related to somebody very important, or what?'

Chesnokoy said nothing for a long while. Then he said, 'I was told only as much as I needed to know – which wasn't much. But reading between the lines, I got the feeling these two are a threat of some kind, and we have to stop them in their tracks.'

'A threat to who?' asked Gorin.

'That's what they didn't tell me. But what difference does it make? When were we ever given the full story instead of a line of bullshit and told to follow orders? At least now we're being well-paid for doing what we're told and not asking questions. Are we all in or not? If so, we need to move right now.' He stood up and waited.

'Fuck it,' Ignatyev muttered softly, his tone sombre. He got to his feet and slapped his friend Kruglov on the shoulder. 'What else are we going to do with our lives – join a biker gang and wear tin helmets and leathers? Fuck that.'

Kruglov shrugged and stood up. 'OK. But where do we go afterwards? Have you thought about that?'

'Anywhere you like, my friend. Personally, I've always wondered what South Africa was like at this time of year.'

SIXTEEN

B y the time I got to see past the fat rear-end of the truck in front of me, with the driver holding the centre of the road trying to see what was causing the hold-up, it was too late to back out. And turning around at this point wasn't an option.

An armed soldier was walking down the line of traffic, checking each vehicle. Beyond him a couple of others were tailing him at a distance, with others standing at the side of the road. They all looked primed and ready for something to kick off.

Logic told me that whoever or whatever these men were after, it couldn't be me. It was unlikely to be Tzorekov, either; it was way too soon for the news of his arrival to have got out and to have activated this kind of response. In any case I doubted whoever wanted to stop him meeting with Putin would have involved the military, no matter how much pull they had. It would have raised too many questions. Or maybe I was underestimating the opposition.

My guess was, any interference thrown in Tzorekov's way would come from forces unconnected with any machine of state.

I made sure the door panel hiding the pistol was secure and waited for the first soldier to stop and look in the car. He did so without acknowledging me, but gave my face the once-over for good measure, with no flicker of emotion. I didn't offer to talk and he didn't look receptive, anyway. He moved to the rear of the pickup and checked it out, his free hand resting right above where the Saiga was hidden. Finally he nodded and walked away to the next in line.

Five minutes later I was on my way again. It was slow-going in the stack of vehicles, but at least we were moving. My only problem was, the red light that should have been showing the Touareg's position was dead. Either the signal had died temporarily or the Touareg was out of range. I put on speed, pushing past three trucks in line and earning a wailing air horn of frustration as I went by. I shared their feeling, but there was little I could do other than keep going and put my foot down. In the short time I'd been detained in the tailback, the traffic had got strung out like beads on a string and the faster-moving Touareg was long gone.

I called up Lindsay.

'Go ahead, Watchman.'

'I need a fix on the Touareg,' I told her. 'We got separated by a military roadblock. Any ideas?'

'I have them on the screen, Watchman. I'd say about thirty-five miles ahead of your location and travelling fast. Are you in the clear?' She was referring to the roadblock.

'Yes, I am. What's the other traffic like? They were several places in front of me until now.'

'They have a lot of traffic behind them and a reasonably clear road ahead.'

'Thanks for that. Listen, I have another question. Wherever Counselor is going, it has to be somewhere specific and safe for meeting up with somebody. He probably doesn't know where that is yet, but somebody on our side might have that information . . . or at least might know somebody who does.'

'I understand. I'll get on it. Do you have someone in mind?'

'Tom Vale. The British have been operating here for years, both commercially and in other ways. They have people who probably know the area well. Ask him for me, will you? The more I know about likely meeting places around here, the better.

Counselor is currently heading north, and I get the feeling it won't be any of the obvious locations. Callahan will know what I mean. Wherever this is going down – if it is going down – it will be somewhere quiet and away from the usual spots. It means a location the main man would know about but not his entourage.'

'Copy that. I'll call Vale now. He's here in New York so he'll probably want to call you back himself.'

I thanked her and disconnected, then focussed on driving. Tzorekov and Gurov had done the clever thing and used the impact of the roadblock to pile on the speed once they were free and clear, and to power past the slower trucks the same way that I was doing now, only a lot further back. I wondered why they had shot ahead. If they had a definite destination in mind, it was either still quite a way off, in which case they were simply getting impatient, or something must have spooked them into putting a foot on the gas.

Yet speed at this point made no sense, if what Lindsay had said earlier about Putin's agenda was correct. I was willing to bet the Moscow veterans' parade was carved in stone, since there would be too much to lose for Putin to show disrespect by not being there. Even if he cut short the visit to the troops in Kursk, I doubted he'd be able to make it to this region until the day after tomorrow.

But that left a whole lot of north-western Russia for a potential meeting place. And something told me it would not be where any of us expected.

I decided to risk it and keep up the speed. If the two men got too far ahead of me, without the tracking signal I'd never find them again in this vastly wooded region. Searching side turnings and tracks in the hopes that I'd happen on their trail would take forever, and with the light soon beginning to fade, that would be a no-go, anyway.

And all the time whatever opposition forces might be on their way here to stop them would be getting closer and closer.

It took over an hour for the tracker light to come on again. When it did, it showed the Touareg was just a few of miles ahead of me and not moving.

I slowed down. If they were doing what I suspected, they'd have stopped to check their back-trail. Both men would have been well aware of what they were up against coming here, and after travelling at speed to get this far, they must have begun to wonder if it could really be this simple.

A lot of the earlier traffic, just like the rain, had thinned out by now, and the road itself, once again bordered by acres of dense conifers on each side after miles of near-open countryside and a broad river crossing, had developed occasional wider stretches of verge. It opened the surroundings to more light and the less oppressive feel of travelling in a long tunnel. I'd passed two small truck pull-ins and a police post, the former temptingly near to getting me in for a quick coffee and some food, the latter less so, but I decided to press on. With the rations I had on board, I wasn't about to starve or dehydrate.

I checked the map, which showed a turn-off to the left. It ran north-west towards the eastern shore of Lake Ladoga and a town called Olonets. From there the road ran all the way north to the top of the lake before veering north-east towards what would ultimately become the Kola Peninsula, or cutting off west again towards the Finnish border crossing near Nirala.

If Tzorekov was playing very cute, he might be close to doubling back by going right round Lake Ladoga counter-clockwise and eventually reaching Lake Komsomolskoye – which was where he might have been heading all along. But somehow I didn't get that feeling. They had now spent several hours on the open road, all the time vulnerable to interception if the opposition had got their asses in gear. By heading direct for the suspected meeting place – if that's where it was going to be – they'd have been able to get close and off the road with plenty of time to sit it out in relative safety and wait for the signal to go in.

I looked at the tracker. It showed the Touareg was ahead of me by a couple of miles but now moving at a consistent rate. It was almost on top of the turn-off and I had a side bet about what they would do, hoping it would be to stay on this road. I slowed some more, giving them plenty of space.

Seconds later they were passing the turn-off and continuing north. I'd won my bet.

SEVENTEEN

'Gentlemen, welcome. Can you all hear me?' Victor Simoyan's voice echoed around the large boardroom of his commercial premises in the Mozhaysky District of Moscow. He was seated at a table, a large oval structure of old but polished European oak big enough to host thirty places with ease, a relic from when this building was a workers' cooperative. The room was easily the most impressive part of the premises, guaranteed to show customers that he valued their comfort while they were here, while not overloading his prices to pay for unnecessary spending on areas that did not call for it.

Right now he was facing the far wall some thirty feet way, on which was a giant screen split into twelve squares. Each square held the face of a man, each dressed in a smart suit and tie, and nodding in confirmation.

On one side of Simoyan sat Evgeniy Koroleg, nursing a glass of whisky and a two-day stubble, while on the other was Lev Solov, the country's deputy defence minister, a man with a narrow face, slanted eyebrows and a widow's peak which detractors had suggested gave him the appearance of a bird of prey.

The twelve men on the video screens were a disparate group from all over Russia, each with his own perspective of what was important in life, which was why Simoyan had struggled to get them all together this afternoon – or rather, this evening, he reminded himself, checking the fading light outside the windows. Still, they were all assembled now, and he could enlarge on the plan he had outlined earlier, person by person, to gauge their responses and see who was likely to be in disagreement. So far, none of them had.

They called themselves the Wise Men, and between them controlled large sections of the fabric of the Russian economy and structure. There was Solov from the defence ministry,

Koroleg in energy and gas, and others holding key areas in the military, manufacturing, technology, telecommunications, banking, aircraft and armaments. All had become wealthy and influential in the new Russia – and all wished to stay that way.

Which was why they had been called together.

Every one of them, thought Simoyan, had assets and futures to protect, and were unwilling to allow anyone – especially an outsider like Tzorekov – to spoil their game by influencing the most powerful man in the land to allow a situation that would see a reduction of spending on military equipment and energy supplies.

'You have all heard,' he began, 'about the traitor Tzorekov's decision to return to Russia in what we believe is an attempt to influence those above us in their decisions regarding the current course on which our country seems set.'

They all nodded, heads moving in unison on the screens. It wouldn't have escaped anyone's attention that he had carefully avoided mentioning Vladimir Putin's name, but that was clearly who he meant. He had already shown them his seriousness by allowing them to watch while his head of security had swept the room with an electronic detector – a device with which they were all well-acquainted in their own lives – to set their minds at rest. Equally, he had pressed each man to do the same in their locations, and had reminded them to be doubly careful about using certain key words or names during this discussion.

'Our latest information is that he has had contact via an intermediary here in Moscow with one at the heart of government, the plan being to meet face-to-face.'

'Where?' The first to speak was Solov, alongside him. 'And how does he plan to do this – by magic? A cloak of invisibility?' He chuckled, drawing an echoing response from the others. 'Has this Tzorekov turned himself into Harry Potter?'

Simoyan didn't rise to the bait. Solov was a political performer and was well known for playing the clown. But he carried a lot of weight and rubbing him up the wrong way would be a major mistake. Let him have his laughs; it was safer to let the tiger roar than take him on by sticking an arm into his mouth.

'We don't know where yet. He is at this moment in the company of one Arkady Gurov, another former KGB officer, proceeding north from Saint Petersburg to a destination so far unknown. But it's clear to us that he is doing so in the knowledge that a meeting is on the cards. There has been mention of "the lakes", but that could be anywhere within five hundred miles and as you know there are hundreds to choose from.'

'Could it be *the* lake, do you think?' This from Andrei Maltsev, the oil and telecommunications mogul. It was known by his colleagues that he had invested in a *dacha*, although not alongside the Ozero Cooperative, on Lake Komsomolskoye, to which he was referring. His holiday home lay on the shores of another stretch of water a few miles away, less prestigious but still protected from the encroachment of the lower classes. As a business competitor had once remarked slyly in his presence, eliciting his lasting hatred, 'Close, Andrei . . . but not close enough.'

'We think not. It would be too obvious – which is a good thing for us. There are security personnel constantly monitoring the area, which would be problematic for anything we may have to do. Tzorekov is not an unknown figure and word would get out sooner or later. If we intend to stop him, it's going to happen somewhere else.'

'You've talked before about this situation,' said Oblovsky, a former KGB man, now an arms dealer. 'We all know the dangers for us as individuals if the current situation changes. But how do you know Tzorekov will try to . . . affect such a change? He's only one man – and still an outsider.'

Simoyan flicked a hand at Koroleg for support.

'We know because he has been heard talking about it,' Koroleg supplied. 'We have transcripts and recordings of telephone conversations. We also know – and you, I suggest, Dmitry must know – how close the two men are.'

'They were, once, that is true,' Oblovsky agreed. 'But now, who knows? Situations and loyalties change.'

'Dare we take a chance on doing nothing?' asked Alexander Kushka, a military consultant and entrepreneur. 'If they have come to the situation already where a meeting, however improbable it might seem, is actually possible, then we are already some way along the road, are we not?' He scowled. 'Wait for the enemy to get too close, and very soon you may become their guest – or worse.'

Solov grinned. 'What's that, Alex – Sun Tzu and *The Art of War*?'

'No, Lev. It's bitter experience.' Kushka gave a smile, his face suddenly genial. 'Of course, I could quote you some better ones if you wish.'

'Let's not,' Simoyan murmured quickly. 'We have a decision to make.'

'Why so hasty?' Maltsev asked. 'This could all be a fuss over nothing. If they are friends, then they have at least a right to meet up, even if we find one of them . . . distasteful.'

'Because we could talk about this for ever, Andrei, and not find a solution until our pants were down around our ankles.' He breathed deeply, then said, 'We stop him or we let him go. Yes or no.'

So far nobody else had spoken. That could be good or bad. They might be either for or against any action to stop Tzorekov, or undecided, waiting to see how the majority would go. As in all groups, there were followers and leaders. He decided to push them.

'You all know the problems we might face,' he said. There is only one way to secure our situation for certain, and that is by taking action before it's too late. Now, who is in . . . and who is out? I need your votes.'

He waited as they made up their minds. Even at this point, when they had clearly all decided on a course of *potential* action, which, God knows, was dangerous enough, he could sense how fearful they were of Putin's reach. Not that he was entirely dismissive of the emotion himself. If any one of these men talked out of turn after this discussion, whether to a friend, colleague, rent boy or mistress, they could all end up facing a firing squad.

'I agree,' said Kushka, flicking a hand in the air, a salute to action.

Solov nodded. 'I also.'

Koroleg tapped the table with his knuckle. 'Yes.'

One by one the heads on the screens nodded and hands were raised in agreement. What they didn't know was that in spite of the theatricals with the security sweep against bugs, all of them had been recorded nodding their agreement to the proposed plan, a copy of which would find a resting place in Simoyan's safe within minutes of this video meeting being ended.

Simoyan smiled. 'Wonderful. And if it were needed, which it isn't, I have the deciding vote and I say yes, we stop the traitorous bastard in his tracks and bury him somewhere they'll never find him!'

Seconds later the screens began to click off as each man disconnected.

'How, exactly?' Solov queried, when the large screen went black, 'do we stop Tzorekov? We haven't talked about that.'

Simoyan shrugged. He'd expected this question at some point; he just hadn't seen it necessary to discuss the finer details with all the others. 'The only way we can. Permanently.'

'And the means of accomplishing this?'

'Do you really want to know? I'm pretty certain the others don't.'

'Call me curious.'

Simoyan shrugged. 'Very well. I've given this a lot of thought. We cannot – we dare not – rely on anyone who will wish to remain in the area afterwards. Whoever does this will have to disappear – and for a long time.'

'You mean to use criminals?' Koroleg rumbled. 'They'd be cheap, I give you that – and disposable. But totally unreliable in the meantime. They'd sell us out in an instant if they saw a profit.'

'Very true, which is why we won't be using them. For this assignment we need people with a proven track record of such work, ready and willing to leave the country afterwards. We cannot afford any mistakes.' He studied them carefully. 'We all stand to lose everything, otherwise.'

'So who, then?'

'I have a team in mind.'

'A team?' Solov looked at him. 'Not current serving personnel, I trust.' He had a politician's fear of the military having within its ranks members who would turn on their own leaders for money – or worse, ideology.

'No. They were, once, of the highest order. But they are now very disconnected and will remain so afterwards, I assure you. You and each of the others, by the way, will be receiving a bill detailing your equal share of their fee.' He smiled like a shark, enjoying the moment and sensing hesitation at this point. It was amazing, he reflected, how rich men hated spending money on non-business ventures, even at the promised inevitability of making even more money further down the line.

Koroleg said, 'How long will it take to get them together?'

'No time at all. In fact, I have them on standby.'

It was a lie, actually, since the team was already up and on the move. But neither of these men needed to know that. Simoyan had merely anticipated the group's agreement and set the machine in motion. Wasting time was as anathema to him as wasting money.

'What about outside interference?' This from Solov. 'Has there been any chatter from the British or Americans?'

'Well, that's really part of your expertise, isn't it, being defence? What do you think?'

Solov tipped his head in agreement. 'It's almost certain that they must know something of Tzorekov's plans, in my judgement. They may play genial host to dissenters like Tzorekov, but they monitor their movements very closely, just as we would in similar circumstances. They will do anything they can to bring instability to this country.'

A politician's answer, thought Simoyan. In other words, he had no idea. 'Exactly. For that reason we're doing some monitoring of our own. Any whispers from the embassies, any unusual movements or changes in personnel, especially in the north, and we will know.' He snapped his fingers for emphasis.

Koroleg said, 'You can cover all of that? Seriously?' He looked and sounded sceptical.

'We have and we will. Seriously.' Simoyan stared hard at him until he looked away. It was a blatant show of strength in the face of doubt, and it worked.

'Good. How do you plan to react if you hear anything?' said Solov.

'Very simply.' Simoyan made a show of taking a cell phone from his inside pocket and dialling a number. The other two watched while it rang out. When it was answered, Simoyan said simply, 'You have the green light. Go.' Then he switched off the phone, dropped it to the floor and ground it beneath his heel, a brutally significant display of his commitment to security.

'That's how,' he said casually. 'One phone call and a team will be on its way. Like the one I've just despatched. The game, gentlemen, is on.' He clapped his hands and said, 'Any more questions?' When neither of the men ventured to speak he gestured at a side table where drinks were waiting in a small refrigerator, the bottles visible through the glass door and beaded with icy condensation. 'In that case, our business is concluded and I propose a toast to successful ventures.'

As he stepped away from the table he glanced at his watch. The team he'd selected should be in the air very shortly. A few hours from now and they would be doing what they were good at; what they'd been hired to do. Hunters.

Hunting the biggest game of all: men.

EIGHTEEN

Airman Technician Maxim Datsyuk was bored. Isolated in one of the auxiliary flight monitoring rooms of the Main Air Traffic Management Centre on Leningradsky Prospekt, Moscow, he'd been staring at his screen for several hours now, trying to determine a flow pattern of night traffic around the city's skies. On attachment from the Ministry of Defence Flight Safety Service centre at Shaykovka air base, Datsyuk was here to broaden his experience and, as his MOD supervisor had suggested, to teach the civilian sky-watchers a thing or two about emergency traffic control procedures the military way.

Yet here he was in a windowless room where he was certain he'd been sent simply because they didn't know what else to do with him. He was beginning to feel like a spare dick at a wedding, ignored by the other staff and receiving little or no welcome or help from his hosts. He yawned and sipped at a bottle of water. He'd have preferred something stronger, but taking alcohol while on duty – even as a visitor/observer – was against regulations.

He shook his head and changed screens, zooming in to bring up the radar feed of the area north of the city. There was little traffic to speak of this late, other than the usual authorized late-night cargo and emergency flights, and the ever-present police helicopters monitoring ground traffic and supporting law enforcement operations. If he could find something interesting to show Gretsky, the fat and sullen civilian supervisor he'd been assigned to, it might get him taken a little more seriously, instead of being sidelined to this rabbit hole.

He played with the screen, picking up transponder signals and data tags at random and checking them against a list of codes he'd been given by one of the few friendly desk-jockeys in the building. Nothing remotely interesting; mostly long-established utility traffic on pre-planned flights and not likely to be changed as long as the Moscow Zonal planners had holes in their—

Whoa. What was that?

He sat up straight. An ADSB beacon. He clicked on it to bring up the detail. It was a code he hadn't seen before. **Trapdoor Z5993**. Interesting. The aircraft was a helicopter – an Ansat-U military utility job – current altitude 300 metres on a 25-degree track heading N-N-E beyond the city suburbs. Probably ferrying a bunch of officers back to base from a late-night cocktail party. But no other data. And no transponder signal.

OK, so the military didn't have to follow all the rules, but even so. He dragged the keyboard closer, checking the log for queried codes and feeding in the beacon number. Not a thing, save the taunting 'No Search Results'. Was this something a little special, maybe? A spook flight carrying FSB personnel or a minister on a hush-hush trip? If so it might account for the unusual number.

He chewed on a fingernail and thought about what to do. As a visitor/observer he had authorization to track flights while building patterns for later use in creating computer models, but not to contact them. Yet the comms function was sitting here unused. What would be the harm?

He decided to call them up, in case they were listening on the local frequency. To hell with it – he could label this as a potential safety issue. That's what he was here studying, after all. And what was the worst they could they do if they didn't like it? Send him to a field radar hut in the Urals? Hell, he'd seen worse.

'Ansat-U heading N-N-E this is Main ATM Centre, Moscow, please confirm destination and route, over.'

No answer.

He repeated the call. And a third time. Nothing.

He logged the time, position and direction of the flight and sent a note up the line to the duty supervisor, checking the list to see who was on tonight. Shit. It was Gretsky, who almost never responded to any messages and generally treated him like dirt. He was probably sleeping in the store cupboard next to his room right now and wouldn't give a rat's ass about what was happening in the sky until it fell on his head.

To his surprise Gretsky came right back.

'What the hell is this report, Datsyuk? Are you trying to screw with me?'

'No, sir. Not at all.' He was surprised at the tone of venom in Gretsky's voice. 'I noticed the flight because it has a beacon number which doesn't show up anywhere.'

'How do you know that? Are you an expert all of a sudden?'

'No, I'm not saying that, sir. I checked the log and this one doesn't figure.'

'You did what? Who gave you permission to do that? Did I say you could do that?' Gretsky's voice was almost a squeak now and rising.

'You didn't have to. We run these checks all the time down in Shaykovka; some aircraft don't have a detailed flight plan or they switch off their transponders – even their radios. It's standard procedure when one of the three elements is miss—'

Gretsky yelled, 'Like I give a shit what's standard procedure in freaking Shaykovka! This is a *civilian* facility, not military, you dumb fuck! And I *know* what the three elements are, thank you very much – I don't need a lecture from you!'

'But the code—'

'Code nothing. It was probably an echo. In case you forgot, you're here as an observer, Datsyuk. That means you observe but you do not interfere, you understand me? Now check yourself out; you're off duty until tomorrow.'

Maxim swallowed hard. Ouch. He'd really touched a sore spot, although he couldn't understand why. He decided not to mention that he'd tried making contact with the helicopter; it would probably give Gretsky an aneurism, the fat bastard.

'I didn't hear an answer, Datsyuk! Are you listening to me? You're off duty.'

'OK, I understand. Got it, sir. I'm leaving now. Over and out.' He banged the receiver down, the sarcasm probably lost on the fat man, and turned off his monitors. Jesus, these civilian time-servers didn't know they were born.

Echo, my ass.

NINETEEN

Victor Simoyan was woken from a fitful sleep by a soft buzzing sound. He turned over and slid open the drawer of the bedside table. Taking out the cell phone inside, he slipped out of bed, careful not to wake his wife, and left the bedroom. He walked along the landing to his home office, which was equipped in similar fashion to his workplace.

The cell phone was a throwaway containing numbers he liked to keep separate from his usual business and domestic matters. He studied the screen to see who was calling. Probably one of the Wise Men, having second thoughts and pissing in their pants in terror at the idea of being found out. He'd thought that coming home and getting some sleep while the team got into position for the operation might keep them off his backs for a while, but evidently not.

He was surprised to see the name of the caller and debated for a moment ignoring it. But instinct told him that could be a mistake.

'What is it, Gretsky?' he murmured. He sat in his office chair and poured a whisky. He rarely got back to sleep once roused and had a feeling this call wasn't going to be good news. Gretsky was one of many individuals around the country that he kept on a small retainer, guaranteeing a flow of information on all manner of subjects where knowledge was key.

Like many functionaries Gretsky was a weasel, but weasels had their value. As an Air Traffic Control supervisor, his inside knowledge allowed Simoyan to gain first-hand details of certain flights of interest anywhere in the country and beyond its borders; details that might prove useful for future plans. In return, like all his sources, Gretsky enjoyed a regular sum of money paid into a secret account. Right now the only topic he could think of in Gretsky's viewfinder was one involving Chesnokoy and his team of mercenaries, and a certain helicopter travelling north.

'We have a small problem, sir.' Gretsky's voice floated down the line in a near-whisper, as if he were crouched under his desk to avoid being overheard. 'A problem with the flight situation.'

'Tell me.'

'Um . . . we currently have a visiting observer from the military down here learning how we do things. He's a young man, of no great importance or talent, but he's keen and ambitious, and is currently on duty observing traffic patterns and procedures. Personally, if it was down to me I wouldn't have him around, but—'

'Get to it, Gretsky. What's the problem?'

He listened as Gretsky outlined the conversation with the visiting ATC. The news wasn't good, but he'd heard worse. So some eager beaver of a visiting controller had spotted and reported an Ansat – the Ansat with Chesnokoy and his team on board, as it happened. Slightly unfortunate but by itself it wasn't a huge problem.

'He spoke to you about it?'

'Yes, sir.'

'Fine. Then you can contain it.'

'Well, I can contain Datsyuk, yes, sir – that's the name of the controller in question. I must stress that he went way beyond my strict instructions in what he did—'

'Is there any danger he'll talk about it outside?' Simoyan asked coolly. That was the nub of the problem; if this leaked out, it could throw the entire plan into disarray and threaten them all. In which case he might have to take steps to deal with it.

'I'm sure he won't, sir. He's from the Ministry of Defence Air Safety Service at Shaykovka and they have strict rules about divulging confidential information. He's here for a short while only – a short-term transfer only. He'll be gone in a couple of days. I just thought I should alert you—'

'Quite correct, Gretsky,' Simoyan said, interrupting him before he could gabble any further. He made a note on his desk pad. 'Make sure this man stays away from any further probing and keeps his mouth shut.'

'Of course, sir. I will. There is just one more thing, sir.' Gretsky sounded as if he were having trouble breathing. 'It has just come to my attention that he tried to make contact with the flight to verify its course and destination. You see, I took the precaution of placing a recording facility on his assigned workstation, and played it back. Again, I must stress that he had no authority to make contact; he was supposed to be observing traffic movement only, not interfacing with it. Fortunately he was unsuccessful.'

By all the saints, Simoyan thought savagely, don't these bloody people ever get to the point? 'So why mention it, then?'

'When there was no response he logged the sighting on the system as an unidentified craft with elements missing.'

'Elements *what*?'

'It means no radio, no transponder signal and no flight plan. But it had a beacon signal and that's what triggered his interest; turns out it was an old beacon attached to a military aircraft that was supposed to have been decommissioned a couple of years ago. The beacon was still operative and emitting a signal.'

Simoyan felt himself go cold. It might go unnoticed, it might not. The worst case scenario was that somebody higher up with a rule book up his arse might see it and start asking questions about unusual night flights with outdated – but ultimately traceable – beacons. And that could ultimately lead right back to himself. 'So delete the report. Override it. Do whatever you have to do. Make sure it never appears.'

'I can't.'

'What?'

'It's already been circulated and archived, as all reports are. It can't be deleted or altered.'

'Seriously?'

'I'm afraid so, sir. I can't. I mean . . . there's no way. But there are dozens of such reports every day and it's quite probable that nobody will notice this one.'

Simoyan stood bolt upright in a burst of energy. 'You *think*? Gretsky, your assumption is redundant. If you recall, nobody was supposed to *notice* a decommissioned Ansat leaving Moscow and heading north. Nobody was supposed to be in a position to *notice* a signal and start asking questions. Isn't that what you promised me would be the case – that if it were seen you would ensure it was passed off as special military traffic?'

'Yes, sir, that's quite correct, but I—'

'Then I suggest you make that your main priority. And make sure this Datsyuk doesn't put his interfering nose anywhere near another monitor. Understood?'

'Yes. Yes, of course. I've already seen to it and sent him home. I'll make sure he doesn't get the chance to do it again.'

Simoyan cut the call and dropped the cell phone on the desk. Then he snatched it up again and began to dial a number, before changing his mind. He'd been about to speak to Chesnokoy and warn him, but that was futile. There was nothing the former soldier could do about his situation other than to follow orders and complete the mission.

He finished his whisky and went back to bed, ignoring his wife's grumbles. As he waited restlessly for sleep to claim him, he found a distant, nagging voice telling him that this wasn't over. Not by a long way.

TWENTY

High above the carpet of trees and an occasional glimpse of water, and shielded by the encroaching darkness and a ceiling of low clouds, Alex Chesnokoy and his three companions were unaware that their journey had been noticed and logged. Sitting in the cabin of an Ansat-U light utility helicopter, they were too focussed on trying to ignore the buffeting of the weather outside and the thrashing cacophony of the rotors overhead.

Nobody was talking; it was a habit they'd given up a lifetime ago, when too much chatter from a colleague during an operation usually betrayed a nervous disposition – something nobody wanted to hear going into a hot zone. For now each man was concentrating on thoughts of what lay ahead while trying to push aside the darker concerns about what might be awaiting them when they landed. As for now, getting them there in one piece was up to the experts at the controls.

The pilot was a former major, a specialist with many years of experience flying Spetsnaz troops into battle zones. Flight operations in lousy weather had long been part of his life, taking men and equipment into the air when others were happier being grounded. Alongside him sat a former lieutenant navigator, also with special forces experience, whose ability to find his way in atrocious conditions had kept them working together long past most men in their positions. Now they worked for private individuals as well as taking on occasional jobs for government departments with lots of acronyms but few faces. They had been well paid for this job, and what the four men behind them were going to do on this trip was none of their business.

Chesnokoy was checking a small electronic box on his lap, no bigger than a cell phone, waiting for a signal to show up on the map outlined on the screen. They were still too high and far away, he figured, but getting closer all the time, if the navigator was doing his job properly in this shit weather. If the target had continued on the same road after the tracker had been attached, there weren't too many places they could go off the main route to the north. But if they did, and the tracker signal came up, it shouldn't take too long to home in on their location.

He sat back and closed his eyes. Waiting; it was always about waiting. What was it someone had once said about war? Months of boredom interspersed by moments of terror. They'd certainly got that right.

After receiving the 'go' for this assignment, he'd ordered his colleagues out of the apartment and into a small removals van out back. Each man had carried a heavy-duty canvas holdall, from where they had taken camouflage uniforms and boots, changing quickly from their civilian clothes once the van was on the move. Their discarded clothes had been placed in their bags for use later on.

If there was to be a later on.

Arriving under cover of dark at a small airfield several miles away from the Golyanovo District, they had found the helicopter and two-man crew waiting and ready to go. Within minutes they were in the air and heading towards the north-west.

The helicopter lurched suddenly, dropping fifty feet and causing each of the men to look up and grab their seats. One or two may have even offered a prayer to whatever god they favoured to keep this godless lump of metal, glass and electronics in the air where it belonged, instead of plunging into the black waters or the spears of trees, where lay certain death either way with no chance of escape.

Chesnokoy inspected their faces in turn. He could read them like a book and had absolute faith in each one. He was experienced enough to know that no soldier, no matter how skilled, could be entirely free of fear in the face of the unknown. Those who pretended otherwise were a danger to themselves and others, and rarely lasted long. Fear was what made you cautious enough to survive – if you were lucky – and gave you that edge to succeed where others might hesitate and fail.

And these three were at least honest enough with each other to not try hiding their concerns; that only made them stronger and more reliable.

He had a feeling they'd need it for this job, which had been sold as a simple task of taking out two men, one of them old, who were 'a perceived and serious threat to the state', as Victor Simoyan, the man who'd recruited him, had said. Chesnokoy had worked for Simoyan before, and the arms manufacturer had made a good case for accepting the job, along with the conditions he'd imposed about disappearing afterwards. But Chesnokoy had learned a long time ago that nothing was entirely free from risk, no matter how persuasive the sales pitch.

There was also the unusual amount of money on offer: a third paid up front and the rest on completion, along with documentation to help the men disappear. He'd talked to other freelance contractors and had come to the conclusion that the sum promised was usually in direct proportion to the dangers involved. Maybe this one was one of the rare good deals. Time would tell.

'Hey, look.' Georgi Gorin was staring out of the window and nudged him with his elbow. 'I'd rather be down there than up here.' He was pointing at a flicker of lights below, and Chesnokoy realized they were looking down at a vehicle travelling along a road. It seemed frighteningly close, and even closer were the glimpses of treetops between them.

At that moment he caught a movement against the console display in the pilot's cabin and looked up. The navigator was waving at him to put on a headset hanging from a communications point behind his head.

He did so and said, 'Why are we so low?'

'We're using a military flight corridor as extra cover,' the man explained. 'We've turned off the transponder so we're not emitting a signal, but if we get pinged by radar they'll think we're part of the regular traffic. No questions, no lies.'

'Is that likely?'

'It's happened already. We heard a call earlier from a civilian ATC in Moscow wanting to know who we were and where we were going.'

'What did you say?'

'I didn't. It's none of his business. Hell of a thing, though; I don't how he spotted us – as I said. We'd turned off the transponder.'

'So where are we?'

'That's what I was going to tell you. We're still on course but we've got a solid front of rain coming in dead ahead. We're going to have to put down on the first bit of clear ground we see. Tell your men to get ready and brace for a rough landing.'

'No.' Chesnokoy leaned forward. 'You land when I say so. Keep going or go round it.'

'We can't. If we hit it head on, this weather will blow us out of the sky, and going round it isn't an option – it's too big. We have to land.' The navigator's face showed briefly as he was thrown sideways in his seat, a pale oval beneath his flying helmet. Chesnokoy wasn't certain, but the man looked scared.

'Don't be a fucking pussy,' he snarled. 'Keep going!' As he spoke, he saw a spot of red appear on the tracker unit on his lap. At last: the signal was calling. It was weak but definitely there. If this box of tricks was working correctly, the target looked to be about twenty miles away and slightly to the left of their current heading. Good navigation or pure luck? Who cared – it was time to get going.

The pilot came on the wire. 'We land when *I* say so, not you,' he said calmly. 'I promise you, if that weather front hits us this crate will bounce like a ball and won't stop until we're splashed in pieces all over the landscape below. Now, are you ready to try winning a pissing contest against Mother Nature or do we land and let the weather go by? We won't lose more than about twenty minutes and we'll soon make up that time. In any case, don't you have a signal to lock onto?'

Chesnokoy considered taking out the Makarov semi-automatic he had in his holdall and shooting the navigator. That would show who would win the pissing contest. But the weather chose that moment to prove the warning correct by flipping the helicopter to the right and down as if by a giant swipe of the hand. The twin engines howled in protest as the pilot fought to regain control, swearing loudly over the noise and seemingly hauling the machine back from the brink of disaster by sheer muscle-power and spit. 'See what I mean?' the pilot shouted, once they were flying relatively level again. He sounded angry and ready for a fight. 'What do you want to do? Try staying up here and die? Or land? It's your fucking choice!'

Chesnokoy bit down on his tongue, then shouted back, 'Very well, land. But you'd better not cause us to lose the target or I'll shoot both of you.'

There was no response, but the helicopter immediately began to lose height as the pilot took it down under the directions of the navigator, now using a night vision device to find a clear landing area below.

On the other side of the cabin, Ignatyev, who had always hated flying, groaned and vomited on the floor.

TWENTY-ONE

The road in front of me had opened up as darkness fell, as if the traffic around me had found other places to go for the night. I figured it couldn't be long before Tzorekov and Gurov decided they'd had enough and found somewhere to rest up. The weather seemed to be worsening by the hour and my wipers were having a hard time clearing the screen. I'd seen no signs of hotels in the area, although there had to be something catering for weekenders and long-distance travellers. But until the two men stopped, I had to keep going or risk losing them in the middle of nowhere.

As the road dipped between another long strip of trees on both sides, with nothing but blackness beyond and above, I felt a vibration through my elbow where it was resting against the glass of the side window. At first I figured it had to be the condition of the road, which was steadily getting pretty much Third-World crappy. But I realized after a moment that the vibration wasn't being transmitted through the frame of the vehicle.

I lowered the window, letting in a blast of cool air and a shower of rainwater, and the echo of the engine and road noise bouncing back at me off the trees.

I slowed down and did a quick 360-degree check. There was nothing behind me and nothing immediately ahead. Forget either side – that was black and blacker. The flickering tracker light on my cell phone showed the Touareg was about five miles in front of me, and had been holding a steady speed for some time. It was good going considering the state of the road and the amount of surface water they had to plough through.

I slowed some more, letting my speed bleed away until I was doing no more than twenty. The reduction of speed, engine and road noise meant I could hear better, even above the pounding rain, although it still wasn't crystal clear. But something was out there . . . I could feel it. Now I'd got the window open, the vibration I'd felt earlier had translated into a definite drumming in the air – and getting louder. Then I had it. It was a sound I'd heard too many times before.

A helicopter. The thudding sound of the rotors was unmistakable. But in these conditions? Somebody must be desperate.

I heard Lindsay's voice. 'Watchman, come in.'

'A little busy right now,' I told her calmly. 'What's up?'

'Sorry, but I just got in a fresh satellite feed tracking aircraft in your area. There's a helicopter moving up on your position right now—'

She stopped speaking because I was holding the phone out the window so she could hear what I was hearing.

I brought the phone back in just as she said, 'Is that what I think it is?'

'Sure is. I've got company and it's about half a click away and coming in fast. But I don't think it's me he's after. Wait one.'

A faint light had appeared off to my right, showing briefly through the line of trees. It wasn't much, probably no more than a running light or the flash of an instrumentation array off the cockpit. But seen from my low perspective, I figured the helicopter was about 500 feet up and by the varying pattern of flight, was being shaken like a rag by the force of the wind and rain. Too much of that and it might start to come apart at the seams.

'I have to go,' I told Lindsay quickly. 'I'll call again later.'

'Copy that, Watchman.'

I switched off and checked the road ahead; I could see maybe a half-mile to a mile of blacktop with no vehicles or obstructions and no signs of habitation. We were pretty much in the middle of nowhere. I slowed to little more than a crawl and kept one eye on the helicopter as it came up level with me and began to move past. By now it was losing speed and altitude until it reached treetop height. Whoever was flying it must be an expert or crazy – or maybe a little of both. One error and they'd crash and burn among the trees, with nobody but me right now being any the wiser.

Then the engine note changed and the machine flared suddenly, the nose going up for a moment before it sank with amazing elegance, and disappeared from sight.

I switched off the headlights and stopped, then jumped out of the car, waiting for the sound of a crash. Nothing. Instead I heard the whine and the telltale whup-whup of the rotors slowing down. They'd landed.

I got back in the car and edged forward a couple of hundred yards until I figured it was safe to pull off the road. A quick check of my cell phone to make sure the tracker light was still flickering up ahead, and I decided to take a quick look. I was taking a chance stopping like this, but instinct was telling me that whoever was in that helicopter was no errant traveller who'd lost their way, but was connected in some way with Tzorekov.

If they were out here flying in these conditions, it was because they wanted to – or had to. And that meant I needed to see who they were.

I climbed out, taking the Grach 9mm and the night vision scope with me, and locked the doors. Then I scooted across the road and into the trees, where I ducked down and tuned in to the night, allowing the atmosphere around me to settle.

The scope was a godsend. It stopped me walking into a ten-foot flood-ditch just off the road, and showed me the way through the treeline roughly in the direction of where the helicopter had landed. And if I had any doubts, I could smell the stench of aviation fuel in the air and the harsh residue of exhaust fumes lingering in the vegetation before being swept away on the wind.

I took it slow, treading carefully over the underlying blanket of pine needles and broken branches littering the ground. I was counting on the weather giving me some cover, and the knowledge that anybody travelling in a noisy helicopter would be feeling slightly deafened for a few minutes afterwards until their hearing returned to normal.

A hundred feet later and I was looking at a twin-engine utility helicopter with a four-blade rotor, sitting in a clearing. It looked like an Ansat but I couldn't see any markings. Whoever the pilot was, he should have taken a bow for getting them down in one piece in such lousy conditions.

As I watched, the clamshell-style doors opened, one up and one down to form the steps, and two men emerged. Both were armed with handguns, just visible in the interior light in the cabin, with two more men standing behind them. Another two were at the controls up front.

I eased back in case they had night-vision goggles, and slipped behind a small pile of logs. Whatever these men were doing here, it didn't look like good news.

The first two stepped away from the helicopter and disappeared into the darkness, shoulders hunched against the wet. Either they were going for a comfort break or checking out the scenery. Something told me the latter. I kept my head down, and minutes later one of them walked past my position before returning to the helicopter and meeting up with his colleague. Whoever he was, he moved through the trees like he knew how and I put his age at somewhere in the thirties.

As soon as they were together, one of the other men inside stepped down from the cabin and stood looking down at a cell phone, apparently oblivious to the rain. He was taller than the others and broad across the shoulders. The light from the phone showed up a face with strong cheekbones and a beak of a nose, and I had a feeling this was the man in charge. It took me a second or two before I realized that he and the others were dressed in camouflage uniforms and jump boots.

Something in the way the big man was standing, and the manner in which he was holding the cell phone, looked odd. It was only when he turned to look to the north, then looked down to check the phone again, that I realized what he was doing. He was confirming a location against his current position.

I eased away and hurried back to the pickup. Armed men, military or ex-military, flying in close to zero-visibility conditions miles from anywhere and being forced to land. A wild explanation might say they were Russian special forces on a field exercise; but somehow I didn't think so. Most military chiefs will hesitate to risk valuable men and machines in training unless absolutely unavoidable.

And the fact was, these guys weren't miles from anywhere; they were up close – too close – to the same godforsaken patch of remote forest and lakes as Leonid Tzorekov and his bodyguard.

My only question was, how could that happen?

TWENTY-TWO

On the side of a tree-covered hill thirty miles inside the border with Finland, two figures were huddled inside a concealed observation post. Sergeants Robert Cross and Joe Cundell had parachuted in three nights ago using the HAHO – high altitude, high opening – technique to drift across the border, and had concealed their chutes deep in the ground where they would never be found. After force-marching – or tabbing, as they called it – overland to their present position, they had dug in and set up the BAE Systems-manufactured Blackbat stealth drone ready for flight. From here they would watch out for the signal from the target vehicle they would hopefully see on the screen of the control unit, before sending the data to a receiving station near London.

Cross was awake with Cundell catching up on some sleep while the opportunity allowed. Both men were highly experienced and had worked together before, in Afghanistan and Iraq, setting up Forward OPs – observation posts – and living for days in dangerous terrain, constantly exposed to possible discovery with little or no chance of survival. Back then they had contended with mostly desert conditions, dry rations and hot days; at least here they had trees, cool air and water – lots of it – to soften the assignment.

Cross checked the screen of a handheld motion detector for signs of movement. They had planted several monitor spikes in the ground around their position, which would alert them to anything larger than a dog approaching by means of a tiny light showing the direction of the potential threat. So far, the spikes had remained silent.

He leaned across and ran his eyes over the Blackbat, checking again for signs of damage to the casing that could signify a possible malfunction. If this bird didn't work at this late stage in the operation, they would have no option but to up sticks and tab back out all the way to the border, where they would be eased across to safety.

Satisfied he had done as much as he could, Cross sat back and tuned into the night, shutting out Joe Cundell's soft snores and subconsciously counting down the minutes to launch time. Their biggest moment of danger would be when they released the drone from a clearing close to the top of the hill. They needed very little space for the flight take-off, since the machine would hit vertical lift almost immediately. But sudden powerful gusts or an increase in rainfall at the wrong moment could be disastrous. There was also the risk of hunters in the region, who might spot them as they moved to and from the launch position.

He flicked back the cover of his watch. Ten minutes to go. Enough for a quick bite and a drink. Then it was suck-it-and-see time. He nudged Cundell with his foot and watched as his colleague came awake, hardly moving but alert and ready to go.

He couldn't see clearly in the dark, but he knew Joe would have reached instinctively for his weapon. Except on this trip there wasn't one. No guns allowed, just some camera equipment to go with the drone as cover in case they were blown, and papers from a wildlife production studio back in the UK. They might not be sufficient to explain how they had wandered across the border without realizing it, but it was worth a try.

They ate quickly, absorbing as many calories as they could. Like sleep, food was something to take in whenever you could, because you never knew when the next opportunity might present itself.

'You ready?' Cross said, and waved his satellite phone.

Cundell nodded. 'Let's play spy planes.'

'Christ, don't even use that word.' Cross thumbed the speed dial number and waited while the call went through. It was answered after ten seconds, the soft voice of a female comms operator coming all the way from GCHQ, the UK Government Communications Headquarters in Cheltenham, Gloucestershire.

'Go ahead, Blackbat One.'

'Ready to fly. Five minutes.'

'Copy that, Blackbat One. Ready to receive. Good luck.'

Cross cut the connection and stowed the phone in his jacket, and both men crawled out from their OP. They took the drone and control unit with them, and wore night-vision goggles.

It took three minutes to reach the clearing, and another two to check that all was clear and ready to launch. The wind was minimal and the rain had stopped.

It was a small window and possibly the only one they might get for a safe launch. Once the machine was in the air, it would virtually fly itself on a pre-set course, adjusting to the elements even under fairly extreme conditions. The greatest hazards were while it was close to the ground, but it had been designed specifically for this kind of operation. Cross lifted the drone above his head and nodded at Cundell, who switched on the control unit.

The speed with which the drone reacted still surprised Cross, even though he'd spent many days training with the machine. With barely a hum from its small motors, it lifted out of his hands and disappeared into the night sky, the black, non-reflective casing invisible even from a few feet away.

The two men retreated to their OP, Cross leading the way while Cundell kept an eye on the monitor showing the machine's height and direction. They had fed a straightforward grid pattern into the computer to cover the initial search area, and the drone could be relied on to do its job. If they didn't pick up a signal after thirty minutes, it would be simple enough to change the parameters and start again.

Back in the OP, Cross called in to GCHQ.

'Blackbat One. Up and flying.'

'Copy, Blackbat One. Out.'

They ate again and settled down to wait. This was the worst time of any covert operation, when all they could do was sit and wait, monitoring the screen and motion detectors and hoping the drone stayed in the air and undetected. The sleek contours of the body combined with the powerful motors made it perfect for night-time use, but if a strong weather pattern closed in, all their hopes could be dashed by a chance wind throwing the craft off-course. And right now that was a distinct possibility. If the drone did go down, all they could do was hope to find it by following the GPS signal and then start tabbing fast for the border and home.

Then Cundell said softly, 'Gotcha, baby. Talk to Daddy. OK, we've got a signal. Target acquired.' He grinned, his face just visible in the reflected light of the screen. 'I think I'll celebrate by making a brew.'

Cross nodded, sharing the relief of a job at least starting out right. 'I'll do it. You keep an eye on the birdie.' He moved across the space to break out a drink.

'What the hell . . .?' Cundell swore softly. 'Look at this.'

'What?' Cross instinctively checked the motion detector screen, but it was dark.

'I flicked the dial just to check we were in the clear, and picked up a second signal.'

'Could be a radio beacon . . . or a local military comms site.'

'I don't think so. It's coming from the same co-ordinates as the other one.' Cundell turned the screen so that Cross could see it. Sure enough, a signal was coming in, but it didn't bear the signature of the one they'd been told to expect. 'Maybe it's the second vehicle – the one we're supporting. He wouldn't be that close, though, would he?'

Cross shook his head. Their briefing had been short on details about who else was involved, since theirs was a distance-support only assignment with strictly no local communication or contact. Drop in, run the drone for as long as it took, feeding back information as required, then tab out again without leaving a trace. They were experienced enough to know that the kind of task they'd been given was in support of an operative on the ground. Who he was and what he was doing hadn't been disclosed, but they were both savvy enough to realize that some poor guy was out there on his own in bandit country, and relying on them to provide electronic backup.

'If it was our guy, why would he be carrying a tracker? Maybe it's a freak echo.'

'No way.' Cundell studied the screen again. 'It's definitely in the same location. And I mean, the exact same – like on the same body frame.'

'Shit.' Cross tried to figure out what it meant, but there was only one conclusion he could draw.

Somehow the target vehicle had picked up a second tracking device.

He picked up the satellite phone and dialled in. 'We'd better report in. If somebody else has joined the party, our guy could be in all sorts of trouble.'

'Fine. What do we do in the meantime?'

'We carry on. He's relying on us.'

TWENTY-THREE

'Watchman, come in.'

'Go ahead. Lindsay.' I could guess what she was calling about and she quickly confirmed it.

'That helicopter that came close to you,' she said. 'It was an Ansat-U military aircraft, currently listed as non-assigned. We checked all flights and it originated from the Moscow area via Vologda. We haven't found a flight plan and if he has a transponder, it's switched off. But it is carrying an ADSB beacon which showed continuous emissions except for a short time around Vologda. It only became visible again to our monitors just before reaching your location.'

Somebody was being extra cautious. If it was listed by the Russians as non-assigned, it could mean almost anything, even a euphemism for non-operational or private. They must have flown at very low level from somewhere outside the immediate Moscow area. A major city like that, you didn't fly through it without letting air traffic control know where you were. In these troubled times, that was a quick way to have a MiG-31 closing on your ass with a finger on the button.

Once clear of the main Moscow-Vologda corridor flight zone, they had ducked out of sight somehow. After that, if the pilot was capable – and he clearly was, from what I'd witnessed – he'd kept low to the ground and skipped under the radar like a hockey puck all the way to this dark and dense neck of the woods.

It told me one important fact: whoever was on board liked to move in the dark. And travelling in these conditions, they must have got a solid reason for risking life and limb to be here.

But why here and why now?

I confirmed that it had been an Ansat and added, 'I have four on board with two crew. The four were in camo gear and armed. They looked and moved like regular forces but I couldn't see any insignia.'

'Copy that, Watchman.' She hesitated and I heard a voice in the background. Then she came back. 'I think we might have an answer on that. Wait one, please.'

'Watchman?' It was Callahan. 'I've just had a call from GCHQ in the UK. It seems we have another party tracking the Touareg. Three days ago a two-man British Pathfinder team was inserted north-west of your location with airborne tracking capability. They were put in by Tom Vale to assist in finding and tracking Counselor in case you struck out. They just reported in, saying they've picked up a second signal from the target vehicle.'

Double damn. So that was how they'd done it: they'd managed to get a tracking bug planted on the Touareg. All the helicopter crew had to do when they got here was lock in on the signal, just as I was doing. As for the Pathfinders, it would have been nice to know that there were more friendly bodies in the field than me, but that was strictly a need-to-know thing and I understood the reasons for not telling me. What I didn't know couldn't harm them if I came unglued.

But that still left me wondering about the identity and intentions of the bozos in the chopper. If they weren't regular troops, they could only be ex-military or contractors for hire. But what was their purpose?

I checked the tracker light. It was still there, but on the edge of the system's ability to hold the signal for much longer. I had to catch up with Tzorekov and fast.

I took a chance of starting the engine and drove as quietly as I could until I was well out of earshot of the men in the helicopter. When I was far enough up the road I turned on my sidelights and put my foot down. Another mile and I put on the main lights and hit the gas.

The signal became stronger after thirty minutes, and I figured Tzorekov must have stopped somewhere. The where was soon apparent as I saw a sign for a truck stop up ahead, with a handful of vehicles but not much sign of movement. The lights inside the restaurant were still on, so when I was certain there were no Touaregs sitting in the parking lot out front, I pulled over and went in.

It was cosy inside, with the windows steamed up and the hiss of wind across the roof. There were only four customers, all men with faces like hammered tent pegs, most of them hunched over their food and looking like they'd been hauled through a hedge. Long distance truckers; too many miles, the wrong kind of food and never enough sleep.

I ordered take-out coffee and the middle-years lady with a beehive hairdo behind the counter obliged by selling me a vacuum flask with a pretty pink casing to go with it. She kept smiling at me behind her eyelashes all the way through filling it without spilling a drop, which I guessed took some practice. So I paid up and left before she got round to telling me what was really on her mind.

Back on the road I gradually reeled in the Touareg again to a safe margin and kept them there. As long as the tracker kept doing its thing or Tzorekov didn't do something radical, like throw in a sudden change of direction, I should be fine.

Which of course, is exactly what he did. One second he was there, on the road in front, then the signal light went off-road and heading away from me into what looked like big tree, big bear country, with no signs of life.

I slowed down and checked the phone was working. It was fine. But the tracker light was now away from the main route and still going strong.

I lowered the window. The map didn't show a road but that didn't mean there wasn't one. As long as I didn't miss it, I should be able to stay on their trail. The rain had really slacked off now, and the wind with it. It might only be a lull, but it was all the opportunity I was going to get.

I decided to call Lindsay. 'I need some help. They've gone off-road. Can you ask the team to double-check the signal for me?'

'Copy that, Watchman. Call you back.'

Even as she was speaking I caught sight of a sign in the headlights. It was a billboard on a wooden frame showing a schematic for a cabin village, the sketches showing hunting, fishing and cross-country skiing facilities. There was also a canoe pinned to a metal rack to show they were close to water. Or maybe they just liked the decoration.

Whatever. Cabins for weekenders and hunters; an ideal place for a stopover. I called up Lindsay and told her where I was headed, and she confirmed she was running a check.

I followed a rough metalled road for about two miles, winding deeper into a vast belt of trees while hoping I didn't meet the Touareg waiting for me. Then I saw another sign telling me I had a hundred metres to go. I switched off the main lights and nosed into a crushed gravel turnaround in front of a wood-framed hut. There were lights on inside but no signs of the Touareg. I parked out front and went inside.

An old woman with a flat face and long grey hair hanging down past her shoulders looked like she was about ready to close up for the night. But she perked up when she saw me and even gave me a smile. She was chewing on her gums and pointed at three cabins on a large wall-map to show they were vacant. I counted three others that weren't and decided business must be slow.

I nodded at a picture of a cabin sitting against a splash of blue and dropped enough cash on the counter for one night. She snatched it up before I could change my mind and looked at me as if I was going to ask for a receipt. I didn't, which seemed to be right, and she handed me a key and a hand-drawn map showing the way to my cabin. It was about a hundred yards away down a track through a belt of trees, so I thanked her and got back in the car. As I pulled away, the office lights went out and I saw her scuttling away down the road at speed. I hadn't seen any signs of a house, so I had no idea where she was headed.

Maybe she was a hobbit.

Half a minute later the headlights lit up a plain log cabin right out of an old Davy Crockett movie. It had a pitch right on the water's edge just like the schematic in the office had showed, and a small jetty with a covered boat tied up alongside. The air was heavy with the tang of fish, dried mud and some other stuff I didn't like to think about, but I hadn't expected the Ritz. I dumped my stuff on the inside, which was basic, rough-hewn and would appeal mainly to hunters who liked to drink themselves unconscious after a hard day's killing. Then I checked everything was secure and headed for the door to go on a walkabout.

'Watchman, come in.' Lindsay's voice sounded in my earpiece.

'I'm here.'

'We have confirmation. The location is listed as an unofficial hunters' lodge area. We don't have any details, but it doesn't look very big.'

'It's not,' I told her. 'I think I'm going to be picking up some cooties tonight.'

I heard her laugh and disconnected before she could come back at me. As I stepped outside and closed the door I heard a familiar whup-whup sound drifting across the lake, rising and fading on the wind. The helicopter.

These guys weren't giving up.

TWENTY-FOUR

Arkady Gurov waited until Tzorekov was asleep before stepping outside the cabin and closing the door softly behind him. The old man had barely said a word for the past three hours, other than to talk about how things were changing too fast and complaining about the food, which was tinned stew and potatoes, heated on the small stove. It was unlike him to find fault, but then, the situation they had put themselves in was hardly what they were accustomed to.

This entire journey was far from ideal for a man of Tzorekov's years, Gurov knew. They had known from the beginning that this was going to be a difficult mission and might end in disaster, and Gurov had tried more than once to counsel his boss to seek another way of performing the impossible. But, dogged as ever in the way that had made him such a success in the KGB and later, in business, Tzorekov had insisted that the outcome would be for the good of them all.

Gurov wasn't so sure, but he trusted his boss with his life. And that trust, he figured, was probably going to be tested to the limit sooner or later.

He'd first picked up the distant murmur of an engine while making a quick recce around the outside of the cabin shortly after their arrival. A truck on the main road, perhaps, but the trees played tricks with sound. More likely a hunter out late in the woods.

Tzorekov was inside, heating up the food, and appeared not to have noticed. At first Gurov wasn't concerned; there were several military facilities in the region, and any night-time movement could be a vehicle on a training exercise or a navigation test. But instinct had made him go back outside a few minutes later on the pretext of getting something from the car, and he'd recognized the sound for what it was: a helicopter. He'd judged it to be about five kilometres away and getting closer.

He stepped lightly along the jetty, carefully balanced on the balls of his feet. The boards were weather-worn and uneven, some shifting alarmingly in places, and he doubted the owners of this place put much effort into maintenance or repairs. He reached the end of the wooden walkway and stood still, allowing his eyes to become accustomed to the dark and to pick out the lighter tones of the stretch of water before him.

With stillness came the soft sounds of night creatures; a fish plopped out on the lake and an owl called some distance away in the trees, echoed by another. A ripple of water was echoed by the hiss of wind in the trees. They were lonely sounds, isolated and natural. But that was all. No engine noise.

He turned and walked back to the cabin, a sense of unease settling on his shoulders. He was city born and bred, but that made him all the more suspicious of environments he didn't know, and therefore doubly cautious. He had no reason for suspecting that their presence in the country had become known already, but he was experienced enough to accept that nothing stayed secret for very long, especially when it concerned a man like Tzorekov.

Before re-entering the cabin he scanned the perimeter one last time, then checked the safety on the semi-automatic. With the benefit of hindsight it seemed pitifully inadequate now; he should have acquired some heavier firepower, although he knew Tzorekov would never have allowed it. He'd had a hard enough time keeping the pistol. But the old man was always open to persuasion, if a good case was made. He hadn't argued strongly enough and was now stuck with little more than a pea-shooter against . . . whoever the hell was out there.

'What is it?' Tzorekov was awake and huddled under a blanket. He looked tired and drained of energy, but still had a glint in his eyes. He'd clearly noticed whatever restless energy Gurov was giving off.

'Nothing,' said Gurov. 'The night, mostly, and fish and this shitty weather. How are you feeling?'

'Nothing? For nothing and a bunch of fish you take that gun? Come on, Arkasha, don't try kidding an old man. You heard something.'

Gurov felt embarrassed. It wasn't often that Tzorekov used the diminutive form of his name; usually when they were alone or in family situations. But this was different. This carried a tone of mild reproof.

'I think it was a helicopter,' he said finally. 'Sorry. But it's gone now.'

'Gone? Or you merely stopped hearing it?'

'OK, I stopped hearing it.' He smiled at the old man's perceptiveness. At the same time he felt some relief; at least now there would be no point hiding anything. 'It could be nothing; this area's full of training camps. Probably some junior pilot on a night-flying exercise, poor sod.'

'Bullshit.' Tzorekov sat up. 'They're out there and we both know it. The bastards know we're coming – probably know why, too. They'll do anything to stop us, anything to preserve the status quo.'

'True. But who are "they"?'

'Fuck, who cares? The Siloviki . . . the Ozero Cooperative . . . the imbeciles who want to take us right back to the days of the Soviet . . . or the jumped-up dictators who think they can run this bloody country *and* the surrounding states better than Putin or anybody else. We're hardly short of candidates.' He stared at the stove as Gurov made tea. 'Personally, I put my money on a mix of all the above.'

'Such as?'

'There's a new group I've been hearing about; formed by breakaways unhappy with the pace of things. They're made up of politicos, military and intelligence people and call themselves the Wise Men. Can you believe that? As if they alone hold the only valid answers. What arrogant pricks!'

'Do you know any of them?' Gurov asked. He had never broached this topic with Tzorekov before, if only because it wasn't on his radar and because there was precious little he could do about it. As long as they both stayed outside Russia, outlaws in all but name, they were disconnected, involved only by association and history, like so many others who had put themselves out of reach.

'I know one of them.' Tzorekov nodded abruptly, and slapped a heavily-veined hand on the bed. 'Victor Simoyan, the tub of lard. He's got ambition and he's greedy. I've been studying him from a distance.' He looked up as Gurov handed him a mug of tea. 'You know what a kingmaker is, Arkasha?'

'Of course. Not that we have them here in Russia.'

'You're wrong, my friend. We do – and Simoyan is one of them. He won't try to run anything himself because he hasn't the talent and he knows he'd get fucked eventually by his so-called friends. But he knows people who want to do it and that's our big problem: people like him don't stop to consider the wider implications – what the Americans are fond of calling the bigger picture. Simoyan and his type will blunder us into a new age of warfare because they're too greedy, too stupid and lack the vision to see where it will lead us.' He sipped his tea. When he spoke again, his voice was soft, almost saddened. 'That is why, my friend, we must do this thing. We have to try to make a difference. This planet cannot withstand another big war.'

Gurov said nothing. But it wasn't Tzorekov's words that silenced him. In the momentary silence as the old man drank his tea, he thought he'd heard the sound of an engine. He walked over to the small window looking out over the lake. He couldn't see anything out there in the dark, but he didn't need to. They were there; he could sense it.

'Did you really,' he said casually, 'tell the British what we were doing? Or the Americans?'

Tzorekov seemed surprised by the question. 'I had to. It was important that they knew – that somebody knew, in case . . .'

'In case what – we disappear?'

'Yes. What we are doing, I've said it before, is vitally important. Somebody has to try this. I've achieved much in my life, Arkasha, but it will be meaningless if it all comes down to knowing what is happening but standing by and doing nothing. There are too many who stand by and do nothing and . . . I don't want to be one of them.'

'Did you expect them to help us? Is that why you told them?'

'How would they? Anything they do would be seen as an act of aggression and used against us. It would be worse than useless. No, we're in this alone. The best the Americans or British can do is stand on the sidelines and watch. And pray.'

'Well, let's hope they've got a direct line for the praying bit, then,' Gurov said easily. 'Talking of lines, when do we expect to hear from Valentin?'

'Who knows? Soon, I hope. He knows we're here and waiting – and he knows how important this is.'

Gurov nodded. The sooner the better in his opinion. If his instincts were right, it wasn't a big war that might be their first and only problem, but a much smaller one landing right here on their doorstep.

Later, as he put his head down and waited for sleep, Gurov wondered if they should be moving from here. If Tzorekov was right and a team was already searching, they could be in the gravest danger. But was that realistic in an area as remote as this? And was running too soon and at night any less dangerous than staying until daylight?

TWENTY-FIVE

I checked out the other three occupied cabins. They were spaced out randomly through the trees, all fronting on the water and with their own jetty. The first two were dark, with off-roaders outside and piles of boots and other wet-weather gear strung from hooks under the roof overhang. One of the cabins had a detachable outboard motor chained to the veranda posts and a five-gallon jerry can standing a few feet away. I sniffed at the lid. Gasoline.

The Touareg was parked alongside number three, and like the others had its own wooden jetty. A wisp of smoke was coming from the cabin's stove-pipe chimney and a yellow light showed through the window.

I heard a vague rumble of voices coming from inside, and stayed back in case Gurov was feeling jumpy or had put out motion detectors. If he was in full protective mode I didn't want to tangle with him, much less try explaining what I was doing here; as far as he and Tzorekov were concerned, I didn't exist.

I ducked under the tail of the Touareg and ran my hand around, hoping to feel the second tracker device. But it was a no-go; whoever had managed to put it there must have found a good place to hide it, and I didn't dare shine a light to find out where.

As I slipped out from underneath, I could still hear the helicopter, the sound alternately fading and rising as the wind shifted. It sounded louder close to the ground than it did when I stood up, and I figured the sound was being transmitted across the surface of the lake.

I doubled back to my cabin and collected the night scope, then headed off round the shore towards the sound of the rotors, which was now fading. But it was the fade of a dying engine, not distance, and I guessed they'd found somewhere to land.

There was a track of sorts through the trees, and although overgrown and littered with brushwood, was close enough to the water to keep my bearings and clear enough to keep up a fast pace. I used the night scope to avoid obstacles and stopped every few yards to check the way ahead. I didn't think anybody would have made it out this far yet, but running into opposition at this stage would put a real kink in my plans to remain invisible.

After fifteen minutes I sensed another shift in the wind, bringing with it the smell of aviation fuel. Then I saw a flash of light about a hundred yards away; there for a second, then gone. I stopped and focused the scope, and through the tangle of foliage picked out the curved shape of the helicopter fuse-lage. It had come down in a clearing close to the water, and when I swivelled the scope, I saw a long jetty pushing out into the lake with a number of small shapes tied up alongside covered in tarpaulins.

Movement. I sank down, slow and easy. If these guys knew what they were doing, they wouldn't fight their way through the woods the way I'd just had to do; they'd jump in one of the boats and take the easy route.

I wormed my way forward until I could see more clearly. There were four, no five, men gathered next to the clamshell door to the main cabin. They were probably discussing tactics.

So where was number six?

Then I saw him. It was the big guy I'd seen earlier, and he was walking back from the water's edge. He called to the others and waved an arm towards the boats. They split up, one man and the crew members staying by the helicopter and two joining the big man at the jetty, where they began to check out the boats. They were unlikely to find one with an engine, but they wouldn't need one; instinct told me these guys would be adept on the water with oars and muscle-power, where they could make a silent approach.

As they split away I could see that they were carrying assault rifles.

The big man gave a sharp whistle and waved his arm in a circle. It was a signal for the helicopter to take off. The crew members and the man with them climbed on board and moments later the engines began to turn over. It was a wise move. He was making sure they didn't all get caught out if anything went wrong, by keeping the transport mobile and out of harm's way. He was probably also hoping to fool anybody listening into thinking they had left.

Time to go. I backed out and jogged back to the cabins. At a guess it would take the men fifteen, maybe twenty minutes to make the trip by boat. It was going to take me a little less than that but it would be tight.

I was sweating by the time I got there. I stepped onto the jetty outside my cabin and checked the lake through the scope. For a second I saw nothing. Maybe I'd been wrong and they were here for some other reason.

Then I saw a flicker of movement. They were hugging the shore and moving at a steady pace about half a mile away. No splashes, no fuss, just the roll of their shoulders as they powered the boat along in a way that spoke of military training in covert night-time raids.

I ducked back to the cover of the cabin. Whoever these guys were, I didn't want to wait to see what their intentions were; if I did that I'd be too late. Night movement plus assault rifles could only mean they had come here for one thing.

And I had to stop them.

I contemplated using the Saiga. A couple of well-placed

shots would put holes below the waterline, and they'd begin to sink in no time. But that would make an open display of armed protection – and I wasn't supposed to be here. There was also the question of intent. I didn't know for sure what these guys wanted, although I was ready to bet good money on them not being here for a weekend's fishing. But starting a gunfight when it wasn't strictly necessary was upping the ante way too soon. Call me cautious, but if I could put them off their stroke without starting a minor war, that was fine by me.

For any attack, disruption is the first stage of defence. It's like fitting extra window locks; if your potential attacker isn't real serious, and sees no advantage in wasting time or effort overcoming obstacles, they will give up. If they're serious, they will attempt to overcome it there and then or step back and regroup. That's when you know you have a fight on your hands.

I went outside and hurried through the trees to the cabin I'd checked out earlier – the one with the jerry can of gas. It was heavy enough to be holding at least a couple of gallons, which should do nicely. I toted it back to a point a hundred yards beyond my cabin, where the trees stood some way back from the water, and thought about how to play this out.

If the men were homing in on the Touareg's signal, they already knew approximately where it was. All they had to do was follow the lead and walk right up to the cabin where it was parked. Easy job.

Except that I wasn't going to make it that simple.

I took the lid off the jerry can and let most of the contents glug into the water. The smell of gas was ripe but there wasn't much I could do about it. It wasn't exactly eco-friendly, either, pouring it into the lake, but neither is an assault rifle on full-auto. That done, I checked on the boat's progress. I couldn't hear it yet, but I figured I had maybe ten minutes before it got here.

I went back to the cabin and grabbed a gas lighter, a spatula from the limited kitchen tools by the stove, a disgustingly grey towel left by a previous visitor, and a couple of fire-starter cubes. I emptied out two plastic bottles of water from the car, then collected my haul and jogged back to where I'd left the jerry can of gas.

Still no sign of the boat, so I got to work; they wouldn't be long now. I put the cubes under a tree where they would stay dry, and half-filled the plastic bottles with the remaining gas. Tearing the towel into strips, I stuffed a strip into each bottle and shook them up until the fabric was soaked through. Then I walked back to the water's edge. The smell coming off the surface was less obvious now, and I hoped the mix of wind and water hadn't dissipated my surprise too much. Gas being lighter than water, it would float. If the men in the boat picked up on the smell, I was hoping they would assume it was a memory remnant of their flight in the helicopter. Helicopters – especially the military kind – give off a lot of exhaust gases which stick to the clothing and follow you like a bad reputation.

I took my two plastic Molotovs and placed them off the path closer to my cabin, where I could find them in a hurry. Having backups is essential in this kind of action, and preparation is half the battle.

By the time I got back to the waterside, I could hear the rhythmic slap of oars and the occasional rumble of wood on wood. They had probably muffled the oars with cloth to reduce the sound travelling across the lake, but under cover of darkness, nothing was going to be perfect for long.

I was mostly hoping they were counting on nobody being awake to hear them coming.

I heard a voice moments before I saw the boat slipping around a pile of brushwood jutting out into the lake. I could also hear their breathing now, sounding harsh and laboured after their efforts. In the green light of the scope I saw two men bent over the oars and a third crouched in the stern, holding a rifle. They were about twenty yards out and running parallel with the shore, and moving at a steady pace. Something in the boat's position, however, indicated that they were slowing and beginning to turn in slightly. I took that to mean that they weren't going to head straight for the cabins and the jetties, but were looking to come ashore and go the rest of the way on foot using the cover of the trees.

Which suited me just fine.

I waited until the boat was almost level with my position, then lit both fire cubes, and used the spatula to flick them one after the other as far as I could out over the water.

TWENTY-SIX

asoline. Chesnokoy had begun to pick up the familiar smell in the air as the boat neared the target area. It was sharply pungent over the dull, muddy aroma coming off the lake, an alien smell in this otherwise natural environment. He dismissed it as spillage from outboard motors used by fishermen during the day. What he couldn't see, and might have been more concerned if he had, was a slick of film in the water ahead, spreading out slowly as the wind began to shift the surface layer away from the shore.

'Easy!' he muttered, as Kruglov pulled too hard on his oar, causing it to jump out of the rowlock with a dull clatter. The two men were getting tired; they would have to step ashore soon and go the rest of the way on foot, exercising a different set of muscles. Even now, at an estimated three hundred metres from where the signal was pulsing out from the tracker on the target vehicle, he was beginning to feel too exposed. Like his men, Chesnokoy had done more than his fair share of amphibious landings over the years, but had never quite lost the sense of vulnerability brought on by being on open water. You couldn't change direction or dive into cover like you could on solid ground, nor could you avoid being bunched together with others, presenting a nice target for the enemy to hose down with bursts of deadly fire.

He tapped Ignatyev on the shoulder and pointed to a spot a hundred metres ahead. They could land there and prepare themselves before making their way to the target. At least then they could spread out and approach it from more than one direction, just in case they were expected. With ex-KGB men, no matter what their age, you never took anything for granted.

Ignatyev dug his oar in hard and the nose of the boat swung round as Kruglov kept rowing. These two didn't need any coaching; they were two halves of the same unit, sensing what each was doing and reacting accordingly.

Chesnokoy scanned the shoreline through the night scope on his rifle. It consisted of thick brushwood and trees all along here, with few landing places. But there was bound to be one shortly, if only because the fishermen would have made sure of it for landing and building illegal fires to enjoy their catches. All they would need was a space to push the boat in and jump ashore. There was no sign of movement that he could see, although the vegetation here was densely-packed and near-impenetrable.

He felt hot with anticipation, and wondered if he was simply out of condition, or was finally losing the battle-hardened confidence he'd gathered around him over many years of campaigns around the globe. It had to happen one day, he knew that; it hit every soldier eventually. But please God, not yet, not right now. He'd get this job done, and with the payment he'd receive, he could start looking for another line of business.

Earlier, before the helicopter had landed, he'd told the men to test-fire their weapons. It was more a psychological means of getting their hands in after a long lay-off than of ensuring the guns worked properly. They had gone at it eagerly, Ignatyev and Gorin firing single- or three-shot bursts while Kruglov let loose an extended volley into the inky blackness that was the water below. Gorin had commented sourly on the need to come back later and pick up the dead fish, but it had been enough to introduce a much-needed touch of humour and help them prepare for what lay ahead.

He checked their position relative to the shore. Another fifteen metres or so to go. He leaned over and dipped his hand in the lake, dashing water into his face. It felt and cool and refreshing, yet . . . oily? *And the smell.*

In the same moment Chesnokoy realized he'd just coated his face with gasoline, he saw a spot of yellow light curve out from the treeline. It appeared to hover for a second, before dropping towards the water, closely followed by another.

In a flash the surface of the lake was alight, a carpet of

flames licking out towards the boat like a hungry monster, waiting to embrace it. Ignatyev was nearest, and gave a cry of alarm and instinctively raised his arms to protect his face against the heat. He dropped his oar which slithered out of the rowlock and disappeared over the side into the flames. Chesnokoy smelled burning hair and reached out to grab the man's shoulder, yanking him backwards into the body of the boat out of further harm's way. He didn't have time to check his condition but turned to Kruglov and shouted, 'Keep going!' He pointed to a stretch of clear water just beyond the fire. 'Dig and paddle!'

Kruglov understood immediately. He got to his knees, and lifting the oar out of the rowlock, spun it round and grasped it halfway down, then dug the blade hard into the water as if paddling a canoe. Trying to dig and row, effectively steering the boat from one side with the oar in the rowlock was next to impossible, especially in these conditions. But Kruglov was skilled in boats and could paddle and dig like a champion, even with such an unwieldy implement.

The last of the flames brushed over the boat's prow, and Kruglov ducked, then dug in hard once more to propel them into a stretch of water close to the shore. Chesnokoy waited for the keel to hit the bottom before jumping out and dragging the boat until it was firmly grounded.

Leaving Kruglov to look after the injured Ignatyev, he slipped into the trees and began scanning for a sign of their attacker, his finger on the trigger.

TWENTY-SEVEN

I hit the path running before the men in the boat got through the flames. Their night vision would now be compromised which gave me a momentary advantage, but I didn't underestimate their powers of recuperation. If they got organized quickly and managed to spread out among the trees, I'd be in trouble.

Their quickest and easiest route to the cabins was along the path; any other way meant fighting through a tangle of brushwood and trees. As my cabin was going to be the first in line, I pulled my pickup back up the track and into cover. No point in giving three pissed-off, fully-armed men anything on which to vent their anger. Then I hunkered down to wait and got ready for a hot contact.

They had to come past me to get to Tzorekov, and I was determined to put them off before they got there. The element of surprise was now gone, but that was the trade-off when disrupting an attacker's plans: there might be a violent knock-back to contend with if they didn't get the message first time round.

As I checked through the scope a figure stepped out of the trees and crept along the path into the open. He was carrying an assault rifle with a big scope and stopping constantly to scan the ground ahead. I stayed low and out of sight. The other two men had to be somewhere close by, ready to back him up if he got compromised.

There was only one way to find out. I ducked behind the cabin wall and lit the first fuse. This was going to have to be quick and dirty. The backup would be waiting for something like this to happen, and I'd only have a split second to get a reaction without getting shot. I stepped to the corner and lobbed the bottle high into the air. If they were both using night-sights, the flare of light would be enough to blind them for a few seconds before they could react.

Using plastic bottles is more effective than glass, since the plastic is thin and will usually split, even on contact with soft ground or grass. Glass, on the other hand, will sometimes remain perversely intact, spilling a small amount of the fuel from the neck but without accomplishing the task needed.

And what I needed right now was shock value.

As I moved back I caught an image of the bottle making a perfect arc through the night sky. It hit the path near where the man was crouching and split open with spectacular effect. He gave a yelp as flames burst across the ground all around him, catching his legs as he tried to jump back out of the way. He had good reactions but not good enough. Tongues of fire wrapped around his ankles as he dropped to the ground and rolled around, trying to extinguish the flames and get into cover.

Then I caught a faint rattle from the trees off to one side, and a section of the cabin wall exploded, a bunch of fragments flying past my face. Here was the backup. A good one, too; he'd been able to spot and zero in on me in spite of the flare of light. Worse, he was using a silencer and I'd seen no sign of muzzle-flash.

So where was number three? Maybe they'd left him back at the boat to cover their escape.

A voice called from the trees. The reply when it came from the man on the path was succinct and forced, but he didn't sound as if he was ready to give up just yet.

I picked up a small log from the stack behind me, and hurled it away in the direction of the other cabins and the lake. It hit the ground and tumbled end over end, by luck a close enough approximation to the sound of somebody running. At least I hoped so. I waited for the next move.

It wasn't long in coming and I almost got caught out. There was a scuff of footsteps close to the cabin and I just had time to pick up another log and swing it as a figure came charging round the corner. He was very fast; he had his arms raised with the assault rifle held up high and managed to block most of the blow from the log. He twisted sideways and struck out with the butt of the rifle, catching me a glancing blow on the shoulder. But he was already off balance and beginning to fall. I turned with him and hit him again with the log. This time I connected with the side of his head and he grunted once before hitting the ground and rolling past me, carried by his own momentum.

End of story.

I checked him over in case he was playing possum. He was out cold. It really wasn't his night; he smelled of burnt cloth and one leg felt bare where the fabric had burned away. What was interesting was the assault rifle he'd dropped. It was short and stubby and by the feel of it I guessed it was something special, like an AS Val, with a permanent night-vision scope and flash suppressor. That accounted for the lack of noise when the bullets fired by his colleague had almost taken my face off.

'Kruglov?' A voice called out from the dark.

So that was his name.

'*Kruglov!*'

Kruglov wasn't going to answer.

I was about to check through the rifle's scope for movement when Kruglov's pal decided he'd had enough of waiting. He switched his rate of fire to fully-automatic and hosed down my corner of the cabin. As I hugged the ground and waited for the chunks of wood and filler to stop raining down on me, I heard the sound of footsteps running through the bush. They were heading away from me and I knew instantly what he was doing: he was going for Tzorekov alone.

I ran towards the jetty and veered off to follow the edge of the lake. I wasn't worried about the gunman seeing me down here; it was low down and gave me enough cover. It was also the shortest distance to Tzorekov's cabin, where I had to intercept him.

I had to hand it to them, these guys were serious. They'd come in fast and were using military-grade equipment. It was special forces stuff but I still wasn't convinced they were serving personnel; if they were, they'd have flown in right over the cabins and abseiled down and it would have all been over within minutes, job done.

I came to a clutch of trees growing right down at the lake side, and slipped into the water up to my waist. The going was muddy and soft, pulling at my boots. A tangle of weeds felt like snakes around my ankles, bringing back childhood memories of wild swimming in lakes and rivers and the fear of feeling you were suddenly going to be pulled under, never to be found.

I pushed on, trying not to make a noise and watching for signs of light from the other cabins. If the other residents had slept through the past ten minutes they must be drunk or drugged. If not, and they had seen the fire display, they were simply keeping their heads down and minding their own business.

As soon as I had a decent amount of scenery between me

and the shooter, I came up out of the water and moved into the trees.

I figured I was now about fifty yards away from Tzorekov's cabin. If the attacker was following the signal from the Touareg, all he had to do was move in the general direction and he'd trip over it. Which meant I had to place myself in the way and wait – or stop him getting anywhere close.

I opted for stopping him. If he saw the cabin and got past me, all he had to do was find a window, then open fire and riddle the interior with gunfire. Tzorekov and his buddy Gurov would be turned into burger mince. But if I engaged him before he got that far, it might be enough to put him off trying.

I checked the assault rifle by feel. It was covered in dust where it had rolled around in the dirt a few times, but these weapons were made for a rough life. If it let me down I was going to write a serious letter of complaint to the manufacturers.

TWENTY-EIGHT

'What is it?' Tzorekov was awake. He threw his blanket aside and sat up as Gurov stepped across the cabin to the window.

'It's nothing. I'm just checking something.' Gurov was staring out over the lake. He could just make out the line of the jetty against the water, but not much else. He'd heard something too, but he couldn't make out what. It had been enough to drag him from a light sleep, but not quickly enough to put an image to the memory. And there had been a flash of light glowing briefly before being extinguished. Not torchlight but something bigger and less defined – a naked flame?

'Stay here,' he said, and stepped outside, the gun in his hand. It was probably nothing; a hunter perhaps, out late when he should have been fast asleep or dead drunk. But he had to make sure.

Silence.

Then came a snapping sound, rapidly repeated. It wasn't far, maybe two or three hundred metres, and he felt the hairs on the back of his neck stir with a distant memory. He'd heard a noise like that before, while training with the FSB. He turned and went back inside. 'Quick, we have to move – now!'

'Why – what's going on?' Tzorekov demanded, but he gathered up his clothes and headed for the door, his instincts and faith in Gurov taking over. Answers could come later.

'The bastards are here, that's what.' Gurov grabbed his things, checked they had left nothing behind, then headed outside after his boss.

They bundled their gear inside the Touareg and Gurov handed the gun to the old man. 'If you see anybody in our way, shoot them. Don't wait, just shoot.'

Tzorekov took the gun and wound down the window. 'What if it's a hunter?'

'Too bad. It will teach him not to go around killing innocent animals. Ready?' Gurov turned the ignition and eased the Touareg forward along the track towards the road, ready to stamp on the gas and hit the lights. He was praying that the engine noise wouldn't alert anybody to their departure but right now it was the only option he had. If it was a hunter out there, blundering around in the dark, it had to be one armed with a silenced automatic weapon; he'd heard that snapping sound often enough not to be mistaken.

He flicked on the main beams for a second to see the layout of the track, then switched them off again. It was enough to cover some distance before switching them on again for another look.

They reached the end of the track and came out in the clearing in front of the office. The space was empty and the office lights were out. He stopped and turned off the engine, then got out and jumped onto the hood.

Absolute silence.

Wait. An engine noise. Distant but audible, a high-pitched whine. A helicopter. The same one he'd heard earlier?

He got back in and hit the gas. This wasn't good. He felt sick with guilt; he'd been a fool to have waited for daybreak

– they should have got out while they could. Now they'd been tracked down and the search was closing in.

As he set off along the road, he was wondering how the hell the followers had managed to find them.

TWENTY-NINE

I knew the cabin was deserted before I got there. I'd heard the sound of an engine but it had been too soft to locate the source. Now I knew. Gurov would have been alerted by the noise and the light from the lake, and had taken off fast.

I ran past the open door, across the space where the Touareg had stood earlier and continued into the trees. I still planned on stopping the opposition, even though their quarry was gone. Whoever they were, this was just the first attempt; they would keep on trying until they got lucky.

I heard a shout. It was far enough away but I knew what it meant: they had given up. They must have guessed the two men had lit out and were now regrouping to take up the hunt later.

I jogged back to the cabins and made for the path to the lake. The man whose gun I was carrying was gone from outside my cabin, and I figured his pal had picked him up. There was only one place they could have been making for.

The distant whine of the helicopter told me that.

I continued as quickly as I dared on their trail, cutting off briefly down to where the boat had come ashore. The smell of gas and burned brushwood still hung in the air, but there was no sign of the men. The boat was still there, sitting low in the water about twenty feet away, with one oar hanging over the side like a broken arm.

I carried on along the path. If nothing else I could give them a send-off and hopefully make it seem like a waste of their time coming back.

The Ansat's engines burst into a full-throated roar when I

was still a hundred yards away. They were taking off. I put on speed, but as I reached the edge of the clearing I saw lights rising through the foliage ahead and the branches bending back under the powerful down-draft of the rotors.

The roar became a clatter as the machine reached a couple of hundred feet and the pilot took it sideways over the treetops with the helicopter equivalent of a racing start. I dropped to one knee and aimed at the main cabin. I didn't want to kill anyone or bring down the machine, even if I thought I could with such a light weapon. That would attract too much attention and be like sticking my finger in a hornets' nest. The local military camps Lindsay had mentioned would notice it and in no time the area would be flooded with police, army and emergency personnel.

But the necessary follow-on to disruption of an attack is to counter-strike and, if further action is required, harassment. It didn't have to be fatal, but it did have to appear deadly in its intent.

Whoever they were, I wanted to let them know that they had a fight on their hands.

One. Two. Three. I couldn't hear the shots but I felt the recoil of each one against my shoulder. At that range I couldn't miss and the men inside the flying tin can would certainly hear the ping of impact.

And in a helicopter, even a light military workhorse like this one, already operating under difficult conditions and very close to trees, taking live fire makes you feel very vulnerable.

I turned and jogged back to the cabin.

THIRTY

'What the fuck was that?' The pilot yelled, as he appeared to be hauling the Ansat into the air by sheer muscle-power alone. His navigator turned to stare at Chesnokoy and the two wounded men, seeking answers.

'We're taking incoming fire, you idiot,' Chesnokoy shouted back angrily. 'I assumed you'd been shot at before.'

'I have and I know *what* it is – I mean what the hell have you got us into? This was supposed to be a drop-and-carry assignment, not a damned war zone.'

Chesnokoy ignored him. The less this idiot knew the better. But even he must have known this was no simple logistical exercise. The first thing they had to do was get away from here in one piece, then decide what to do next. That meant talking to Simoyan, the man who'd hired them. With Kruglov nursing a sore head and what looked like a badly smashed arm following his contact with the mystery man at the cabins, and Ignatyev virtually blinded by the brush of fire sweeping over him in the boat, he was going to have some explaining to do. But he was damned if he was going to run away with his tail tucked between his legs. He still had Gorin, who was worth two very good men, and given a chance to regroup, he'd be back in the fight and wipe out whoever had done this.

'You look worried.' Gorin leaned across and spoke in his ear. 'And scared.'

Chesnokoy bit his tongue. If there was one man alive who could say such a thing to him and get away with it, it was Georgi. They had shared too many bad moments, some terrifying, some horrifying in the extreme; but that was in the white heat of an operation when they all knew the risks facing them before going out. But this . . . this was different.

'I'm not worried,' he shouted back. 'I'm pissed!'

Gorin said nothing and went back to tending the two injured men, while Chesnokoy tried to ignore the feeling welling up in his chest. In truth, he was afraid of no man on the planet. At least, no ordinary man. But suddenly he *was* afraid and it wasn't a nice feeling. Was it fear of failing? Of losing his men? Or was it the fear of losing the money they'd been promised for this operation and the opportunity it presented for him to get out of this business and make a new start?

He had no idea. All he knew was, he had a score to settle with the person who had done this, otherwise he'd never experience another peaceful moment in his life. If there was one thing he hated, it was losing a fight and having to retreat.

He took a deep breath, suddenly aware of how drained he felt after the mad dash through the trees. Struggling to drag Ignatyev along the path while using his radio to call up the Ansat, he'd been filled with rage and a sense of frustration at the turn of events and desperate to go back to the cabins and wreak havoc on whoever had been waiting for them. But he was now two men down and a weapon missing, and in the unaccustomed position of being on the back foot.

'Get those engines turning *now*!' he'd yelled as soon as the navigator's voice responded.

'Ready and waiting. What the hell happened back there?' The man had sounded calm enough, but was clearly not keen on hanging around any longer than necessary.

'Don't ask questions – we're leaving the moment we're on board!'

Moments later they had broken through the last of the trees into the clearing, and seen Georgi Gorin waiting at the foot of the clamshell doors, armed and ready. Chesnokoy had heaved Ignatyev unceremoniously up the steps, while behind him Kruglov, still dazed from his contact with the mystery figure in the trees, stumbled against him and cried out as his damaged arm was sandwiched between them.

The moment they were all aboard with the doors closed, the aircraft had lifted off and begun to turn. Chesnokoy braced himself and helped Gorin grab the two wounded men as the pilot took the machine up and away above treetop level, aiming for maximum speed and lift. Once they were level he helped them buckle in to their seats and got himself belted in while Gorin began to check Kruglov's arm.

He tossed the radio on the floor of the cabin; he had no use for it now unless he decided to hurl it at the fool of a pilot. It wouldn't be logical or professional, but right now he didn't feel much of either and wanted to smash something. What a fucking mess.

There was nothing for it. He took out his phone and dialled the number he'd been given. For use only in extreme emergencies, he'd been told, and keep it brief. Well, this was an emergency, he decided. A big one. And he'd keep it brief, all right.

Five rings. Seven, Ten. Twelve. He was about to hang up when it was answered with a single word. Even over the roar of the engines battering his head, he recognized the gravelly voice immediately. 'Yes?'

He stuck a finger in his ear and said calmly, 'It's Chesnokoy. I need more men. Armed and ready to fight.'

THIRTY-ONE

Victor Simoyan put down his phone in disbelief, and sat back to stare at the darkness outside and consider what he should do. What was that strange saying he'd heard a visiting British trades unionist mutter one day? *It never rains but it pours.* He'd never thought much about it, dismissing it as some kind of trite British working-class utterance. But now it seemed to have taken on a clear meaning.

From the start this project had seemed such a simple thing to accomplish; send a group of trained and highly-skilled men with nothing to lose and a substantial reward to gain, to find two targets, one old, one younger, and make certain they never surfaced anywhere ever again, alive or dead. Just like the men who would deal with them, they had to vanish.

What the hell could go wrong?

First the call from Gretsky about a nosy air traffic controller picking up the Ansat's beacon signal, which was worrying enough. The thought that some mid-level functionary might pick up on the log that the pilot had filed and send it on up the line to gain some personal commendation for attention to duty had been sufficient to kill any further ideas of sleep, in spite of the whisky. He'd come into the office instead, preferring the functional surroundings of his workplace to the chilly atmosphere that would prevail if he were to disturb his wife's slumbers. Now this call from Chesnokoy – ironically, in the same Ansat, which he was beginning to think might be jinxed.

'What's happened?' Evgeniy Koroleg was sitting slumped

in a chair across the other side of Simoyan's desk, nursing a glass of whisky. He'd arrived five minutes ago as if summoned by some telepathic message, also unable to sleep and in search of reassurance that what they were doing couldn't possibly go wrong.

As usual he looked a mess; a three-day beard under a heavy moustache, and crumpled clothes Simoyan wouldn't have been seen dead in, even at his own funeral. Like Simoyan, he had been waiting ever since the team had been given the order to go, anxious to hear news that the 'problem' of Tzorekov had been dealt with and they and the rest of the Wise Men could relax and carry on their business as normal. Or maybe get some sleep instead of sitting up all night long.

'A slight setback,' Simoyan said more easily than he felt. 'Chesnokoy's run into a little problem.'

'What sort of problem?'

'The kind that bites. I think we may have underestimated Gurov and his ability to protect Tzorekov.' He reached for the throwaway cell phone and flicked through the limited directory. These were mostly related to certain people the authorities would view with some alarm if his links to them were ever made public.

'What are you going to do?' said Koroleg. He was looking worried and finished off his drink in one throw, then stared into his empty glass. 'Hell, what have we started?' he added.

'What we'll do is keep going and finish it. What we've started is a fight to ensure our survival.' Simoyan dialled a number, then leaned forward so that Koroleg had to look him in the eye. 'Don't make the mistake of going soft on me now, Evgeniy. This is just the first move. Teething troubles. Once we've dealt with the traitors, we can rest assured that the situation will continue to our benefit; to Russia's benefit. Don't forget, you're in this all the way; there's no backing out now for any of us.'

'I know that, of course. I'm not suggesting otherwise.'

'Good.' There was a click as the call was picked up at the other end. He sat back and said without preamble, 'I need more men to join Chesnokoy. Four should do it. Liaise with him on this; you have his number. Make sure he heads towards the airfield outside Saint Petersburg and stays there until dark. He can pick the men up there. Same conditions as the others and an extra twenty per cent if they get it right. If they don't, tell them not to bother coming back.'

He listened for a moment as the person on the other end spoke, then said, 'I think the Ansat is going to be required for at least another two days and nights. Yes, I know what I said, but the situation has changed. I'm sure you can square it with everyone involved. Tell them it's being serviced or repaired, tell them anything you like, make them an offer they can't refuse. Just make sure it stays in use and off the board, you hear me? And that means flying only at night. Oh, and you'd better sort out some medical help; Chesnokoy ran into some trouble and has two injured men. Find some-where secure and quiet to keep them.' He cut the connection and put the phone back in the drawer. Picking up his whisky, he rattled the ice cubes in the glass with a gentle shake of his wrist.

'Who was that?' Koroleg asked, now looking alarmed. 'The Ansat's a military helicopter, isn't it? How the hell did you get one of those?'

'A man,' Simoyan replied bluntly. 'A man who provides services. That's all you need to know. Right now he is a provider of logistics and men. Men like Chesnokoy.' He gave Koroleg a cool glance that conveyed a deliberate message. 'The kind of men I use when somebody fails to live up to my expectations.'

Men like the two he was considering sending after the air traffic controller named Datsyuk, who had noticed rather more than he should. It might not be necessary, but the risk of his report becoming more public might outweigh any chance he had of sitting back and doing nothing. After all, if the source happened to have an accident – easy to do in night-time Moscow – that was at least one part of the problem dealt with permanently.

But he wouldn't tell Koroleg about that. There were some things that were best kept secret.

He poured more whisky for them both and decided to wait

until dawn. Things often appeared much simpler with the start of a new day.

THIRTY-TWO

I t was raining again by the time I got back to the cabin. Heavy and relentless, it was going to make visibility even harder once I was out on the road. I checked the Touareg's tracking signal. It was still there but not strong. Sooner rather than later, with the head start they'd got, they would drop off the edge and I'd lose them. I had to go after them but first I had to contact Langley. This assignment was getting hotter and I needed to know what I was up against. I still wasn't convinced the attackers had been regular forces, but thinking and knowing weren't the same. I got inside the cabin and checked the weapon dropped by the man I'd hit.

As I'd thought, it was an assault weapon; a Russian AS Val silenced sniper's rifle. It only had a few rounds left in the magazine, but it might prove useful. The model had been around for some time, but beyond that I knew little about it or where this one might have come from. However, I did have its serial number and identifier on the side of the receiver, which housed the trigger assembly and main working parts. And that gave me an idea about checking who the assault team might be working for.

I called Lindsay.

'Go ahead, Watchman.' Quick off the mark and economical as always. It was good to hear a friendly voice.

'I need you to see if you can run a background check on a weapon,' I said, and gave her the serial number and description. 'I think it could be off the black market, in which case numbers close to this one might have been circulating on international police files of weapons stolen in batches from armouries or military depots.'

'Got that. Anything else?'

'Yes. That helicopter you saw earlier is back in the air. If you can get a trace on where it's going, it would help. I'd also like a heads up if it looks like heading back this way.'

'Copy that. I'll keep you posted.'

'Another thing. I'm close to losing contact with Counselor. Can you get the Pathfinders to monitor and feed back his progress until I'm back on board?'

'Of course.'

'Good. After that you should ask Vale to get them out of there.'

'Is there a specific problem?'

'Not yet, but there might be. I'm only guessing but I think the other team are contractors. Even so, if the people they work for have any juice they might use local military and intelligence assets to scan the area for unusual signals.'

'One moment, Watchman. I have someone for you.'

There was a click and Brian Callahan came on. 'What happened?'

I gave him a potted version of events and repeated my suggestion that the observers sent in by Tom Vale should be sent out of the area in case things hotted up. By accident or design, the situation could become compromised at any moment, and fewer bodies in the field would be a good idea.

'Copy that; I'll pass it on. I take it you had contact?'

'Affirmative. Four men by air. They're now down to two plus two walking wounded. But I don't think that's going to stop them. They'll be back.'

'I think you can count on it. It's a setback but if the people behind them are who we think they are, they have too much to lose to give up easily. Be prepared for additional bodies.'

'Copy that. Any word on movement from Impaler?' If Putin did make tracks for this end of his empire, he could well be dragging a posse of observers behind him, not all of them friendly. Either way it might make the field a little crowded. And unlike being able to go to ground in a city, getting caught in the open out here would take some explaining away.

'We've got nothing yet. We're watching those close to him. If he moves, so will they.'

I signed off and dragged my gear out to the car. More than anything now I had to keep a close tail on Tzorekov. Whether

Putin moved or not, whether he agreed to a meeting with
Tzorekov directly or via an intermediary, Tzorekov had
placed himself in a tough position. The opposition would be
out to stop him at all costs, and now they knew somebody
else was out there and ready to fight, they'd come back with
all guns blazing.

Worse still, they had one big advantage in their favour: the
other tracker was still on the Touareg, pinpointing precisely
where Tzorekov was headed.

A couple of hours of hard driving later, as I was beginning to
think I'd never catch up, I got lucky. The signal from the
Touareg became stronger. I slowed down. A large metal sign
by the side of the road was showing a schematic of a power
plant sitting on the banks of a river. It was old and rusted, the
paint peeling badly, but in the headlights I caught a glimpse
of the old Soviet-era graphic of a workers' paradise, with
muscular and smiling men and women in flat caps and scarves,
all marching towards a new age that had long since gone.

I checked the signal. Unless the tracker had become
dislodged, they were no more than a couple of miles away
and not moving. I hadn't seen another vehicle for over an
hour, the last one a logging truck that had nearly swept me
into the trees on a sharp corner. But suddenly I was feeling
beat and needed to get some sleep, if only for a few minutes.
A deserted building might be an ideal place to stop for a while,
especially if there was no risk of losing the Touareg. I could
always call for the Pathfinders to give me a reading, but I
preferred to stick a little closer to Tzorekov if I could. The
one thing I couldn't do was continue my assignment if I was
so tired I got wrapped around a tree or the front end of a
big truck.

I dropped my speed to a crawl and came to a bridge spanning
the river. Beyond it I saw the faint outline of chimneys and a
huge blockhouse of a building outlined against the sky. I
switched off my lights and stopped the car. I climbed out and
did a quick tour of the car to drum some feeling back into my
legs, which felt stiff and cold. Then I got out the scope and
took a look at what lay ahead. It was a monstrosity in green,

of concrete and metal with crumbling walls and trees growing through the sides of the structure. The once-substantial river that had serviced and powered it was now a long way down and little more than a hundred yards across.

I focused on the approach to the main building. I was hoping there was no security in place. Many such facilities like this in Russia kept a caretaker on site to keep away scavengers and squatters. What I needed was somewhere quiet to put the pickup under cover and get my head down. But first I had to find the Touareg.

Then I saw it. They'd had the same idea as me.

I was looking into the dark interior of a huge bunker of some kind. It had double sliding doors that were wide open, with one door hanging on its rails and looking like it hadn't moved in decades. Although deep in shadow, or perhaps because of it, I saw a flare of red light. It was no more than a second or two, but it was enough to show the outline of the Touareg, which had reversed in against the back wall. The flare had been from the brake lights. Then the shape of the vehicle changed as the front doors opened and Tzorekov and Gurov climbed out. They went to the rear and opened it, and took out something that looked like baggage. Moments later they walked out of sight.

I went back to the car and considered my options. I couldn't stay on this side of the river and hope to provide any kind of cover for Tzorekov if the helicopter came tracking in on their signal. The speed they had in the air would outweigh mine to react on the ground by a long way. But to drive across the bridge now was to risk putting myself under the spotlight, especially if I encountered another vehicle coming the other way and Gurov heard the engines. One might be acceptable but in his jumpy state, two might make him take a closer look.

I drove across the bridge, foot light on the gas pedal. The feeling of exposure I got while passing the open latticework between the vast metal struts was like being a target on a high-wire. I was hoping Gurov was even more exhausted than I was and not watching me right now. The plant was far enough away to be out of normal earshot, but sitting down the river like it was, sound would travel more easily along the water.

I drove past the gated entrance to the plant and found a pull-in three hundred yards beyond it, sandwiched between trees. It looked as if it was in occasional use by truckers, but right now I had it all to myself. I reversed into the trees and cut the engine, then set my internal alarm to sleep for thirty minutes.

THIRTY-THREE

Up close, even in the green light of the scope, the twin gates to the power plant looked big and intimidating. At some point there had been chains fitted and locked in place, but they had since been cut away and one of the gates forced back just enough to allow a vehicle through.

I stepped through the gap. The surface of the road had crumpled and was full of potholes. It was impossible in this light to see whether any other vehicles apart from the Touareg had passed this way recently. A nice layer of mud to show up tyre tracks would have been ideal but I was out of luck.

A crumbling cinder-block guardhouse stood fifty yards inside the gates, another reminder of times past. Grey and austere, it was as welcoming as a tank trap. I checked it over through the scope on the Val first to make sure it was clear, then moved in to make sure there were no surprises waiting – like Gurov with an itchy trigger finger. It would be too humiliating to be shot by one of the people I was supposed to be protecting.

Closer inspection showed the structure was empty. It had long ago been gutted and stripped of anything useful, a case of individual free enterprise taking over from rigid state control. This included the sliding windows for checking vehicles, staff and visitors in and out, and the inner doors and other fitments. I left it and moved to the river side of the approach road where there was a grass verge, and began walking towards the power plant.

It was easy going, with plenty of cover if I had to get

out of sight fast. I came to a bend and saw the river side of
the building where it jutted out over the water. The rest of the
structure was out of sight behind a line of trees coming right
down to the road. I used the scope and saw that whatever had
once been built for drawing water off the river had now
collapsed, and there was no way for anybody to bridge the
gap. I crossed the road to where there was a backdrop of trees
and continued moving round the bend until I could see the
whole sweep of the building, including the bunker where I'd
seen the Touareg.

The space in front of the building was the size of two foot-
ball fields, and had once been a truck and vehicle park. Getting
across to the bunker meant having to skirt around the edge
under cover of the trees surrounding the site. It was going to
take time, but it was the only way of staying off Gurov's radar
and not being caught flat-footed on open ground.

I took it slowly, checking for obstacles. The ground inside
the treeline was rough underfoot and tangled with undergrowth,
but thankfully free of fences or other barriers. I finally got
close to the corner of the bunker, and stood studying every
inch of it for signs of Gurov. I wasn't going to underestimate
him or the fact that, to him I would be an intruder – and a
potentially dangerous one at that. He would be alert for any
opposition to what he and his boss were doing, and whether
he was old-school KGB or more recently their successor, FSB,
his reaction would in all likelihood be instantaneous and deadly.

And out here there would be nobody to witness what he
was doing or how he would dispose of the evidence.

Once I was satisfied I walked across to the building and
slid round the edge of the nearest giant door into the interior.
It was like stepping into an aircraft hangar, with the ceiling
high above and that oddly conflicting feeling of enormous
space somehow contained, the kind that made you instinctively
want to shout simply for the comfort of hearing the echo.

The Touareg was fifty feet away. Beyond it were two doors,
one at each corner, leading into the main building, each with
steps leading up to a small platform. Both doors were closed,
but I couldn't see any signs of locks or chains. In the centre
of the wall between them was a large steel shutter affair which

I guessed covered hoppers for loading coal into the plant. There were no viewpoints overlooking the bunker interior, so I crossed the open floor and looked through the Touareg windows. I couldn't make out much detail inside, just a couple of boxes, probably supplies, some bottled water and wet-weather clothing spread over the rear seats.

I considered for a moment seeing if I could locate the other tracking device. If I could destroy that the team pursuing them would be flying blind. But that was assuming they didn't now have more up-to-date information about where Tzorekov and Gurov were heading. I decided I had to find them first. If the helicopter team did come calling, I couldn't do much to protect the two men if I didn't know where they were.

I moved across to the left-hand stairs and up the steps. With no way of knowing what was on the other side of the door, I had to tread carefully.

I tested the door. It was closed but not locked. I edged it open enough to put my ear close to the gap, and heard the soft echo of voices. I pulled the door further and slipped through. I was in a large passageway with two doors along the left-hand wall and a pair of double doors at the far end about forty feet away, where a flicker of light showed. Water lay on the bare concrete floor, pooled around a scattering of broken and mouldy plaster where damp had got into the structure. The smell was musty, the air chilled and unwelcoming.

I checked the two doors first. They opened into what I guessed had been offices. They were now bare and open to the elements where the windows had been stripped out, letting in years of rain and snow to assist in the gradual deterioration of the building's fabric.

That left the double doors at the far end. As I started forward, I felt a hint of a crackling sensation under my foot, and stopped. This was too risky. The floor was layered in grit, and I could see where the two men had already passed by, leaving crushed fragments in their wake. It was like a natural intruder alert, and I really didn't need to be here right now. I stepped back and retreated through the door. Now I knew where the two men were, I could check out the rest of the site in case I needed to find a quick way out.

But first I had to look for the second tracker. I slid underneath the Touareg and felt around the underneath, digging my fingers into all the nooks and crannies. I ghosted over the tracker I'd left there, and working on the basis that whoever had bugged the vehicle would have had little time to do it, focussed on the areas close to each side.

Nothing.

That meant it had to be under the hood or inside the vehicle itself. And that could be a problem. I've never yet come across a hood that lifted without a sound; they're noisy because they're made of thin metal and in a space like this the sound would be magnified several times over. To add to it, modern vehicles come fitted with anti-theft alarms and this one had a telltale red indicator glowing in the front. But I was guessing that whoever had placed the tracker would have had the same thoughts as me and avoided the hood. Maybe I was being too clever but that left the inside.

I looked around. Several lengths of heavy-duty rubber tubing were tacked against the wall nearby, with a couple of others lying on the floor where they had fallen. I judged the distance from the car and decided they would do nicely. All it would need was a flick and they would fall right where I wanted them.

It was hammy but it would have to do. You have to work with what you've got.

I tried the tail door, ready to reach up and pull the wiring loose and make tracks for the open if I had to. Silence. Just the click of the lock and the interior light came on.

Two seconds later, so did the alarm.

Damn, it was loud. I closed the door again, reached across to the stack of rubber tubing and pulled a couple away from the wall. By the time they hit the roof of the Touareg with a dull thump, I was sprinting for the great outdoors. Hopefully, the picture would explain everything.

I hit the corner just as I heard a shout coming from inside the building. Gurov, I figured, with fast reflexes and probably armed.

I ran for the trees and kept going.

THIRTY-FOUR

I must have dozed off when I got back to the car, because I came awake to the faintest glow of dawn in the sky and the buzz of the cell phone in my ear. It was Lindsay. I checked my surroundings through the windows before picking up the call but I was still alone.

'Watchman, I have Tom Vale for you.'

Vale came on without preamble, his voice brisk. 'I've found someone with local knowledge. I called him last night and he's ready to go as soon as it's daylight.'

'Good work – thanks. Who is he?'

'His name is Sedgwick – Robert Sedgwick; he's a commercial attaché out of the embassy in Moscow currently working on a trade project alongside the Consulate-General in Saint Petersburg. He knows the region well and is pretty sure he knows the location they're most likely to use for a meeting.' He read out the number of a cell phone. 'He'll be waiting for your call when he lands.'

'Is this place approachable?'

'He described it as a lakeside dacha. It's been used by Impaler before, a couple of years ago. It was closed down by the government not long afterwards, but Sedgwick says it's still kept running, although nobody has been seen there apart from a skeleton staff. He'll brief you face-to-face, maybe take you to within sight of it. He can meet up with you within a couple of hours as long as it's near water and in daylight.'

'He has a plane?' It had to be one of the small floatplanes that served the area around here and used the lakes as landing areas. I was surprised a British diplomat had one, but maybe things were a lot more relaxed up here than I thought.

'He has access to one with a pilot. He conducts cross-border trade visits and conferences in the region for British and Russian chambers of commerce, so he has a fair degree of leeway.'

'I take it he's not one of yours, then?' I meant his employers, MI6, Britain's Secret Intelligence Service. I trusted Vale without question, but it's nice to know who I might get to meet with, especially in the field.

Vale wasn't offended; he would have asked the same question himself in my shoes. 'Not at all. We've used his local knowledge from time to time, but he is what it says on his badge.'

I thought about how to get together with Sedgwick in a way that was safe for him. If he wasn't an MI6 regular, he'd be operating outside his usual comfort zone. I didn't want to put him in danger, and if we relied on cell phone contact, we could easily miss the other's call and waste the day. I had an idea.

'If he knows the area, it's best if he chooses a location where he can land safely and I'll meet him there.' Although the region was peppered with lakes, I wasn't sure they were all accessible by floatplane.

'Good point. We can use the Pathfinders to keep an eye on Counselor for you while you're gone. I have the data on your location and will send you coordinates for the rendezvous as soon as I get word from Sedgwick.'

I turned off the cell phone and drank some water and ate some fruit, then checked on the tracker signal. The Touareg was still here, but I decided to check on Tzorekov anyway, just to be sure. I made my way through the trees to a point where I could see the Touareg. It was still parked where I'd seen it before and the strips of rubber I'd knocked over had been moved. I watched for a while to see if there was any sign that the two men were going to make a move, but the place was quiet.

I figured if they were in no hurry to leave, it was because they were still waiting for confirmation of a location and a time for the meeting.

Two hours later I got another call from Lindsay. I was back in the car and fixating on a huge mug of fresh coffee. With cream. If nothing else it helped pass the time.

'I'm sending you some co-ordinates from Vale,' she told

me. 'He told me it's the information you requested for your meeting.' Then she added brightly, 'How are you?'

How was I? It was an odd question and I sensed the experienced hand of Tom Vale behind it. Brian Callahan might be responsible for running this operation, but I knew Vale would be taking a close interest in the actual mechanics. Me, in other words.

'I'm good. What did he say?'

'Who?'

'Vale. I know he said something.'

'He didn't . . . I mean, not much.' I could almost hear her confused blush.

'Like what?'

'He said the waiting was the most difficult part of an operation and that you might like to hear the sound of a . . . a friendly voice. It was his idea, I promise. I'm not breaking protocol. And Callahan agreed.'

I couldn't fault their interest, I had to give them that. And I knew why it was. The stakes for this assignment must be very high indeed, and that alone would be enough of a driver behind their thinking. Keep the operative active and alert whenever possible; engage and detect any doubts or concerns and give whatever support was available, relaying any relevant information to the Clandestine Service Officer in charge – in this case Brian Callahan. And Tom Vale would be thinking exactly the same. Leaving a field operative in the dark from time to time was sometimes inevitable, especially in a fast-moving scenario when communications were not always possible or advisable. But it isn't good practice.

That wasn't the only reason they might be concerned, however. Although I was in secure and encrypted communication, I'd come through a hard contact with the opposition, and was now having to wait for something to unfold. The succession of adrenalin surge from the fire-fight with the men in the helicopter, then a period of inaction, when I wasn't sure whether my presence had been detected or the men I'd come into contact with had merely assumed that Gurov was the aggressor, would be an alternate high and low. And for some operatives that was a killer combination, when mistakes could be made and uncertainty would be at its highest. For some it bred a sense of paranoia that could eventually begin to chip away at the mind.

'Tell Mother Goose to stop fussing,' I suggested. 'But thank you all, anyway. As soon as I get the co-ordinates I'll be on my way. Make sure the Pathfinders keep an eye on the target and to watch their backs. I still don't know how connected the guys from last night are, but I'm pretty sure they'll be back with extra help and looking for anything out of the ordinary.'

'Copy that.'

'I suppose their toy has camera capabilities – like the one you sent over to watch my back last time?'

'That's correct. Kind of you to remember.' The smile in her voice told me she knew what I was referring to. She had taken a shot on enlisting the help of an unarmed, high-altitude drone to give me a picture of everything on the ground while running for the border in Ukraine. It had been a lifesaver in more ways than one and I hadn't forgotten it.

'Don't suppose they have any other gadgets on board, do they?'

'You mean lethal ones?'

'Yes.'

'I asked about that. Mr Vale said this one's too small . . . but they're working on it.' She paused. 'Do you think he was joking?'

'I wouldn't bet on it. If he gets one any time soon, tell him to get it in the air.'

'I will. Stay safe.'

I waited for the co-ordinates to come through, then fed them into my navigation system. The location was a lake about thirty miles away. Given a decent road, which was doubtful, that meant an hour's drive. Lindsay's message said there was a bar at the lake along with a boating and fishing hire store billed as ideal for weekend enthusiasts from the city, so the arrival of a plane wouldn't stand out. Sedgwick would be there in one hour thirty minutes.

I made sure the Val was securely out of sight and the pistol close at hand, then set out for my rendezvous.

THIRTY-FIVE

'Y ou're going out? But it's so early.' The voice was soft,
feminine and sleepy, and came out of a tangle of
bedclothes that, until the early alarm had woken him,
Robert Sedgwick had been sharing cosily with Elena Semenova,
a young model and marketing assistant. They were in his small
third-floor rented apartment not far from the centre of Saint
Petersburg, and had been sharing the space for the past three
weeks, since meeting at a trade party thrown at the British
Consulate in Smolninskiy Raion. It had been lust at first sight
in Sedgwick's limited experience, but it was slowly turning
into something deeper.

'I have to. I'm sorry. It shouldn't be long – out and back
today, I hope.' Sedgwick stepped over to the bed as Elena
emerged, hair tousled, and elegantly and unabashedly naked.
Blonde and slim, she had enviable cheekbones and the kind
of skin most women would have given their right arm for, and
which he found irresistible to the touch.

'Where are you going? Anywhere interesting? Oh, don't
tell me – embassy business. I shouldn't ask otherwise you
might have to shoot me.' She brightened up at a thought.
'Maybe I could come and keep you company! We could have
lunch together.'

He kissed her back. 'Sorry – I'd love to but this is strictly
business. I have to go talk to a group of officials and believe
me, it won't be fun and could be a long day.' He was surprised
at how easy he found it to tell the small lie, and felt instantly
guilty. Elena didn't deserve lies and he resolved to make it
up to her as soon as he could. For now, though, duty called
and it was a summons he couldn't refuse. A short flight to
a lake he knew and a meeting with a man whom he had been
assured he could trust implicitly, and he could be back here
in no time.

Although as a commercial attaché he wasn't compelled to

become involved in any way in the more clandestine nature of his country's foreign office, he felt some internal pressure to assist where he could as long as it didn't get him expelled for 'activities incompatible with his status' as a diplomat. In addition, he had been assured that it was his local knowledge only that was required, after which he could leave and return to his normal duties, his brief absence being explained by London to the embassy in Moscow.

'Do you have to?' Elena murmured softly with a delightful pout, taking hold of his arm and sliding her other hand under his jacket to caress his ribs. 'I was looking forward to a day in bed.' She laughed and tried to pull him down, but he grinned back and resisted, much against his better judgement.

At forty-eight, Sedgwick was divorced and free to play the field. But he was also aware of the dangers inherent in being a diplomat in Russia, and took his position seriously, even if, as he was doing now, he was skating a little close to the edge. He was also realistic enough to question what Elena found attractive about him. He was no real catch – a fact his ex-wife would have been delighted to confirm – and although still upright and in possession of his own teeth, was almost twenty years her senior, a fact he found discomforting.

He retreated out of range while he still could and picked up his briefcase and a thick jacket he always wore when flying. It was invariably chilly in the plane he used for his regular trade trips. As for the briefcase, it held nothing out of the ordinary, but since receiving the call last night from the man named Tom Vale, whose function he was only vaguely aware of and didn't wish to pursue too closely, he was focussing on making his day seem outwardly as ordinary and mundane as all his other days.

Elena looked resigned and shook her head, which had the effect of gently shaking other parts of her body which instantly drew Sedgwick's eyes. 'I understand. In that case, perhaps you can bring me a little present to make up for deserting me.' She smiled to soften the words and sat back against the headboard, hand folded demurely in her lap, a stance that only served to emphasize her other assets.

'I'm not sure I can do that,' he murmured, his throat suddenly dry. He tried not to look at her body and failed. 'Unless you have a sudden desire for freshwater fish or wood carvings. Maybe some bear's teeth if I can find them?' He stopped speaking, aware that he had said too much, and walked towards the door before he gave the game away entirely. 'We can go shopping in the city centre tomorrow, I promise. Will that do?'

She smiled and blew him a kiss. 'Of course, my darling. Have a nice day.' She patted the bedclothes. 'I'll be waiting right here when you get back.'

Sedgwick closed the door of the apartment and hurried downstairs. He had thirty minutes to get to the small airfield where Andrei, his usual taxi pilot, was based, and less than an hour's flying time to reach the destination of the lake which he would convey to Vale by text once they were airborne. Hopefully, if Vale was right, he could be done with whatever small task he was needed for and be heading back to Saint Pete and Elena by lunchtime. That was, he thought, as he emerged onto a rain-soaked street, if the weather allowed. On the other hand, in his experience, Andrei would never allow a spot of rain to stop him taking to the air and earning a day's fee.

As Sedgwick was making his way by car to the small club airfield outside the city, Elena was finding herself at a loss. Her modelling and marketing work were intermittent at best, and she had few friends she could call on at such short notice. The day looked like looming ahead of her with precious little to do. She jumped out of bed and headed for the shower, suddenly resolved to be positive. She would clean and tidy the apartment and have a nice meal waiting for when Robert returned. She wasn't the best cook in the world, but she was eager to learn and hadn't managed to poison him yet.

As she went to step under the spray, she heard her cell phone ringing. She checked the screen and saw it was Monika, a woman of indeterminate years and glacial beauty who was in some way connected with the modelling agency.

She hadn't quite worked out what Monika did there, but she often seemed to be hanging around recently and had always been very pleasant and chatty.

'Hi, Monika.'

'Elena. How are you today? Can you take on a last-minute photo shoot? The model we'd booked has dropped out. An overdose of coke, apparently, stupid girl.'

'Of course. Who was it?'

'Oh, I forget. We won't be using her again, anyway.' The comment came as an aside, without emotion, a reminder for Elena of the cut-throat nature of this business.

'Where and when?'

'I'll text you later with the details. It's in the city so you won't have far to travel. I'm surprised you're not busy cosying up with your new boyfriend.'

Elena hesitated. She hadn't talked about Robert to anybody as far as she could recall, although she had a feeling a couple of the girls might have seen her out with him. Still, it was the kind of business where news travelled fast and gossip even faster, and she felt rather proud to be able to say she had a boyfriend – and an English one at that. 'Actually, no. I was, but he's had to go out of town today at short notice. A phone call earlier. So suddenly I'm free.'

'Oh, lucky him. Anywhere interesting?'

'No idea. He wouldn't say, but he took his thick jacket so I know he's taking an air taxi somewhere. He does that quite a lot, from Morotevo.'

'What, and he didn't take you with him?' Monika sounded shocked. 'Why do men get all the fun?'

'I know. He said it was a boring meeting with a bunch of officials, so he couldn't take me. He did offer to bring me back a present, though . . . as long as I liked wood carvings or freshwater fish.'

'Yuk . . . how romantic. Wood and fish. Sounds like he's going up north, then. From Morotevo, you say? There's a flying club there, isn't there? I always thought I'd like to learn to fly someday.'

Elena was surprised. She couldn't see Monika behind the controls of a plane. Somehow the idea of her elegantly manicured fingers coming into contact with a joystick simply didn't match, but she didn't say so. 'What's this job you mentioned?'

'Oh, don't worry – I'll confirm you're doing it and text you with the details. 'Bye.'

As Elena got in the shower, she felt a surge of excitement. A modelling job – any job – could be the beginning of something good, and just at the right time. She couldn't wait to tell Robert all about it – he'd be so pleased for her.

Barely a hundred yards away, in a small apartment block on the other side of a park, the woman whose full name was Monika Kolokova dialled a number. The apartment she was in had been rented under an assumed name on a short-term lease, unfurnished and bare, save for a camp bed, curtains at the windows and a hanging wardrobe with three changes of clothes. Kolokova was currently dressed in leisure pants and a fleece top, and smoking a long cigarette. She had been awake for several hours, monitoring a surveillance device placed in Sedgwick's apartment across the way, and needed the nicotine to keep going.

'Yes?' A man's voice, matter-of-fact. A voice in the information chain of which she was a simple link.

'The man named Robert Sedgwick is on his way to Morotevo to catch an air taxi north. Very short notice, according to Semenova. He wouldn't tell her where or why, although that doesn't normally stop him; the idiot's like a love-struck calf.'

The man's voice remained flat, showing no interest in her opinion. 'Morotevo. Got it. You can stand down until further notice.'

Kolokova switched off the phone and began to pack away the surveillance equipment. She made a mental note to arrange a make-do photo assignment for Semenova. She knew a magazine proprietor who would help, no questions asked. No point having told the lie only to have the dumb girl asking questions later when no job materialized.

THIRTY-SIX

When Sedgwick arrived at the small airfield outside Saint Petersburg, a single-engine amphibious Cessna was waiting. It was early for the small club field and nobody else was in sight. Most of the pilots here seemed to fly purely sociable hours, and rarely turned up until after nine.

Sedgwick breathed a sigh of relief. He didn't want to go through the usual range of hearty greetings and questions about where he was going, especially today. At any other time he would have been able to give a thoroughly truthful answer, entirely verifiable and innocent, even boring, and usually concerned with logging, tourism and acquiring licences for inbound trade from the UK and contact details for outbound shipments of wood and other products from this region. By now he was fairly well-known at the airfield and, he suspected, had long been marked down as a bit of an oddity from the British Consulate who liked flying off to talk to loggers, hunters and anybody else with an interest in trade.

It was a long-term commitment and one he enjoyed, but he always had to question how long it could last. The kinds of trade opportunities to and from here were limited in comparison to manufacturing industries in big cities, and he constantly expected to hear that he was being recalled to perform a more valuable function elsewhere where the potential was much greater.

He parked and locked his car and walked across to the plane, expecting to find Andrei in the cockpit ready to take off. But the plane was locked. He walked round it, wondering if the pilot was off in the clubhouse, which was an old WW2 structure from the field's days as a fighter airbase. Just as he was debating ringing the man, he heard a vehicle approaching and saw a car skid to a stop outside the clubhouse. Two men climbed out, one wearing a flying jacket, and walked across to meet him.

'Who are you?' Sedgwick asked. 'I was expecting Andrei.'

'Andrei's sick,' the man in the flyting jacket replied bluntly. 'I'm the replacement.' He was a similar height and build to the usual pilot, but younger, somewhere in his early forties, with a sallow complexion and a two-day stubble. He wore hiking boots and jeans, and stared at Sedgwick without an ounce of welcome.

'Sick? What's wrong with him? I spoke to him last night and he was fine.'

The pilot shrugged and said nothing.

'Can we get going?' This was the second man, who was balding, stocky and dressed in work pants and an old combat jacket.

The pilot looked at Sedgwick and said, 'Well, are we flying or not?'

Sedgwick nodded. 'Of course.' He felt a tug of concern. It was a familiar feeling in this country when well-laid plans were suddenly thrown into disarray with no real explanation or apology. He thought he'd get used to it over time but he never had. The feeling that any disruption might be deliberate and caused by outside forces never went away entirely, and he knew that colleagues at the embassy and consulate often felt the same way.

He handed a slip of paper with the co-ordinates to the pilot and climbed on board, strapping himself in, closely followed by the other passenger, who promptly buried his nose in a day-old newspaper. Sedgwick would have preferred to listen to the usual friendly chatter from Andrei about his family in the city, his children and grandchildren – even his exploits as a contract pilot in South America – but that wasn't going to happen on this trip.

Five minutes later they were rushing down the runway and lifting into a dull, cloudy sky full of threatened rain. Sedgwick had seen this part of the country too many times to be fascinated by the landscape below, and he soon found the early-morning call from Vale and the trip out here catching up with him. His eyes became heavy and he fell asleep, thinking of Elena.

At the controls, the pilot levelled out and checked his passengers in the rear-view mirror. Unseen by Sedgwick, he caught the eye of the other passenger, who lifted his eyebrows and went back to his newspaper.

THIRTY-SEVEN

Arriving anywhere for a meet in unknown terrain with somebody you've never seen before carries its own dangers. People aren't always who or what they're supposed to be, or don't always match the description given. They might also have their own suspicions and fears about the situation, so don't behave the way you expect, either. Some are calm, some edgy, some look as if they might freak out and run the moment you say hi. Some don't turn up.

But some simply smell wrong from the start.

I've been through the process too many times for it to be new to me, but there is inevitably a procedure to follow. If you can, you get there first and scout the area. You check routes in and routes out – especially the latter – and you put a mental tag on anybody who looks like they really don't fit.

The lake was called Avego and looked like any other patch of water where fishing was the primary activity. There was a kind of beach area, where trees had been cleared to give access to the water, and above that a tackle shop and a café/bar, with a big barbecue area out back. Rock music was blaring out from a speaker on the wall of the café, and if it upset the fishermen, who in my experience prefer peace and quiet, they didn't seem too keen to complain. Not surprising when I saw the owner, a huge bearded wrestler-type with a heavy gut and arms like a bear.

There was a hut with boats for hire, some with outboard motors. But that was it. It was hardly a mecca for tourists, and investors clearly hadn't discovered it as the go-to place to build a marina and a watersports centre for up-and-coming rich kids from Saint Petersburg or Moscow. Even the weather seemed to agree that it really wasn't worth the trouble, and low clouds over the lake and surrounding miles of trees were dark and heavy, as if to put off any idea of anyone being here for fun or leisure.

I parked the UAZ and walked down to the water. I passed a few old men on the way, mostly wearing multi-looped jackets and carrying fishing poles, and figured this was as good as any place to meet; there was enough activity to look casual and if anybody here was working undercover, they were world-class actors and mostly way too old to be in the undercover business.

A few boats were already out on the water, and a large buoy a hundred yards out from the shore looked like it might be used for floatplanes tying up. I decided to grab myself a coffee and some breakfast at the café, where I could watch Sedgwick come in and land.

It didn't take long. Two coffees and some scrambled egg and potatoes later, I heard the buzz of an engine and saw a couple of the old boys checking the sky. Minutes later a floatplane came in low over the water, then zoomed skywards and began to come around for a landing approach, before touching down with a hop and a skip.

I watched a boat go out from the shore and tie up at the buoy alongside the plane. It brought back three men. The pilot was obvious; he wore a flying jacket, jeans and boots and the kind of face used for delivering bad news about weather, landing, taking off and pretty much anything else. The second man was balding, heavily built and looked like he might be going fishing if only he could find a rod. The third man couldn't have been anything but British. He stepped out of the boat clutching a puffer coat and briefcase, and marched away like Montgomery at Alamein.

I stayed where I was. And felt the hairs move on the back of my neck.

I was busy watching the other two men. The pilot seemed to lose interest in his passengers immediately and turned to watch the boats out on the lake. Baldy was walking up the beach on a path diverging away from Sedgwick, but occasionally throwing a glance his way as if keeping him in sight. If he really was a fisherman, I figured the first place he would go to would be the tackle shop, to kit himself out for the day.

But he didn't. He slowed and loitered, pretending to be interested in an inflatable boat with an outboard motor. Lucky for me, being out in the open as he was, he stood out like a bull in a milking parlour.

Sedgwick had picked up a tail.

I took out my phone and dialled Sedgwick's number. It was safe to talk because I was the only customer in the café and I could see the *chef du jour* cum owner was out back gutting fish. I didn't want Sedgwick coming into the café, as that would target us both and I needed to get him away from his follower.

When he answered, I said, 'Keep walking, Robert. Don't stop. Go towards the parking lot and turn right. Follow the path into the trees round the side of the lake and I'll join you there. Don't look back.'

To be fair he tried. He'd slowed to take out his cell phone, then did a double-step when he heard my voice, trying to absorb the instructions and looking up towards the parking area. Then he continued on his way. It had been enough to tell anyone watching him where I was calling from, but I needed to make sure I hadn't misread the situation. I was using him as a lead, but he wouldn't know that. I figured his tail would want to keep him in sight to see what he was doing, and would soon react.

And that's what Baldy did: he lost interest in the boat and set off up the beach after him.

I called Lindsay. 'I have Sedgwick in sight, but he's got company. Tell Vale. Sedgwick either talked about this to somebody or he's being watched and somebody picked up on his movements.'

'Is he in danger?'

'Not from me. Vale might like to check his background, though, just in case. It could be nothing – an overreaction by the local FSB watchers to a consulate worker suddenly going out of town, something like that.'

'Copy that. I'll pass it on.'

I cut the connection, dropped money on the counter and got

a nod from the bearded man out back. I stood just inside the door studying a bulletin board while watching Baldy to see how far he would go.

Correction. The pilot was in on it, too. He'd dumped any interest in the lake and had moved up to stand alongside Baldy. They waited to see where Sedgwick was going, then kicked off after him. No fuss, no overt signals, suddenly they were all focus. It told me all I needed to know; the way they had moved was too slick to be low-level embassy personnel watchers. These guys were serious.

I went back to the car and picked up the Grach. I was hoping I didn't have to use it. But carrying the silenced Val, although more useful, would be impractical if I was spotted by any of the fishermen in the area. Even they might raise more than an eyebrow at the idea of an assault rifle being used to catch freshwater fish.

I ambled off after the two men following Sedgwick, and hoped their assignment was to follow and report, and not to do anything drastic before I got there.

Sedgwick had picked up a couple of hundred yards start on me and was moving at a decent clip, which I put down to nerves. I'd noted the path as a meeting point on arrival; it followed the edge of the lake, which I figured was a good half-mile long and a quarter wide. If the path went all the way round it was a good distance to walk, and even better to lose the two heavies on his tail.

I hit the trees and followed a parallel route, keeping the path in sight. I had no worries about the two men seeing me, as they were too focussed on Sedgwick to be checking their own backs. I also had them in profile against the water, so I could easily keep track of them and see them the moment they decided to make a move.

Moving away from the beach and the café was like stepping off the planet. Apart from the occasional distant pop of a gun from up in the woods, everything else, the talk, the rock music and the hum of engines, were gone, deadened by the hiss of the wind in the trees. It was sombre, too, like being in a church. The conditions worked for me; if I managed to get Sedgwick away from Baldy and the pilot without any rough play, we could talk. On the other hand, if I had to deal with the two men, the quieter the surroundings the better.

Once we got round the longest side of the lake I angled towards the water. It brought me to within fifty yards of the two men, who were walking along in file, like day trippers enjoying the scenery. Moments later my plan for a peaceful talk went down the toilet.

The pilot snatched at his jacket and took out a cell phone, and dropped back a few yards while waving at Baldy to keep going. He held the phone to his ear while giving what looked like a running commentary on their progress, shaking his head and gesturing towards Sedgwick and at the surrounding scenery. He even turned and checked his back trail, before shaking his head and stopping to listen to whoever was on the other end.

Baldy, meanwhile, was now more than a hundred yards away. He looked like he'd been designated as the Number Two guy for the day and was simply keeping Sedgwick in sight while his colleague did the talking. He'd glance back occasionally to see where he was, but I got the feeling he was merely waiting for instructions to move. The most obvious point to me was, they weren't trying to catch up with Sedgwick, but merely keeping him in sight.

Waiting to see who he was meeting.

THIRTY-EIGHT

The path Sedgwick and Baldy were on had taken a turn away from the lake, where a vast pile of ice-age boulders had been thrown up, making access to the water impossible. From my elevated angle I could see the path narrowed here, too, twisting and turning through a jumble of rocks and clumps of vegetation. It was a great place for an ambush.

Even as I thought it, the pilot took his phone away from his ear and reached into his flying jacket. When he took out his hand he was holding a gun. He began to walk faster, then shouted something I couldn't pick up, before breaking into a run. Baldy, who was now even further ahead, heard him and also began to run, disappearing after Sedgwick down a slope in the path behind a clump of trees.

The situation was easy to read: it had gone critical. They'd been given the order to move in and dispose of the problem.

I covered the ground on the run, aiming for an interception point along the path. I was trying to avoid the tangle of brushwood and fallen branches as much as I could, thus alerting the pilot to my approach. But he was so intent on following orders he didn't hear me coming.

When he finally did cotton on, alerted by the loud crack of a branch I didn't see, it was too late. He turned his head and slowed, his mouth forming a surprised 'O', and tried to bring up the gun and run at the same time. It didn't work. I slammed into him broadside before he could aim, taking him off the path and over the edge into a gulley. He gave a yelp on the way down but it was muffled by his body spinning over and over.

I skidded down after him, hitting roots and fallen branches on the way, and jumped down the last few feet to the bottom of the gulley. The pilot had lost the gun but came up fast, his face covered in dirt and looking murderous. He opened his mouth to shout a warning to Baldy, so I moved in and hit him hard in the side of the neck. He staggered back and tried to shout again, but all he could manage was a croak. It was obvious I'd hurt him. I dropped my arms and waited for him to come at me. He took the bait and rushed in, piling onto me with a flurry of punches and strikes that were a blur but ineffective, apart from one that made my ear sting.

I waited for him to take a breath, then grabbed the front of his flying jacket and pulled hard. It wasn't what he was expecting; fighters usually try to keep a distance and throw punches, as he'd been doing. Getting in close was counter-intuitive. As he came towards me I ducked my head and smashed his nose, then followed up with a piledriver to his midsection.

He went down and lay gasping, his face covered in blood, then gave a shiver and lay still. When I checked closer I found a pool of blood spreading out from the back of his head. He'd hit it on a sharp rock and was dead.

I went through his jacket and came up with a wallet. I stuffed it in my pocket. Right now wasn't the time to check out his credentials; I had to see where Baldy had got to and stop whatever he was planning to do.

When I came up out of the gulley, there was no sign of him or Sedgwick. The path here was like a rollercoaster, ducking and diving as it followed the contours of the land around the lakeside. I started to run, hoping Baldy hadn't anticipated his orders and gone in hard after Sedgwick. It was tough going, mostly stubby grass with an underlay of hard rock and tangled tree roots, but beaten to a solid base over the years by the passage of many feet.

As I rounded a corner I saw Sedgwick. He was kneeling in the middle of the path with Baldy standing over him, a gun pointed at his head. Sedgwick looked sick.

There are times when the only reaction is action. No talking, no negotiating and no trying to go for the man. In any case I knew I'd never make it. All he had to do was pull the trigger. He couldn't miss.

Without breaking stride I brought up my gun and shot him.

He was punched backwards off the path and rolled away into the long grass. I kept my momentum going, my gun aimed ready to make a follow-up shot if he came up fighting.

But he was dead. My bullet had taken him in the throat.

I did a couple of deep bends to catch my breath, then checked the body and came up with another wallet. I turned to see how Sedgwick was doing. He was sitting on the ground and shaking his head.

'Good morning,' he said, then promptly threw up.

I let him recover. Some events take you like that.

When he was ready he stared at the man and said, 'Who was he? What the hell is going on?'

I checked Baldy's wallet. It held cash, a credit card and a photo ID with a federal agency name and logo I'd never seen before. Jesus, had I just killed a cop?

I tossed the wallet to Sedgwick and checked the one from the pilot. Same ID, same logo.

'What is that logo?' I said. 'Is it official?'

He shook his head. 'It's a fake. I've seen it before. The logo says they're the Federal Security Division for the Safety of the State. It's meaningless. They're actually a security contractor based in Saint Petersburg. They've done work in Iraq and Afghanistan, mostly using Russian veterans but pulling in others, too.' He handed back the wallet. 'They've been under investigation twice by the authorities but so far have been given a clean bill of health.'

'Investigation for what?'

He brushed some leaf mould off the front of his coat where he'd fallen over and picked up his briefcase. 'The usual stuff: mafiya dealings, extortion and other criminal activity, some connected with certain government ministers and others.' He wiped his face with a handkerchief and turned to spit into the grass. 'Excuse me.'

'Oligarchs?'

'That's the old term now largely regarded as pejorative. The new ones especially are sensitive on the issue and like to think of themselves as serious businessmen.' He pulled a face. 'I believe the American mafia took the same approach.'

At least it meant the two men weren't FSB. But it begged the question how and why they came to be here in the first place. 'Are you being watched for any reason?'

'I'm always being watched. We all are. But I don't fit the traditional mould of a British diplomat because I travel around a lot and meet a lot of ordinary people. I think it bothers them because they can't explain it.'

'Perhaps they think you're a spy.'

He shook his head. After a moment he said, 'It's not that. I have a local girlfriend.' He shrugged. 'To some that's a lot worse than spying – it's subversive.'

'Well, good for you. But why these two and not the usual embassy watchers?'

'Two? There's another one?' He looked around.

'Your pilot was in on it.' I jerked a thumb behind me. 'He's back there. He lost interest.'

Sedgwick looked confused. 'I've no idea what's going on. Really.' He scowled. 'Although there was something odd this morning, at the airfield.'

'What?'

'The usual taxi pilot, Andrei, didn't turn up. The other man did and said Andrei was sick. Yet he was fine last night when I spoke to him, and he never misses the opportunity for a fare.'

'And this one?' I pointed at Baldy.

'He acted like another passenger. It's not unusual here to find yourself sharing rides. I didn't think anything of it at the time, although he didn't seem exactly friendly. Most Russians are, believe it or not.'

'I hear you.'

I decided to get Lindsay onto it. It was a remote possibility, but if she could track down one of the names it might point to whoever had sent the men after Sedgwick.

'Come on,' I said, 'we'd better get out of here. You can show me the lake.'

We covered up both men as best we could, using brushwood and handfuls of pine needles, then hiked back to the car. On the way, Sedgwick kept looking at me as if he wanted to say something. In the end I said, 'It would be good if you said what's on your mind, otherwise the tension will kill us both.'

'Sorry. It's just that I'm not used to this kind of . . . situation.'

'Lucky for you. What is it?'

'The men back there. Did you have to kill them both? I know the one with me was going to shoot – and I'm grateful, so please don't misunderstand me. But was it strictly necessary with the other one?'

'If it's any consolation, I didn't set out to kill anybody. But there's no point taking a bible to church if you don't intend using it.'

He gave a weak grin. 'Is that an example of American home-spun wisdom?'

'No. It is what it is. They weren't going to take you back alive, and would have shot me without a second thought for being in the wrong place at the wrong time.' I described seeing the pilot talking on the phone. 'Just before I got to you he received orders from somebody which made him reach for his gun. He was also looking around a lot – and it wasn't because he didn't want to be followed; he was expecting you to meet someone. He didn't know I even existed, so when nobody showed up he was told to dispose of you. There was no going back from that.'

He stopped in his tracks. 'But why me? I'm nobody. What the hell could they have against me?'

I really didn't want to tell him what I thought. Being in the same stretch of woods as Tzorekov and Gurov and the kill team in the helicopter was all a bit too close. It made me think that Sedgwick taking off in this direction had rung alarm bells somewhere, and whoever it was who was trying to stop the meeting had decided to latch onto anybody even remotely connected with the British embassy who showed a sudden interest in the area. The same would have applied to US embassy personnel.

'Is there a connection?' he said.

'With what?' I urged him to carry on walking until we reached the parking lot. The sooner we were away from here the less danger there was of being tied in with the two dead men when they were found.

'With the reason that brings you here. The location for a meeting.'

'What did Vale tell you?'

'He didn't. He said he wanted possible locations for a high-level meeting in the area; somewhere secret. I said there was only one place I could think of, about ten miles from here.' He stopped again. 'Does this involve Putin?'

THIRTY-NINE

Sedgwick was either smarter than he seemed or lucky. I figured on the former. If I tried lying, he'd smell a rat and refuse to cooperate.

I decided to keep it brief. 'There's a man newly arrived in the area hoping to talk to a senior member of government to calm down the current situation. There are others who don't want that meeting to take place. I'm here to make sure it goes ahead. That's it in a nutshell.'

I followed his directions leading north away from the lake. After a while he said, 'This man you mentioned; is he American?'

'No. Russian.'

'An outsider.'

'Correct.'

He nodded and I could see he'd already worked it out. Like I thought, smart. 'Putin's in a difficult position,' he said finally, the diplomat never far under the surface. 'He's the most powerful and charismatic leader – and the most popular – that this country has had. He has detractors but he also commands huge respect. That very situation means he can't, or shouldn't, be seen to be taking advice or counselling from just anybody. And I mean, anybody. He's Russia's strong man, so why should he listen to outsiders? He's powerful, yet constrained by his own success and charisma. And there are forces here who are desperate to see that the status quo doesn't change.'

'The military.'

'Undoubtedly. And those in government. But there's a strong group of business leaders – mostly those in charge of Russia's biggest energy, financial and mineral industries – who don't want the gravy train to stop either. A strong Putin means they can continue to expand. If Putin changes course in any way, their strength is diminished.' He waved a hand. 'Logically, that's not exactly true because Putin taking a softer line on certain issues means an opportunity for expansion of inter-national trade once sanctions are relaxed. But they don't see it that way. They want continued growth.'

It was pretty much what Vale had told me.

'I guess there's your answer,' I said. 'Who other than people connected with the state would have the means and interest in stopping this meeting taking place . . . and trying to find out what you were up to coming here? They must be ready to jump on anything to trash the whole idea.'

We drove in silence for a while, then Sedgwick directed me down a forest track. 'I've only been here once. It doesn't lead to the house but to a point overlooking it. It used to be wider but they've allowed it to grow over to discourage casual visitors. There is a main way in which leads to the front entrance, but if they've got security in place we'd be walking right into them.'

We were now hemmed in on both sides by vegetation and overhanging foliage, and I twice had to stop to drag fallen branches out of the way. Eventually we reached a point where we began to climb a steep slope between the trees, and the track petered out.

'It's on foot from here,' said Sedgwick. 'I hope you're ready for a walk.'

I looked at his footwear, which consisted of what the British would call stout shoes. But they were hardly hiking boots. 'More ready than you are.'

He got out and stamped his feet. 'Don't worry about me. My parents were hard-core Ramblers' Association members.' He looked at me and explained, 'That's hikers to you. They would go for twenty-mile walks at the drop of a hat and my father never wore boots, only shoes. Mind you, he did slip and fall off a mountain a couple of years ago, so it got him in the end. I suppose there's a moral in there somewhere.'

He led the way up another slope, pushing through a tangle of foliage and occasionally stopping to get his bearings. Then we emerged into a small clearing overlooking a lake. Below and to our left was a vast wooden, single-storey villa with verandas, shuttered double windows and interconnecting shingle roofs. Standing in a large plot of land it had gardens and lawns stretching all the way from the trees at the back down to the water's edge, with two jetties and a boathouse. The place was like a billionaire's dream and totally out of place here, yet somehow oddly fitting.

I took out my scope and scanned the building. There was no sign that it was occupied, but the shutters didn't allow me to see inside. It looked enormous, solid and deserted. And ideal for a meeting.

But there were obvious setbacks. In security terms the place was a nightmare. I wasn't surprised it had been largely abandoned by the government. A halfway decent sniper would be able to sit up here and take out anyone who showed themselves.

The people responsible for security would need a small army to cover all this ground and water, but even then a good operator would find a way of getting through.

'Who else knows about this place?'

'Surprisingly few, I think. It was built by a Swedish timber magnate in the 1920s who did a lot of business with the then Soviet Socialist Republic. They gave him permission to build it in recognition of his trade record. It's known about locally, but it's pretty much avoided simply because it's there.'

'It looks abandoned.'

I handed Sedgwick the scope. He studied it carefully before saying dryly, 'I suppose you have the rifle to go with this thing?'

'I do'

'It's Russian made.'

'So is the rifle.'

'You took it off somebody?'

'He let me have it.'

He shrugged at the mootness of the point and stared at the house through the scope for a moment, then handed it back. 'Take a look at the trees to the right of the house.'

I did and eventually detected the vague shape of a vehicle among the trees.

'You're pretty good at this, Sedgwick. Is that a security detail?'

'No. There's a husband and wife team who keep the place going, plus a daughter, I believe, but that's it. Since nobody comes here there's no reason for security. It was used for a summit about thirty years ago and one more recently, but since then I think it's been pretty much forgotten. Nobody wants to take on the responsibility of closing it completely; it's one of those acceptable links with the past that the Russians like to quietly ignore but not do away with altogether.'

I took one last look before deciding on my next move. Supposition and guesswork weren't going to help here and I needed to take a closer look. If the house looked spick and span, then it was ten to one they were ready for an important arrival.

Sedgwick read my mind. 'You're going down there.'

'You stay here. I'm going to take a look around. I won't be long.'

I slipped away before he could argue and hit a path down through the trees.

It took me ten minutes of hard going to reach the treeline bordering the grounds of the house. I waited to get my breath back and studied the building through the scope. Just as I'd thought from up the hill, it looked shuttered and closed, a relic consigned to history. But I could only see one side from my position.

I worked my way round to the rear of the property where I could see the approach road. It was covered with a layer of pine needles and clumps of grass, but clearly still in occasional use, as I could see from the twin lines of tyre tracks. I could also see the vehicle that Sedgwick had pointed out. It was an elderly Lada and hardly the kind of car issued to security personnel.

The rear entrance to the house was through a pair of double doors under a sagging portico, with a glint of glass inside which I guessed was another set of doors. Beyond that I couldn't see a thing.

I jogged across the tangle of grass that had once been a lawn and fetched up alongside a window. This one wasn't covered by a shutter and I could see a large kitchen that looked like something from another age. It included a huge cooker and an open fire, with a long table down the middle and some equipment I could only guess at. It looked deserted and unused, with a film of grime over the window glass and the table misted with a layer of dust. I moved along the wall to another window, this with one shutter hanging off the wall, the hinges rusted through. It gave me a view down a long corridor running the entire length of the house to a similar window at the front. Cloth-covered shapes were dotted around, possibly shielding chairs and small tables, and a roll of paper had been laid on the floor over the carpet, which looked past its best with patches of mildew at the edges.

I moved to the next window in line. This looked like a library or study, with empty bookcases lining the walls and a few shrouded shapes pushed together in the middle.

I gave it two more windows on the other side of the house

before deciding that if this was the place for a meeting, the
housekeepers hadn't got the memo.

I hiked back up the hill and found Sedgwick where I'd left
him. We walked back to the car and I drove down the track
to the road. He didn't say much when I described what I'd
seen, and I guessed being alone for a while had given time
him to think things over. The reality of what had happened
earlier was beginning to hit home. Delayed action shock; I'd
seen it before.

'You realize you won't be going back on that plane, right?'

He nodded. His face looked grey but he was holding it
together. 'I know. What will I do? I mean, if the people behind
those two men are connected to the government, this isn't
going to stop here, is it? I'm sure to be called in. And when
they find them both—'

'Don't think like that.' Called in meant being summoned
to explain himself. I figured it must be pretty high on the list
of things to avoid for diplomats, and felt genuinely sorry for
him. He'd found himself involved in something that was none
of his making and for which he hadn't been trained. Diplomats
weren't supposed to get themselves in running fights or activities that might get them kicked out of the host country – or
imprisoned – but there was no way round this one for
Sedgwick. His job here was probably over.

'But what should I do?'

'Get out,' I advised him. 'Pack your bags and get on the
first flight home. Your job here is shot and if the people who
sent those two bozos after you decide to, they'll take it out
on you if only to divert attention from themselves.' It was
brutal but I had to get him to see the reality of the situation.
Suddenly his world had been tipped upside down and he was
going to have to make some serious adjustments.

'But I don't know anything else. I'm a commercial attaché
– it's what I do. And what about Elena? I can't leave her behind.'

'Your girlfriend?'

'Yes.' He told me in brief terms about his divorce, how
he'd met this girl at an embassy party, a model, and they'd
had a couple of dates and it was now something else. It

sounded ordinary and uncomplicated, and yet so predictable, especially in this part of the world. I probably looked a bit cynical about the attraction between them, because he got defensive and angry.

'I know what you're thinking,' he said sourly. 'Elena's part of a honeytrap and one day I'll wake up and she'll be gone along with whatever information she thinks she can get out of me. Either that or she's just looking for a free ride to the west. Well, you're not the first to think it or even say it, but it's not like that.' He flushed deep red. 'I know I'm probably being a fool, but what the hell kind of information could she get from me, anyway? I talk business and trade and boring figures that mean nothing; I spend my life in meetings and awful parties where everybody pretends to like you – even your own colleagues. If she is looking to get to the west on my back . . . well, good luck to her.'

'Don't knock yourself out,' I told him. 'I hope she's genuine for your sake. And maybe she is. For now, though, you need to think about getting out.'

'I know. But how do I get home? We're miles from anywhere.'

'There will be other planes.'

'How do you know that?'

'Because there aren't many cars here for the number of people around. They had to get here somehow, and flying is the easiest way. You can hitch a ride.'

He stared at me. 'Christ, how do you do it?'

'Do what?'

'Notice stuff. Details like the number of cars and people, the layout of the terrain. I could see you doing it earlier; you evaluate everything and know exactly what to do next. And dealing with those two men – you didn't hesitate. You saw what was about to happen and stopped it.'

'It's my job. It's not a conscious thing – it's what I do. You'd be the same if you did this work.' I didn't mention the down side of the job; how if you didn't develop the skills of having 360-degree vision and a retentive memory you didn't stay in it for long.

'But it's a skill. It's incredible. Don't you ever feel . . . I don't know – afraid?'

'Sure. Lots of times.'

'And that doesn't overwhelm you?'

'I don't let it. If I did I'd have to find another line of employment.'

The truth was, that thought probably scared me more than anything. The idea of a future with no challenge and no aim, of having to join in with others in a job I'd hate; that wasn't me. Not that I was about to admit that to Sedgwick, who was already feeling lost. Hopefully he'd get over it.

Instead I said, 'Don't underestimate yourself, Robert. You came out here knowing there had to be more to this. I mean, who wants a meeting in the middle of the woods in Russia to ask questions about a house on a lake? It was hardly a real estate deal. And Vale; you know what he does, right?'

'I suppose so. I was pretending I didn't.' He looked glum, the reality he'd denied finally sinking in. 'He's with Six, isn't he?'

I didn't answer. 'You knew there were risks taking on a job for him, yet you still came.'

He tried to smile. 'Maybe I have a secret taste for danger – is that what you're saying?'

'No. I think you weighed up the pros and cons and decided to do it anyway because it was expected of you. That takes courage.'

'Let's hope the ambassador and the foreign office see it that way.'

As we pulled back into the parking lot at the lake I could see two more planes out on the water. Everybody was going about their business and the scene looked calm and unhurried. It wasn't the kind of atmosphere where two dead bodies had been found, but I didn't think it would last for long.

'Tell one of the pilots you got stranded by your wife and need a ride back. With luck he'll understand and give you a guy's discount.'

'I will, thanks. What about Elena? Should I call her?'

'And tell her what? Leave it until you get back. If she looks genuinely happy to see you and not even slightly puzzled, then forget about it and take her with you.'

'But what if I'm wrong and she did talk to somebody?'

'Then that somebody is probably the bad guy, not her. Did you tell her where you were going?'

'No. At least, not in so many words. As I was leaving I made some crack about buying her a present of carved wood, but I don't think that would have done it.'

'It was enough. It told her you weren't going into the city. And that isn't city wear.' I pointed at the puffer coat he was still carrying. 'That left the woods. If anybody was monitoring your movements, it would have been enough to ring some bells. A call to Elena would have confirmed it.'

'God, that's awful. I've been stupid.'

'Don't sweat it. If they were watching you, the moment you headed for the airfield they'd have figured something was happening anyway and followed you. You have to allow for random – it happens.'

I left him with that thought and drove away. The first thing I did on the road was get onto Vale at Langley and tell him he had to stage a rescue mission for two via the embassy in Moscow. Hell, Sedgwick had been helping MI6 in the first place; the least he could do was stand up for the guy when he needed a favour in return.

FORTY

'So what was so darned urgent that it couldn't be dealt with in a phone call?' CIA Assistant Director Jason Sewell was feeling testy. He'd been dragged out of his office at short notice on orders from the White House, to attend a meeting in the CIA building with two visitors, and to bring CSO Brian Callahan with him. He sat down and waved at Callahan to take a seat across the table. They were in a meeting room for twenty, but there were just four people present.

Angela Thornbury took a seat and gestured at the man who had come in with her. 'I'm sure you know Alastair Davies, Deputy Secretary at the Department of State? He's here with me at the request of the Secretary.'

Sewell and Callahan gave the obligatory nods of recognition to the newcomer. Davies was tall and thin, with a shock of dark hair and an enviable tan, and wore his suit as if born to it. He smiled fleetingly, then looked around the room as if seeking the recording equipment he probably thought might be embedded in the walls and giving a lingering look of suspicion at the communications console in the centre of the table.

Sewell let him look. He'd never find it. He'd met Davies on a couple of occasions, the moments so fleeting he couldn't quite recall where or when and barely long enough to remember his face much less get to know anything about him. He'd pegged him immediately as a professional public servant and therefore to be treated with caution. Quite why he was here now was a puzzle, but he suspected it might have something to do with the mauling Brian Callahan had given Thornbury during her last visit. Maybe she felt the need for a big hitter like Davies to protect her, and this was going to be some sort of payback for Callahan to endure. He couldn't off-hand think of any other reason for the Clandestine Service Officer to have been included.

'So what's this about?' he said. 'Callahan here has a mission to run and it's in an advanced stage.'

'Don't worry,' said Thornbury with the ghost of a smile. 'We won't keep either of you long. We thought it best if you both heard what we have to say, then you can go back to your duties.'

Sewell and Callahan exchanged a look. *Duties?* What the hell was this woman on? Made it sound like they were janitors.

'Go ahead,' Sewell said quietly.

'We,' Thornbury said smoothly, gesturing to include Davies, 'in consultation with the Secretary of State, have come to a decision about the Counselor mission. In light of recent and ongoing developments in the situation with Russia and its . . . neighbours, there have been extensive discussions as to the advisability of the operation currently being undertaken by the CIA in the north of that country. It has been drawn to everybody's general attention that the current talks between the two countries are at a delicate stage, and anything which threatens to unbalance our position in the talks is to be avoided. Especially a covert operation involving a man like Tzorekov.'

Sewell pursed his lips at the preamble, as unclear as it was irritating. He thought he'd become adept over the years at interpreting the convoluted speech patterns of Washington bureaucrats, but this was threatening to kill that idea entirely.

'Say what?'

Thornbury didn't miss a beat. 'It has been decided that in the interests of ongoing developments between the two countries, to impose a change of priorities vis-à-vis the Watchman operation.'

'Vis-à-vis?' Sewell thought this didn't sound good and was about to say so but Callahan got there first and went for the jugular. 'What the heck does that mean?'

'It means, Mr Callahan, that we're pulling the plug. With immediate effect.'

'What?' Sewell felt his blood pressure rising like an express elevator. 'You're ending it? Why?'

'Because we no longer see the advantage to the US of continuing to be seen backing an initiative that may well go against us. There is also the question of having the operation entirely in the hands of an unattached individual over whom you have at best a transient control. It's simply far too risky. The president agrees and we therefore have to instruct you and the British participants to cease all activities and withdraw all personnel from the area.'

'Nice of you to include us in those talks.' Brian Callahan sat back with a look of disgust. 'When exactly was this decision made?'

Thornbury flushed, no doubt recalling their last meeting. Before she could speak, Davies leaned forward and gave a conciliatory smile. 'My apologies, Brian – you can blame me for that. I should have included you both at the outset, but events have been moving a little . . . rapidly all round. We figured it best to talk it out first around the table between the White House and the State Department, then make the appropriate decision where it affected the CIA and its active partners.'

'I have a question,' Sewell interjected. 'Were the British

included in your around-the-table discussions, or are they only now hearing about this, too? You might not know this, Deputy Secretary, but it was they who brought this initiative by Leonid Tzorekov to us. It was they who suggested that we be included in view of the close alliance between our two countries, and the potential ramifications involved whether Tzorekov succeeded or not.'

'I'll bet a dollar,' Callahan said quietly, his eyes on Thornbury, 'that Tom Vale doesn't know yet. Does he?'

'I find your tone offensive, Mr Callahan,' Thornbury retorted sharply, with a quick glance at Davies. 'May I remind you that you do not decide policy on these matters – that's our job.'

Callahan was unruffled by the obvious reprimand. 'Yeah, and I'm only the sharp object out front that does some of the digging – I get that. Well, let me remind you, Ms Thornbury, that it was only a few days ago following your earlier *policy* decision and at your specific request that we sent a man out into the field – inside Russia – to help secure Mr Tzorekov and his companion on their way to this proposed meeting. Watchman has been undercover since then and is beyond our help if anything goes wrong. Had you told us about this even twenty-four hours ago, we could have avoided some of the problems he has already encountered by pulling him out of there.'

'He was aware of the risks, wasn't he?' said Davies. He was looking at Sewell and ignoring Callahan altogether. 'Frankly, this defensive attitude isn't helpful, Jason. I cannot stress enough that the reversal of the decision to help Tzorekov was made after much discussion and because the chances of our involvement being discovered and broadcast could be severely damaging to the US and any future dealings with President Putin and his ministers. Yes, it's unfortunate that we have to withdraw support for the mission, but you have our full backing to take whatever steps are necessary to get your man out of the country. Short of sending in other assets, of course.'

'What, none?'

'None. That's non-negotiable.' He pressed the point of his index finger on the table in emphasis. 'Nobody else puts a toe across the Russian border or anywhere near it. That decision comes from the very top.'

'What about the British personnel? There are two of their men out there, monitoring the situation.'

'We will be talking to the relevant people in London as soon as we can to confirm any actions they might have to take on the issue.'

Sewell looked shocked. 'You don't even know about Tom Vale, do you? Your briefing didn't even get that far.' He threw a look at Thornbury that should have had her bursting into flames where she sat. She gave a cool smile in return, but looked suddenly uneasy.

'Pardon me?'

'Tom Vale, the senior MI6 officer who brought this to us in the first place; he's here in this building right now, as Ms Thornbury knows. It would have been courteous, don't you think, in view of his involvement, to have included him in this meeting?'

'My apologies, I didn't realize.' A sharp flick of his eyes towards Thornbury was the only indication that Davies was telling the truth. 'Be that as it may, this is the end of this mission. I'll talk with Mr Vale immediately we're finished here.' He stood up. 'I'm sorry, gentlemen, but having missions terminated at short notice can hardly be unusual. Changes of policy can't always take account of the situation on the ground. For the reasons outlined, this was unavoidable.'

'So what happens to Tzorekov?' Callahan had remained seated. He was staring at Davies with open disgust. 'This leaves him right out on a limb. We're supposed to be protecting him! Don't you care how this goes down?'

Davies looked unmoved. 'It's unfortunate, but the decision to return to Russia was entirely his. As I understand it, he was going in without any commitment from us anyway, and doesn't even know your man is there, am I right?'

'Yes, that's true—'

'Then there's nothing we can do about it. As to your man – Watchman? I'm sure he'll find his way out. Good day, gentlemen.' Without waiting for their response, he turned and walked out.

As his footsteps faded along the corridor, Thornbury seemed to realize that she had been left behind. She stood up and said, 'I must be going, too.'

'Wait.' Sewell reached forward to the comms console and pressed a button. 'You'll need an escort to see you out. Security protocol, I'm afraid.'

'Why?' She look flustered. 'Deputy Secretary Davies didn't have one.'

Sewell smiled thinly. 'But you're not the deputy secretary, are you? You get an escort, like it or not.'

She looked stung by the words and tone, and stared at the two CIA men in turn. Her jaw flexed with anger. 'You had better hope,' she muttered, 'that your man doesn't get caught. If he does there are going to be some changes around here. Personally, I don't give a damn how this goes *down* as you put it. But I do not intend going down with it. That I promise you!'

As she finished speaking there was a knock at the door. A uniformed guard entered and stood waiting.

'Escort Ms Thornbury to the exit, will you?' Sewell said calmly. 'And make sure she signs out on the way. If she refuses, lock her up.' With that he turned his back on Thornbury, waiting until the door closed behind her before saying to Callahan, 'I want to keep Watchman running. This isn't over yet.'

Callahan looked surprised. 'Are you sure? You heard what Davies said.'

'Sure, I heard him. But he didn't put a timescale on it, did he? Whether we pull Watchman out now or in twenty-four hours isn't going to make a pile of difference to him one way or another. But it might gain a whole lot more than their "change of policy" has reckoned with.' He stood up. 'Let's give Tzorekov and Watchman a fighting chance. We owe them that.'

Callahan nodded with smile. 'Twenty-four hours. You've got it.'

FORTY-ONE

'Watchman, come in.'

'I'm here. Go ahead.' I was halfway back to the power plant and stuck in a long line of trucks when Lindsay called. I could see a logging truck in the ditch on one side of the road, and the remains of another on the opposite side. There was nothing much left of the second cab, which had been destroyed by three logs coming adrift from their chains and ploughing through it on their way to God knew where.

I still felt bad about leaving Sedgwick and the situation he was in, but it was out of my hands. Vale had promised to do all he could to help him, so I had to be satisfied with that.

'Watchman, I have a lead on the numbered item you mentioned,' Lindsay said, and I knew she was talking about the assault rifle I'd taken off the Russian. 'It came up almost immediately. It's one of a batch of twelve similar items originally designated for unspecified military use about five years ago. We don't have specific details but a police report since then lists them as having been taken out of military use and allocated to a specialist anti-terror unit in southern Ukraine. The items were stolen before they could be put into service.'

For 'unspecified military use' read special forces. 'Good work. How did you find it?'

'We got lucky. Several similar items turned up in Europe, specifically Munich, Belfast, Northern Ireland and Sardinia. Interpol issued a general warning because of terrorist implications involving the G8 summits held at or near these locations. The information on their history was supplied by the Russian authorities but only after some international pressure to come clean.'

As she said, it was lucky. Information from the Russian authorities on stolen weapons was rarely made available to the outside world. Some arsenals and depots had been raided over the years by criminal gangs looking for weapons to feed a hungry market. But there were also records of remote depots closed down and left with minimal security measures, where weapons had been discovered still packed in their original crates, unlisted and forgotten until somebody came along with a ready cash bribe and a flat-bed truck.

Mostly it would be the traditional AK-47 model which was a big attraction to the open market. But specialist weapons like the Val were bad news and the Russians knew it. If they got into the wrong kind of hands and a signature was left behind, it might point the finger rather too directly at Moscow being connected with acts of terrorism by association. It didn't take me much further forward to finding out who the opposite team were, but it did tell me who they weren't. And any information is better than none.

'I have a couple of other items I'd like you to check,' I said, and read out the names from the wallets I'd taken off the two men at the lake. 'It's a long shot but I have good reason to think they're ex-military contractors with service in Afghanistan or Iraq.' I had no idea if they would have used the same names but if they did turn up on any records of military contractors working there, it would at least confirm that they weren't FSB, and might tell us who last employed them.

'Copy that, Watchman. I'll get on it.'

'Have the Pathfinders still got a signal?'

'Affirmative and still in the same location. The last flyover was timed at thirteen minutes ago and recorded as strong and clear.'

'Good to hear. Now heading back there. ETA as soon as I can get out of a truck jam.'

'Truck jam? I never heard of one of those.'

'You haven't lived. Nose-to-tail fumes and noise.' I summarized what I'd found at the house on the lake, then cut the connection and sat back to wait for the jam to clear.

It was late afternoon and the light was fading by the time I got through and hit open road. It had turned out to be a long day and I needed some sleep. But first I had to make sure Tzorekov was where I'd left him. As I got nearer I checked the signal and finally picked up a reading when I was about ten miles out from the power plant.

I left the car in the same pull-in I'd used before and made my way through the main gates and down to the main building. Knowing the layout made moving around a lot easier.

Not that it helped much.

The Touareg was gone.

What I did find was my tracker, balanced on a small

pile of stones where the Touareg had been, and where it would be impossible to miss. Gurov, I figured, had a twisted sense of humour.

It had remained hidden longer than I'd expected, but its discovery presented me with a new problem. Now Gurov knew somebody had been following him he'd be more on his guard than ever.

I checked out the rest of the building, starting with the long corridor and the space beyond the double doors where I'd seen the light the last time I was here. Empty. Nothing to show anybody had been here in a long time. I went through the remainder of the site, but it was a vast space of nothing to see, long ago stripped of anything useful and now just a shell slowly rotting away.

I headed back to the car and called Langley.

'Houston, I have a problem.'

'Copy that, Watchman. What's up?'

I told Lindsay about the tracker. 'Can you get the Pathfinders to check the second signal? If that tracker was missed I still have a chance of staying on Counselor's trail.'

'Copy that, Watchman. They're on down time at the moment, as I understand it, charging batteries. I'll get back to you as soon as they get back in the air.'

I disconnected and drank some water and ate a few biscuits, then put my head down. It was pointless driving anywhere; daylight was going and Tzorekov could be anywhere in hundreds of miles of forested roads and tracks.

Old military saying: when in doubt, eat and sleep.

FORTY-TWO

Victor Simoyan stood in front of the video screens on the boardroom wall and said, 'Gentlemen. My apologies for calling another late conference but I wanted to bring you up to date.' He smiled at the waiting faces. So far nobody had backed out, he noted. 'I know we're all impatient to see this matter concluded, but it may take a little time yet.' He waved a newspaper carrying details of President Putin's visit to Kursk, to inspect troops at a base in the south of the country. 'So far we have no indication that this timetable is to be changed – a good thing. However, we must continue with our plan, just in case. It can do no harm to deal with Tzorekov while he's within our reach.'

'A question, Victor,' said Kushka, the military consultant, his voice transmission gravelly. 'What's the situation with your team of hunters? Have they located the target?' His voice was soft, carrying a faint hint of criticism, like the schoolmasterly figure he so closely resembled.

Simoyan began to wonder if he knew more than he was letting on. 'Indeed, Alex,' he replied coolly. 'They found them very quickly, as I expected. But they did run into some opposition on the way.'

'What kind of opposition,' asked Solov, 'could take on a team of . . . what was it, four experienced men I think you said? Tzorekov's an old man and Gurov's probably gone soft in exile. Or are you saying there are others who have joined the mix?'

Simoyan tried to ignore the worried expression on Solov's face, but he was aware that the other men were looking concerned by the possibility of a setback. What had no doubt seemed to them a simple task of stopping two men from getting even close to a hoped-for meeting with President Putin was beginning to look less likely, and he knew what they would be thinking: should they get out now while they thought they could or see it through to the end before failure came staring them in the face?

'There is no need for panic,' he reassured them, and took a walk around the room, knowing they would follow his every move. He had long ago mastered the art of holding an audience, even one as high-powered as this, and knew it was simply a matter of convincing them that all was well and under control. What he couldn't do was string them along; each one of them had resources he could only guess at, and Solov and Kushka especially had the means and the capability of checking what was going on if they thought he was denying them the whole truth.

'Two of the men we sent after Tzorekov,' he explained, deliberately using the 'we' to remind them of their shared responsibility, 'have been hurt and are no longer able to contribute to this operation.'

'Hurt? How?' This from Oblovsky, former KGB man now arms dealer.

'Gurov must not be as soft as some might have imagined. He saw them coming and arranged for a reception. However, I've already arranged for replacements and four others will be joining Chesnokoy as we speak. They have fresh orders and will deal with Gurov and Tzorekov tonight.'

'Are you sure you have nothing else to tell us?' Kushka again, his voice almost teasing.

'Not quite.' Simoyan took a deep breath. Bloody man – he did know more than he should. He wondered if there was any way he could deal with this idiot when all this was over. Maybe a car accident or a random mugging – something painful but not fatal, to teach him a lesson. 'The biggest asset we've always had in this country, gentlemen, is information – or, should I say, sources of information. Go back as far as you like and you will find that society operated on data, on knowing about people. We're a nation of informants, did you ever consider that? Huh?' Nobody said anything, so he continued. 'You know it and I know it, a chicken doesn't fart in Vladivostok without it being heard here in Moscow.'

'All very poetic,' said Maltsev, the oil man. 'But it doesn't answer the question.'

'Actually, Andrei, it does.' Simoyan gave a tight smile. 'Because it serves as a warning to us all. I have just been advised of an incident involving a British diplomat working out of the consulate in Saint Petersburg. He made an unscheduled trip by plane to Lake Avego early this morning.'

'What's at Lake Avego?' Maltsev sounded bored, and Simoyan decided that he simply lacked the imagination to be troubled by unexplained events that were just a little too close to be a coincidence. He was probably dreaming of his latest mistress and counting down the minutes before he could be with her again.

'Nothing. It's where some people go to fish and get drunk

– which is why I was concerned. This particular man has been described as a little unusual in the way he conducts his day-to-day activities but I'm reliably informed that fishing and alcohol are not among them. As soon as I heard he was flying out there I arranged for two men to follow him. Any member of the British diplomatic corps who suddenly takes off for an unscheduled trip to the very region where there is the other lake we all know about is worth a close look, in my view.'

'What happened?'

'I don't know. The men have not responded to calls.'

There was a lengthy silence while they all took in the implications, eventually filled by Oblovsky. 'Gurov again? If so, how? I thought he was old KGB. He is not Superman, is he?'

'No. He's not. I believe there must be others in play; somebody we don't know about. The last the two men were heard of was while they were following the diplomat to what they concluded was a pre-arranged meeting place. But nobody turned up – at least, not that the men could see on their last phone contact. In view of that they were given instructions to deal with the diplomat. Since then there has been no contact.'

'But the diplomat,' Kushka said sharply, 'you ordered his death?'

'I had no choice. If he was involved and his contact failed to show up, allowing him to go back to Saint Petersburg and raise questions would have brought the attention of the FSB. We could not risk that. It was better that he simply met with an accident.'

'What happened to him?'

'I have no information on that. I have sent a man out to the lake to find out.' Simoyan took a deep breath. He could feel the situation beginning to slide away from him. He stepped forward, bringing himself closer to the camera and projecting his face onto each of their screens in close-up. It was a move that had worked before with others, when he had a deal to sell. 'But that is not the issue, my friends. The diplomat is not the problem. I can say categorically that he would not have been capable of dealing with the two men.'

'How do you know that?'

'I have my sources. Somebody else must have intervened; somebody more . . . adept.'

'Then it's obvious.' Oblovsky threw a hand in the air. 'The diplomat must have got himself a bodyguard. Was this man Gurov anywhere nearby, perhaps?'

'No. It would appear not.'

'So what now?'

'We wait. The renewed team are flying in tonight and will hard-target Tzorekov and Gurov . . . and anybody else who stands in their way. Gentlemen,' he added, 'this is not finished. We will prevail. But you must be patient. I promise this will be brought to a satisfactory conclusion very soon.'

FORTY-THREE

Maxim Datsyuk couldn't believe his eyes. Damn – it was that beacon code again; the one he'd seen leaving Moscow airspace and heading north. The same one Gretsky the Fat had given him such a hard time over. This time it was way to the north-west near Saint Petersburg. Man, whoever this guy was, he likes to get about.

He was about to play safe and ignore it but temptation took over. He ran another check to make sure he wasn't imagining things, then cocked an ear for the sound of footsteps in the central corridor. He'd been placed on an earlier shift tonight by Gretsky, on condition that he stay away from the live monitors with comms connections and use the robot screen only, and to confine himself to studying traffic movements and nothing else. And then only until 22:00, at which point he was to leave the building.

He checked his watch. It was already 22:30 and he was already overstaying his welcome. But try as he might he couldn't bring himself to leave this thing alone. He was convinced something was going on in the air up north, and that Gretsky must be deliberately turning a blind eye. It had to be, because even Gretsky as an experienced supervisor couldn't be so lazy as to be bordering on the negligent. Maybe he knew about the movement and was being paid not to make waves; it happened and he wasn't so naïve as to think it didn't. Bribes and kickbacks were a feature of the black economy, especially if, like Gretsky, you had information to sell.

Whatever the reason, he was being drawn to keep on watching by a force more powerful than his fear of being kicked back to his home base. Just as long as Gretsky didn't take the unusual step of dragging his fat arse downstairs to check on him, he should be all right.

And here was the proof that it hadn't ended.

The signal was now just north of Saint Petersburg, moving due north, altitude 250 metres at 190 km/h. Whoever this guy was, he liked night flying.

He watched its progress, holding his breath, a silent blip on the screen, wondering where it had been hiding during the day. He'd made a quick search the moment he'd come on shift, but nothing had shown up; just the normal traffic, nothing out of the ordinary and no weird codes or idents. He'd checked out a few military flights up and around the large blobs that were Lakes Ladoga and Onega, the twin waters to the north of Saint Petersburg, but they were routine and easily verified. He'd added them to his study anyway, just to show Gretsky he'd been doing what he was here to do.

He started back-tracking on the recorded data to see where the beacon code had gone after leaving Moscow airspace. There it was, heading towards Vologda, some 400 km to the north. OK, that was nice and normal. Sort of. But after touching the Vologda area, that was it. No landing data available – at least, not where it would have been noted officially.

He tracked it further, rattling the keyboard with an increasing sense of urgency and excitement as it routed wide around the city to the west, then turned north again. Damn, this really was looking like spooks all over. He'd assisted in a couple of training exercises involving Spetsnaz units and those guys just loved pretending to hide for the sheer hell of it. He figured they did it to build their mystique, like wearing balaclavas, jeans and tough-guy Kevlar vests with lots of pouches and waving crazy-looking weapons like something out of Mad Max.

Right, so where did this flight go after reaching the Vologda traffic zone?

It didn't. The darned thing had disappeared. *But how?*

He went back to the current screen. There was no point searching any further on the other one; the pilot must have landed somewhere, rendering his signature silent. With no transponder signal either, he'd gone dark. Maybe he'd had to refuel and have some repairs done. Ah . . . there it was, now heading towards the north-east, approaching Lake Onega. It still didn't explain how the signal had gone silent past Vologda then reactivated leaving Saint Petersburg. Unless it was a simple malfunction. Hell, they happened all the time, he'd seen that in the military.

He checked the current logs again, to make sure he hadn't missed anything, looking for **Trapdoor Z5993** or anything remotely similar. Nothing came even close. So who the hell was this guy – and what was he doing?

Maybe it wasn't military at all. A dope run? Could be. Dope or arms . . . maybe it was a mafiya deal using a military aircraft. He'd heard stories from colleagues in the MOD who'd been used to track those kind of people and provide a location so the anti-narcotics units could be waiting to greet them when they touched down, usually finding a couple of military guys or cops involved in the gang. The bigger gangs were increasing their reach and becoming more and more open in the way they operated, as if they didn't give a crap about the authorities, like they were untouchable.

Thinking of his colleagues brought a face to mind. A face who had been around a long time and might recognize this thing for what it was. It was risky, though, especially if Gretsky the asshole ever got wind of it. Still, what was risk if it wasn't fun? And if it came to anything good, he might get a commendation for being so vigilant. Now that wouldn't do his career any harm at all.

He bobbed up out of his chair long enough to make sure he was still clear. Nobody close; a few voices in the distance and somebody shouting at a pilot who seemed not to understand basic instructions about staying well away from Moscow airspace unless he wanted to get shot down. He sat back down and picked up the phone, dialling a number from memory.

FORTY-FOUR

I n the communications centre at Langley, Lindsay Citera was using a satellite feed to watch a display similar to the one Maxim Datsyuk had been studying, showing the movement of aircraft close to the area where Watchman was waiting. Untangling the traffic during the day was a real headache due to the volume of flights represented by a spiderweb over the city and surrounding region. But as the flight schedules diminished and night crept in, a different pattern emerged and the tangle became much more simplified and easier to follow.

'Uh-oh.' She was perusing an expanded screen of an area to the north-east of Saint Petersburg when she saw a blip moving to the north-east. The beacon code was **Trapdoor Z5993** and was the same Ansat-U military chopper she'd tracked right over Watchman's position twenty-four hours ago. She hadn't picked up a beacon code immediately before. But there it was now, plain as day. It was following a flight path away from the normal routes and had so far changed direction twice, heading out now over a large lake identified as Ladoga. Some lake, she thought; it must be over a hundred miles long.

The blip wasn't moving fast, which meant it was probably encountering heavy weather, confirmed by a quick glance at the weather map. She watched its progress and remembered clearly hearing the noise of the rotors while talking to Watchman the first time, and feeling a shiver go through her at the idea that it was almost on top of him and how vulnerable it must have made him feel.

She shook her head in annoyance. Focus, Citera; that's crazy thinking. This is real and happening right now. She hit a series of buttons to capture a coloured screen grab of the helicopter's course, a graph of blue dots over green. It seemed to be jinking more than was necessary through weather, and she wondered if it was doing so to avoid overflying sensitive areas. The idea was reinforced when she noted that after each change of course, it eventually resumed the same heading.

And that was straight for the area where Watchman was waiting.

She keyed the contact button. 'Watchman, come in.'

A few seconds went by. Silence. 'Come in, Watchman.' She couldn't help herself, she felt her stomach flip. Had something happened? Maybe he was away from his radio.

'Go ahead.'

Lindsay breathed a sigh of relief. His voice sounded heavy, as if he had just woken up. 'Sorry to disturb you, Watchman, but there's an Ansat-U heading your way out of Saint Petersburg. It's the same one I saw near you before. It's moving slow and changing course periodically, which reads as if they're flying low and careful, but always returning to the same heading. It's guesswork but their ETA on you at their current speed is anything between forty-five minutes to one hour. That's four-five to one hour.'

'Copy that. Sounds like he's coming back for another try. I'll get on it. Any news from the Pathfinders on that signal?'

'I have. They've got their bird in the air and are currently sitting on the second signal roughly forty miles north-west of your location and static. Sending you those coordinates now.' She keyed in the details and sent them off.

'Got that. What's in the area at Counselor's current location?'

Lindsay turned to a second screen. 'Another lake . . . lots of trees . . . and some kind of track off the main road. I don't have a name but it looks small, maybe a half-mile long.' She heard Watchman moving around and the sound of a car engine starting.

'Thanks for that,' he said, his voice firmer and louder. 'On my way. Keep the information coming.'

Lindsay watched the helicopter creeping across the screen in a relentless course to the north-west. If it continued on that heading it would pass right over Watchman's current position, a predator looking for its target. She shivered, unable to help feeling a tinge of apprehension.

FORTY-FIVE

Maxim was nervous. He'd used the number he was calling a couple of times before, when he'd needed to check a matter of procedure while on shift at the Shaykovka air base. Perhaps because of that the number had stuck in his mind. But that was army work; this wasn't.

'Yeah, what?' The familiar growly voice answered. It was Denis Romanov, his Air Force supervisor. He sounded sleepy and bad-tempered, like a bear woken too early from hibernation and looking for somebody to bite.

'Hey, Denis,' Maxim said cheerfully, fingers crossed. 'How are you, my friend, sir?'

'What? Who the hell is– *Datsyuk*, is that you?'

'In person, boss. I'm great, thank you for asking.'

'As if I care. What the holy hell are you doing calling me at this time, you young dick! I was asleep, in case you hadn't noticed the time. What do you want? Don't tell me you got bored already working for those wussy civilians in Moscow ATC.'

'Actually, I've got a little problem, Denis, and I need your sound advice. I wouldn't be calling if it wasn't important.'

'Don't tell me: you met a girl who told you she's a model and she's the love of your life and you want to settle down and have twenty kids. Wow. Great news. Fucking ace. Good luck and goodnight. Ring me when she dumps you, you moron. Better yet – don't bother.'

'Wait! This is serious. At least . . . I think it is.'

A long sigh. 'Go on, then. Hit me.'

'Have you ever heard of a beacon code anything like Trapdoor Z5993?'

He heard a scrambling noise which told him Denis was sitting up in bed. 'Trap-what? Say again.'

He repeated it.

'Where the hell did you get that from?' Denis sounded surprised . . . and suddenly wideawake.

'I saw it last night and tonight, in two different places.' He described the route the aircraft had taken from Moscow to Vologda, and now heading north from Saint Petersburg. 'I tried calling them up last night to ask for confirmation of a flight plan, but they didn't respond.'

'What? I thought you were on observer attachment only. Did they give you the authority to do that?'

'I am. And no, they didn't. But I figured, what's the harm? I mean, it's a safety issue, right, having unidentified flights roaming around the skies at night? What if it was terrorist related or a flight in trouble . . . with the pilot fallen ill or something?'

'Yeah, of course. Keep telling yourself that, Einstein.' Denis's sarcasm had a harsh tone of reproof. 'If it was either of those, it would have landed by now and stayed down – or crashed somewhere, in which case, same thing. You just got bored, didn't you, and decided to stick your nose where you shouldn't. Admit it.'

'No, I . . . well, I guess.'

'I knew it.' Denis went silent for a moment, then said seriously, 'Now listen to me, young man, and listen good. You've got a bright future ahead of you, because you've got a few more grey cells than the average no-hoper we get down here.'

'Thank you.'

'Don't interrupt when I'm shouting. However, bright as you are, there are some things you need to know, like *not* assuming you're bulletproof. Incidentally, I hope you didn't log this flight.'

'Why?'

'Christ. You did, didn't you?'

'Is that bad?'

There was a brief silence, then Denis said, 'You'd better hope not. Listen, the code you picked up is not a standard signal. It's a special. If I'm right it's from a batch of beacons used a few years ago, fitted to a number of light military helicopters to track movements. If I remember correctly it was part of some scheme devised by a pencil-head in the Defence Ministry to chart military movements using or crossing commercial flight paths. It was supposed to be a safety thing but got abandoned when it became too complicated; in other

words when the data began to show up too many utility helicopters being used by senior officers and ministers out on
non-official business.'

'What kind of business?'

'What kind of–? Are you that really that naïve? Lady-friend
business, you dope. Private parties with benefits. Secret meetings. Stuff they weren't supposed to be doing and probably
involving money and drugs. Anyway, the beacons were all
ordered to be stripped out and destroyed, which was obviously
a decision made at ministerial level to cover a few asses and
avoid prosecutions.'

'So why is this one still showing up?'

'Wha – how would I know? Maybe they missed one, maybe
the machine you tracked was decommissioned and sold off
before they got round to it. They auctioned a whole flight of
utility helicopters about two years ago, knocked down to a
bunch of third-world heads of government who wanted a flying
bucket to show the starving masses how important they were.
Maybe,' he added with heavy emphasis, 'this *particular*
machine was kept on to be used by departments who don't
exist. *Do you get what I'm saying, Maxim?*'

Maxim swallowed. Oh, no. 'You mean a black flight?'

Denis made a stifled noise. 'God, how I wish you hadn't
said that. But yes, one of those.'

Maxim's head was whirling. He'd heard about black flights.
The guys at the base talked about them all the time. Ultra-
secret security and military in nature, they were the stuff of
films and novels, and were rumoured to fly from remote locations that weren't on any map, slipping across borders without
leaving a trace and dropping men and equipment in places
that never appeared in the news until something went bang,
by which time the men were long gone. 'So what should I do?'

'Do? You do nothing, you imbecile. Forget you ever saw
it, hope the pilot didn't hear your call, or if he did, wasn't so
pissed off he'll report it to his spook superiors and have you
thrown in jail; hope your dopey civilian supervisor forgets
you mentioned it and that nobody else sees the report you
filed because if they do you'll be getting a visit from somebody unpleasant. And from this moment on, learn to keep

your head down. Black flights are called that for a very good reason: nobody is supposed to see them, and if they do they're supposed to keep their mouths *shut*. Now, get yourself back down here as soon as you can where your talents will be exploited to the full by a grateful military establishment who will work you to the bone for little reward. *Good night!*'

The connection went dead. Maxim put the phone down and sat looking at his reflection in the monitor, which had gone into sleep mode. Boy, he'd never heard Denis sound so mad before. What the hell had he done?

He flicked the keyboard to wake up the screen. And there it was, still moving; the same code, now tracking further north than ever.

He turned off the screen and logged out. He had to get out of here now and take Denis's advice. He could always explain away logging off later than he should have done by saying he'd been sick; too much cheap food and beer. Tomorrow morning he'd ask for a transfer back to his home base. They'd probably be glad to see the back of him, Gretsky the Fat most of all.

He signed out of the building's rear staff entrance and pulled the door closed behind him, waiting for the click of the lock and wondering where he could get a drink. Even this late there would be something open. He needed something a little stronger than beer . . . maybe vodka or whisky, something to deaden the fears suddenly whirling around in his brain. *Black flights?* God, how stupid have I been . . .

He turned to walk across the narrow service road to the parking lot and found a car parked right outside the entrance.

Two men were standing alongside it. They were looking at him.

As he went to walk round the car, one of the men stepped out in front of him and blocked his way. A scuff of noise at his back and he sensed the other man moving in behind him to block his retreat.

'Maxim Datsyuk?'

'Yes.' Maxim's gut flipped and he felt sick. This was bad. Very bad.

'We'd like to talk with you. Get in the car.'

FORTY-SIX

C hesnokoy stared fixedly at the screen of the tracking monitor, waiting for a signal to come through and confirm that they were heading the right way. He forced himself to sit back and be patient as the Ansat rotors thumped out their familiar beat overhead, and he felt himself finally beginning to relax. Action at last.

There were worse places to be than the cabin of a military helicopter heading out into the dark; at least it meant he was doing something instead of sitting around.

After the seemingly never-ending torture of having had to wait all day to get the helicopter checked over for critical damage and the new team to arrive, night had fallen and they'd been able to get back in the air. As he kept reminding himself, they were under strict orders to fly only under cover of dark, and to stay well away from the attentions of the regional air-defence systems around Saint Petersburg. Meeting a Sukhoi fighter jet with the pilot's finger on the trigger would be an ignominious ending he preferred not to encounter. And he had too much to do to want to end things now.

The first thing on the list was to locate the targets once again, to deal with them and place a check in the box that said mission accomplished. The sooner he got the signal telling him where they were, and was able to give the order for the pilot to go in, the happier he would be.

Deep down, however, he knew it probably wouldn't be that simple. Uppermost in his mind all day had been the man who had attacked them at the lake and taken out half his team; the man who had come out of nowhere and caught them with their pants down and almost taken down the helicopter in the process.

As the pilot had explained with frightening and furious clarity once he'd inspected the damage, one of the bullets had come perilously close to wrecking the rear rotor assembly, impacting against the housing and sending splinters into the main drive. Chesnokoy had no idea what that meant in technical terms, but was realistic enough to know that the pilot's anger came from having seen a similar outcome before and knowing it could have been catastrophic.

He stared at the men around him. With Kruglov and Ignatyev seriously out of action, he was now going to have to rely on Georgi Gorin, sitting next to him, and the four new arrivals he'd picked up at the abandoned military base near Puskino north of Saint Petersburg. He didn't know them, didn't recall their first names and didn't really care; they were there to do a job. As long as they obeyed orders and could use the weapons they'd brought with them, he expected nothing more of them.

Their nominated lead was a tall, dark-skinned man with piercing eyes. He'd given his name as Kasbek. Chesnokoy figured he was a Chechen, like the man alongside him, Kelim. He'd worked with Chechen Muslims before many times and had nothing against them as soldiers. They fought well and died hard and he could respect that. Politically they were crazy and uncontrollable, in his view, but that wasn't his problem. He couldn't remember the names of the other two men; only that they were native Russians from around Saint Petersburg and hadn't spoken all day, seemingly content to clean their weapons, over and over, as if it were a sacred ritual. That suited him just fine. Good soldiers didn't have to talk, just fight.

That thought brought him back inevitably to the mystery attacker. What was the name of the younger of the two targets? Gurov. That was it; a former KGB man. But did he have the skills to have done the damage he'd caused? Somehow he didn't think so. He couldn't say why, only that some instinct told him the man who'd laid the fire trap on the water, who'd used a Molotov to disrupt their approach and pretty much kicked their arses back into the helicopter, was military trained to a high degree. KGB men learned to fight, he knew that, and many were former military men. But the attack down at the lake had been spontaneous, quickly planned, controlled and effective. And that pointed to somebody who'd done it before – and in the recent past.

Damn, he could almost admire the tactics used, even if he did want to kill the man so badly it gave him a headache.

His cell phone buzzed in his chest pocket. He took it out. It was Simoyan calling from Moscow.

'I have information that might prove interesting,' the gruff voice intoned. 'Two men went missing yesterday at a location west of Lake Onega. They were watching a foreign diplomat at the time.'

'Perhaps they got lost in the woods,' Chesnokoy replied. What the hell did this have to do with anything? He had enough on his plate without—

'Hardly. They were actually with him at the time. The diplomat has since returned to Saint Petersburg.'

'Who were the men?' It might have been better to ask who the diplomat was, but he had a feeling it wasn't the case of a man in a fancy suit suddenly going rogue and disposing of his FSB watchers.

'Good ones. Extremely good. I've used them before. They weren't the kind to get lost.'

'So what's the connection with us?'

'We believe the diplomat was planning to meet up with your two targets.'

Chesnokoy acknowledged the information and signed off, a sudden leaden lump in his chest. Damn it, he'd been right: there was somebody else out there. Somebody capable of taking out two good men. If they hadn't made contact with Simoyan, it could only mean they were dead.

He saw the navigator waving an arm, signalling him to put on the comms headset.

'What are we doing exactly?' the man asked, when Chesnokoy pushed in the jack plug. 'We're flying into a black soup here, with a dense weather pattern right ahead of us. An area this size we can't see anything on the ground unless we know where to look.'

Based on the last known position of the targets, Chesnokoy had given them the same heading towards the lake. But that wasn't where he expected to find them. If they had any sense they'd be long gone by now and trying to hide.

'When I know, so will you,' he replied, and waved the tracking monitor. 'Until then, keep going.' Rain or no rain, he thought; this is not over until I see the bodies.

FORTY-SEVEN

'They should have made contact by now.' Tzorekov was in a black mood, made worse by the discovery of the tracking device at the power plant along with a flat tyre.

'They will do so soon, I'm sure,' said Gurov. He was trying everything he could think of to penetrate the cloud of pessimism that had descended on Tzorekov. The tracker hadn't helped, found while scraping caked mud away from the axles. It had been placed underneath the car's body, tucked out of sight from a casual inspection. The combined discoveries had made Tzorekov voice the possibility that this venture might be fatally flawed.

Immediately the tyre was in place, they had packed up and driven hard to get clear of the area. The older man had said little on the way, huddled in the passenger seat and staring out of the window as if he might see whoever had placed the tracker on the car descending on them across the vast area of treelined hills either side of the road.

Even now, having eaten, his mood was grim and withdrawn as if retreating from the harsh reality that seemed to be rearing up before him.

They were seated in a small bar-restaurant at a hunting lodge some sixty kilometres north-west of the abandoned power plant. Seeing the sign, Gurov had insisted they take the opportunity to eat a meal while they could. Tzorekov had shrugged, showing little interest. The menu was limited but the food edible and filling. Washed down with local beer, it should have been enough to make any man feel that there was hope in the air.

But it hadn't worked.

'You know that, do you?' Tzorekov muttered. 'I wish I had your confidence.'

The 'they' in question was actually one person, a man named Valentin Roykovski, Putin's former driver and long-time link between the former KGB colleagues. The last contact from Roykovski had been five days ago, when they had begun their long journey here. Roykovski had been firm then in his assurances that a meeting would be possible, even probable. If they could be in position, he'd suggested, for when Putin's engagements in the south came to an end, he would make sure a time and location was provided as soon as he knew the details.

Since then, silence. Two calls to Roykovski's home number, risky though that had been, had elicited no response.

'We should have checked the car before now,' Tzorekov added quietly. 'It was an unforgiveable lapse for which I blame myself.'

'Not so,' replied Gurov. 'It was my responsibility – I should have expected it. Somehow they managed to intercept us and plant the device.'

'How would they have known precisely when we were coming? We've been very careful about communications – and we've been with the car the whole time.'

Gurov shrugged. 'I don't know. I've been thinking about that, but . . . maybe something we did alerted them to our plans. You know we've been under occasional surveillance, so they might have chosen that moment to see us leaving. But placing the tracker? I don't know.'

'Are you sure it wasn't when you heard the alarm go off back at the power plant?'

Gurov shook his head and pushed his plate away. 'Absolutely. The device was caked in mud and grit from the road; it had been there at least two days.'

'At the airport, then? There has been nowhere else.'

'Maybe. I must confess I didn't think they would latch onto us that quickly. I'm sorry.'

Tzorekov reached out to touch the younger man's hand. 'Arkasha, you mustn't blame yourself. This trip was bound to be full of hazards, we both knew that. This has come a little early, I admit – but now we know about it and can prepare ourselves. If anybody wishes to launch a direct attack on us, they will find themselves blowing an old power plant to pieces.' He grunted with the first smile he'd given in a long time. 'At least that will save the state some money, eh?'

Gurov opened his mouth to say something, but Tzorekov held up a hand. He was looking at a small television screen on the wall behind the bar. It was broadcasting a news bulletin from Moscow, the picture showing a plane arriving at Domodedovo International Airport. It cut away to show a familiar pale figure flanked by security men and aides, walking towards a clutch of reporters, held in place by security police, the air alive with the flash of cameras.

President Vladimir Putin, arriving back in Moscow from Kurtz.

Tzorekov said nothing, but his face was studied in concentration. He watched as the strap line summarised the scene, describing Putin's return and his intention of going directly into the city centre for a meeting with his ministers over the sanctions currently being applied against Russia and Russian businessmen by the United States and European Union.

'I don't believe it,' said Gurov softly. 'It can't be. What's he doing?'

But Tzorekov shook his head. 'Patience, Arkasha. Patience. These things are never simple. There are formalities he has to go through, you know that. The world stage is watching. But we will see. We will see.' He sat back, nodding confidently, but there was no mistaking the way his face had drained of colour on seeing the broadcast. 'This is just disinformation. That's all.'

But Gurov wasn't listening. He had stiffened in his chair and was looking past Tzorekov's shoulder towards the entrance.

A man had stepped through the door and was looking directly at them.

FORTY-EIGHT

already knew what I was going to do when I caught up with the Touareg. The plan wasn't ideal but it was the best of the alternatives on offer. It meant breaking my usual operating procedures, but I couldn't see any other choice. There was too much to lose if I didn't get this right.

I'd followed the co-ordinates given to Lindsay by the Pathfinders, which led to a small restaurant off the road close to another site advertising hunting and fishing. It was strictly a weekend kind of place, with garish lights and advertising hoardings for Baltika beer showing through the rain, and lots of parking. It was the first eating place of its kind I'd seen for a long while. Rough and ready it might be, but when you can't get steak, burger is a luxury.

I counted a car and two pickups out front, but no Touareg.

'You sure about the co-ordinates?' I asked Lindsay, scanning the area through the scope. 'I can't see the vehicle.' I was a hundred yards back on the side of the road with the lights off. I didn't want to go in until I had to, and scaring off Tzorekov was definitely not part of my plan. Neither was getting shot by Gurov if he was feeling jumpy and keeping his eye out for followers.

'Checked and double-checked,' Lindsay replied. 'The signal's loud and clear. I have a small structure on-screen but no identifying tags. The satellite image I have is a couple of days old and looks like a bar or a small store. There's some parking out back, perhaps for deliveries and employees, and I have a track leading away at the rear towards a small lake.'

'Good to know. Where does it go after that?' I was hoping there was another way out of here.

A slight hesitation, then: 'I'm zooming in . . . now. The track goes past the lake and into the forest. Could be a logging trail; there are open areas a few miles on that look like controlled clearance sites, then . . . yes, the track meets up with another road about five miles away which heads east towards another large lake. I don't have a clear sight of the track's condition, though; you might be facing a rough ride.'

I got out of the pickup, the Grach in my coat pocket. 'I'm going in for a closer look. Keep an eye out for that helicopter, will you? Give me a shout if they look like joining in.'

'Copy that, Watchman. Good luck.'

I locked the pickup and crossed the road into the parking lot. It was mostly gravel and hard core, puddled with rain-water and patches of mud. Close to the building, which was a single-storey wooden construction, they had painted rough white lines for parking. I was beginning to think I had lucked out and that the second tracker had also been found and dumped, when I stepped round the corner of the building and hit pay dirt.

One Touareg, parked in the shadows.

It was hidden from the road, which was good, but from the air it would show up clearly to anybody looking down. A static target.

I stood for a moment, reconsidering my plan. Making contact with a person I'm shadowing can be a risky business. The line of work I'm in usually means the people involved are on the edge of something risky, like the intelligence field or special operations. It makes them wary of everybody around them, being confident that they can get by without some guy riding shotgun, otherwise they'd have asked for it in the first place. Since they're not expecting me – and usually they're not – having me pitch up out of nowhere can look all kinds of suspicious. They either respond with concern or annoyance, mostly at their having failed to detect my presence, or even some hostility. Explaining to them that my job is all about me remaining invisible doesn't always help; they mostly like to think they can cope just fine.

There was nothing for it. If the flight Lindsay had identified leaving the Saint Petersburg area really was the same one I'd seen previously – and shot at – then standing here and hoping they'd get lost or run out of fuel was pointless.

I walked into the restaurant.

Inside was warm, dry, homely and pretty much empty. An array of old photos around the walls gave the atmosphere an ancient, musty feel, as did the series of animal heads mounted on wooden plaques. I saw a bear, a couple of wolves and some kind of deer. Nice.

Three guys in ancient padded jackets and pants were sitting on one side, spooning up some kind of soup and chewing large hunks of bread. A woman in an apron at the back was pouring coffee behind a counter, and smiled at me like I was the grim reaper come to call.

Tzorekov and Gurov were over by a window in the corner.

Tzorekov had his back to me but Gurov saw me immediately. I could tell by his body language that he was ready to go active. He was wearing a coat, even though it was warm, and he had his hand inside pretending to scratch his chest. But I was betting he had more inside there than chest hair.

I nodded at the woman behind the counter and shook some raindrops off my shoulders, then walked towards the table adjacent to the two men, taking off my coat and dropping it on the next chair. I kept my hands well clear of my body, and when I sat down, left them resting in plain sight.

Gurov was pretending not to look but followed my every move. He was as tense as a gun dog and clearly didn't like me being so close. He looked very pale in the yellow light. I wasn't sure if it was his normal colour or whether the tension of the trip was beginning to tell on him.

When Tzorekov turned his head to look, I picked up the menu and said quietly, 'Mr Tzorekov, I'm here to warn you that an Ansat-U with armed men on board is on its way here, tracking a signal from your car. They're the same men who attacked the cabins at the fishing site and you have no more than thirty minutes to get clear of this place.'

He was good. Very good. He might have been a long time out of the KGB, but he hadn't lost his ability to remain cool in a crisis. He studied me for a moment, stretching out a hand to stop Gurov, who had stiffened when I began speaking and was pulling his hand out of his coat.

'And you are?'

'My name doesn't matter, but you found my tracker back at the power plant.' I looked at Gurov. 'Thanks for not smashing it – they're pretty expensive and I have to account for all equipment.' I was joking but they didn't know that. I was deliberately keeping the talk flowing to show I wasn't a threat. If I was I'd have come in all guns blazing.

'You're American.' It came like an accusation. Gurov was looking pissed, which I figured was a mixture of professional pride at not having spotted me, and a lingering suspicion that I might be lying in my teeth and be something much worse.

'Actually I hold both US and British passports – although I don't expect either to help me much here. I was asked to shadow you in and make sure nothing happened along the way.'

'How do we know that? We're supposed to believe you, just like that?'

'You landed at Pulkovo and stayed in the Solokna Motel for one night. Then you drove east and headed along the E105, turning north after Ladoga, where you encountered a military police roadblock. If I was going to be a threat I could have done something anywhere along the road or back at the lake. Do I need to say more?'

'These men you say are coming after us,' Tzorekov said. 'Who are they?' He'd looked exhausted and old when I first sat down, but there was suddenly an energy about him that jumped the space between us. Maybe he was one of those rare types who thrives on conflict and challenge even when they know it might be a losing battle.

'I think you probably know who they are – or, at least, who they represent. The Wise Men want to stop you meeting with anybody important.'

He looked shocked at the mention of the group. I wasn't showing off what I knew, merely displaying that I knew enough about what was going on to have been well briefed.

'We didn't ask for help,' said Gurov. He appeared to have got past the gun dog response, perhaps because Tzorekov was still holding his arm. But he was still in a feisty mood. 'Who sent you?'

'People who want the same outcome as you.'

Tzorekov nodded. 'Why did these men not continue their attack on the cabins? What stopped them?'

'I did. I persuaded them to change their plans. When they left they had two walking wounded but I suspect they went for reinforcements.'

'One man?' Gurov muttered. 'And you "persuaded" them to leave?' The scoff of disbelief was missing, but the scepticism was there in buckets. No cynic like a KGB cynic, I guess.

'I had the advantage of surprise.'

'You say they are following a signal?' Tzorekov said, waving that aside. 'How do you know that?'

'Because I followed the same signal. I just got here first.' I wasn't about to mention the help I'd had from the Pathfinders, which would have been a step of information too far. An outsider by choice Tzorekov might be, but hearing there were foreign troops on the ground in his mother country would probably undo any good we were hoping to accomplish. Pride was pride and he was strictly old school at heart.

'But I checked the car,' said Gurov. 'I found your tracker.'

'There were two. They managed to place another one. Thing is, I'm not very far ahead of them and I guess as soon as they lock onto your signal again, they'll come in fast to finish the job. You need to get out of here.'

'But how will we find this device? It could be anywhere on the vehicle.'

'You tell me. Did anybody get close enough to your car in the past couple of days to plant it?'

They thought about it. Then Gurov's jaw dropped. 'The soldier at the roadblock. He opened the back to inspect the interior. He told us they were looking for a deserter.' He looked annoyed, probably at his own failure to realize what had happened.

'I think we should go.' I waited until I was sure Gurov wasn't going to blow me out of my socks, then stood up carefully and headed for the door.

FORTY-NINE

'I have them!' Chesnokoy saw the signal flicker and go stronger. It was them, definitely. He released his belt and moved forward to pass the tracking monitor to the navigator. 'This is where we have to go. Quickly.'

The navigator nodded and reached for the onboard computer, feeding in the co-ordinates before checking the device and handing it back. 'It doesn't look as if they're moving.'

'No. They probably don't know we're coming. Let us hope it stays that way.'

'What do you want us to do when we get there?' The navigator was pointing to the map on his computer read-out. 'We can find somewhere to land and let you off nearby or go in closer. It's up to you.'

Chesnokoy grinned at the thought of taking out the targets wherever they were. It was time to finish this. Then he could think about finding the other man – the one who had caused them such damage and inconvenience. 'Go in as close as you can. As soon as you have visual, find a place to put us down.'

'And if there isn't one?' He was referring to the carpet of trees.

Chesnokoy turned and gestured at the coils of rappelling ropes by the door. 'Then we'll go in the old-fashioned way.'

He moved back to his seat and signalled for the men to get ready. If Gurov was prepared for their arrival, there wouldn't be time to stroll around and take it easy; they'd have to move in hard and fast. He watched them as they went through the ritual of checking their weapons, followed by the dozen other little things soldiers did before going into battle; tightening belts and buckles, doing up buttons, looking at their watches, tying and retying bootlaces and looking at favourite photos or charms. To fighting men it was a habit as common as eating and drinking, and to each individual, just as important.

After going through his own readiness check, he sat back and waited for a signal from the navigator that they were coming in on the target. He felt a keen sense of excitement. This was it; they were nearing the end.

FIFTY

The rain had intensified, a steady downpour that instantly ran down my neck in an unerring stream as soon as I stepped outside. We ducked round the back to the Touareg and found the tracker inside three minutes. Gurov unlocked the rear door and switched on the light, and we both began checking every inch of the compartment, running our hands around each corner and cavity.

Gurov found it and swore as he held it up; it was no bigger than a matchbox with a wire transmitter aerial and a magnetic strip to hold the box in place. It was a neat piece of equipment and I wondered which government equipment store it had come from, legally or otherwise.

'Bastard!' Gurov muttered. 'The roadblock was a fake!'

Tzorekov was more pragmatic. 'It shows they have great reach, these people. It's always the way: if you have connections and influence, you can get anything you wish done.' He turned away and climbed into the Touareg.

I figured there was plenty of time for philosophical discussions later. Right now we were on borrowed time. I grabbed Gurov's arm; he was about to drop the tracker on the ground and stamp on it.

'What?' He looked ready to fight but I ignored him.

'I can use that.' I took it from him and nodded at the Touareg. 'You two get going. They'll be here any minute.'

'What are you going to do?'

'I'll lead them away with this.' I held up the tracker. 'You focus on putting some distance between you and this place and finishing what you came here for.'

He gave me an odd look, then glanced quickly towards the

front of the Touareg. I suddenly got the feeling that all wasn't well in the Tzorekov camp. He was hiding something.

'What?' I hadn't been going to ask if they had a location for their meeting yet; I'd figured they wouldn't tell me and in their place, neither would I. It was enough that I was checking their backs. But something in Gurov's expression told me he had a problem he wanted to get off his chest.

'We have a serious situation,' he said simply, and I could sense how difficult he was finding it to tell me. 'We haven't heard anything from . . . the person we expected to have contact with.'

'A go-between?'

'Yes. But also, Putin has just arrived back in Moscow.' He jerked a thumb towards the bar. 'There was a television broadcast.'

'So why are you here? It's in the middle of nowhere.'

'When the contact last spoke to us, he said we should aim for this region, maybe heading a little further north. He said that a specific location didn't matter and he would give us co-ordinates where a meeting could take place. All we had to do was stay invisible.' He sighed as if it had all been a waste of time.

'So it wasn't going to be Komsomolskoye?'

He looked surprised again, but nodded. 'You have been well briefed.'

'What does he think?' I nodded towards Tzorekov.

'He is concerned . . . but resolute. I have to respect that.'

'But?'

'I think maybe Putin will not be coming. I think this meeting will not happen.'

Gurov was in a tough position. Like any bodyguard, there was only so much he could do to offer guidance to his boss. In a case like this, Tzorekov's good intentions looked like trumping caution and realism. And that was always going to be dangerous.

We were getting wetter and in more danger the longer we stood here. Since I couldn't affect their hopes or plans, I just had to hang in there, like Gurov.

Right now it was time to go.

'I hope it works out,' I said, and meant it. I didn't wait to hear any arguments, but turned and jogged back to the pickup.

'You there, Lindsay?' I started the engine.

'Right here, Watchman. You have fifteen minutes, no more. They're now flying parallel to the road but the way they came in on your location so far, they're zeroing in on the signal. What's your plan?'

'Uh . . . actually, not sure yet, just flying blind and hoping to luck. I'll be in touch. In the meantime ask the Pathfinders to continue watching Counselor's vehicle. The weather's closing in again here, so they'd better watch their drone doesn't go AWOL.'

'Copy that. Uh, which tracker will they be following?'

'The original.'

A slight hesitation. 'Please confirm, you've put your original tracker back on the Touareg?'

'That's the one.' I'd slipped it back inside while Gurov was swearing about the roadblock, sliding it under the mat in the corner.

'And the alien?'

'I have that with me.'

'Copy that, Watchman.' She sounded cool and professional but I could tell she wasn't. Underneath her words was a whole lot of surprise, the sort which said, Are you freaking nuts?

'Keep me advised of their approach. Oh, and you might tell Callahan, there's some doubt in the camp about this meeting taking place.'

'He knows. He just told me Impaler's back in Moscow. Does Counselor know?'

'Yes. But I think he's in denial. He's got too much hope invested in this. They haven't heard squat from their contact.'

I signed off and hit the gas and took the pickup through the parking lot and onto the track behind the restaurant. On the way I saw the Touareg's tail lights disappearing down the road heading north. At least Gurov had listened to me instead of arguing. I hit a long section of single-lane cinder track bordered by trees and bushes, wide enough for trucks with occasional passing places. Lindsay had said this was logging country and she was right. I saw cleared sections of trees in the headlights and deep ruts in the earth where logs had been hauled out and loaded onto flatbeds, churning over the ground and revealing fresh earth glistening in the headlights. Elsewhere, neat piles of wet logs stood waiting for removal.

I drove for a good ten minutes, bouncing around like a beach ball and throwing up gouts of muddy water, and passed close by a small lake on my right, shown as a glimpse of silver through a thin strip of trees. This was nowhere near as fast as the road I'd come here on, but I was short of choices and had to work with what I'd got. All I wanted to hear right now was that the helicopter was following me, not the Touareg.

I soon got my wish.

'Watchman, come in.'

'Here.'

'The signal has just passed the bar where you stopped and . . . is now turning east – I repeat, turning east. It's now on your track although they've reduced speed. Is that the rain? It looks heavy on my current weather map.'

'Sure is. How far behind me?'

'I estimate no more than five miles and closing.'

'Copy that. And the Touareg?'

'Wait one.' She went silent for five seconds, then said, 'They're heading north, speed steady.'

I hit an uphill section of track that had me sliding back on my seat and made my ears pop. I changed down a couple of gears and stamped hard on the gas as the engine began to labour under the strain and the wheels began to skid. Getting caught out here with a car going nowhere wasn't exactly what I had in mind. I'd be like one of those little ducks in a fairground shooting gallery, except the men in the helicopter could simply sit up above me and hose me off the road at their leisure.

The engine picked up and the tyres suddenly bit deep on something firm and we shot forward. A clatter of stones hit the underneath as we swished sideways under the rush of power and the nearside wheels dipped into a rut. I kept going; slowing now would lose valuable ground and momentum and I had to get over this hill and see what was on the other side if I was to stand any chance of getting out of this in one piece.

I hit the top of the rise and felt the nose dip and bounce,

and had to fight the wheel as I hit a series of deep ruts going downhill. It was like being shaken by a giant hand, with everything inside the pickup jumping around and a worrying metallic rattle coming from somewhere underneath my butt. Trees flashed by either side of me but I couldn't see the terrain off the track and figured it would be best not to find out. Going off here would be a one-time thing only and it was probably a mandatory slow section for logging trucks so they didn't lose their loads on the downslope. Unfortunately, I didn't have that luxury. Every minute I lost was giving a hand to the helicopter, and with night-vision equipment, which I guessed they must have, they'd soon be seeing me as clear as day even through the rain.

'Lindsay, give me a reading.'

'Watchman, you're approaching the road I mentioned before. If you turn left and follow it for fifteen miles, it joins up with the road you just left and continues north. Turn right and it circles a large lake some twenty miles long.'

'And the chopper?'

'Now three miles behind you . . . and closing.'

Three miles. If the pilot put on even a hint of speed, he could overtake me in no time at all. I had almost no margin for error.

'Check the map for me, will you? How close to the lake does the road go and what's the tree cover like?'

'Trees everywhere, Watchman, either side of the road and right down to the water. There's no clearance work showing up just here. Further, the road runs parallel to the lake in a fairly straight line for approximately ten miles, with turnings off on that side only for access to the water. But no secondary routes out that I can see.'

In other words once I got onto the road past the lake, I'd have to stay on it for miles. It would be like sitting in a shooting gallery, where the men in the helicopter would find me pretty much out in the open. The only alternative was to go down one of the dead ends with only one way back.

Some hell of a choice.

'Watchman you have approximately half a mile to go to the road.'

'Copy that. I'm turning right. Keep me advised.'

I put on speed. The track here was less of a roller coaster and solid, and I guessed the logging company had put in some extra work to the surface to make sure the trucks got out safely with their valuable loads. A sign flicked by, nailed to a tree. It showed a junction up ahead. I kept on going but got ready to slam on the brakes. Slowing now would just play into the pursuers' hands.

Suddenly I was there. I stamped hard as I saw a hoarding right in front of me painted with a large red 'T' to show the road going right and left. Part of the hoarding was missing, as if taken out by some large teeth, and a section of bushes and trees on the same side had been flattened. Somebody had been dozing and hadn't see the turn coming.

I had just enough time to turn off my lights to see if there were any other vehicle lights coming either way, then switched them back on again and hauled on the wheel, turning hard right and scattering mud and cinders off the tyres. I straightened up and hit the gas again, and found I had a clear if undulating road, a decent surface and the pickup was no longer shaking itself to pieces.

I saw lights up ahead. A block of four, two low down and two higher up. A large truck. It gave me something to aim at. But now the weather had turned really nasty; hard, slanting rain bouncing off the screen and hood and turning the road surface into a glistening mirror. The wipers could barely cope and I could feel the tyres beginning to lose traction whenever we came to a bend. Still, if it made it tough for me, it was probably worse for the pilot behind me.

Then Lindsay came on, proving everything was relative.

'Watchman, they're right on your tail!'

FIFTY-ONE

'Why are you slowing down? Keep going!' Chesnokoy had grabbed the comms headset and was shouting at the pilot as he sensed the helicopter losing speed. He could see the signal on his monitor dead ahead and could almost taste the pleasure of consigning the targets to their fate and completing the job.

'Two reasons,' the pilot shouted back. 'One, I can barely see anything in this shit! This is insane weather – we warned you about this!'

'So you did – so report me to the aviation board or whatever they're called. What's the other excuse?'

'A local military base ATC controller is demanding an identification code. In other words, who the hell are we and what are we doing flying through this section of airspace? He's called three times now on a local frequency and I think he's getting pissed at being ignored.'

'Let him. We came this far with no questions asked, didn't we?'

'Actually, we didn't. We had queries but nobody seemed too bothered when we didn't respond. They just assumed we were a military flight on a mission. But this is a sensitive area with a number of training bases, and they like to know who's around.'

'So we're another training flight on manoeuvres. What's the problem?'

'One of the bases is less than fifty kilometres away and is a special training wing with Ka-Five-Two Alligators. If they get suspicious and send one of those bastards up to take a close look at us, we'll be in deep shit. They're fast and nasty.'

'Won't they be as blind as we are in this weather?'

'No. The Alligator's an all-weather craft with missiles and automatic thirty-millimetre guns. If they don't like the look of us they'll come right in – and bad weather for them doesn't exist. They'll simply fly right through it and blow us away.'

'So what do you suggest? Only don't say we should stop – we do not stop, you understand?'

'At least let me reduce speed and change height. If we continue like this our luck is going to run out. We'll hit a hill with tall trees or a radio mast – or an Alligator will knock us out of the sky. Are you really so keen to die?'

Chesnokoy looked around the cabin at the faces of the men. They couldn't hear the exchange but the atmosphere told them that something was wrong. They looked nervous – even Gorin, who wasn't frightened of anything, was shaking his head. The others were clinging onto anything they could and staring at him as if he'd gone mad.

He swore loudly. Losing ground at this point in the chase went against everything he'd ever learned. If you had your target in your sights, you didn't pull back and you didn't veer off course. But the pilot was right: this weather *was* insane and if they encountered any obstacle, natural or military, they wouldn't know about it until it was too late.

'Very well,' he replied. 'But whatever you do, stay on his tail.'

The pilot's reply was brief and sour, followed by a change of direction. 'I'm pulling over water,' he explained, 'to avoid the trees. We can lose height safely here and maybe stay below the base radar. We'll be flying on a parallel course to the target but a little way behind.'

'Why? Why not keep up with him?'

'Because he can change course in an instant. If he sees a way out he can slam on the brakes and turn within a few metres. We can't. If we're alongside him, we'd lose him and in this muck we might not find him again for some time, by which point the Alligator might be chomping on our tail.'

Chesnokoy gave a grudging assent. He was right again. The pilot would have performed this kind of chase many times before and knew all the moves.

'Do it.'

FIFTY-TWO

I felt the downbeat of the rotors before I heard the engines. There was a thudding sensation over my right shoulder and a rattle on the windows, which I at first took to be gusts of wind. But it was too regular for that and I realized my luck was running out.

They were here.

I used the gears to slow down. I had to keep my lights on

or risk running head-on into a large tree, or worse, driving right off the road. But if I used the brakes, the super-bright flare of red would show up a long way off, even through the trees, and that would give the helicopter pilot a point to fix on. I wasn't keen on slowing but there was no way I could outrun them. Instead I was looking for a turning where I could lose myself for long enough to plan a way out of this.

I just hoped the pilot wasn't carrying missiles and decided to let them do the work so he and his pals could go home to nice warm beds.

The next thing I saw was the treetops flailing towards me against the sky, as if being pushed by a giant hand, then bending further as the downward pressure increased. Bits of foliage started hitting the car and landing all around me, adding to the general distraction, and I figured he couldn't be very far off my right shoulder.

'Watchman, come in.'

'Still here.'

'I have the helicopter right alongside you, but he's being queried by an air traffic controller at a local base. Do you copy?'

'Yes, I copy. What's the likelihood of them sending someone along to check him out? I could do with some help right now – even from the Russian military.'

'That's a no, Watchman. They've given him repeated warnings about restricted airspace, but I think it's a bluff; nothing in our data shows anything other than some over-fly restrictions at certain times – and tonight doesn't seem to be one of those.'

I hit a stretch of road that veered close to the large lake on my right. I couldn't see the water through the trees straight-away, but I knew it must be down there somewhere. Then I had it, a glint of paleness that showed the trees here were spread thinly along the shores of the lake, their tops little more than twenty feet or so above me, where the road was taking an elevated position.

'Lindsay, can you see any turnings off here? I need an escape route.' As I finished speaking, I saw movement off to my side, and a large, dark shape drifted into view. It was pretty much at my eye level and out above the lake. The pilot must have been virtually skimming the water to keep it there, and I could just make out the soft glow of lights in the cockpit. It was great flying at any time, but in this weather and at night it was close to spectacular. Pity was, right now I wasn't really up to appreciating his skill the way that I should have done.

'You have one coming up in approximately one quarter mile, repeat one quarter mile. It shows up here as an access track to the water. But there's no visible way out that I can see.'

'Damn. Where's a friendly missile-laden Sukhoi when you need one?'

'I hear you. I'll call one up, shall I?' I heard the attempt at humour in her voice, but she also sounded strained. I wasn't surprised; sitting in her comms bubble, which I knew would be a small, gloomy space surrounded by equipment and lights, she could see little of my outside world save in terms of maps, screens and digital read-outs. Trying to imagine the reality on the ground beyond those limitations would be like a child trying to visualize a monster under the bed. I'd been in the same situation myself a couple of times, and it wasn't easy.

Then I saw the turning up ahead, marked by a white pole and an arrow. It seemed to disappear into a black hole among the trees and I figured the track dipped sharply towards the water, allowing access for fishing and boats.

I slowed some more, making the engine howl in protest, and hauled the wheel round as I came level with the sign. The hood dipped alarmingly as we left the road and the headlights showed a steep track marked by ruts, descending into a dark hollow formed by trees and bushes, with passing-places. I braked hard before I got too far down and turned off the lights.

Seconds later the dark shape of the helicopter glided past not a hundred yards away, smooth as a killer shark on the hunt. I could feel the vibration of the rotors beating against the windscreen and setting up a gentle rocking motion of the car. Bits of foliage dropped around me and I could see the treetops bending.

I took the alien tracker out of my pocket. It had done its duty; it was now time to lose it. I threw it out of the window, then reversed back up the track and out onto the road. I drove for a good half mile without lights, then pulled into the side of the road and waited.

The pitch of the engine changed from a distant flutter to something heavier and charged. It was turning round and coming back. I watched as it went past my position, homing in on the signal I'd left behind.

I gave it a couple of minutes, then eased onto the road and headed north, continuing back the way I'd come.

Now I had to find Tzorekov again and take up where I'd left off.

FIFTY-THREE

'W hy have you slowed down?' Chesnokoy lifted his head as the engine note dropped and the helicopter slewed round.

The pilot didn't answer at first, then said, 'The target stopped, just like I said he might. He must have seen a turning off the road. Don't worry – we still have the signal.' He got a nod of assent from the navigator.

'Where? I don't have it.' Chesnokoy shook the tracking monitor. It had stopped working, the signal gone. A malfunction? He tossed it to Gorin to keep checking and moved across to the window as if he might see the target standing down there in the dark waiting for him. But all he could see was blackness stretching away to infinity, and a pale glow of reflected light from the flight controls.

The helicopter tilted sharply as the pilot brought it round on a tight, 180-degree turn and began to go back over the course they had just taken. 'Have your men check through the starboard windows,' the pilot called. 'Look for lights among the trees. He's in there somewhere about five-hundred metres ahead.'

The throb of the engines took over and each man watched in the hope of seeing something, anything that might give them a target on which to fasten and vent their frustration.

'I've got a signal.' Gorin held up the monitor and pointed towards the shore. 'He's right out there in front of us. But he's not moving.'

'He's hoping we've missed him,' Chesnokoy shouted. 'Let's prove him wrong!' He pointed at the ropes. 'Stand by! Two of you, go down and report. Take the monitor with you.'

The two Chechens, Kasbek and Kelim, were the first to move, Kasbek clipping a radio to his combat jacket and slipping the tracker monitor in his pocket. They picked up a rope each while Gorin attached himself to a safety line to help them out. As he opened the door a burst of wind and rain flowed inside, a welcome blast of freshness after the overheated atmosphere of the cabin so far.

'What do you want us to do if the target's down there?' Kasbek queried.

'There should be two men – one old, the other younger. Watch out for the younger one – he's a fighter. Hold them and call me.'

'And if they don't want to be held?'

'Simple. Kill them and drop them in the lake.'

'What's the plan?' the pilot asked, butting in while keeping the helicopter level.

'Take us in over the trees at the shoreline,' Chesnokoy replied. 'Two men will rappel down.'

The pilot nodded. 'Moving in. We'll look for a clear spot. Have them call in their descent. I don't want to get too close to those treetops.'

The helicopter drifted sideways across the water, gradually gaining height over the trees until the navigator called out that they were over a small clearing. He looked back and gave the thumbs up for the two men to go.

Gorin clapped Kasbek on the shoulder and the Chechen was gone, dropping into the dark and followed quickly by Kelim. Each man carried an assault rifle slung across his chest and wore a balaclava to cut down any chance of being seen in the dark. The speed and skill with which they dropped showed they had done this many times before.

Chesnokoy watched them go with professional appreciation, and almost wished he could have gone down there with them.

This was the element he'd most enjoyed as a soldier: the physical demands, the excitement and the part of being a team. All the rest was incidental.

But something told him this wasn't going to be quite as simple or as exciting as it seemed.

It wasn't long before his instincts were proven correct. After calling in their descent to the ground and landing safely, Kasbek eventually reported back after searching the area. He sounded short of breath.

'There's nothing here; just a track leading up to the road with fresh tyre marks at the top. They must have come part of the way down, then reversed out. We're just checking the road.' Minutes later he was back. 'Nothing. They've gone.'

Chesnokoy shook his head in frustration. He was beyond swearing. Gurov had fooled them. But how the hell had he known what to do? They hadn't announced their plans to anybody, yet somehow Gurov must have sensed they were coming and had taken steps to evade them.

'What about the signal? The device must be down there somewhere.'

'It is,' Kasbek replied. 'I have it here. It was dumped by the side of the track.'

This time Chesnokoy did swear, long and loud. How the hell were they going to find the target now? 'Check for mud on the road,' he said. 'They'll have left tyre tracks when they turned out. Then wait there – we'll land and pick you up.'

FIFTY-FOUR

In an apartment block on the outskirts of Moscow, former government chauffeur Valentin Roykovski checked his phone calls and emails. He had just returned late to the city after a couple of days' absence in a government health spa, courtesy of his past service as a driver and aide for the president, who had also just flown in to Moscow, from Kurtz in the south.

There was one missed call from his sister, one from a garage reminding him about a due service on his car . . . and two from an unlisted number, one leaving a voice message.

He pressed the PLAY button and heard the familiar voice.

'Valentin, my old friend. We haven't spoken in so long, for which I apologize. We must get together and talk about the old days. Please call me as soon as you can.'

He played it through again. To outside ears it was merely a message from a friend, playing catch-up after a long absence. The voice was that of an old man, cajoling and intimate as old friends can be, but with a subtle hint of reproof. To Roykovski he sounded desperate.

Leonid Tzorekov.

He stood for a moment, wondering how to play this. He caught sight of himself in the mirror over the shelf holding the recording machine. He adjusted his silk tie and smoothed down his hair, which was silver grey; paused to look at the backs of his hands, where liver spots showed in the skin. The curse of old age, he decided, like so many other ailments.

Like old friends calling in favours out of sentiment; favours they no longer deserved.

His former boss was busy, he knew that, tied up with issues of state. And his last message to Roykovski earlier that day had been unambiguous.

There would be no meetings other than those on government matters.

None.

It was, Roykovski reflected, the right decision. The timing and circumstances were all wrong. There could be no deviation from the current course. To do otherwise would be to attract criticism from the president's enemies waiting in the wings, both inside Russia and beyond its borders. It was a tough decision but that was part of the burden of leadership.

Time for a drink, he thought. It was late but to hell with the spa's advice – he hadn't had one in forty-eight hours. There was plenty of time to sleep later. And what the doctors didn't know couldn't hurt them.

Before walking away, he reached out and deleted the voice message.

FIFTY-FIVE

'Watchman, come in.'

'I'm here. What's happening in the big wide world?' Morning had come with a chill breeze and the promise of more rain. I'd unpicked myself from the passenger seat of the pickup and opened the door a couple of minutes earlier, stepping outside and doing some quick stretching exercises to loosen up. Three hours of poor sleep wasn't exactly a new experience for me, but it was never exactly welcome. Now I was ready to move on.

'The Pathfinders have reported tracking Counselor's signal, currently north-west of your location and static. The co-ordinates are on their way to you now. They report that they're close to the edge of their operating range and can't guarantee to hold it much longer.'

'Good to know. I'm about to set out. As soon as I find the target again you can tell the guys to bug out for home – and say thank you for me. Is there anything else I should look out for on the radar? That includes military roadblocks, cops and helicopters with angry men on board.'

Her voice developed a smile. 'Nothing on those, Watchman. There are military training units at various locations in the region – I'll send you a graphic in a second. There are none near you right now, but there is a camp on a line between you and Counselor's current location. It's listed on our database as a specialist training school, confirmed and updated as of one month ago.'

I knew the CIA and other agencies, including the US military, kept a regularly updated check on all known facilities as a matter of course and shared the information among themselves when it suited them. Right now that sharing could be of real value to me. 'What sort of specialist?'

'Sniper training and winter survival for regular troops looking to step up.'

Great. Special forces intakes, in other words; hot to trot and eager to prove themselves worthy of selection. They'd be out in all weathers and conditions and wouldn't be advertising their presence. They would also look on anybody out and about in the area as potentially part of the testing procedure they were going through. I'd have to steer well clear of them.

'I lost sight of the helicopter during the night,' Lindsay continued. 'They must have put down and gone dark. Did you have any contact?'

She meant did I shoot anybody but was too polite to ask outright.

'No. I was a good boy and stayed out of sight. But they weren't fooling. I think they'll be back.'

'Copy that. I'll keep an eye out.'

I thanked her and signed off, then had a field-style breakfast, which was water, a can of juice and a couple of energy bars. It would do me fine until I got something better. I'd had about an hour of hard driving after leaving the lake before I gave up the chase and found a place to pull in and get my head down. With no visible signal to follow it meant Tzorekov had headed for the horizon beyond my tracking range. Right at this moment he could be anywhere and certainly wasn't going to wait around for me to buddy up to him again. Now he knew I was here and what I represented, I was nothing more than a distraction – and a danger for him and Gurov if I got picked up.

I stamped around the pickup a couple of times to warm up, then changed the magnetic decals on the pickup back to the logging company. The best way to not stand out was by blending in like a local, and you couldn't be more local around here than a logging contractor. Then I hit the road, keeping one eye on the skies in case the helicopter popped up on my tail. I had no cover now and the roads were few and far between in this area, which gave them a far smaller area to cover. I didn't know what kind of electronics they had on board or whether it included cameras, but it was a safe bet to assume that they hadn't come armed only with opera glasses and a borrowed road map.

*   *   *

Another roadblock. I'd been driving for less than an hour when I rounded a long bend on the side of a hill and saw brake lights up ahead. I wasn't too surprised; I'd overtaken a few trucks and slow cars along the route but seen oncoming vehicles neatly spaced out, which meant something was breaking up the traffic flow like an accident – or something a lot less welcome.

I started to brake, looking for turnings. Nothing doing. A solid belt of trees lay on one side with a deep ravine on the other behind a metal barrier. A half dozen soldiers were standing on each side of the road, this time with a light armoured vehicle and a GAZ-Tigr utility to back them up. And instead of one man like the last one I'd seen, they were moving in pairs along the lines of vehicles, checking each one.

'Lindsay, come in.'

'I hear you, Watchman. Go ahead.'

'Have there been reports of any radio chatter from military bands? I have a roadblock up ahead of me and no way out. It might be nothing but I could use a heads up if I have to run.'

'Nothing specific on that, Watchman. There have been news reports about a clampdown on all non-essential flights north of Moscow, but no details given. It could be a random exercise but it's being described by observers and some of the press as a show of strength after Putin's visit to the south.' She paused. 'I see a track off to your right, but I think that might be too late.'

It was. I was stuck and would have to sweat it out. I checked I hadn't left anything out, like the cell phone or the weapons. But the car was a convincing mess of food wrappers, empty water bottles and some fruit on the front passenger seat. We loggers can be real slobs.

I grabbed an apple and took a large bite. One way of disguising a foreign accent is to talk through a mouthful of food. It isn't foolproof but works more often than not, especially if the people asking the questions are themselves a little jumpy. There was also a second reason: I was sending out the silent message that anybody apparently calm enough to be chewing an apple can't be too nervous about being stopped by cops or troops.

A pair of soldiers arrived, one each side of the pickup. They had assault rifles at the ready and were standing back in a way that showed they were trained and ready in case anything kicked off. I nodded a greeting and carried on eating, hoping they weren't looking to have a chat. Both men gave me the dead eye, ducking to get a good look at my face, and I waved the apple. They seemed relaxed enough, but they were professionals; if they had any suspicions they were sitting on them.

The one on my side checked out the logging company decals on the side of the pickup, taking his time. When he looked through the window at the inside, he pulled a face. Maybe he was a neatness freak. He gave a quick glance at the back space then looked over the top at his colleague and waved him on, before turning to jerk a thumb at me to get moving and take my mess with me.

I was more than happy to comply.

As soon as I got through the roadblock I called Lindsay again. The delay hadn't been too long but I still didn't have a signal from the Touareg.

'Copy that, Watchman. I have a location from the Pathfinders as of ten minutes ago. Coming through now.'

'Thanks. Got that.'

As I signed off and put my foot down, I glanced in the mirror. The GAZ had pulled out from the side of the road and was coming after me, flashing its headlights. I wondered if it was me they wanted or if they were simply telling me to clear the road. But there was nobody else around.

It had to be me.

FIFTY-SIX

'We need to refuel.' The navigator was looking back at Chesnokoy. 'We have thirty minutes flying time left and are within two minutes of a small depot. Beyond that we will be reducing our flight time and will lose more time coming back to refuel than is practical.'

Chesnokoy nodded. 'Do it. But make it quick.'

After an uncomfortable few hours' sleep, they were back in the air and heading north along the road from the lake. After touching down on the road to pick up the two Chechens, Gorin had jumped out and confirmed that mud tracks led from the lake and turned left, showing the target vehicle's direction of travel.

'That bloody Gurov,' he'd muttered, climbing back aboard. 'I can't wait to get him in my sights.'

Chesnokoy shared the sentiment, but some instinct cautioned him about assuming that Gurov was to blame for leading them on a dance. Surely he wouldn't have endangered the man he'd been protecting for so long by doing that? What if he'd miscalculated and they'd managed to catch them out in the open? It didn't ring right.

'How safe is this depot?' he queried. Although they were operating under the radar and being given help to avoid being questioned too closely, that situation would not last indefinitely. Neither would they stand too close an inspection by one of the military's 'paper' soldiers wielding a clipboard and a sense of self-importance.

'It's fine as long as we land, refuel and leave immediately. We have a clearance code as a Spetsnaz training mission but only as long as we don't run into one of their unit observers. Your men will have to remain on board and out of sight, though.' He flicked a hand at his own face. 'In fact it might be better if they wear their masks.'

Chesnokoy gave the order for his men to don their balaclavas and get ready for landing. He thought having the men stay on-board and concealed was over-elaborating the issue but was content to take the precaution. He trusted Gorin to know the score and keep his head down; like himself, the former sergeant had spent a lifetime knowing when to talk and when not to; when the seemingly innocent man standing next to you round the camp fire was actually reporting back on the cynics, the disgruntled and the dissenters. But he didn't know Kasbek or the others. All it needed was a careless word from one of them and their cover could be blown in a second.

'Prepare for landing.' The pilot's voice drifted over the

comms system. 'There are other flights here, some with men onboard. I'll land away from them and wait our turn. Nobody gets off, OK?'

'Agreed.' Chesnokoy looked round each man in turn and signalled that they should stay onboard and keep their faces covered. In most places a group of men dressed in combat gear with their faces masked would attract a level of attention out of the ordinary. Russia's Spetsnaz troops were the best of the best and were accorded the appropriate level of mystique and admiration by the public. But among other military professionals there was always a degree of interest that went beyond that. Some would be looking for individuals they might know, looking to put a face to the figure and bask in the glow of a shared acquaintance.

And that could be disastrous.

The pilot circled the depot, housed at the end of a small airfield with a few buildings and a repair facility. He touched down and switched off the engines, then got out and walked away towards the buildings to sign off a fuel voucher.

Chesnokoy stayed where he was, eyeing the rest of the field. He counted three other military helicopters and a fixed-wing plane. Several men in combat or flight uniform were standing in groups away from the machines being refuelled, some looking at the Ansat-U with interest. New arrivals, he thought; always of interest to soldiers bored with waiting and looking for the opportunity to exchange some gossip.

Twenty minutes later the pilot still hadn't returned.

'What's the hold-up?' said Chesnokoy.

The navigator shook his head. 'Could be anything. Probably some lazy clerk who doesn't want to put himself out. We have an open docket to take on fuel; it was guaranteed the same as the one we used in Saint Petersburg. They get picky sometimes, demanding extra codes and ID.'

Chesnokoy sat back and took a deep breath. Don't sweat it, Alex, he told himself. It's probably some typical military pencil pusher flexing his authority because it's the only way he can.

Then Gorin touched his arm and pointed through the window. Three men in combat gear were walking towards them.

They had left a group clustered around a Mil Mi-24 attack helicopter, squatting on the field like a giant dragonfly, bristling with guns and missiles. As the men got closer it was possible to see they were wearing blue-striped T-shirts under their jackets. They looked tanned and fit, and walked with the brazen confidence of elite troops.

'Great,' Gorin muttered. 'That's all we need – a bunch of hulking paras looking to make new friends.'

Or GRU Spetsnaz, thought Chesnokoy sourly. The *telnyashka* striped T-shirt was worn by naval, army and airborne troops, the color of the stripes denoting which branch of the service they came from. But some soldiers with few brains liked to wear them for the buzz even if they weren't entitled.

He watched the men and felt a drumming sensation building in his chest. Anywhere else in the world, faced with nosy civilians eager to meet a bunch of soldiers, he could have bluffed his way out with no trouble. Or told them to get lost.

But this was different.

He pulled the mouthpiece of his comms headset close and said quietly to the navigator, 'Don't let these idiots onboard, you hear me?'

'Got it.' The navigator unclipped himself and climbed out, and walked across to meet the three men, two senior sergeants and a captain. They stood and talked, with the captain gesturing at the Ansat-U and lifting his chin in a query.

The navigator shook his head. The captain frowned and said something else. Again the navigator shook his head, this time moving slightly to block the path of one of the sergeants who looked like walking past him.

Chesnokoy felt his blood pounding. He dropped his hand and picked up his pistol, a 9mm Makarov. The other men saw the movement and were instantly at the ready, reaching for their own weapons.

'Nosy bastards, aren't they?' said Gorin. 'This could get messy.'

'Stay calm,' Chesnokoy warned them, feeling a lot less relaxed than he probably sounded. 'Let the fly boy do the talking.'

'What if it doesn't work?' said Kasbek. 'He doesn't look very convincing to me.'

'He'll do fine, don't worry. He's been round the block a few times; I'm sure it will take more than a para captain to scare him off.'

'I hope you're right. If they find out we haven't got official clearance, we'll be an open target.' He licked his lips but Chesnokoy noticed he had his hand on his rifle ready to fight.

'We have official clearance all right,' he said lightly. 'It's just not *official* official.' After a second or two he saw Kasbek's lips move in a smile, and the others did the same. They might be in an awkward situation, but they could all appreciate sticking up a middle finger at officialdom whenever the opportunity arose.

Then he heard a voice snapping out orders and saw the navigator returning to the Ansat on the double. The man doing the shouting was their pilot, who marched straight up to the captain and issued a stream of invective at him, jerking a thumb away towards the Mil in a way that was impossible to misunderstand.

'Piss off, junior, in other words,' Gorin translated, 'and go fly your own machine.'

Everybody relaxed and lowered their weapons.

The pilot jumped aboard. 'There was a query with the paperwork, but it's sorted out,' he explained. 'Petty bureaucrats, even out here.'

'And the captain?' Chesnokoy thought the pilot was a lot less calm than he sounded.

'The snot in the fancy T-shirt, you mean? He's part of an inspection mission. He demanded to know our names and unit details so I told him to get lost and go polish his medals.' He settled himself into his seat and put on his helmet, then said softly to Chesnokoy over the intercom, 'Something doesn't feel right about this. I don't want to worry your men but they're querying all "non-essential" flights in the region. That means anything that doesn't qualify as a training flight or special operations will be shut down for an unspecified period. The captain said they were considering grounding any that fail to show proper identification and mission plans. I think that means us.'

'Did he say why?'

'No. Instructions from the Air Transport Agency, he said, but that's bullshit; they don't give orders to the military. Somebody must have rattled the bars somewhere and everybody's jumping to attention. Could be a terrorist exercise or some such crap. I suggest we carry on and refuel; to leave without it would look very suspicious and we're dangerously low on fuel as it is. With luck we can fill up and get out of here before Captain Parachute grows some balls and comes back with an order to ground us.'

Chesnokoy nodded. 'Let's do that. Then we can go hunting. I feel the need to shoot somebody.'

FIFTY-SEVEN

'Lindsay, come in. I'm going to need some fancy map reading.'

'Copy that, Watchman. I have your location.'

'I've got a Russian military muscle-wagon on my tail and it looks like he wants to take a closer look. I can't let him do that but I won't be able to outrun him on this road before he calls up some help, so I need an escape route.'

'Copy that. Running map overlay now. Get ready to follow my call.' She sounded amazingly calm and I hoped she had some tricks up her sleeve. If the soldiers in the GAZ knew the area at all, it would be way better than I did and they'd react very fast to any change of direction. But maybe between us we could fool them.

'Watchman, two hundred yards, left!'

I was already hitting eighty when she said it and I just had time to see the turning coming up before I had to haul the wheel round and stand on the brakes. The tyres protested and I prayed they'd hold out and not start to shred under the further round of abuse I was about to send their way. Then we were facing left and the nose was dropping into a black void before we hit ground and I saw a track heading away into a long dark tunnel of trees.

I floored the accelerator and felt my guts heave along with the suspension as we hit a rough patch before levelling out on a slightly better section of track. Trees flashed by close on both sides and I heard the slap-slap of low-hanging branches bouncing off the bodywork.

When I looked back I saw the GAZ had turned off the road after me and was closing fast. Whatever had caught their attention and made them come after me, I had a feeling wasn't about to go away.

I had once ridden in a Humvee on a high-speed raid and knew the things it could do in the hands of an experienced driver in spite of its size. I figured the GAZ would be little different. And if the men inside had an itch to catch me, they would simply play it out by staying right on my tail until I ran out of road or hit something.

'I need some fast turns, Lindsay,' I said. 'These guys are serious.'

'Got that, Watchman. Wait one. Checking I don't send you down a dead end.'

I waited, doing my best to keep the pickup on the track while trying to ignore the way the GAZ was gaining on me as if I was standing still. Just my luck – they probably had a rally champion in the driver's seat who knew this area better than his own mother's face.

'Three hundred yards right.'

I waited until I got real close to the turning before I hit the brakes again and drifted round to my right, just squeezing into the opening and missing a tree by a whisker. I felt the tail beginning to wobble before I slammed my foot down and regained control, then we were on our way again into another section of tree-lined track.

'And two hundred left.'

This time I used the handbrake. I felt the tyres beginning to lose traction but I was ready and already pulling on the wheel to steer into the turn before we got there. Just for a second I felt the left-hand wheels leave the ground before the pickup decided it didn't want to play rollover and slammed down again, shaking my teeth.

The lights behind me had gone, but I was sure it was only

temporary. I kept my foot down hard and prayed nothing big would step out onto the track to play chicken. At this kind of speed it wouldn't take much to knock me off-line with no way of stopping a fatal impact in the trees.

The GAZ lights flickered behind me. The handbrake move had caught him unprepared; with no brake lights to alert him, he'd overshot the turning and been forced to reverse. But now he knew what I'd do next time and he'd be ready.

'Watchman, you have two more turns before reaching an intersection with a road which will take you back to your original route.'

'Got that. Waiting on your call.'

We were on another long stretch, which put the ball firmly back in the GAZ's favour. He was already closing on me and I figured the pickup must have been abused more than I'd figured because it was beginning to labour and feeling very sloppy.

I now had only the vaguest idea where I was and which direction I was headed. I was completely in Lindsay's hands, and in spite of her skills at keeping me out of trouble, we couldn't continue this duel much longer. Either the GAZ driver would get tired of the chase and call down some help or he'd try to shunt me off the road. Neither choice was going to help me, so I was going to have to put him off his game.

'Six hundred right and counting.'

She was giving me plenty of warning now, and with her overview of the terrain she must have seen that I was fast running out of options. No turns meant I'd lose the game.

'Four hundred.'

I took my foot off the gas and allowed my speed to bleed. This was going to be a one-time trick and no repeats.

'Three hundred.'

The inside of the pickup was now ablaze with harsh light as the GAZ began to close the gap with his full beams on, and I could hear the heavy growl of the engine coming up behind me. If he was hoping to intimidate me into stopping, he was having the opposite effect; if I slowed down any more, he'd be unable to stop and would run right over me.

'Two hundred – and it's a must-turn!'

Ouch. A right-angle turn with no alternatives. This time I couldn't choose to keep going even if I wanted to. Good to know.

I wondered if the GAZ driver knew it.

I hit the accelerator again and began to pull away, catching him by surprise. But it was a momentary thing only and he soon began to catch up until he was only yards off my tail. He was also sounding the horn to add to the confusion. I figured he was probably getting mad now and saw no reason to try and stop me. That meant he'd go for a rear-end shunt and wipe me off the road.

'Coming up now!'

This time he got the full benefit of my brake lights. Up this close and focussing intensely on my rear end, it must have been like having a bright red flashlight stuck in his eye. For a second he was so close I thought this was it as the gap between us shrank to nothing. Then there was no time for thinking as the turning came up on my right. I took my foot off the brake pedal and pulled on the handbrake, and as the nose of the pickup edged into the turning, I saw the GAZ slide past my rear end and continue on down the track.

Except there was no track for him to follow, just a solid wall of trees.

FIFTY-EIGHT

The weather had closed in tight by the time I got the first hint of a signal from Tzorekov's car. I was pushing hard out of a long valley dipping between mist-shrouded hills when I saw the first flicker. It looked weak at first, growing steadier as the road lifted sharply towards the peaks.

The ground flattened out at the top and dropped slightly after a half mile on the other side, giving me a brief view of trees and a couple of small lakes, and a river snaking away in the distance.

The nearest lake of the two was about a mile away. It had

a large clearing just off the road, like a make-do parking lot, and a pontoon floating in the water about thirty yards offshore. I used the scope to check the area and saw a single vehicle sitting beneath the trees near the water. Dark green. A 4WD.

The Touareg.

I checked the map. If Tzorekov had finally got a location for his meeting, maybe this was the place.

I called Lindsay and asked if she could see any buildings in the area. If there was going to be a meeting, it had to be inside somewhere. A quick bird's-eye view would save me a lot of driving.

'Got that, Watchman. Nothing in sight. It's just a lake.'

'Copy that. Thanks.'

A pause, then: 'Are you OK, Watchman? That last bit seemed . . . hairy.'

Hairy. That was one way of describing it. 'All in a day's work,' I said breezily. 'I wouldn't have done it without your help, though. That was impressive work. Say, did I say thank you?'

'I took it as read. And you're very welcome.'

I sat and watched for a while, feeling the residue of adrenaline after the chase filtering out of my system. I'd seen no signs of activity after leaving the forest track, and figured the men in the GAZ had not called it in for some reason. Maybe they'd got fed up sitting by the side of the road and I was the nominated sucker to be pulled over and hazed to relieve the boredom. Once I was sure they had given up the chase, I'd pulled over and ripped off the decals just in case.

I checked the Touareg again. I could see one man inside but it was too indistinct to tell if it was Tzorekov or Gurov.

Then a slim figure stepped out from the trees. Gurov. He walked over to the passenger side of the Touareg and stood there, presumably talking to his boss, but didn't seem in too much of a hurry to get back inside. Waiting for somebody, perhaps?

I gave it another twenty minutes to see if they were going to move. Sitting here for too long was crazy. I was still concerned about the helicopter. Without the tracker, the men in the Ansat now had no way of finding the Touareg, but having seen the layout of this region, the very simplicity of the road system and lack of buildings in the area was likely to act against Tzorekov remaining invisible for ever. All the helicopter had to do was follow the more obvious roads and sooner or later they'd get lucky. The lack of moving vehicles alone meant those of us down here would stand out clearly from the sky, and if they had cameras on board, they wouldn't need to come too low to check out any that looked good.

And if I could see the Touareg, so would the helicopter. Surely Gurov knew that. So what the hell was he playing at?

I got back in the pickup and drifted down the road, keeping an eye on the skyline. I was on a long, winding slope between huge swathes of conifers, and for much of the time it was like being in a sheer-sided tunnel, cutting out a lot of light and most of the horizon. Then I caught a glimpse of water through a clearing, and stopped, backing up a few yards so I had a clear view.

Gurov was still standing by the passenger door, staring out across the lake as if he hadn't got a care in the world. I could see the wind ruffling his hair and he might have been any city dweller out in the wilds for the day to get some fresh air in his lungs.

But something was wrong; I could sense it from here.

To hell with caution. I drove the rest of the way and entered the approach road to the lakeside, driving slowly. Gurov must have heard me coming but if it bothered him he didn't show it. He was leaning against the side of the Touareg with his hands in his pockets. I parked beneath the trees and walked across to him. I had my hand on the Grach but something told me I wasn't going to need it.

He finally turned and watched me approach. He looked relaxed but it was the stance of a man who suddenly didn't know what to do with himself.

I had a bad feeling and glanced towards the Touareg, where I could just make out Tzorekov sitting in the passenger seat. He looked as if he was asleep.

'What are you doing?' I asked Gurov. 'You know they're still searching for you.'

He said nothing for a moment, then straightened himself up. 'It does not matter,' he said softly. 'It is over.'

'What? Have you heard something?'

He shook his head. 'No. Not that.' He nodded towards the front of the car and drew in a deep breath. 'Leonid is dead. A heart attack. A little more than an hour ago.'

I walked over and opened the door. Tzorekov's skin was grey. His eyes were half-closed and he had a look of something that might have been pain etched into the tilt of his mouth. I checked the pulse in the side of his neck. He was cold.

'I'm sorry,' I said, as Gurov joined me. He had a faraway look in his eyes and I could see he was hurting. He'd evidently been far closer to Tzorekov than any normal bodyguard, more like a son than an employee. A son who had joined in this crazy journey into Russia that his father had decided was worth a try, come what may because it was important. But having come this far, he'd seen his father die, his wish unfulfilled. No wonder he was in pain.

'Did you know?'

'That his heart was bad? Yes. He had been sick for some time but nobody else knew. He insisted on that. He refused to tell them, saying he had one last thing to do.' He shrugged and added softly, 'He wanted to come back home. That, too, was part of the sickness, and why I cannot be truly sad for him. But I am sorry he did not accomplish his mission. It was a good thing to want to do.'

'What will you do now?' I said.

He stared at Tzorekov and shook his head. He looked thinner than ever in the morning light, his cheekbones prominent and his skin stretched tight with emotion.

'I don't know. First I must bury him.'

'Here?'

He nodded. 'It is what he would have wanted. Once a Russian, always a Russian. This is his homeland.'

'And then?'

'Then I don't know.' He leaned into the car and lifted out Tzorekov's body. For such a slim man it took him no more effort than if it had been a small child, and he did it with the utmost care.

'Do you want my help?'

'No. This is for me to do. He would have wanted that. But thank you.' He hesitated, then added, 'Leonid was very grateful for what you have done. You have put yourself in great danger for him. For us. I thank you, also, but you should go home now.'

I didn't say anything, just nodded in acknowledgment.

As he walked away into the trees bearing the body of his boss, I detected a faint rumble in the air. It could have been thunder but I doubted it. Then it became a thudding sound, distant and just about audible, interrupted only by an occasional shift in the wind, but definitely there. I turned and walked out into the open and scanned the horizon, checking the grey skies over the hills and trees. I knew sooner or later that I'd see a dark shape come into view.

I jogged back to the pickup and retrieved the Saiga from its hiding place in the rear bodywork, and slipped in a fresh magazine. I looked for Gurov but he was out of sight.

'Watchman, come in.'

'Here, Lindsay. Go ahead.'

'The beacon signal I saw before is approaching your location. It's about ten miles out. It appeared out of nowhere. Sorry, I wanted to warn you sooner.'

'Don't sweat it. I'm ready for him.'

'Oh.' A slight pause while she digested the meaning, then: 'What's your situation?'

'The deal's off. Tzorekov's dead.' I relayed what Gurov had told me. She took the news without reaction, but I knew she'd be hitting buttons in the background. This was a complete game changer and everybody would have to be briefed. She probably had a feed going through to Callahan's office and was giving him the heads up. No doubt it would throw a few heads in the State Department into a spin, but there was nothing that could be done about it.

Some missions end like that; no winners, no losers, no medals, no gain.

'Copy that. And the other man?'

'He's dealing with it.'

'What will you do now?'

'Head for home. Are those Pathfinders out of here?' I had no doubts that if things got very hot from here on, there would be a lot of attention being thrown this way from the various military facilities in the area. You couldn't have a firefight even in these remote parts without somebody asking questions.

'Orders confirmed; they're on their way.'

The distant thudding had intensified. It became louder and the sound changed as the Ansat popped up over the trees about a mile away and wheeled round towards the lake, sinking towards the water. I didn't know how they'd found us but logic and a knowledge of the local countryside and roads must have played a part. There wasn't so much traffic in this area that they could get too easily confused.

'Gotta go,' I told Lindsay, and cut the connection. I checked the Saiga's magazine again out of habit. Full. Made sure the scope was firmly in place and the lens clean. Tight and clear. What I hadn't done was checked the sights were good, but there was one good way to rectify that.

I sighted on the helicopter. It jumped into view, the two men in the cockpit clearly visible. I scanned towards the side and rear, and a man's face and shoulders appeared in profile at the door. He looked to be shouting and was pointing forwards, and I realized he'd been given the heads-up by the pilot.

They were coming straight for me.

It was time to get busy.

I aimed at the rotors and fired twice, the rifle jumping with a satisfying jolt against my shoulder. The shots sounded horribly loud in this quiet location, the noise spinning out across the lake and echoing off the trees, making a clutch of birds in the branches behind me fly off in panic, wings beating like someone shaking a newspaper.

I didn't wait to see the results; I grabbed the Val and turned and ran for the trees on the other side, away from where Gurov had gone.

FIFTY-NINE

J ason Sewell took his seat at the head of the table and
wondered what this latest call to order was all about. Deputy
Secretary Alastair Davies had requested it this time, and
he had an uneasy feeling in his gut. If he was correct, Davies
had found out that Watchman hadn't been called out of Russia
yet and was going to try roasting the two CIA officers for
not moving fast enough.

Down the table were Tom Vale and Brian Callahan, but
there was no sign of Angela Thornbury. He hadn't wasted
time asking why – he'd already heard on the grapevine that
she had moved on, for reasons unspecified.

'I'm sorry to call you out this early,' Davies began. 'I know
you fellows are in the final stages of tying up an operation,
but I felt you should know that the Tzorekov situation is
moving towards some kind of conclusion.'

'How so?' said Sewell. He wondered how much Davies
knew, if anything, of his decision to keep Watchman running
for another twenty-four hours.

'Well, what we know for certain is that President Putin is
firmly back in Moscow and doesn't look like going anywhere
due to urgent commitments. Furthermore, I've been advised
that Valentin Roykovski, Putin's former driver, has just checked
out of a health spa and is also back in Moscow.'

Sewell was puzzled. If this was a roasting, Davies was taking
the long way round. And how did he know of Roykovski's
movements?

Davies read his mind. 'Don't worry, Jason, we're not
doubling up on your work; I had a feeling I didn't know as
much as I should so I had somebody run a check on Thornbury's
briefing notes. Roykovski's name popped up and we ran him
past our embassy liaison in Moscow. He was Tzorekov's
planned go-between, right?'

Sewell nodded. He'd wondered if Davies had been briefed

fully on all the details from the first meeting with Thornbury, and clearly he hadn't. 'We had strong evidence from Tom Vale, here, that Roykovski has been acting for some time as a go-between for passing messages between Putin and Tzorekov. We suspect the president was probably being ultra-cautious about not being seen having dialogue with a man generally regarded as an outsider, for fear of under-mining his own authority. He has good reason, as it turns out.'

'Fair enough. So where does that leave Tzorekov? Is he likely to keep trying?'

'We're not sure. Our last take from Watchman was that Tzorekov was still counting on a meeting of some sort. He was merely waiting for a time and a place.'

'Watchman's talked with him?' Davies looked surprised. 'I thought he was supposed to remain at a distance. Isn't that the way he usually operates?'

'Usually, yes. But he can't always call the tune. Sometimes he has to go in close.'

'Right. Like he did with Ed Travis. I heard about that.' He smiled. 'No need to worry – something tells me you haven't yet pulled Watchman out of there, am I right?'

'Correct. We wanted to give it a last shot.' Sewell held his breath, wondering if this wasn't going to go stratospheric and call into question his ability to do his job.

'Good decision. As for Tzorekov's thinking, could he have another contact he can use?'

'Not that we know of. Tom?' He turned to bring in Tom Vale.

'Sorry,' said the MI6 man. 'We're as much in the dark as you. Tzorekov had faith in Roykovski being the one. If Putin has decided on another go-between to keep this thing going, we don't have a name.'

Just then the communications console in the centre of the room gave a discreet buzz. At a nod from Sewell, Brian Callahan reached out to take it. He listened for a moment, then said, 'Thank you, Lindsay. Wait one.' When he looked up, his expression was grave. 'That was a message from Watchman. Tzorekov's dead. He had a heart attack.'

Amid the silence that followed, Davies stood up and straightened his jacket. He looked at Callahan and Sewell and said, 'You'd better get your man Watchman out of there. If it wasn't over before, it certainly is now.'

SIXTY

I t was instantly darker under the canopy of tangled branches, and I hoped it was thick enough to prevent me being tracked by the men in the Ansat. If they had a thermal imaging camera on board, it wouldn't take them long to pin me down, but I was counting on them trying to find me and draw me out, rather than hosing down the entire woodland in the hopes of scoring a lucky hit.

There are two ways of stopping a potential attacker: one is by making it clear that any confrontation will be costly and painful – to them. But that's tough to do for one man against a machine. The men in the machine will always consider themselves in a superior position by being invulnerable against all but obvious superior firepower. And I didn't have that advantage.

The other way is to demonstrate from the get-go that you intend to fight hard and will take them all out if necessary. Even if you don't get them all, you might inflict sufficient damage to reduce their capability and confidence to zero.

I wasn't about to scare them, I knew that. But neither were they going to let me go; I'd already hurt them once and they weren't going to forget it and go home. So I was going to have to wait my chances and go for a war of attrition.

After grabbing what arsenal I had out of the car, I got a couple of hundred yards into the trees before I slowed down and slid behind a large trunk with a view out across the lake. I couldn't protect the pickup if the bad guys wanted to trash it out of malice, but I didn't want to isolate myself too far away from my only possible means of escape. If they decided to drop men at intervals along the shore, eventually they would box me in and the ending would be predictable.

The air here was filled with the aroma of mud and pine sap, reminding me of similar circumstances in other places. It's not unusual when faced with imminent conflict to see a kaleidoscope of previous experiences tucked away in one's memory, some helpful, some not. Right now the main thing I could recall was having a heavy-duty rifle with the kick of a mule and armour-piercing shells. Pity was, armed with the Saiga, the Val – which only had a few rounds left – and a semi-automatic pistol, that particular memory wasn't going to do me one bit of good.

I kicked away at the layer of needles and twigs beneath me, digging a hollow of sorts and giving me a firing point with some degree of protection. It wasn't great but as the old story goes, any foxhole will do.

The engine noise was getting louder as the helicopter began edging along the shore close to the water. I could see the tactics the pilot was using; flying overhead gave them a foreshortened view downwards, further restricted by the move-ment of trees. If I hugged the roots, they might never see me but I could see them and fire into their underbelly. But looking inwards from the water, they could see between the trees and get a better view of any movements against the slope.

The treetops closer to me began shaking as they were buffeted by the downdraft, the wave effect moving towards my section of the lake as if an invisible hand was running across them, smoothing the way. The water, too, was rippling as the machine edged lower, until a fine spray began to blow across the surface, forming a cloud of vapour running across the lake and reflecting the light in a multi-million tiny particles.

The helicopter came into view. It was about eighty yards out and moving with great deliberation. Two men were standing in the open doorway behind another man, sitting with his legs over the edge and his feet resting on the steps of the lower half of the clamshell door. He was cradling an assault rifle across his chest and wearing dark glasses. All three were in full combat gear, but like before, without insignia.

The man sitting down must have seen something, a flash of colour, maybe, a change in light as the foliage around me moved, because I was being very still. He swung his rifle down and watched for a moment, his glasses like large black buttons in a dark face.

Then he grinned and lifted the weapon in a smooth movement and pulled the trigger.

I fell back just in time. The trees around me were ripped apart by a long burst of gunfire, smashed branches and foliage raining down all around me. Something hot burned my shoulder and I felt the sting of a wood splinter pierce my cheek. I brushed it away and as soon as the firing stopped, risked a quick look.

He had emptied his magazine but was using two mags back-to-back; that is, a fresh magazine taped upside-down to the other. All he had to do to reload was unclip the empty, spin it round the other way and clip the new one in place without losing time or momentum. It wasn't the most professional way of using a weapon because the open top of the second magazine could easily pick up dirt and become jammed. The two mags also added to the weight and created an imbalance to the weapon. But some fighters did it to look good and only found out the bad practice when it was too late.

Now it was my turn. I rolled round the tree and brought up the Val just as he swung his rifle back towards me.

I don't know if he'd seen me or not, or whether he'd been trying to intimidate me into breaking cover. Either way, it didn't work the way he wanted. Before he could pull the trigger I fired a three-shot burst, aiming for the main body mass. I had to show that this business was going to be costly to them, and that I had the means to fight back. The sound of the suppressed shots was remarkably low, little more than a rattle beneath the silencing canopy of the trees. The men in the helicopter wouldn't have heard a thing. But the effect on the shooter in the doorway was dramatic.

The first two of the three rounds hit him high on the chest. The third I figured went somewhere over his shoulder into the interior of the cabin as he was knocked back under the double impact. He slumped back, dropping his rifle.

The pilot must have reacted by instinct as the other men shouted, or maybe it was the noise of the missed round impacting on his machine and ricocheting around the inside. The helicopter dipped and rolled slightly, turning away from the shoreline. The effect was enough to flip the shooter forward and out of the door.

One of the others tried to grab him but he was too late.

The shooter dropped into empty space, the safety line paying out behind him, and came to a brutal stop below the helicopter, where he hung like a broken doll.

I fired a couple of rounds at the open doorway, and one of the other men leaned out and fired back, brushing the trees around me. Then he dodged back and the helicopter veered away under power, roaring up and across the treetops out of my sight.

I checked the Val's magazine. Two shots left. It would be time soon to try out the Saiga.

SIXTY-ONE

'Cut him loose!' Chesnokoy shouted, and made a chopping motion at the man nearest the door. The man, whose name Chesnokoy couldn't recall, turned and stared at him, then gestured down at his stricken colleague on the end of the line.

'He's only wounded,' he protested. 'We should pull him back up.'

But Chesnokoy shook his head. 'He's finished. We'd never be able to pull him up and he'll just drag us down. Cut the fucking thing!'

The man shook his head, a flicker of desperation on his face. Then Gorin stepped across the cabin and produced a razor-sharp knife. He pushed the man aside and sliced through the safety line.

For a long moment the wounded man seemed to hang there, spinning on the end like a top, his mouth working as he waited to be pulled to safety. Then gravity took over and he was gone from sight, plummeting into the water far below.

'We should go back for him,' Kasbek shouted. 'He landed in the lake.'

'No,' Chesnokoy replied coldly. 'It would have been like hitting concrete from this height. Leave him – he's gone. We need to finish this thing now.'

Kasbek looked across at the navigator, who was leaning out from the cabin to see what was happening. He shook his head and made a slicing motion across his throat to indicate that it would be a waste of time.

Chesnokoy meanwhile, was checking over one of the rappelling ropes. He made sure the coils were not tangled, then grabbed the comms headset and shouted, 'I'm going down! Find me a clearing up the slope.' He slung his assault rifle across his chest, watched by the others.

Gorin stood up and pulled the other rope close to the door. He yelled, 'I'm coming with you.'

Chesnokoy nodded and gave the ghost of a smile. 'Like the old days!'

The pilot took them back over the trees to a point up the slope away from the water. The navigator was watching the terrain for a clearing, and signalled when he saw one. It wasn't large, an area where several trees had fallen in domino fashion in high winds. But it was enough for two men to land safely.

As soon as the navigator gave the thumbs-up sign, Chesnokoy and Gorin were out of the door and sliding down the ropes as fast as they could, aware at any moment that the gunman on the ground might see them and open fire. If he did, they would be sitting targets.

They got down safely and dodged quickly into the cover of the surrounding trees. Chesnokoy got his bearings, checking the trees through the scope on his assault rifle. He estimated that they had landed roughly 400 metres away from where the man had been shooting at them, but on higher ground. That was both good and bad; good in that it gave them the advantage of viewpoint, looking down towards the target, and bad because he would have the advantage of sighting on them against the skyline if they weren't careful.

The two men began moving down the slope some fifty metres apart, carefully avoiding fallen branches and tangles of brushwood. The ground here was liberally scattered with pine needles, which made for soft going, but they were aware that the man below them had thick cover in his favour. If he had seen them rappelling down, all he had to do was wait for them to work their way down the slope towards him.

Chesnokoy took several deep breaths to calm his nerves. He felt angry – angrier than he'd been in a long time. This job had turned into a nightmare. What had been described to him as an easy mission, to go after two men, one of them old and beyond being a real opponent, had become something very different. Somehow another person had inserted himself into the field, and that person had taken them apart and made them look like amateurs, choosing the ground on which he fought and not even showing himself.

Well, that was going to change, he decided. The man was now up against someone who had fought on these terms many times before. This was the kind of warfare he understood – man against man.

SIXTY-TWO

I watched as two men made their way down the ropes to the ground. I couldn't do anything because I hadn't got a clear enough line of fire, and shooting on the off-chance of a hit would give away my position to the observers in the helicopter. With their eagle's-eye view of the forest floor they would be able to cover the area with deadly fire the moment I showed myself.

I moved slowly across the slope, using the scope to locate the two men as they slipped into the cover of the trees. They were good; they moved quickly and with the minimum of body showing before ducking into cover, using the ground in a way that told me they were experienced in this kind of guerrilla-style warfare.

I slid left, further away from the parking lot area into denser trees where the ground cover was thicker. Somehow I had to isolate the men one from the other, to stop them working as an effective team. If I didn't, they'd begin to herd me until they got me where they wanted. The best way I could achieve that was to put them in line away from me so that the man furthest away couldn't open fire easily without endangering his partner.

I made my way down the slope until I saw the glint of water through the trees. The ground here was more open where some clearance work had been done, but there was still plenty of cover if I needed it, as long as I kept an eye on the approximate positions of the two men gunning for me.

As soon as I was as low as I could get without getting my feet wet, I turned and started running along the shore. The helicopter was somewhere high above the trees further up the slope. It was easy enough going, but I was braced all the way for the sound and impact of a shot. I vaulted a couple of fallen trees, tore through a section of bushes, but all the time keeping as close to the water as possible. It was hot work and the temptation to stop and splash my face was huge, but I kept moving, leading the men further away from the parking lot into denser trees.

I was counting on at least one of them having radio contact with the Ansat, and if he did and failed to keep up with me, sooner or later he'd bring the helicopter back into play.

And that's exactly what they did.

I heard shouting, and a series of whistles. They were signals, keeping each other appraised of their positions so that they didn't run into each other – or worse, start shooting at the wrong target. Then I heard a familiar sound. It began as a rumble and became a thudding, and when I looked out over the water I saw the Ansat wheeling down and round and coming in towards me like an arrow.

The sheepdog had found the target.

I stayed close to the water's edge and stepped in front of a large pine tree, keeping it at my back. I was deliberately making no attempt to hide from the helicopter, and figured the pilot had me in his sights and was transmitting the information to the two men on the ground. The trees around me were silent now, save for a faint hiss of wind through the branches, and the rain had reduced in volume to a slight drizzle.

It was kind of spooky, watching the Ansat coming in at me and how everything else around me seemed to pause as if holding its breath.

I heard the snap of a branch on the slope behind me. A hundred feet away, at a guess. One of the men must have worked his way round, seeking to keep the advantage of height while leaving his colleague to move down and take me from the side.

Clever move. This was as close to being bracketed as I wanted to get. Now it was time to change the game.

The vibration from the helicopter was increasing as it closed in, and I felt the downdraft effect on the trees around me, and saw a mist of spray lifting off the water.

I stayed where I was, watching the Ansat. The two men in the cockpit were looking right back, probably trying to figure out what I was doing and why I wasn't running.

Cat and mouse.

I waited until they were a hundred and fifty yards out, then lifted the Val and fired the last two shots. I was aiming at the cockpit and through the scope saw both shots strike home, scarring the glass.

The Ansat wobbled. It was pretty unnerving, seeing two bullets smash into the glass right in front of you, and I could imagine the conversation going on inside.

I was right; the pilot turned his craft, but he wasn't running. Instead he was presenting the open doorway, where one of the passengers was standing, assault rifle to his shoulder ready to open fire.

But by then I had tossed the empty Val into the water and slipped behind the tree, giving him no target to aim at.

He hesitated, probably asking for more details of my position, so I gave him what he wanted. I edged round the tree and fired two shots with the Saiga, the noise after the silenced Val dramatically loud in comparison. For a moment nothing happened. Then the man in the doorway dropped sideways and disappeared from sight.

Another one down. But I nearly didn't get to see it.

The response was fast and furious. The man I'd shot was replaced by another, who simply hosed down the area where he thought I might be, changed magazines and repeated the exercise until the helicopter pilot decided he'd had enough and pulled away out over the water. Most of the shots went into the trees high over my head, and I heard a shout from one of the men on the slope behind me, who must have felt the wind of a passing bullet.

Rough justice. But it didn't stop them.

Two shots came from above me, slamming into the tree by my shoulder and tearing off a great chunk of bark. Moments later two more came from my right, snapping through the branches overhead and sending down a shower of debris. Damn, the other guy had moved very fast and figured out where I was. He'd also given his partner the opportunity to move while I was distracted, a clear signal if I'd needed it that they knew what they were doing.

I heard a scuff of noise. It sounded like the brush of combat jacket material against branches and came from just a few yards away. They badly wanted to finish this and were coming in fast, taking chances and banking on me keeping out of their way and not exposing myself.

Another noise, this one closer. I stood up and swung the Saiga, and focussed on a figure coming out of cover thirty yards away. He was moving fast and heading slightly away from me. I fired twice but missed.

I should have turned and raced away along the shore towards the car. At least, that's what he would have expected me to do. But the helicopter was still out there and I knew that was what they would be waiting for. The moment I tried to cross open ground to the pickup, the men in the Ansat would have me in their sights.

Instead I faced up the slope and veered right, effectively running between the two men.

Suddenly a small tree to my right exploded under a hail of gunfire coming from my rear. I threw myself to the ground, desperately twisting round to cover my rear and flank. In the same instant, a figure came charging out of the trees, rifle levelled ready to finish me off.

I pulled the trigger and caught him high on the shoulder. But it wasn't enough to stop him; he staggered but kept coming.

Then the game changed altogether. Three shots, sounding flat, loud and very fast came from up the slope to his right.

Handgun?

The effect was stunning. Already in full motion coming towards me, the man was hit from the side and knocked clean off his feet. He dropped into a pile of brushwood, the rifle spinning away and slamming into a tree. I could see he'd been hit badly and wasn't about to offer any further resistance, but I wasn't about to stick my head up and see how he was doing. Then a movement showed higher up the slope on my left and I spun round, finger tightening on the trigger.

It was Gurov.

He stood there motionless. He didn't try to duck under cover, or even put out a hand to stop me firing. He still looked pale and thin but now seemed more determined and focussed. He jerked his chin away towards the area behind me, and I held up one finger.

He nodded and scrambled down to check on the man he'd shot, then straightened up and shook his head.

Then he turned and walked away, vanishing into the trees towards the parking lot without looking back.

The message was abundantly clear; he'd come back to even the odds, maybe pay me back a little for helping out on their way here. But now he was off to complete what he'd set out to do for his former boss.

I turned and checked out the tress where I'd heard the other man moving after I'd shot at him.

There was an area of unrestricted light some hundred yards away, which I figured must be a large clearing. I could see some felled logs lying around, the trunks trimmed of branches ready for pulling out and loading on trucks. Then I saw a flicker as a figure moved against the light and out of sight.

The helicopter was coming closer. The sound had been growing steadily, and I knew what he was doing: the man on the ground was calling him in, using him like a giant metal sheepdog to push me towards his gun.

I couldn't stay where I was; they would see me too easily

and I'd be an easy target. The only way to avoid that was to move towards the man on the ground, making it difficult for those in the air to open fire without hitting him.

If I took him out that might dissuade them from taking it any further.

SIXTY-THREE

'Putin's back in Moscow.'

Victor Simoyan had received the news earlier with relief, tinged with an instinctive degree of scepticism. Never be certain of anything until carefully checked out.

'You know this for sure? It's not a feint? He could have changed planes on the way.'

'It's not a feint. I can vouch for it because I saw him myself.' The caller was a former presidential aide and probably knew the president better than most people. If he said it was Putin and he was firmly in Moscow, that was it.

'Where is he now?'

'Heading into a meeting with the cabinet to discuss sanctions imposed by the Americans and the European Union. He boarded a plane in Kurtz with his party and flew direct to Domodedovo. He was met there by an international press group and two ministers, where he held a photo shoot before being taken to the city. There is no way it was a staged presentation and he cannot now go anywhere else – his schedule is locked down tight.'

Simoyan breathed a little easier and thanked the caller. That laid to bed the use of a double, a ruse which had been rumoured for some time when Putin needed to be in two places at once. The accredited foreign press corps knew Putin's face like their own mothers, and their cameras would have picked out even a slight variation in his appearance.

But staged it almost certainly was, even if very few people were aware of why. If ever Putin had wanted to send a clear message, this was a classic. It announced to those who were watching, in Russia and abroad, that there would be no chats in remote lakeside *dachas*, no meeting with outsiders, whatever their shared history. No retrenching, no cutbacks, no caving in to foreign threats and sanctions.

Instead it was going to be business as usual.

But first it was time to call off the dogs. Permanently. He picked up his cell phone and dialled one of the special numbers. When it was answered he said, 'That final solution you said you could deliver for me. Is it still available?'

'I think we can manage that. When do you want it?'

'Set it in motion. You have the beacon code?'

'I'm watching it right now. It's currently active and moving over a remote area of lakes and forest. It's as if they don't even know they're giving out their location.'

'That's because they don't. How long?'

'Thirty minutes after I give the "go", no more. Then it's over.'

'The extra payment will be made into your account within a few minutes.'

'Thank you. It's nice doing business with you.'

'What of Chesnokoy's two men wounded earlier?'

'Wounded men?' The voice held a hint of raw humour. 'I have no idea what you mean.'

Simoyan cut the connection and sat back with a sense of relief. There was a man after his own heart; venal by nature and not afraid to make hard decisions. There should be more like him. He was about to make another call when the cell phone rang. He checked the screen.

Gretsky. What the hell did he want?

'Yes?'

'I've been getting calls about Datsyuk,' the air traffic supervisor began quickly, his voice low. He sounded frightened. 'Some guy named Romanov at Shaykovka air base wants to speak to him. What do I tell him?'

'Why ask me?' said Simoyan. 'How would I know?'

'Because he never reported in for duty after we last—'

'After we what?' Simoyan's voice was soft, the three words uttered slowly and heavy with threat.

'Nothing. I mean . . . he hasn't been back and I thought something bad . . . had happened.'

'Maybe something did. He's young, did you not say that? Young men get into trouble all the time.'

'Of course, yes. But—'

'In any case, how would his movements concern me?'

'I don't know. I'm sorry, but I don't know what to tell Romanov.'

'Tell him nothing. He's probably on a drunk somewhere. Then go home.'

'Home? Why?'

'To see your wife and family. And perhaps to remind yourself how precious they are to you.'

He cut the connection before Gretsky could speak again. Silencing Datsyuk had been simple; a bottle of vodka in his pocket and a body in the river . . . it happened every day. The city was so lawless and people from out of town simply didn't realize the dangers. Maybe another accident was called for. But that was for later. Right now he had a more important event to arrange. He began the round of calls to bring the other Wise Men together. This was a video conference they were definitely not going to be reluctant to attend.

SIXTY-FOUR

Chesnokoy waited for a signal from Gorin. But there was nothing. He'd heard the three shots and identified them as a semi-automatic. Nine millimetre almost certainly and not from the man they had been pursuing – the shots had come from a different section of trees.

He didn't waste time worrying who that second shooter might be; whoever it was he'd taken out Gorin, and now it was two against one the other way. The wrong way.

So be it. He took out the radio. 'This is Chesnokoy. Come in and get me. Look for a clearing to your south, close to the water. But be careful – there are now two of them down here.'

'Got that.' It was the voice of the navigator. 'ETA on that clearing two minutes.'

Keeping an eye out for signs of movement among the trees, he watched as the helicopter came into view out over the water, heading in a wide curve to make its approach over the clearing where he was standing on the edge of the trees. The clatter of the rotors changed in tone, echoing back across the water and making it sound as if there were two helicopters out there, one louder than the other.

He shook his head. He needed to get out of this business. He'd lost too many good friends and spent too much time facing the prospect of joining them if he carried on much longer. It was time to find something else to do.

But first he had to finish the job. The green Touareg he'd seen while coming into land was Tzorekov's, and the old man couldn't be far away. He couldn't understand why he would have got himself trapped in this back-of-beyond place but it was going to be the old man's biggest mistake – and his downfall.

The Ansat came in fast and began to turn ready to land. Kasbek – or was it one of the others? – was standing in the open doorway, his assault rifle across his chest, the wind tugging at his combat jacket. He raised a hand in greeting, and turned to say something to somebody inside.

Then his head jerked back round and he looked up towards the peak above the lake, and froze, his mouth dropping open.

What the hell was he—?

Chesnokoy spun round to follow his look, an awful premonition coming to him as a separate sound travelled across the water towards him.

It hadn't been an echo after all. There *were* two helicopters.

For a couple of seconds he saw nothing. Just endless grey clouds hanging low over the peaks and the ever-present curtain of rain, now thinner but forming a film of silver-grey against the sombre carpet of trees.

Then he saw movement: a dark shape against the grey, too solid to be cloud, too big to be a bird, wheeling out of the murk and settling on a level flight facing the Ansat. He felt his gut go cold and turned to stare at the man in the door of the Ansat, who had his head turned away and looked as if he was shouting instructions at the pilot.

He looked back. The newcomer was a good kilometre away and closing. It looked big, and even through the rain Chesnokoy recognized the outline and stubby wings of a Mi-24 gunship. And beneath the wings he was sure he detected the slim shape of rocket pods.

The machine settled to level flight, and Chesnokoy felt sick. He'd seen that stance before too many times to be mistaken.

They were going to open fire.

Before he could take it all in, he saw a flash from beneath the right-hand wing. A split second later a slim smoke trail arched away and a dark shape began to climb, increasing speed at a bewildering rate.

'*No!*' he screamed. '*No!*' all the time realizing it was no use. Nothing was going to stop this happening. *Shturms*, he thought automatically, the professional side of his brain clicking in despite the horror of what he was witnessing. Radio-guided missiles with laser range-finders. Tank busters also effective against helicopters, like the one now firmly in its sights.

The air seemed to crackle with energy as the missile surged in on its target through the rain. Chesnokoy could only watch as the Ansat tried to climb out of the way, engines screaming as the pilot reacted to the warning and tried to haul it clear as if by muscle-power alone. But it was too little too late; the Ansat simply didn't have the raw power or speed for such a desperate manoeuvre.

Chesnokoy covered his face in horror, unable to watch the final moments of his men. This hadn't been suspected, and none of them would have been watching for it. His last glimpse was of the missile arcing down a split second before it impacted on its struggling target.

He didn't need to see the effect, knowing that if he looked he would see the Ansat broken into pieces and falling from the sky, leaking flames and smoke, men tumbling from the inside, already dead and smashed beyond recognition.

When he finally looked up, the Ansat was gone, a heavy pall of black smoke rising from the edge of the forest showing where the remains had struck the shore. A number of trees nearby had burst into flames, crackling with an angry spitting sound as spilled fuel ignited, their tops burning fiercely like grisly black candles on a funeral cake.

Beyond it, the Mi-24 was already turning away and heading towards the distant peaks.

Mission accomplished.

Chesnokoy heard the snap of a twig behind him. He turned and saw a man standing at the edge of the clearing. He was holding a rifle. At first Chesnokoy thought he was a forestry worker or a hunter, come to see what had happened. Dressed in a heavy coat and pants, with the bottoms tucked into boots, he seemed to blend in with the background.

But there was something about the way the newcomer was standing, relaxed yet ready to move, that made him look again. And the rifle was no hunting weapon. It was a Saiga assault rifle fitted with a night-vision scope.

He thought about bringing up his own weapon, but he knew he'd be dead before he got his finger near the trigger.

SIXTY-FIVE

Victor Simoyan looked at the men assembled once more on the screens at the end of the room. They had been waiting for news following his call – and now he had it, the final confirmation they had all been waiting for.

'Gentlemen,' he announced almost breezily, 'we have played our best cards and I am pleased to report that there will be no meeting between the traitor Tzorekov and . . . anybody else. He will no doubt go back to London with his tail between his legs.'

The faces on the screens smiled in satisfaction, some applauding, some rapping the desks or tables before them with their knuckles in appreciation. If there had been a line open to Moscow Exchange right now, they would undoubtedly have been fantasizing about a marked jump in figures against their various company interests. Not that that would happen for a while just yet – but it would, he was certain of it.

'Fantastic!' said Maltsev. 'Now I can go to Monaco as planned and deal with some important business.' He grinned widely, the light flashing off his spectacles.

'You be careful you don't burst a blood vessel filling in all those forms,' warned one of the others with a wry look.

'Gentlemen, please.' Simoyan hated to ruin their pleasure, but he had a duty to remind these men about some practical facts. 'I am sorry to burden you with messy details, but there are one or two items we need to be clear on before we go any further.'

'What kind of items?' Solov, the deputy defence minister was looking at his cell phone. 'I'm sorry, but I have to go. A meeting . . .'

'I won't take long, Lev, I promise. First of all, we have to ensure that nothing of what we arranged, or what we discussed here, will ever leak out. If it does, you can be assured that we will feel the full force of the state. And like each one of you,' he added softly, looking at each man in turn, 'I have enemies who would be happy to contribute to my downfall.'

There was a short silence, then Maltsev said, 'What could they do to us? We have clean hands; we haven't raised a single finger against the state. Tzorekov was an outsider.'

One or two of the others nodded in agreement and Simoyan looked at them, barely managing to hide his contempt. Typical of so many businessmen, he reflected. They were painfully naïve when it came to matters of political and legal inter-pretation, and seemed unaware of how easily the house could come tumbling down around their ears.

'You think that argument will save us?' he retorted. 'Have you not heard of the charge of conspiracy? We used armed mercenaries, we "borrowed" a military helicopter and equip-ment, we paid off certain people to assist us by looking the other way, we paid others to openly conspire with us in a plan that some would interpret as raising a hand against the highest office in the land. You think if the president had agreed to finally attend this meeting in person he would have been quite so understanding of us conspiring to eliminate his old friend, Tzorekov? Somehow, I don't think so.'

'What are you saying, then?' Kushka was wearing his usual schoolmasterly expression. 'What else do we have to do?'

The others murmured in agreement, the mood in the room changing dramatically as they sensed some unwelcome developments ahead.

'I'm saying we have to clean up behind us. Dispose of any liabilities.'

'You mean the two men who were wounded earlier?' said Oblovsky.

'Already dealt with.'

'What about the others?' Solov tapped the table softly. 'They're still out there, are they not? What do you intend doing about them?'

'I've already taken steps to ensure that none of them returns. All links back to us will be severed. This matter, gentlemen, simply never took place.'

'How will you do that?' asked Oblovsky. 'We don't even know where they are until they report back, do we?'

'Actually, I do.' After calling Gretsky and confirming that the Ansat was sending out an ADSB beacon code showing its altitude and location, he'd had an idea for wrapping up this business in one fell swoop. The beacon was like writing the Ansat's position in the sky for all to see. Especially those with the ability to arrange for an attack helicopter to follow the signal and make a pass, blowing it out of the sky.

End of problem.

'So?'

'So it is my sad duty to report that an Ansat-U helicopter with a number of criminals on board today strayed into a live firing range with tragic consequences for all concerned.' He waited for reactions or protests but they were all too stunned to speak. He searched their faces for dissent, for weakness, for even a hint that one of them might buckle and lead to disaster for them all.

'God almighty,' whispered Maltsev. 'All of them?'

'You don't fool around, do you?' said Solov.

'Me? I don't know what you mean. It was an unfortunate

accident, that's all.' Simoyan sounded innocent, but his next words belied that completely. 'Just bear in mind, gentlemen, that such accidents happen every day . . . and in all walks of life.'

The silence from the men on the screens was total.

SIXTY-SIX

I watched as the man in front of me made his decision. A host of conflicting emotions were chasing across his face before his shoulders finally dropped. He wasn't giving in, though; I could tell that by looking at his eyes. He was simply recognizing the futility of attempting a move he knew wasn't going to come off – for now.

He dropped the rifle he was carrying and lifted his arms away from his sides. I could see the effort of will it took him to do that; how he was hating every split second, knowing that if I was going to open fire, he wouldn't have a cat's chance in hell of stopping me.

I motioned with the Saiga's barrel for him to sit. He did so, sinking into a squat and placing his hands on the ground. I walked closer to check him for other weapons. Up close he was big and hard-boned, with broad shoulders and a blade of a nose. His eyes were watching me with caution, but behind that look I could see a whole turmoil going on.

He was suffering.

I saw no reason to humiliate him further, but I had to be sure I was safe. I patted my pockets and pointed to his jacket. He indicated his side and said, 'Makarov.'

'Take it out. Put it on the ground. Be very careful.'

He did so, lifting it out with the tips of his fingers and thumb. I knew he was within a professional's ace of being able to flip it and start shooting, but he'd have to cock it first and even he must have known he'd never make it in time. He placed it on the ground and pushed it away.

'Any others?'

'No.'

I stepped forward and kicked the Makarov out of his reach. He didn't move, but watched while I did it with the kind of detachment of somebody only vaguely interested, with no real concern at the possible outcome. I guessed he was in deep shock.

'American?' he said, and sank onto his butt, lacing his fingers and placing his forearms on his knees. It wasn't a good position from which to jump up and fight, especially against a gun, and he wanted me to know it.

'Doesn't matter what I am. You were here to stop Tzorekov?'

He shrugged. 'It was my job.' He spoke good English with a strong accent, and I figured he'd picked it up over the years mixing with troops of various nations. 'And you?'

'Protecting him. That was my job.'

He almost smiled. Two opponents acknowledging the other's position.

'What's your name?' I asked.

'Chesnokoy. Alexei.'

'All your men?' I nodded at the burning remains of the Ansat, which took that moment to send up a vivid gout of flame followed by the vibration from an explosion. The smoke was drifting into the sky in a huge pillar-like formation, and spreading out on the wind and rain to form a blanket over the burning trees below. The pop-pop of burning fabric and rubber, and the occasional louder report of a burning cartridge going off were the only other sounds.

'Yes.' He turned his head to glance at it, then looked back at me. His eyes were full of pain and fury, although I didn't denote much direct hostility. A professional soldier after all, recognizing that there was nothing to be gained by showing anger. All that did was blind you to opportunities for seizing back the advantage.

'That didn't look like a friendly-fire accident. What was it?'

'It was not friendly. We were—' he searched for the right word, then said – 'betrayed.'

'By who?'

'The man who hired us.'

'Name?'

He hesitated for a second, then shrugged and said, 'He is Simoyan. Victor Simoyan.' He spat on the ground to demonstrate his contempt for the man. 'He makes weapons . . . and lots of money. He also uses people.'

'How many were you?'

He held up both hands, showing eight fingers, and added, 'Also pilot and navigator. All gone.' His eyes glittered. 'But not all here.' He was acknowledging my part in the contest, but whatever the means, he'd lost all his men. It would have been a very bitter pill to swallow.

'Two were wounded,' I pointed out. 'Burns.'

He shook his head. 'He will kill them, too. If they are not dead now, then soon.'

'Why?' I meant, why was it ending this way for them?

'Because that is the way of these things.' He shrugged almost fatalistically. '*Biznismen* – they have no honour. Not like soldiers.' The way he said the word '*Biznismen*', which meant exactly what it sounded like but was definitely not a compliment, told me everything I needed to know about the kind of person who'd hired him. Simoyan and others had been protecting their pockets and status and now they were making sure they protected their backs, clearing up the mess by making certain nobody got back to talk about it.

I walked around him and picked up the assault rifle, slinging it over my shoulder, then collected the Makarov and put it in my pocket. I was going to walk away from here and I didn't want him coming after me. He had good reason for doing so and I didn't assume for a second that he lacked the guts or determination to want me dead. As it turned out, I was only half right. He had guts in spades.

He didn't turn to watch me, but dipped his head, and I realized he was waiting for the shot that would send him to join his colleagues. He was a fatalist at heart.

When I walked back in front of him, he looked suspicious, then surprised.

'We've done enough, you and I,' I told him. 'This is over.'

'For me, maybe.' He shrugged again. 'Some win, some lose.'

'For all of us. Tzorekov is dead.' When he raised his eyebrows I added, 'Heart attack. He was an old man. Sick.'

He nodded. 'So, all of this for nothing. And Gurov?'

'Gurov's gone.' I pointed away over the hills. The truth was, I didn't know where he'd gone but it didn't really matter. He'd been well-trained and would disappear into the land-scape and make his way into whatever kind of future he had waiting for him.

'You can manage from here?' I was being polite but I wasn't going to be noble enough to offer him a lift out of here. Once he got over his shock at what had happened, it would be like having a silverback gorilla in the car with me.

'Of course.' He didn't look at me, but stared out across the lake.

'You know, if you go after this Simoyan, you'll die,' I said. It wasn't really any of my business, but I felt I had to say it. I also knew what I'd have said in his position.

'Maybe. Maybe not. But if I do not try, I should be dead, anyway. They were good men. They did not deserve this.'

There was nothing more to say, so I turned and walked away into the trees, back towards the car. This was Chesnokoy's country and I figured he'd do the same as Gurov, only with different aims in mind. Gurov would survive but I wasn't certain Chesnokoy was that interested, beyond dealing with the person he knew had organized the gunship to take out the Ansat and everybody onboard. The same person who'd hired him in the first place.

Victor Simoyan. It was a name I hadn't heard before. Whoever he was, he must have had some pull to have been able to arrange all this. I'd be looking out for his name over the next few weeks, to see what happened. Whoever or wher-ever he was, he was going to need some serious protection when Alex Chesnokoy returned from the dead.

I called up Langley. It was time to go home.

Lindsay came on.

'Go ahead, Watchman.'